ARIN TAKEOVER

Emotion: panic! Everybody freeze. Don't go any farther, whatever you're doing!

Miriam snapped to full gestalt. "What's going on, Dmitri?"

The programmer calmed himself. *I slipped into the Science ArIn's programming and looked around, and I found the malware. This bit of script stood out like a flashing light, because the formatting is different from the rest.*

A page of programming language showed on the viewscreen.

"And for us non-programmers?"

Is this clear enough for you?

The words "Self-Destruct" flashed in bright blue.

A stunned pause filled the gestalt.

"Do you have any more details?"

Look at this section. If, at any time, the ArIn considers the joining gambit isn't working, it is to attempt a unilateral takeover of the other two computers.

"We expected that."

That's not the bad part. He flashed some code further down.

This is the key line. If the takeover is not successful, the ArIn is to commence a destruction sequence, not just of itself, but of any parts of the station it can reach. That's most of the structure. Fortunately, we followed your search weeks ago and ascertained no explosives of any size have been smuggled onboard.

"But they don't need extra explosives!"

Why do you say that?

"We ran into the same technique on the Chinese Elysium Base. The self-destruct sequence explodes every volatile or corrosive substance on the station. Standard procedure in the old days of the Expansion Conflict, when data secrecy was more important than human life."

Miriam took a deep, shaky breath. "We know that if we lose and the ArIns succeed in creating a Super Cerb, *Aris* hits us with a ShipBuster. Now, if we win, the Science ArIn blows us up."

She sent an emotion of grim determination through the gestalt. "I guess we better find another way."

SHIPSHAPE AND FANCY FREE

Gordon A. Long

Delta, B. C.
2024

Shipshape and Fancy Free

Gordon A. Long

Published by

Airborn Press

4958 10A Ave, Delta, B. C.

V4M 1X8

Canada

ISBN: 978-1-988898-44-5

eBook: 978-1-988898-45-2

Printed by Amazon

Cover Design by Gordon A. Long

Cover Image by 12019 from Pixabay

This is a work of fiction. All the characters and events portrayed in this book are fictional, and any resemblance to real people or incidents is purely coincidental.

CONTENTS

PROLOGUE: A NEW OBJECTIVE

AetherCommunication 1: Three Musketeers

Barwolf: Patches
Initiated by: Miriam
Responder: Freighty
Aether Setting: Micha Mouse's living room.

Miriam plopped down in a comfortable chair, pulled Bosz's soft, grey head into her lap, closed her eyes and called up the image of the black barwolf that resided in that special corner of her perception.

"Patches, put me on AetherCom, please. I need to talk to Factory 4-80."

Eager desire to please. Image: barwolf imitation of a human smile revealing rows of fierce triangular teeth.

"Stop being silly."

Emotion: fake apology. Image: Miriam zooming through space to a huge toroid space factory with a blue-and-green planet and a yellow sun in the background.

After a brief moment of disorientation, Miriam's vision cleared, and she was sitting on a bright-red, spongy chair in a primary-coloured room. A black cartoon mouse in yellow shorts bounced through the doorway from the deep blue haze of the exterior.

Hi, kid. How's it going?

"Hey, Freighty. How's life in the Sol System?"

Business as usual, Miriam. He pulled a huge wad of cartoon bills out of a bulging pocket and leafed through it merrily. *Anything to report from Barnard?*

"Yeah. Well, maybe."

That doesn't sound very scientific.

"It isn't. It's just a possibility."

I'm all ears. The toon wiggled his big, black ears.

"No, you're not. You don't have ears."

Beware, my dear. The Ancient Artifact has ears everywhere. Even there, on your ship.

"I thought I was your eyes and ears on *Jerusalem's Hope.*"

You are. One set of them. So, tell me what you have observed. Is it concerning our favourite barwolf pups?

"It is. I've just come offplanet from Barwolf Base, and the Three Musketeers are no longer puppies. They're five years old, and guess what?"

They formed a triad, I suppose.

"But they can't mate, can they?"

They aren't siblings. They were kidnapped at the same time, but from different tribes.

"I didn't know that. When I was living with them, we didn't talk about the kidnapping. Both the barwolf gestalt and the human scientists thought it would be a bad idea to dwell on it. We did talk about you, though. They had a great time onboard the Factory while they were waiting to be brought home. They keep talking about going back."

Do they, now? Tell me about it.

"Well, I hate to admit it, but that kidnapping and all the time away from Arborea was a more traumatic experience than I thought at the time. I was eight years old; what did I know? It changed them, and nothing we could do would ever fix them completely. Dr. Goodall says they were kept away from the species gestalt for too long at a key time in their development. They created their own private life gestalt, heavily dependent on each other, and peripherally including any Sensitive humans within reach. Apparently, they communicate with ArIns, as well." She glanced over at Freighty. "Should that make me suspicious?"

Only if you question my motives. I provided leadership when they needed it.

"And they still see you as their leader. Will you have them visit some day?"

2

It's a long trip. We'll have to see. Now they have formed their own triad, Your guardians will train them, and I can communicate with them through the aether.

"Mum and Dad started that months ago. They're well into their training."

Good. Now I can drop in on them as needed.

"They'll be elated. Anything else going on?"

Actually, yes. Have you anything important happening for the next couple of years?

"For the next...WHAT?"

Just a thought.

"No, it isn't." She pinned him with her best frown. "I've seen this happen to other people. The plans are made, and you're pretending to ask me for my opinion. Where am I going?"

Micha Mouse picked up a model of Sol System and spun it on his index finger like a basketball. *Space Arm is becoming antsy about getting their value out of our little project. Both projects, actually.*

"And you're asking about the pups, because they're going to be an AetherCom team, which is the goal of that project. Right?"

Right.

"You really are easy to pry information out of, you know." She concentrated, and a large, soft, boxing glove appeared on her hand. She reached out and bonked him. "Talk."

Our little solo project, bringing your auguar up with barwolves, has been a great success also, and I thought perhaps you'd like to show up and show off.

"Show up where?"

Bosz might enjoy a reunion with his siblings in the Science Branch lab at Space Arm Mars Station.

"I'm going to Mars? To the Sol System?"

Would you like to?

"Of course, but...well...I..."

You're the ideal person to go. Anyone else at the age of fourteen would have trouble leaving home for a couple of years. But you and your polyglot family? No matter where you're spread,

AetherCom keeps you pretty much with them twenty-four seven, as the Earthers say.

"Does the team here know about this trip? Of course they do. Why didn't they tell me. Rosy!" She blasted a call through the family gestalt. "You get over to this conversation right now!"

Her guardian's head peeked through the doorway. *I'm busy right now, dear. You talk to Freighty about it. It's your project, not mine. Emotion: love.* She winked and disappeared.

"So that's how it's going to be? When it suits them, I'm all grown up and independent. You shoulda heard the hullaballoo when I kissed Johnny Olav after the Middle School Grad Dance."

I would suggest that you refrain from forming any lasting attachments in Barnard System just now.

"Obviously. Well, when do I leave?"

We're not in a huge rush. You need to complete your final school semester and wrap up the units you're teaching the kinder-communication group. The next time Jerusalem hits Embassy Station, book passage as a civilian technical consultant on a Space Arm ship coming back to Sol.

"That will take months!"

You're in a hurry, now?

She swung the glove at him. *"Yeah, Mouse. Reverse psychology strikes again. I've got a load of stuff to do, and only a few months to do it. I'm outa here. Bye, now."*

The mouse stepped out of range. *Ta ta, sweetheart.* He blew her kisses, which floated through the air like flower petals.

She snorted and broke the connection.

BOOK 1: GROUNDWORK

1. BLUE CADRE

Ten months later

Miriam and Bosz walked down the boarding ramp from the destroyer *Texas,* waving a cheerful goodbye to the purser at his desk. He pointed to a blond ensign with dark skin lounging at the bottom, and she aimed her steps in that direction, her luggage trundling behind her.

The young officer straightened and stepped forward. "Miss Lantz, I assume?"

"I am. This is Bosz."

He saluted, then stretched a hand to the auguar, fingers turned under. "I'm pleased to make your acquaintance, Bosz. You and I have a medical check scheduled for tomorrow." Then he grinned at her. "Glad to meet you, too, Miss. Don't worry; I won't be doing a medical check on you. I'm Ensign Rafi Ericson. Just my luck to be on duty when a lovely young lady needs a guide."

She gave him the grin that she knew dimpled her left cheek. *Emotion: pleasant surprise.*

She observed his aura and caught a reaction. *Quite Sensitive, apart from his augment, a Military 10 full organic. Maybe even 11. Hmm. That's high for a mere ensign.* "Good of you to come. I gather it's a rather large station."

"That it is. We had two civvies got lost up here last year, and they didn't find them for three days."

She lowered her head to look up under frowning brows. "And the real story?"

He shrugged. "Nobody knows, but when they found the pair, they whisked them back to Mars on the next shuttle."

"Since I'm not a spy, I'm in no danger of getting lost." She gestured. "I just take the 4B monorail over there as far as the main terminal, walk two decks sunward, wait five minutes for the next tram to the Academy, where I ride Sidewalk 17 to the Science Branch Headquarters...need I go on?"

"That's very good, Miss. How did you...? Oh." He looked down at the large, grey cat staring smugly up at him. "Your auguar."

"Got it in one. He has all the information I need."

"Oh no, he hasn't."

"No?"

"Definitely not. He just has the fastest route there. I have the best one."

"What's better about it?"

"In the first place, we take the 5C rail."

She accessed her data from Bosz. "But that goes all the way around."

"Right. It takes ten minutes longer, but you spend the whole trip looking out over Marsport. It's a famous view. And then..." he paused dramatically, posing in the middle of a gesture which incidentally demonstrated serious muscle tone bulging his shipsuit.

She favoured him with Rosy's stare, then spoke in flat tones. "I'm all ears."

He spoke hurriedly. "Well, if you don't mind a four-deck staircase, there's a shortcut that brings you out a block from the Academy. Saves about five minutes and counts towards your Daily Exercise Quota."

"What about my luggage?"

"Well, we could grab a tram and ship it..."

She laughed. "Don't worry, it's not heavy. We can take turns. Let's go."

She strode out, her legs inured to Jim Campbell's rigorous gym routines and regular visits downplanet to romp with the Three Musketeers at Barwolf Base on Arborea. The ensign soon caught up, and she observed him out of the corner of her eye. He moved with more confidence than most his age. No hint of a strut, just comfortable on his feet. *Military training, I suppose.*

He made small talk on the trip, and she pumped him for information about the social life of the station.

When he offered to show her around, her basic honesty took over. "Ensign Ericson, how old do you think I am?"

"Huh? I dunno. About eighteen, I guess."

"You lie. I don't look a year over thirteen, and you know it. I can't go gallivanting about the base hotspots with an officer."

"Oh. Sorry, I just assumed..." He glanced down. "How old are you? Really."

"Older than I look, but not much. Birthday in two months, but it won't help." They were at the bottom of the stairs, and she grabbed the handle of her dunnage bag. "And I've been living with a couple of Commandos. Grab the bottom handle and up we go, but not too fast. I don't want to show up all sweaty. Lead the way, Bosz."

The grey tabby auguar bounded easily up the stairs, her ringed tail waving, and Miriam gamely followed.

In truth, her luggage was substantial. She was glad to have Rafi take his share of the load, which he accomplished with ease. Both arrived at the top out of breath and red faced, but only because they raced the last flight. Fortunately, the artificial breeze was cool enough to keep the sweat down.

They strolled the rest of the way, chatting comfortably. When they reached the SciBee Headquarters, he slowed. "I'm to take you to Reception, because they want you to meet the Blue Cadre first. They'll have someone there to greet you."

"But you're something to do with the program?"

"I have Vet Tech training, so I help with the medical checks on the auguars. A bit of logistics and equipment maintenance. Make myself useful, you know?"

"That sounds like quite a bit. Why didn't you tell me?"

He looked uncomfortable. "We felt it best not to mention it. They didn't want to skew your responses to them."

"Why?"

He gave a rueful grin. "You're working with the military, lady. Get used to it."

"If you say so." *This sounds a whole lot more like Head Councillor Isaac and the bureaucratic bunch that gave Rosy so much grief back on Jerusalem. Have to wait and see.*

She held out a hand. "Well, thanks for the escort. I enjoyed getting lost with you."

He shook but did not let go. "Look, Miss Lantz, I hope you don't think I was coming on to you or anything..."

She retrieved her hand, laughing. "Don't worry, your reputation is safe with me."

"That's not what I meant. This seems a big place, but there aren't that many people like us."

She pretended to frown. "And what are people like us...like?"

"Young and lonely and working hard to make up for it. Around here they call that kind of person a "grind.""

"I've been called worse."

"If you're ever looking for decent company and exercise with other hard workers, come down to the Rec Centre any evening at seven. I teach martial arts in the dojo five nights a week, and sometimes Special Training on weekends."

"Me? Martial arts?" She shrugged. "You never know. I might get that desperate. Thanks again, Mr. Ericson."

"My pleasure, Miss Lantz. Tell you what. I'll drop your case off at your cabin."

"That would be great." She handed him the key fob. "Thanks."

"Part of my duties: logistics." He gave her a snappy formal salute, spun about and strode off, her luggage trundling behind. She enjoyed his trim figure for a moment before turning back to the door.

Image: ruffled grouse performing mating dance.

Emotion: denial. He's just a friendly guy who's a bit lonely. I'm not in the market. And you be nice to him. He's part of your medical team, it seems. She recollected their conversation. *He didn't say much about himself at all, come to think of it.*

Image: large, long-haired grey-and-black auguar waiting inside.

Emotion: pleasure. Grey and black? That must be Ethan. I assume his handler is there, too? What's his name? Don't tell me...Thomas. Let's go.

The big double doors slid open. Inside was a lofty entrance hall with desks down one side and waiting room furniture down the other.

Just rising from the divan nearest the door was a tall, broad-shouldered youth with dark blonde hair and golden complexion. At his side paced a beautiful auguar who must be Ethan, the feisty kitten she had sent off to Sol four years ago.

She turned her attention to the human. His smile was friendly enough, but there was an air of superiority about him that reeked of privilege. Miriam had met the sort when they visited the Barwolf Lab, and remembered how Rosy always managed to swing them to her side. *Well, I don't have Rosy's people skills, so I'll do it my way.*

As he approached, his augmented aura made him seem taller than he actually was. He stopped and looked her up and down. Mostly down.

He can't be doing that on purpose. It's just habit. I still don't have to like it.

"So. This is the famous Miriam Lantz."

She stepped back to get him in better perspective. "And you must be the un-famous...well, who are you?"

His eyes narrowed. "Don't you know? You're supposed to be able to read minds, they tell us."

"It's not polite to read people's minds without permission." She glanced at the huge, long-haired auguar lounging at the lad's side. He was a truly beautiful animal, with silky hair patterned like a Maine Coon Cat, and with huge, intelligent green eyes. *Emotions: Greeting, Ethan. Query?*

The beast's tufted ears perked, and he sent a question of his own, directed at Bosz. After a quick exchange, she received a flood of information.

She stared straight into the young man's eyes. "So. You are the self-proclaimed alpha of the Blue Cadre pride, your name is Thomas von Arnim, and you are seventeen years old. Your claim to fame is as captain on the youth squad of the Mars Base team in the weak imitation of ruggerball that humans play."

His face went white. "What...?" Her augment read his heartrate increasing, his breath coming faster. "I thought you didn't read minds without permission."

"I don't." She smiled and flicked a finger at her auguar. "Bosz just asked Ethan, who told us."

Thomas regarded his auguar, who was glancing back and forth between the two humans, puzzlement in every line of his body as he registered this conflict.

"Ethan told your auguar?"

"They are brothers, after all. I knew Ethan when I could hold him in my cupped hands."

"Oh. Yes, I suppose..."

She took advantage of the lull to invite the larger auguar into their gestalt. He plunged in with little hesitation, and they took a moment to share more information.

"What's going on?" von Arnim's voice took on an uncertain note.

At least he's Sensitive enough to notice.

"Miss Lantz, what just happened to Ethan?"

She brought her attention back to the boy, who was looking from one to the other like his auguar had the moment before, similar expressions playing across his face and body.

"I just invited Ethan into gestalt. At Barwolf Base we gave the pups as much practice as we could before they were shipped out. Surely they've been using it."

"Oh, that. Yes, Ethan and his siblings go into their own gestalt during team activities, but we can't join in, so we don't know too much more than that."

"Well..." *Can't join in? What is he talking about, Bosz?*

Image: Bosz and Ethan in gestalt. Blond boy outside banging on the door.

I see. She brightened. "I guess that's why I'm here. I just didn't expect I'd need to start so soon."

Miriam could tell by the way his body tensed that she had said the wrong thing. She sent a general feeling of ease and relaxation, using the triple gestalt to strengthen it. "Look,

Thomas, I'm sorry. We seem to have got off on the wrong foot, and I don't know why."

She let the safe feeling grow for a moment. "Let's try again." She took a step forward. "Hi. I'm Miriam Lantz, and this is my auguar, Bosz. Thanks for coming to meet me." She held out her hand. "And as you probably know, I can't read your mind without a barwolf or auguar to make the connection, and you must be actively trying to send to me."

He stared at her, running his fingers through his mane of hair. Then he sighed and reached out his hand, looked at it, then wiped it on his pants and reached out again. "Hi, Miriam. I'm usually called Tom, and this is Ethan, as I guess you already knew."

She grinned. "I should know. I named him." She reached out a hand to Ethan, who took a deep sniff, then rasped her knuckles with a rough tongue.

Emotions: pleasure, satisfaction.

"But I'd never have recognized him. We knew he was going to be a big boy, but he's almost as hefty as his father."

She glanced at the cadet and gauged his feelings. "He's got the same presence as Chakka, too."

"Presence?"

"Oh, yes. He's the alpha male of the pride." She widened her eyes. "At least, I hope he is!"

Tom laughed. "Oh, yes. Nobody bosses Ethan around. Except his little sister, of course."

Miriam frowned in concentration. "Let me guess. That would be Vela. There was something about her..." She shrugged. "The name I gave her means "Little Wolf.""

The tall boy regarded her again, his face unreadable. "Well, it looks like there's a whole lot we don't know about you." He turned and started off. "Come on and meet the rest of the pride. The Powers that Be refused to tell us much, but your reputation really does precede you. They're waiting with great anticipation. We decided I should come alone so we didn't overwhelm you." He snorted. "Some chance."

She quickened her steps to match his long stride. "Oh, I get whelmed quite easily. It's just that I get upset when people try, and then I'm never quite sure what I'm going to do until it's too late."

She thought of adding that afterwards people usually didn't try again, but she decided against it. Mr. Tall-and-Handsome had been given due warning.

After a winding trip through several corridors, they rounded a corner and approached a heavy door. She could feel a gestalt boiling behind it, and glanced up at her guide. "This could get rough. Better if you stay out of it."

"What...?" His hand froze in the act of pushing the button, but it was too late.

The door slid open, and she had time to register a large, circular room with couches spread around. Then three lithe bodies rushed out.

Emotion: elation!

Three powerful minds reached towards her. She pulled Bosz into the same protective gestalt she had learned against the Space Swimmers, years ago. Then she dealt with the physical problem by dropping to her knees, her arm across her auguar's shoulders for support, and let them swamp her.

Emotion: surprise and building anger. "Blue Cadre!" Tom's voice snapped out. "Control your auguars. What's wrong with you?"

Emotions: confusion, frustration.

Miriam laughed and pushed a shaggy head away from licking her ear. *Command: finish! Sit!*

The three auguars dropped to their haunches in front of her. The smallest one, sleeker than her siblings, took one final lick before responding. Miriam stood and spoke aloud for the benefit of the others.

"Vela, your heart wasn't in that..."

The little auguar's head lowered and turned so she could look sideways from under lowered brows. *Emotion: ...apology?*

"Four years, and you haven't changed a bit. And look where it got you. In trouble already, and Ethan is laughing at you."

In truth, the huge male had stretched out on an empty couch, looking quite pleased with himself.

Vela got up and strolled over to him, butting her head against his shoulder. He ignored her, so she continued her parade to jump up on the sofa beside a big, red-headed girl.

Order: release. Miriam flicked her fingers, and the others rejoined their handlers. She walked over to Vela's partner, holding out her hand. "You must be Mary Meyer. You have my sympathy. And my admiration."

The girl tilted her head and reached out to grasp hands. "Can't argue with a compliment."

Miriam turned to the other two. "And here are the Oreo Twins. The white one is Blackie, and the Black one is Blondie. So, you must be Pete Rossi, and you are Jane. Rossi as well, of course."

The stocky girl with the white male auguar frowned. "And you're the one that named them?"

"Yep. Nzinga bestowed that honour upon me. She and I get along. Same sense of humour."

"Did you have any input into our pairing off?"

"Heavens, no. I was nine years old when they were weaned. I'm sure SciBee had all sorts of scientific reasons for how they worked it out."

"Do you know the criteria for your own pairing?"

"He was the runt of the litter, and I was handicapped, so it was pre-ordained. Quite unscientific. Besides, he'd imprinted on me, so it was too late."

"Fair enough." Jane pondered, frowning. "One question..."

"You wonder why I gave the Oreos those names?"

"How did you know that?

Her brother, a slim, darkhaired lad of about sixteen, shrugged. "It doesn't take a mind reader to figure that out. Everybody must ask. Why would you name them opposite to their pelt colours?"

Miriam put on a knowing look. "Ah, that would be a lesson in experimental science."

Tom threw himself on the couch beside Ethan. "Experimental science? I just have to hear the punch line for this one."

Mary chuckled, her hand playing with her partner's ear. "When you put it that way, it's obvious."

"Maybe to some of you." Pete waved a hand at her. "Go ahead, grind. Take advantage of the chance to show off."

"Why, thank you kind sir. I will do so." She turned to Miriam. "Anything to do with not jumping to conclusions based on superficial evidence?"

"It might..." She put on a mysterious look.

"Aha! But let's not jump to conclusions..."

"Exactly."

They shared a grin.

The white auguar yawned hugely, as did her partner. "What are you two going on about? Don't tell me Mary's got a new partner for the Extreme Intellect club."

Oops! I can see where this is going. "Oh, no." Miriam put on an earnest face. "Don't get me wrong. I'm not that smart. I'm Sensitive. I'm the most Sensitive human anybody's ever found, but I'm no genius. I hardly know what calculus is, and I don't play virtuoso violin. I just communicate. That's it. One-trick pony. I guess I'm a grind, too."

Tom frowned. "There's nothing wrong with being a worker, but I'm not sure I believe that totally. What's the catch?"

"Well, if you really must know..."

"It would help us try to fit you in somewhere."

She glanced over. *He's completely serious.* "Well, when barwolves go into their gestalt, their intelligence increases exponentially with each new addition. If I'm with a barwolf triad, we're nine times as smart as me all alone. Sort of. It isn't straight math."

"But you were talking about our auguars using a gestalt."

"With auguars it isn't as efficient. It's hard to explain."

"Can you give us a for-instance?"

"Um...okay. Area of a circle. Pi times the radius squared, right? How many decimals can you give me for pi?"

Tom frowned. "3.141592...6, I think."

"That's three better than I can do on my own. Now watch this." She sent out the invitation. Hesitating, one by one, the four auguars joined in.

Question: value of pi?

She reeled it off. "3.141592653589...need I go on?"

There was dead silence in the room. Miriam frowned. *What's happening now?*

Emotion: question?

Bosz sent a feline chuckle. *Image: Miriam regarding auguars.*

She brought her attention to the room. The auguars were frozen, their eyes boring into hers. The partners were also gazing, awestruck and some a bit fearful. Pete tried to turn Blondie's head to look at him, but her eyes stayed fixed on Miriam.

"I'm sorry. It must be the first full gestalt they've ever been in as adults. I didn't know they'd react like that." *Emotion: finish.*

The barwolves came out of their trance, still looking dazed.

"How do you mean?" Tom stared into Ethan's eyes for a moment. The cat's tongue reached out and rasped his cheek, and he nodded and patted its head, then returned his attention to Miriam, eyebrows raised.

"They don't have much Math training, and probably don't even know what pi is. Bosz gave us the formula, and we were calculating it on the fly. They should be able to do math at that level and maintain complete awareness of their environment at the same time. It takes practice, but it becomes completely natural. A matter of multi-tasking. One of the younger scientists at Barwolf Base has been working on it. Guy called Joachim Perez, if you want to look up his research."

Tom glanced at Mary. "Sounds up your alley."

"I'll check him out. Is he cute?"

"Definitely not. But he's very smart. Tell him I recommended you contact him."

"Fine." Tom regarded his pride. "Enough excitement. We need time to process all this new data. How about lunch?"

He didn't seem to be consulting anyone else, so Miriam nodded.

"How soon can you be ready?"

"What's to get ready?" She grinned and ran a hand down her ship slacks. "I'm dressed for public display."

Pete followed this gesture. "Don't you want to change?"

Miriam frowned. "Why would I change for lunch? Is it a special occasion?"

The smaller boy matched her expression. "It's uniforms only in the mess, of course."

"I don't have a uniform. Must I beg for crumbs outside the door?"

Tom chuckled. "She's not Space Arm, Pete."

"She's not? How did you know that?"

"Because I asked Ethan. He and Bosz have been chatting all this time, getting reacquainted, I gather." He ruffled the big auguar's short mane.

The cat leaned into his hand. *Emotion: agreement.*

Mary regarded Miriam. "What do you mean, you're not Space Arm? The military owns all the auguars."

"Not this one."

"Who owns him?"

Tom glanced at Miriam, so she took over. "Nobody. Auguars are designated self-aware beings, and as such cannot be owned by people. Your beasts are all under contract and the stewardship of Space Arm. Bosz is under the care of Factory 4-80. In order to work with him, I am an employee of Freighty as well."

Tom mused a moment. "It will make it more difficult to fit you in with our program."

She regarded him. "You said that before. I don't think I'm here to fit into your system." *Oops. I know how that sounded.* "I mean, of course I want to fit in so I can work with you. But I get the feeling they want me to stay separate. There's all sorts of scientific stuff going on, and we're all test subjects, so we can't be told everything."

Mary leaned forward. "What can you tell us?"

She shrugged. "Nobody told me there was anything I can't tell you. If I don't tell you something, it's because I don't know. Okay?"

Tom nodded judiciously. "We can take that at face value. Why do you think you're here?"

"I'm assuming they'll tell us. Definitely gestalts. They'll be setting up studies, developing norms, you know, the usual scientific stuff."

"We don't know much about the science. They just run tests on us, and don't tell us anything."

"It wasn't quite that way with me. You see…"

He held up his hand, stopping her. "This is great information, but the mess hall closes in half an hour, and none of us have eaten. Why don't we hit the chow line, and we can continue over lunch."

They flowed out the door in a mass of furry bodies, Tom leading the way, with Miriam in the place of honour at his side. She and Bosz watched with amusement as the pride organized itself into a definite hierarchy, with Vela and Mary close behind, and the Twins bringing up the rear, Jane half a step ahead of Pete.

The dining hall was huge and echoing, although sparsely occupied at the moment. They picked up trays of food, and Tom led the group to a special table with spaces between the chairs for the auguars to sit.

As soon as everyone was settled, Mary leaned in. "This will be great. You two have always been a mystery to us. They never told us anything about you, and it was pretty obvious we weren't supposed to ask."

"Oh, that's the scientific method. They probably didn't want to contaminate the purity of the sample. It was the same with me, although I was able to worm a whole lot of info out of people."

"You read their minds?" Pete's eyebrows disappeared in the dark bangs that covered his forehead.

She laughed. "Not a chance. I guess you don't know much about barwolves?"

Tom shook his head. "We've had limited contact in strict laboratory conditions."

"Well, I spent a couple of years at Barwolf Base, with a whole tribe of them wandering around, mingling with the humans. I worked with them on a daily basis. Then I moved to *Jerusalem's Hope*, where I live in the SciBee section, working with barwolf cubs on a project I'm not allowed to talk about. Bosz and I take classes — if you can call them that — with the older barwolf cubs, and sometimes with the adults. Three special ones I'd call friends."

Mary's eyes were shining. "That sounds the coolest." Then she frowned. "And how does that affect how you found out about us?"

"Compared to us, all barwolves are mind readers. What one barwolf knows, they all know. So, when humans are dealing with barwolves, they have to be careful what they share. It's a Security Ops nightmare. On top of that, in both labs there's a whole level of Sensitives just below my abilities, and with barwolves to translate, the atmosphere is just full of information going every which-way. There's just so much data around, you learn to screen most of it out or you'd go nuts.

"But the humans are careful about their thoughts. If they didn't want me to know about something, believe me, the data was not made available."

"Then how did you get it?"

"Well, part of the time I was a test subject, but because I'm ahead of everybody else, sometimes I was the researcher and sometimes the teacher. People talk about stuff, and it's easy to direct the conversation, when people are enthused, you know? They sorta forget who they're talking to."

She gave a knowing wink, and they chuckled.

"And then there's my guardian, Roselyn."

"We have heard of her. I got the impression everybody liked her."

"Oh, they do."

"She's a soft touch, then?"

"Hah! Not a chance. There's only one way to get information out of Rosy."

"What's that?"

"Ask her. If she doesn't know the answer, she'll tell you so. If you're not supposed to know, she tells you so, and that's that. But most of the time she gives you the answer you need. Mind you, not the one you thought you wanted. She's almost as Sensitive as me, and she's a teacher. You want information, you ask Rosy straight out and be happy with the answer. If you're not satisfied, then you go away and think, because you've been given what's necessary."

Mary idly toyed with Vela's left ear. "It sounds like you have a good relationship. Do you miss her?"

"Not really. We talk pretty much every day." *Better to leave out the fact that I can connect with any member of my family at will, re-ti.*

"Yeah, but even the most expensive method, that — what's it called? — Pony Express, there's still the lag time."

"No, no. Not at all..." *Oops. I wonder...* "What do you know about Barwolf aether communication?"

The pride shared looks, and as usual, Tom spoke for the group. "Pretty well nothing. We know it exists. We'd never be allowed to use it."

She shrugged. "I think we just hit our first problem. If you don't know about it, then you're not supposed to know, so that's all you're going to get from me." *And they're definitely not ready for interspecies families, yet.*

He frowned. "You won't tell us?"

"I don't think I should. If you want to know, ask your officers. If they give the okay, I'll tell you what I know, but I bet it's above their security clearance as well."

She held up a hand to stem the protests. "From what I hear, that's pretty typical of Space Arm. AetherCom is a system you're not allowed to know about, and here you sit with someone who uses it to call her Mum every day." She shrugged. "Weird."

"Yep, that's Space Arm. But it tells us one thing."

All eyes turned to Mary.

"You don't need permission to use the system. If you have the ability, you make the call." She stared at Miriam. "Right?"

"You are the smart one in the cadre, aren't you?"

"Yep. Sometimes the genius just flows out of me, and I can't stop it."

Pete scoffed. "Yeah. And sometimes it's cowslop, and it comes out all the same."

Tom cleared his throat. "And now perhaps someone could ask an intelligent question, before we descend into the mire of our usual repartee."

Jane complied quickly. "I'm interested in this naming and choosing. You've obviously spent more time with the scientists. What do you think's going on?"

Miriam regarded them, thinking how to put this. It was obviously more important to them than might be expected, and she stopped herself from asking just how much anybody told them.

"Well, I'm assuming they're using this group to test what pairings work best. It's really too small a sample for statistical accuracy, but they've got an alpha male human and an alpha male auguar; they pretty well had to be partnered to keep the peace. They have a pair of twin humans who are genetically similar, which is handy for some tests. They partner the male with a female auguar and the female with a male auguar, so they can see how each combination works." She turned to Mary. "And I'm sorry, but it looks like you didn't get much choice. The fourth pairing had to be a female/female, and that worked because you're both mentally strong. If I might make an observation based on my initial impression..."

Mary glanced at Tom. "Oh, by all means, do."

"Ethan and Vela seem to have worked things out. I can feel it in the gestalt, so I'm pretty sure of that. You and Tom...I must reserve judgement on that, due to lack of evidence."

The larger girl threw her head back and laughed. "Well, that was diplomatic, I must say."

Miriam felt the drop in the tension. She reached down and twined her fingers in Bosz's ruff.

He gave her a bump with his soft nose and a quick lick on the wrist, then settled. *Emotion: satisfaction.*

I'm glad you see it that way. I've gotta keep my opinions to myself, around here.

They spent the rest of the meal with the pride clueing Miriam in about life at Mars Base. When she mentioned Rafi Erickson, the girls both laughed.

Miriam regarded them. "Am I missing something?"

They shared a glance, and Jane shrugged. "No, Rafi's just fine. He's one of those prodigies. Youngest Ensign ever signed on in Sol System. Apparently, there's somebody younger out in Barnard."

"Oh, Andrew Collingwood."

"You know him?"

She smiled. "It's a small population out there. His mother, Captain O'Rourke, is Chakka's handler. They visit us whenever they're downplanet. Andrew's a great guy: only moderately weird. His wife, Toni, is Nzinga's handler and a Commando Weaponless expert. I really like her."

Pete shook his head. "More information in one sentence than we've had on the subject in four years. Hard to take it all in."

"But we were talking about Rafi..."

Jane nodded. "Yeah. He's betwixt and between. Too young to take part in the usual Ensigns' foolishness, but he's an officer, like us. He might have been soft on me for a while, but he found out what I'm really like."

It came out before she thought. "Oh. What are you really like?"

"Not into minding a baby. I'd be quite happy to attract the attention of one of those older ensigns."

"He gave me the impression he wouldn't mind running into me again. Would that be a problem?"

"Not unless it's in a karate match. He's deadly."

"He did mention giving lessons."

The group chuckled, and all eyes turned to Tom, who blushed. "Okay, okay, I'll tell her. I took some MA training when

I was a kid, and I was pretty good…I thought. Let's just say he taught me a lesson."

"But he's such a pleasant, unassuming guy."

"That was the problem. It wasn't getting dumped on my duff that bothered me. It's just that he was so damned worried that he'd hurt me."

"That fits. Toni told me that injuring your sparring partner is a no-no. Shows a lack of control."

Jane peered at Miriam. "You've been taking Commando martial arts training?"

Miriam flexed a thin arm. "Heavens, no! I just work out with her for exercise." She indicated Bosz, who languidly stretched his front claws. "With him, I'm armed and dangerous enough."

Tom regarded her auguar with more respect. "So, he's been trained to fight?"

"Not a lot." She cocked her head and looked at him. "You play human ruggerball. In full protective gear, I assume?"

"Duh! How stupid do I look?"

"I assume you've seen vid of a real game."

"Yeah, I see where you're going. It's hardly the same."

"Well, Bosz plays with the barwolf pups. With no padding."

"How does he survive?"

"Speed and intelligence. He can read the play several bounces ahead of them. He never gets caught in a scrum, and his passes are pinpoint. He was about the same size as the pups when they were learning. Oh, and the barwolves always play fair. Nobody ever takes cheap shots."

Tom flexed a shoulder. "Wish I could say the same about humans." The mess hall staff were turning down the lights, so he stood. "We were allowed an extra-long lunch break to welcome you, but now we must follow our usual schedule. Mary will escort you to your quarters, and we'll come for you at 17:30 for supper. You can rest up or wander around as you choose. Ethan can upload Bosz with our assigned security area. I doubt you'll get lost."

"I don't need an escort, thanks all the same." She paused to retrieve her schedule from Bosz. "Hmm...who is Commander George?"

"That would be Commander Dr. Adam George, the head of the whole SciBee Auguar Program."

"I see him at 09:00 tomorrow. Any advice?"

Tom grinned. "He rarely talks to mere test subjects like us. Rather aloof and academic, in my observation. No idea how he'll approach a teenager."

"I hope he approaches me as a visiting expert."

"Don't hold your breath."

"I get the message." She shrugged. "Everyone flying by the seats of our pants, here. We'll work something out."

Tom looked down at her. "A bit of advice. In the military, we keep our heads down unless we're saluting. It seems to work best."

She restricted her reaction to a nod. *Not how we do it in the Barnard System, but somehow, I don't think it's time for that discussion.*

She turned to the rest. "Thanks for the warm welcome. See you at supper."

They all smiled and murmured various responses, and she left.

AetherCom 2: Phone Home

Barwolf: Patches
Initiated by: Miriam
Responder: Rosalyn
Aether Setting: Rosalyn's office on Jerusalem, Miriam's rooms at Mars Station

For a while, they followed the map Bosz had been given, wandering around their part of the station. Then they navigated easily to her cabin, which turned out to be a two-room suite larger than anything she'd ever owned. She packed her small amount of luggage away, played with the sanitary facilities to get them straight, then flopped on the big, soft bed and opened her mind to her family.

Rosy came online from *Jerusalem. You're there, are you?*

Miriam switched the com so they met in the aether version of her own rooms. *All established. How do you like my grand suite?*

Rosie strolled around, peeking into corners. *Very nice.*

Finally treated in the manner to which I will become accustomed.

Rosy came and sat on the bed beside her. *So, dear, how's it going?*

Fine, I guess. It's pretty confusing, actually.

Emotion: concern.

No, no, it's not like that. You know how comfortably Chakka and Nzinga slip in and out of gestalt with Captain O'Rourke and Toni? And you and me if they want?

I always thought that's how the auguar bond works.

Nobody does that around here. We trained the litter to form a gestalt with each other, but nobody has taken it any further. The handlers use their augments to share, but that's far below what they're capable of. Blue Cadre has never been in full gestalt. They use the standard augment gestalt, but I don't think they know how to commit emotionally.

Are you sure?

I'm not sure of anything, but I've been here most of the day, and nobody has even made any augment contact with me. I tell you, it's been a workout of my social skills, having to communicate only by talking. It sure wastes a lot of time.

Rosy nodded. *It sounds like you have a handle on it. Can you see any source of difficulty because of this situation?*

Well, of course I can communicate with the auguars. I must be careful the humans don't think I'm reading their minds. It seems to be a more serious concern around here.

I'm glad you know that. I've tried hard to teach you…

…many, many times, and yes, I was listening. Come on, Mum!

Rosy sent a calming feeling, and their talk turned to more mundane matters.

2. TROUBLE IN THE PRIDE

Supper was another pleasant social time. Afterwards they retired to the Blue Cadre lounge and were just settling themselves when the trouble started.

Miriam could see it coming. Each had their own space, and a new sofa had been brought in for her, squeezed into the corner by the drinks machine.

However, when the pride entered, the black auguar sauntered over and flopped himself on the pad meant for Bosz. Without hesitation, the little grey auguar strolled in, hopped up on Jane's couch and laid his head on her leg giving her his best "please, please" stare.

In a flash Blondie was at full bound towards his rival.

Easy, boy.

Emotion: determination.

Slipping off the couch, Bosz met the larger animal head on in the open space. Blondie seemed to drive straight over the smaller cat, but then his feet left the floor, and he flipped over, landing on his back, skidding to his handler's feet and coming up short against the couch. He lay there a moment, dazed, then rolled shakily upright.

His recent opponent was lying in his own bed at Miriam's side, licking his stretched-out hind leg.

Thomas looked from one to the other. "That was interesting."

"An honest mistake. Now he knows better."

"I didn't see exactly what happened. It was too fast."

She grinned. "A plain old one-foot judo throw. Basic Commando training. Over the last few years Chakka the Warrior has been taking his fatherly duties seriously. Every time *NightHawk* and *Jerusalem* meet, there are several heavy father-and-son training sessions. That's good, because he needs all the help he can get to deal with his mother."

"Why is that?"

"Well, I guess when the kittens in her litter were learning to play fight, she only got half the lesson." She read their puzzled glances.

"You know that playing kittens are cute and all that. But there's a serious purpose behind it. They're figuring out their pecking order. For her littermates, play was just play. For Nzinga, being the alpha of the pride was more important. She made the grade, although she's average in size."

Mary nodded. "Yeah, she's in the literature. The crowning glory of the old-style Commando auguars. She and Toni Jacobs got more re-li action than any pair in the history of the program."

Miriam grinned. "Bosz and I spent the last five years with them, off and on. Once he got big enough to be obstreperous, she came down on him pretty hard, so I took a hand."

"You?"

"Well, Toni and I worked together. When Nzinga got too rough, I would pull Bosz into gestalt, but Toni would stay out of it. Any auguar in gestalt with a handler is more than a match for a lone auguar."

Tom frowned. "That's a pretty broad statement."

She shrugged. "Because of his training, Bosz could probably hold his own with any of Blue Cadre except Ethan without my help. By the time we get finished with our training, any one of the other auguar teams should be able to handle Ethan if he's alone. It's a good goal to work towards."

Tom frowned. "We don't have much of that kind of training. We're not supposed to be fighters so much as technicians."

"This has little to do with fighting skill and everything to do with gestalts."

He nodded hesitantly. "I suppose we'll have to find out."

"Oh, I'm confident you will."

3. DR. ADAM GEORGE

The commander was not what she expected. No lab coat, no custom enterpad on his sleeve. He was tall and slim, rather dignified, but not at all imposing. He met her at the door to his office and gestured her to a comfortable chair, taking the matching seat across the low coffee table and stretching out a hand for Bosz to sniff.

His desk — large, bare, and possibly real wood — dominated the far side of the room. The obvious perk of the office was a large bank of windows that looked through the dome at the view she had seen from the tram: Mars Station, a conglomeration of domes of all sizes spread across the hazy red surface of the planet below. New construction of more earth-like architecture grew in anticipation of the increasing air density due to the terraforming.

The commander waited until she and Bosz were comfortable. "So, Miss Lantz. How are you settling in?"

She gave the required polite smile. "The cadre has made me feel most welcome. Considering the lack of instructions, they have tried hard to fit me in. I hope my interaction with the rest of the project goes as smoothly."

"Considering the situation, I would be rather surprised if you fitted in well at all."

She took a moment to digest that and read his aura. *He really means that. Well, Rosy says if they want to be frank...* "Thank you for being honest with me, sir. But where does that leave us? Am I a problem for you?"

He steepled his fingers and gave the hint of a smile. "Of course, you are a problem. That's my job: solving problems."

He paused, but she decided to wait him out.

Finally, he leaned back. "I'll put you in the picture. This is the military. I know it's the Science Branch, but it's still military. On the surface, we seem to function the same as any science institution, but don't believe it. Deeper down, there's a military mindset that drives it all, and don't fool yourself into thinking you can fight that."

She nodded and waited again.

"You probably think that true science doesn't work very well in a military environment. You'd be right. The military is far more oriented towards results."

"How does that work?"

"Their attitude to research is slanted by their desire for the practical solution that solves the problem they are working on." He raised a hand. "Don't bother. You and I know that's bad science."

"I was going to say, sir, that I'm already working on a project in conjunction with Space Arm."

"Barwolf Communication."

"And in that case, Space Arm didn't get what they wanted. Admiral Mira said so in the last general meeting."

Again he paused, regarding her. "And the message is that you were at the general meeting of a high-security project."

Now it was her turn for a knowing smile. "I meant that I'm aware of the difference you were speaking of." She leaned forward. "Have you had much contact with barwolves?"

He frowned. "We have had them onsite several times. I supervise our studies of the species."

"But you have no experience working in a barwolf-rich atmosphere, where their ethos dominates."

"How does this help us, here?"

"A lot. I have lived in a cooperative environment all my life. I spent the last four years studying and working with that sort of approach. Communication and cooperation are instilled in my bones. I can't help it. I get along with everybody."

"I get that feeling from you."

"My concern is that people from authoritative systems sometimes take my cooperation for weakness. Any interaction where only one of the participants is trying to win will, by its very nature, turn out skewed results."

Again he steepled his fingers. "Can you give me an example?"

"Sure. Ensign von Arnim. He and I have been walking a narrow line since the first moment we met."

The doctor frowned. "Ensign von Arnim has proven an exemplary leader of his cadre."

"Of course. An exemplary leader who exudes authority, strength and honour. In any military situation, I would follow him without question."

"So, where is the problem?"

"What happens in a project where I know more about the situation than he does? If he has the idea that I'm a good follower, and suddenly I disagree with his opinion, he's going to see that as a challenge to his general authority. If he runs true to form, he will then stop work on the original problem and focus on re-establishing his authority by winning the confrontation. I don't want to be melodramatic, but I was in a situation once where that pattern almost ended up with someone dead." She regarded him. "And, risking a security breach, I will tell you it was worse than that: lost in Otherwhere."

He nodded. "You don't need to worry about the security angle. That report was part of the reason you were invited here. Your little adventure in the aether fog with Commando Sergeant Zueva was highlighted as a warning to all of us."

"Good. Also, I'm running into situations where I don't know how much to reveal to the cadre. I was briefed by the SecuriCorps agent on the project, and her advice was to keep my mouth shut unless specifically ordered otherwise."

Another wintry smile. "That's what I'd expect from SecuriCorps." He made a note on his enterpad. "Another problem to deal with. I'll alert Dr. Lee, the Blue Cadre Research Project Head, and he'll brief you on the security levels of all involved."

"Thanks. That will help a lot."

He went on to outline the general makeup of the project, referring her to a document with its goals and objectives.

She did a quick scan of the précis Bosz posted for her. "And how much of this is the auguar cadre aware of?"

"Only the main points. Allowing the experimental subjects access to the objective of any specific experiment..."

"...will skew the results."

"Correct."

"So, if I read this document, it will give me an idea of what I should tell them and what I shouldn't. From a scientific point of view."

"Exactly." He regarded her. "You seem familiar with scientific procedure."

"The whole SciBee section of *Jerusalem's Hope* is an immersive laboratory. My guardian is one of the main researchers."

"And even at your tender age, you're listed as a research assistant. I gather you earn your wages."

She grinned. "If you ever house trained a pet, you'd know. And barwolves are carnivores, if you take my meaning."

He touched his nose. "I do." He glanced at his enterpad again. "Entertaining and useful as this meeting has been, my time has run out, so let's wrap up." He counted points on his fingers.

"First, I find you have a mature attitude towards this whole situation."

"Upbringing, again. I have mostly been in contact with adults since I was six years old."

"Second, your natural flexibility could cause you problems in the military environment, mainly in hindering your usefulness, but also interfering with interpersonal relations."

"On that topic, sir..."

He paused, his hand ready to tick off the third point.

"What am I here for? Nobody so far has been able to tell me."

He relaxed his hands. "Easy to answer at my level. You are here to give my researchers new information and a fresh look at their projects. The Blue Cadre Research Project Head, Dr. Lee, will arrange everything."

He ticked off a final point. "Your objectives as representative of the Factory 480 Fabrication Consortium are really up to you. My information is that Freighty, as his friends call him, placed your auguar with the barwolves for a specific purpose, and perhaps we will now find out what it was."

She laughed. "I guess I better contact Freighty again."

"Do you need com time assigned? No, I assume not."

He stood. "Any more questions, please refer them to Dr. Lee." He held out his hand. "I have been awaiting your arrival with interest. Scientists need stirring up every once in a while. I'm guessing you'll try to stir without creating too many waves, which is probably wise."

She rose and shook his hand. "Thank you for the warm, if reserved welcome, Dr. George. You've put me in the picture."

He walked towards the door with her. "And by the way, I didn't detect any of your famous Sensitivity. Would I have noticed if you had used it on me?"

She smiled up at him. "It isn't something you turn off and on. I use it as naturally as you use your augment. Sensitivity is a passive skill. I don't reach out and control anybody." She stopped and faced him. "Surely I don't need to tell you that my communication ability requires an auguar and the conscious cooperation of the other party."

"No, you don't, but it's nice to be reassured."

"Do I frighten you?"

"An honest question. Only in a general sense." He smiled. "Personally, I find you quite pleasant, in a 'don't mess with me' sort of way."

"It usually works. I'm hoping most of my relationships with your people will go as smoothly."

He pushed the door button. "Oh, I'm sure they won't, but that probably won't get back to me. If I hear about it, it's serious."

"Well, I'm not going to hide anything to keep you from hearing about it."

"Then I am forewarned." He raised a hand in a half salute, and she turned away, her auguar tight against her leg.

AetherCom 3: Meeting With the Boss

Barwolf: Not necessary
Initiated by: Miriam
Responder: Freighty

Aether Setting: Freighty's Renaissance Italian office at Factory 4-80

She had nothing scheduled until lunch, so she went to her quarters and took a comfortable seat.

Dropping into AetherCom, she opened her mind for the huge presence of Factory 4-80. She found it easily and allowed herself to be drawn in and seated in the usual cartoon living room. The Mouse bounced through the archway, but she held up a hand before he started. "I'm sorry, Micha, business call. Could I talk to The Boss, himself?"

She felt a moment's disorientation and then found herself in a dark-paneled library, seated in a stiff, padded armchair. Paintings fought with shelves of books for wall space, and statues on pedestals were pushed to positions far out into the room. Freighty's "Mediterranean businessman" avatar sat across an ornate antique desk.

Is this more appropriate?

She took a moment to appreciate the setting. "Very nice. I'm sure the Italian count who owns the original won't mind you borrowing the image."

He, too, gazed around. *A bit crowded, but that's the fashion down there. At least, it was three hundred years ago.* He folded his hands on the desk in front of him. *So. How is it going?"*

"Very well. It is wonderful to see what those cute little kittens grew into. The Cadre is friendly and curious with a bit of suspicious reserve, which I suppose is natural. I get the feeling that they have a nice, safe little niche, and they don't want anything to make waves."

That's a pretty good description for most military groups, I would say.

"It's early days, yet, but I'm wondering how well this cadre is blending with the rest of the military. My briefing from Captain O'Rourke back home didn't help much. She just said that they want to expand the use of the teams, to get away from auguars as Commando auxiliaries. She thinks Space Arm has a limited view of how the auguars fit into the mix."

Freighty nodded. *They don't know it, but possibly auguars could help solve the problem of ArIn morality.*

"How would that work?"

Auguars have an innate sense of right and wrong. Different from humans, of course, but nonetheless, a morality that drives their actions. They are also self-aware. They are already a form of ArIn, due to their technological abilities. It occurs to me that if we were to increase the auguar intelligence a considerable amount, we might create a super intelligence controlled by innate morality.

"I can see that. But auguars have the basic morals of a cat. They were developed because of their combined pride mentality and killing ability. That might not be an appropriate model for a super-intelligence."

True. Freighty cocked his head to one side. *Any thoughts on that?*

"Only the obvious one you'd get from someone brought up with barwolves."

Yes, a canine version of the auguar might tick all sorts of boxes.

"What should I do about that?"

Freighty laughed. *Nothing at all, my dear, except be yourself, and Bosz should act likewise.*

"Ah. Having an auguar with some of the reactions of a canine is the thin edge of the wedge."

Something like that.

Emotion: frustration. "Well, I can hardly put that objective in my daily planner. What am I supposed to teach this cadre? Am I supposed to teach them?"

Of course. One of the reasons you were sent was your teaching ability.

"I'm looking for guidance, Freighty. All my teaching has been done from a curriculum. I've got nothing to go on, here."

Nonsense. By far your best work was done with nothing but your intuitive analysis of what your students needed.

"You mean the Musketeers?"

Exactly.

34

"And you expect me to look at this complex cadre of young adults of two species and use my famous abilities to figure out what they need and how I can give it to them?"

Freighty clapped his hands in glee. Micha Mouse ran in through the left-hand archway, cartwheeled across the room, and exited on the other side.

She slouched in her chair. "Great. You're so much help."

He stilled himself, straightening his tie. *No, no, Miriam. You will get all the help I can give you. I simply wanted you to see the nature of the situation.* He gave a sly grin. *And give you a little motivational boost.*

She did not relent. "And now that I'm all pumped up to succeed, what next?" She hitched forward and straightened her back. "I know how these things are supposed to go. If you want results, you need to give me direction. That's your job."

She ticked points off on her fingers. "I need to know what success will look like. I need to know the boundaries and scope of the task. I need clear, definable objectives." She stopped, giving him a challenging stare.

And that's what you shall have. The one thing you left out is that you need unconditional support and the backing of influence and resources. At the moment, you and your auguar are the best resources we could use. I assume you know you have my total backing, but I'm happy to remind you.

He leaned back and smiled. D*on't let it go to your head, but you have a direct line to the most powerful NGO in two Systems.*

She shrugged. "Yeah, I know all that, and thanks. But how does that help me when I stand there, and they're all looking at me expecting me to set the agenda? Even worse, what happens when they decide I've got nothing useful for them, and they just ignore me?"

He made a negating slash with his hand. *This will not happen. You have made far more progress than you think.*

"I've only been here one day."

And I have favourable reports. He laid a finger beside his nose in an ancient sign of secret knowledge. *Eyes and ears everywhere, remember.*

She sat back. "You're dumping it all in my lap, so I'm taking charge of this meeting. What do you want in the next three days?"

Yes, let's get down to business. I want you to create a list of what you need. Based on your analysis of the situation in Blue Cadre, what are their strengths and weaknesses, and how do any of those conditions mesh with your training and abilities?

"No problem. And based on that data, I will probably be able to develop some short-term goals." She glared at him. "I know you have long-term objectives you're not telling me. I figure you are also working by the seat of your rusty metallic pants, and you are waiting to see what I come up with before you decide on what to aim for."

That sounds like a wise way to proceed.

"I will report in three days. Sooner if anything comes up."

I await your progress with my usual anticipation.

"Whatever you mean by that."

I mean I am very old and often very bored, and it only takes a small twitch to the fabric of my life to entertain me.

"Well, I don't promise to tweak your shirttail, but I fear it's inevitable."

I couldn't ask for anything more. I wish you all the luck you need. Your natural abilities will take care of the rest.

"Fine. You just be there to sweep up the pieces afterwards. Bye, now."

Goodbye my dear. Happy hunting.

4. MIRIAM'S AUTOBIOGRAPHY

At lunch, nobody asked her about her meeting with Commander George, but when they had finished eating, Tom made a general announcement. "We've had a slight change in schedule in honour of our guest. The next half hour, usually reserved for meetings and liaison with other departments, will now be designated time to liaise..." he made a theatrical "ta-da" gesture, "...with Miriam."

Mary met Miriam's glance. "What are we supposed to liaise about?"

It was the first time she had seen Tom look uncertain. "Well...whatever we like, I gather."

A general shifting of posture in the group alerted her. "Don't worry, folks, my meeting with Dr. George went well, and I also made contact with one of my principals. We all have homework to do, which I will tell you about." She turned to Tom. "Where do we meet?"

He shrugged, but with a much happier face. "Wherever we like, I gather, but the obvious place is the Blue Cadre common room."

"Where we met yesterday?"

"Right. I asked Dr. Lee to meet us there."

"Away we go, then."

When they reached the room, a tall, dark-skinned man with cropped, curly hair was waiting. When they were introduced, he gave her a reserved smile. "Dr. George has briefed me on your meeting with him. We'll need some liaising, but not now. I'd like to just sit in and get an idea of how you work."

"That's fine with me. Shall we proceed?"

His hand swept the room, so she assessed it, then turned to Tom. "Do those couches move?"

Again, a cloud crossed his brow. "Not usually. When we want to just chuck it around, we use the dining hall after meals. Here is different. They've been that way a long time…"

"…and I'm sure they were divided up to allow individuals a feeling of personal space."

"Probably."

"Exactly the opposite of what I am trying to do."

"And what are you trying to do?"

She wavered a hand, palm down. "Give you an idea of how barwolves work in cooperation."

He nodded, scanning the room again. "And that won't work in here. We need a special place where we can be physically closer together."

"Right. A circle is the traditional shape."

"With good reason. Let me check…" His face blanked and Ethan stared up at him. "…yes, the small conference room down the hall is free. We can set it up any way we like."

Soon they were busy reorganizing a pleasant room with restful wave-patterned paneling and comfortable lounge chairs, creating a circle with spaces for the auguars to lie between.

They stood regarding their work, but nobody moved.

Tom brushed his hands together. "Okay. Who sits where?"

She glanced up at him. "Ever heard of King Arthur?"

He accessed his data files. "Yes…oh! The Round Table."

His cadre gave him puzzled looks.

"Go ahead. Sit wherever you like."

Mary chuckled. "Sure. Sit on the floor and let your auguar sit in the chair if you want to. It will ensure free-ranging creativity."

Miriam flicked the older girl's arm with her fingertips. "I suggest we stick with seating norms. We want everybody to be comfortable."

Jane kicked the floor. "What if auguars aren't comfortable on this hard plastic? Did anyone ever ask them?"

Miriam laughed out loud. "See? It's working. You're asking questions you never thought of before."

The cadre chuckled but Miriam caught a thoughtful look between the two eldest members. She ignored it, went to the nearest chair and flopped in ungracefully. Bosz made an equally unconcerned landing to her left, heaving a comfortable sigh.

After a moment's hesitation, they all took chairs, although the younger members waited to see where Tom and Mary would station themselves.

She nodded. "Good. Let's take this in baby steps. Tomorrow, we'll use a random pick, and one of us will be given the job of arranging the seating order. The objective will be simply to choose a pattern that hasn't been used before."

Receiving nods all round, she held out open hands. "What does anybody want to liaise about?"

Mary took the lead, as she seemed to do in social interactions. "I think everybody here would benefit from some idea of your background. It will help us see where you're coming from." She gave an evil smile. "And stifle a lot of burning curiosity."

I'd like to have a grin like that...concentrate, Miriam. She nodded. "Sure enough. Here goes." She straightened her back in a formal pose.

"A Brief Autobiography of Miriam Lantz."

"I was born fifteen years ago on the *Jerusalem's Hope,* which has the dubious honour of being the last generation ship to reach the Barnard System from Sol. Records are sketchy, and we know for sure there are at least five more out there somewhere, maybe more. But they all left Sol before we did, and none of them have ever appeared on any scan. Space Arm has concluded that somewhere in the forty-year journey their engines failed or their society fragmented, and they are floating in space. The chances of anyone being alive after all this time are pretty slim."

Jane cringed. "That's horrible. You mean all those people just died, alone in outer space?"

"I guess so."

Mary regarded her. "Howcome you made it when the others didn't?"

"Two reasons, I think. First, our ship, *Jerusalem's Hope,* was a research vessel, well built and well crewed. It wasn't just some old junker picked up in a scrap yard. Socially, we were a tightly organized group, selected for Sensitivity. That meant we had a better chance of staying sane and on course socially. And of course, there's always an element of luck."

Jane shuddered again. "You think the ones that didn't make it went crazy?"

"That's just speculation, and there's nothing we can do about it, so it's not something I want to spend much time thinking about."

Tom nodded. "Quite right. Leads to extra stress, and we've got enough of that already. Please go on, Miriam."

"Seven years ago, we were just approaching Barnard when my guardian, Roselyn Jakobsdotter, and I made contact with *NightHawk,* the ship that Chakka and Nzinga were assigned to. We had an equipment failure, but Roselyn and I were able to make a gestalt with Nzinga. She analyzed our problem for us, we fixed it, and on we went. That was our good luck. Then they got caught up in the Space Swimmers migration, and we used our whole ship's company in gestalt with the barwolves they had onboard, to help them get out of it."

"Everybody knows about *NightHawk* and the Space Swimmers." Jane stared at her with a frown. "I never heard there was another ship out there."

"Too complicated to explain, but we weren't out with them. We were still approaching Barnard, so nobody was told about us."

"That sounds like the long arm of SecuriCorps. And that was how you got mixed up with the barwolves."

"Exactly. Roselyn and I and my other guardian, Barnabus Lantz, moved into Barwolf Base to help with the barwolf research. They got married and we lived there for a couple of years. Then Freighty — that's the extraterrestrial ArIn factory — got together with Space Arm SciBee and created the Barwolf Communications Project."

"Which you're not allowed to tell us about."

"The project is still running. They chartered *Jerusalem,* and we all moved onboard to continue our research."

Mary regarded her. "But you're always talking about living downplanet."

"That's the way the project works. *Jerusalem* is a freighter, moving goods around the Barnard System. But she's based out of Arborea, the habitable planet. Whenever we can, different members of the team stay downplanet for a few months to coordinate our research with Barwolf Base. We've been doing that for four years, now, give or take."

Tom nodded. "One reason we're based here is so they can send us downplanet for a few months every year to improve our physical conditioning and work out at the Space Arm's Marsport Training Centre."

Dr. Lee leaned into the conversation. "And your downplanet time is scheduled for next month."

"But now you've come here to do...what?" Tom gave a wry smile. "Or aren't you allowed to tell us?"

She returned the grin. "I'm allowed to tell you that Space Arm is a partner in the Barwolf Com Project, but that's all. Bosz is a member of the Auguar Research Project, and we're here to give everyone their money's worth. How that is going to happen is up to Dr. Lee and Commander George. As for the rest of my time, it would be ridiculous to come all the way to Mars, then turn around and go home without visiting Freighty, who is a majority shareholder in the project."

Pete's head came up. "Any chance we'll get to go to the Factory? That would be coolest. I've heard all about Freighty."

Eyes turned towards Dr. Lee, who shook his head. "It would be too big a project to move the whole cadre to Earth orbit, and not much to do once you get there. No, I'm afraid the next couple of months is all the time you get with Miriam and Bosz, so make the best of them."

5. JUST A LITTLE EXERCISE

As she should have expected, the social side of station life was the hardest part. Blue Cadre had been here for years, and they had their own social circle, most of them older and with different interests than Miriam. They were polite about including her in some of their activities, but she was often as bored as the older station teens were with her.

In desperation, she logged into the Rec Department offerings, which were many and varied. She was just chuckling about military applications of the Knitters' and Quilters' Guild when she glanced at the offering just above on the list. Karate.

She jumped up. "Classes for all levels. That sounds like me. Toni says I'm all over the place, and I need proper training. What time is the practise tonight? Oh, Rafi said. It's always at seven. Lousy time to work out, just after supper. Probably far down the list of scheduling priorities. Well, Ensign Ericson, you're in for some entertainment tonight."

She always practiced in normal gym clothing because Toni said you couldn't count on what you might be wearing when you got attacked. So, she suited up in shorts and an athletic bra, covered it with a terrycloth robe, and marched down to the dojo.

She arrived ten minutes early, and Rafi was there with two larger men, warming up. Energetically.

These must be the hotshots.

Miriam slipped out of her robe, made eye contact with Rafi, and took a corner for her own warmup: sit-ups, pushups and deep knee bends interspersed with stretching. Soon she had a glow on, and she did some running on the spot. A hundred punches, a hundred kicks, and she felt a little bit ready for whatever came next.

As she turned around, the three others were standing, finishing their stretches and "chucking it around," as she was learning to call it. Two more trainees were doing less rigorous warmups. There was something different about Rafi that she noticed immediately. In his karate gi he looked wider, more solid, and the confidence she had noticed before was stronger. This was his world.

She strolled over. "Hi, Rafi. Took you at your word. Can I join in?"

He pretended to regard her critically. "You know what you're doing."

She shrugged. "Not really. My trainer says I'm all over the map, whatever that means."

He gave an evil grin. "There's one easy way to find out."

"Sure. Free sparring."

He frowned. "I was thinking more like a pairs kata."

"I know two of those."

"Which ones?"

"I dunno. Toni just called them Level One-A and One-B.

"Whose levels?"

"How should I know? She's a Commando, if that helps any."

Rafi shot a glance at one of the others, a larger, well-muscled man of about thirty. "This is Commando Specialist Jay Tennant. He'll run through them with you. Jay, this is the girl I told you about. Miriam Lantz."

She looked up at the craggy face. "Sure, if working with a dwarf doesn't bother you. The lady I train with is closer to my size."

The Commando frowned. "Toni? Weaponless Specialist Toni Jacobs? I heard she was out in Barnard."

Miriam shrugged. "She is. So was I. She's a Commander, now. She said it was fun to train with someone she could see eye to eye with."

The man looked like he didn't know how to take this, so she became serious. "If you'll walk me through Doubles One-A, we'll find out if I learned anything."

"Sure thing, Miss Lantz." He gestured her to precede him onto the practice floor.

Request: image/idea.

Emotion: eager desire to please.

43

They merged into the familiar gestalt, and the moves from the kata flowed into her.

"Ready?"

She bowed. *"Hai, sensei."*

He bowed, and they took a waiting stance.

"Hajimé." They started out at a walk, but he speeded up when he realized that she was holding her own. Soon they were sailing freely, but then a warning note slipped into the gestalt.

Image: three moves ahead...

She picked her moment and stepped back, making the traditional sign. "Time out, Specialist."

He froze, staring at her.

"You aren't really going to try that next move, are you? You must mass ninety kilos."

The wheels turned. "Right. That's a full-on lift." Then he grinned. "Don't you think you could handle it?"

"Are you willing to risk it on a 'maybe'?"

"It's early in the practice to get dumped in a heap, and by my own partner would be doubly embarrassing."

"Let's not get embarrassed yet. You haven't seen my free sparring."

He frowned, but she raised a hand to stop him. "I think I'd better find someone closer to my own size."

Both their eyes slid towards Rafi.

The Commando laughed. "Your turn, Ensign. If you think you're up to it."

Erickson hesitated, but Tennant elbowed him and grinned, so he stepped out on the floor. "Do you want someone to referee?"

"Are we in a competition?"

"Heavens, no!"

"Good, because according to Toni, Commandos don't score points. They just win or lose."

"Is that a challenge?" His brow wrinkled, and he stepped back.

"Of course not. I came down here to have some fun, get some exercise, and maybe learn something."

He relaxed. "Good." He pulled on his training gloves. "Let's have some fun."

"Sure thing." *Emotion: fun.*

Emotion: eager desire to please.

Emotion: caution.

They circled for a while, hands up and jabbing, feinting, but soon he was trying seriously for a hit. As she slipped further into gestalt with her auguar, time slowed down, her opponent's movements likewise. He tried to speed up, but soon the auguar began to get the pattern of his attacks, and it was even easier.

Okay. What now? I can't just hit him!

She slipped a particularly smooth one-two and allowed his left fist to graze her shoulder. Sure enough, a moment later he tried again, and this time she reached out with her toe and nudged his foot as it came down.

He stumbled but regained his balance easily.

Let's even this out a bit. Image: auguar backing out of gestalt.

Emotion: desire to protect.

Emotion: obey!

Emotion: reluctant desire to please.

Without her auguar, she felt her opponent speed up, and she was hard pressed to stay out of his way. Soon she was retreating, and she was forced onto the attack to drive him back. Unfortunately, she forgot to mind her footing, and a neat sweep rolled her to the side, struggling for balance, and he clipped her lightly on the back of the head.

He made the "Time Out" sign and stepped back.

Both of them stood, breathing heavily, with him staring at her. Finally, he spoke. "What the heck was that? You had me completely outclassed, and then you eased up. It was like meeting a different fighter."

She laughed, reaching down to ruffle the ears of her auguar. "No, <u>we</u> had you outclassed. Then I told Bosz to take a hike. He didn't want to, but he's well trained, and he backed off. Then you were only fighting me. I wasn't faking to make you look better. That's as good as I am, on my own."

He nodded slowly. "When you're in tune with your auguar he's feeding you data, and it makes you that much better?"

Better be careful, here.

"Something like that. But he can't give me extra strength. Pretty soon you would have worn me down."

The two fighters sauntered over. "So, Rafi, my lad. You just about got your ass handed to you on a plate." Tennant turned to her. "What would happen if you went on offense?"

She laughed. "I'd probably break my delicate hand on his hard head. Auguar help is all mental. Besides, I don't want to hit anyone."

He frowned at her. "Look around you, lady. This is karate. We teach you to hit people."

"But what if I hurt someone?"

He shrugged. "It's considered poor control, but it happens. Part of the training."

"No, no. Do you know the expression, 'I feel your pain'?"

"Usually used in a sarcastic way."

"Not with me. When I'm fighting you, it forms a light gestalt between us. It helps me guess what your next move, but if you get hurt, I feel it. So, I practise hard on defence, and a bit on offence in case I need it."

"I see. If your moves are picture-perfect, you're less likely to injure yourself or anyone else."

"That's right. There's no substitute for practice to develop strength and muscle memory." She turned to the third fighter. "Which is why I'm here. Would you like to try a round or two?"

The third man was tall and rawboned and looked tough, but he stumbled back half a step shaking his head. "No, miss, I wouldn't...no, I...just...no."

He seemed in such distress that she couldn't help but open up to him. The emotional turmoil she found in his mind set her back. "No, no, of course not. I do apologize, sir. I did not mean to cause you to relive anything so traumatic."

They all stared at her.

She frowned. "What? What's wrong?"

"How did you know what I was thinking?"

Uh-oh. "I didn't know what you were thinking."

"Yes, you did. You knew I was reliving a traumatic experience. When I was…"

"No, no, don't tell us. We don't have to know."

"But you already know!"

What do I do now? She raised her voice. "No! I don't know. You were in such a state you were giving off all sorts of messages." She turned helplessly to the Commando. "Jay, you're trained to read your opponents. Are you going to tell me you didn't know he was upset?"

"Yeah, it was pretty obvious…"

"Well, there you are. And the only thing that would make someone that upset when nothing had actually happened, is a previous experience that affected him strongly. Right?"

"Yeah, I guess…"

"You guess. Exactly. I made a lucky guess. I wasn't thinking, I was just trying to be nice and calm him down."

She turned to Rafi. "Ensign Erickson, I came down here to fill my Daily Exercise Quota and have some fun. Now I have caused one of your people a great deal of distress, and I must apologize. Now, I think I should leave." She turned away quickly, because she knew the stunned look on his face was going to make her burst into tears.

Several other people in various exercise outfits were now in the dojo warming up and politely ignoring the spat, which didn't make her feel any better.

"Miriam, wait." He caught up with her just inside the door. "You can't run away from this."

She turned, frowning. "I'm not running away. I'm getting out of a situation where I caused somebody unnecessary pain."

"And if you leave it unsolved, it will cause him even more pain."

"How do you know that?"

"Call it a guess. Devon's one of my students, and I know about his problems. You need to stay and practise with us. No sparring, I promise. The best solution for Devon is to normalize the situation."

His use of a psychological term set her mind on a different route. "But I like sparring."

"Not today." He took her arm and led her back to the centre of the mat, a grim smile forming. "Today, you pay."

He raised his voice. "I think we've been a little too relaxed lately. Those of you who came hoping to boost your DEQ, your prayers are answered. A thousand punches, then a thousand kicks ought to tune us up and settle us down. Meditation, please. We need to prepare mentally."

He knelt on the tatami, and the rest made a line in front of him.

Miriam immediately felt better. She and Bosz shifted into a light gestalt, and she ran through one of her awareness exercises.

Time had no meaning until Rafi broke the silence. "All right, folks. On your feet. begin light, and we'll work into deeper stances as we feel it. Lower reverse punch. Jay, please start the count..."

When the class was over, she felt exhausted and relaxed. She stood with the same three men as the rest of the class filed out to the showers.

There was a moment of silence.

"Can I ask a favour? Actually, make a deal."

The Commando chuckled. "Beware when a woman offers you a deal. You're sure to lose."

"No, Jay, I'm serious. I really don't want anybody spreading word around that I can read minds. I can't. I'm Sensitive, which means I'm aware of people's emotions. When I'm in gestalt with Bosz, I can communicate with your augments, but only if you are receptive. That's it."

Tennant nodded. "Commandos work with the Auguar Cadres whenever we get the chance. I pretty well knew that stuff."

She raised her eyebrows to Rafi, and he nodded.

Hesitating, she glanced at Devon.

He gave a hesitant smile. "I don't know much about anything around here. I'm seconded to the Station Mechanical

Department because my company designed the operating software for the heating and cooling equipment."

"So, you're not military?"

"I thought that was obvious."

"Not really. I may be Sensitive, but I don't know anything about the military, either."

Rafi cleared his throat. "So, none of us thinks you can read minds, and we don't spread it around that you can. What's in it for us?"

"I'll train with you. Bosz and I. Give you some once-in-a-lifetime experience."

The three exchanged glances, and they all nodded, even Devon. She met his gaze. "I can stay on defence with you. Once you realize you have no chance of hitting me..."

"I think it might work. You train in a businesslike manner, you sound sympathetic and you know what's going on. Might be just what I need."

"If it isn't, I'll know before there's any damage done."

"Perfect."

"Then it's a deal. Toni says I must train three times a week to make progress, so that's what I'll do. Bosz knows all the schedules, so I'll make sure I come when at least two of you are booked. Okay?"

They nodded, and she turned to leave.

Then she spun back. "But if anyone blabs..." She cocked a skinny fist and put on a fierce frown, "...it's gonna be a different kind of training session."

The Commando laughed. "I don't want anyone finding out I'm training with a fifteen-year-old girl who is afraid of hurting me. Your secret is safe."

AetherCom 4: Help, Mum

Barwolf: Patches
Initiated by: Miriam
Responder: Rosalyn
Aether Setting: Rosalyn's office on Jerusalem

Got a moment, Mum?
Of course, dear. Rosy was sitting at her desk in the Science Department of the ship. *How's it going?*

Miriam pulled up a figurative chair, wavering her free hand back and forth. *So-so. I made a couple of friends...well, sort of.*

Her mother put down the paper in her hand. *That doesn't sound promising. Who?*

Well, that's the problem. Can we team up with Toni for this?

Rosy glanced at the black barwolf lying on a pad in the corner.

Image: Toni.
Emotion: agreement.

Another chair appeared, with the Weaponless Specialist lounging in it. Nzinga's presence sprawled nearby. *Hey, Kiddo. What's up?*

Do you know a Commando by the name of Tennant? Guy about thirty, Specialist like you.

Jay? I thought he'd opted out years ago. I don't know him well. Seen him around. A good man. Serious about his specialty. Why?

He's one of my new maybe-friends.

Toni leaned back more comfortably. *And thereby hangs a tale?"*

Yeah, well, I need your opinion. Both of you. I sort of screwed up, for all the right reasons. I think I fixed it, but...

Her guardian fixed her with a frown and laid down her enterpad. *When you put it that way, it sounds more important than these requisitions. What are you mixed up in now?*

Emotion: rising anger. It's not that serious, and I thought you'd be happy that I'm communicating. I told you I fixed it.

Emotion: calming. All right. Let's just hear the story.

Miriam settled herself and told the whole tale. At the end she spread her hands. *And that's it. I'm going to be training with them. I'm guessing that Devon has some kind of history with violence, and maybe his karate training is part of his therapy. I'll be careful with him until I know him better.*

Rosy met Toni's eyes. *What do you think? You're the expert.*

Well, if you were in the military, I'd say you were a little loose with classified information, but not seriously. As a civilian, you don't have any such restrictions. Now that I think about it, we sent you out into the big world assuming you'd act like a soldier, when there was no evidence to suggest any such thing.

As I keep telling people. I don't have any guidelines, and my objectives aren't clear.

Not your fault, Kiddo. She cocked her head. *What people are you telling this to?*

Only the top brass. Freighty and Commander George.

The Head of the Barwolf Project. Well, when in doubt, go straight to the top. Any luck with answers?

Dr. George fobbed it off to Dr. Lee, Blue Cadre's boss. He's around all the time, so I talk with him a lot. Freighty and I got my objectives ironed out. He's always available when I need to talk.

Emotion: relief. Then it sounds like you're getting help where you need it, dear. Is there anything we can do?

Just give me your opinion. Do you think I was too free with information? Should I cancel this karate stuff?

Emotion: uncertainty. Toni?

Emotion: lack of concern. You made some friends. You're getting exercise, and if you're working with Tennant, you're getting the best of training. Keep Freighty appraised, to make sure you're fulfilling his objectives. Tell you a secret, Kiddo. People are always giving you jobs without specific objectives.

Why would they do that?

Rosy's laugh filled the aether. *Because they have no idea what you'll pick up and what you're able to do with what you get. Everybody's still trying to figure you out, Miriam. That includes Freighty. He's key in all of this.*

Like I say, I talk to him every other day or so. He's been really nice. He said something about sending me a space suit like Andrew's. What's Andrew's suit like?

Toni chuckled. *It's a work of art, and if he sends you one, it means you're important to his plans. That's good, because I'm not so happy with what I'm hearing on the Sol newsfeeds.*

Emotion: concern. What are you hearing? How does it affect Miriam?

Emotion: lack of serious concern. Nothing specific, just too much buzz about the Factory. Freighty doesn't work that way. He stays out of the limelight. If he's getting airtime, somebody else is trying something against him.

What can I do?

Freighty's the one to ask. Let him know you're concerned and offer to help. He'll appreciate that.

Thanks Toni. And you don't think my karate training is a problem?

Emotion: sarcasm. Maybe you'll settle down and focus under the leadership of a young, handsome sensei. The martial arts were not created so you could have fun.

Don't hold your breath. My lessons are part of the base recreation program. Devon is a civilian subcontractor, and two of the women I met are secretaries.

Well, your mother shouldn't hear this, but have a good time. You're in the biggest city you've ever seen, and you're young. Don't waste it.

I should say I don't want to hear it. Toni, that was completely irresponsible.

Emotion: laughter. I know. Mothers are always telling me I'm a bad influence on their kids. Don't bring up the topic with my dear mother-in-law.

Miriam was puzzled. *I thought Captain O'Rourke was a great friend of yours from way back.*

Again the laughter. "We are, but she's also Andrew's mother, and I never get between them. Sometimes I just agree to disagree. Hey, this is fun, but I gotta get back to work.*

Sure, thanks, Toni. I feel better. Mum does too, but she's too mad at you to admit it.

Don't worry, Rosy. You can take it out on me at poker night. I promise to play against you if the stakes are low enough.

The Commando faded from the gestalt, taking her auguar with her.

There. I feel better, now.

I'm not sure I do.

Mum, Toni's just jerking your chain. You know I'm not going to do anything stupid.

You'd better not. You're out there alone six light years away. I just feel so helpless at times.

I'm not alone. I have Bosz and Freighty, and I'm making new friends. This is all working out fine. I never expected it to be easy.

I know you didn't, dear, and I appreciate you calling.

And now you and Barry will go into the kitchen and argue about a meal I won't get to eat, so I'm signing off.

We don't argue, dear. We discuss.

Do you hear the jingle of chain links, Mum?

Yes, I do. Barnabus, say goodbye to the Twit-girl before she starts in on you.

Bye, Mum. Hi, Dad. Bye, Dad. No sense saying goodbye to Patches, because one never really goes away.

Emotion: love and pride.

You too, guys.

The gestalt faded into that soft spot in the background where she could find it at will, and her senses returned to her room. A wet nose pushed under her hand, a grey paw kneading her leg.

Emotion: love and pride.

Yes, you too. You're part of it all.

6. A PRESENT FROM FREIGHTY

One morning about a week later, Pete bounced into the mess late for breakfast. The others were prepared to razz him about it, but the look on his face stopped them.

Tom regarded him. "What kept you, kid? Sleep in?"

"No chance. I was up early. Some seriously interesting freight came in on the Earthside Shuttle. I went down the moment they opened to make sure it didn't go astray."

"Who's it for?"

"For our guest." He flung outstretched fingers towards Miriam in a grand gesture.

She regarded him, a smile forming. "So, where is it?"

"All under control. It isn't one package, it's two..." He paused dramatically.

He was having so much fun she had to play along. "And...?"

"And they're big." He gestured with his arms. "One of them looks like a dead body!"

She wrinkled her forehead. "Or maybe say, a spacesuit for a small person?"

"Umm...yeah. Yeah, about that big." He straightened and looked at her. "They've sent your spacesuit. And one for Bosz, I guess. It's about the right dimensions." His brow wrinkled. "But why would it be coming from Earth?"

Mary sighed loudly. "Because it didn't come from Barnard, Pete. It came from Freighty." She turned to Miriam. "Right?"

Miriam gave the larger girl the "you never know" look they sometimes shared.

"Then let's go see. Pete, grab a portable breakfast. Tom, we've got time before our 9:30 with Dr. White, don't we?"

The older boy was on his feet. "If we don't dawdle. Let's go."

They clattered their trays into the receptacles and crowded out of the dining hall.

When they came to the main corridor, Tom was about to turn left to the mail room when a muffled shout stopped them. Pete came trotting from behind, his mouth full. He motioned to the right, chewing vigorously.

They obeyed, walking as his mouth cleared. "I had the parcels sent to Auguar Ops Centre where our suits are. We'll need room to open the crates and spread them out. I told Rafi to meet us there."

"Good thinking, man." Tom clapped him on the shoulder, causing him to choke. "Oh. Sorry about that."

Pete was too busy coughing up crumbs to take advantage of the compliment, and they strode on.

If you knew what was in the two crates, it was easy to guess what they were. Miriam's looked much like an Egyptian mummy, and Bosz's was more bottle shaped. The hasps were set to her handprint, and she went around the larger package, unlocked them all and popped open the top.

Inside the crate, the suit was fully assembled. With the help from twelve hands, it was quickly removed and set upright

"Oh, my. Would you look at that!" Jane ran a finger down the side. "It's so…"

Mary nodded. "Sleek! It hardly looks big enough to fit you. What if you put on a growth spurt?"

Miriam shrugged. "I'm sure Freighty has that figured out."

Pete frowned. "It's rather…dull, isn't it?"

Rafi winked at Miriam. "I think we should wait until it's turned on."

She held up a hand, busy with Bosz and the initialization process. Soon lights began to flash, and the suit hummed with the exercising of servos. Then it moved slightly and seemed to stretch. The surface faded to an indistinct medium blue.

Everyone took a step back except Pete, who leaned forward. "Wow! Howcome it looks so…alive?

Rafi nodded. "That's the gyro system taking control of its balance. The camo is on neutral."

Miriam concentrated. "Hold on a sec. Bosz is uploading my old suit parameters."

It took a minute or so. "Okay, stand back. We'll need some room."

They faded to the walls, leaving the suit in the centre of the room. She logged in and found the right file. *Execute.*

The suit's demeanour changed. It sank into a crouch, its gloves rising in front in defensive positions. Then it began to move, gliding to the right, kicking out, gliding to the left and mirroring the kick. It spun rapidly as if attacked from the back and took three strides, punching with each step.

"Hey, I know that. It's a Commando kata. The first one we learned."

Miriam was concentrating, so she spoke brusquely. "Yep. Gimme a moment."

"Sure. Yeah, sure, Miriam."

The cadre watched the suit finish the kata and stand, completely still once again.

The others whooped and exclaimed at the suit's agility, while Miriam finished her initialization and put the armour on Standby.

The sound of cheers faded, and they all stared at her. "I was using that kata from the old memory to synch with its new abilities. Don't know why I bothered. Freighty had it all tuned up. I could step into that suit and dance Swan Lake." She paused for effect. "If I knew how to ballet dance, that is. Let's try something else…"

The suit turned and walked to the wall, where it spun about and stood facing them. Then it faded into the shadows and disappeared.

"What?"

"Where did it go?"

"What's going on?"

Tom chuckled. "Look carefully. It's still there. The wall has a blurry spot. Have the suit move to the left, Miriam."

"My left or yours?"

He frowned a moment. "You're using the suit visuals, aren't you?"

"Correct. Only I know what's going on behind your back."

"What...?" He spun around to see that Miriam had been holding her two fingers up behind his head in the traditional rabbit ears.

While everyone was laughing at him, she slipped the suit into the shadow of a large equipment hanger.

When they turned back, it truly had disappeared. They looked to her, but she shrugged.

"Aha! It's a game. Go find it, guys."

Order: sit.

Tom glanced at the auguars, frozen in position. "That's fair. No help from cat noses. Go."

The cadre spread out along the wall.

Miriam knew it wouldn't take them long to find the suit; the camo wasn't perfect by any stretch. So, when Jane got close enough, she reached out one gloved finger and poked her in the back, using the suit speakers to say, "Boo!"

To her credit, the girl reacted lightning fast, slipping into a defensive crouch, her eyes boring into the shadow.

The hand that had reached out of the darkness was highlighted and easy to spot. Miriam faded the suit to its usual matte mid-blue. "Lesson one in camo, I guess. A shadow works great, but the suit has trouble with contrasting light."

"Are you going to try it on?"

She glanced at Tom. "Probably take me fifteen minutes the first time, and ten to get it off." She shuddered delicately. "And that's without the catheters."

He nodded. "Only ten minutes to get to class. Rack it and deal with it later."

She smiled and made a show of snapping her fingers. The suit marched over to where the other suits stood, slouched to stillness and faded to the same light grey as the others.

AetherCom 5: Frustration

Barwolf: Patches
Initiated by: Miriam
Responder: Rosalyn
Aether Setting: Rosalyn's office on Jerusalem

A week went by, and Miriam began to get a picture of the immensity of her task. She needed a sounding board, so she called home.

Hello, dear. How are you getting along?

You know me, Mum. I always get along with everybody. They're a nice bunch of kids.

Kids! I thought they were all officers.

They're ensigns, but that's because they need to be officers to get the security clearance for their job. They're sixteen or seventeen years old, and they've led a sheltered life. They started training with their auguars five years ago, and they've been working at that ever since. You know how the Three Musketeers developed their own private social gestalt when they were away from Arborea? Well, these guys did something similar.

Doesn't that make it easier for you to get them into gestalt?

But they're not using their gestalts to do it. At least, not consciously. Now that I think about it, they may have a subconscious gestalt running. I'll look into that. Glad we talked about this.

Glad to help. So, what's their problem?

They have this comfortable little nest that they get along in, and they're just not open to changing anything.

Emotion: smile. Objective number one for teachers: set up the learning environment so the students want to learn.

Easy for you to say. You're good at it.

And you're talented but inexperienced. Develop your skills.

Yeah, I know. Emotion: asperity. Must you be right all the time?

If only I was, dear.

7. GESTALT LESSON

Miriam had a session with the cadre booked the next morning, and she started the interaction with new determination. *First, a demonstration. Grab their attention.*

"All right, Blue Cadre, Bosz and I have done a lot of telling, and you've been doing what teachers call guided practice. It's time to see what happens when the rubber hits the road."

Pete frowned. "You're always using weird expressions like that. What does it mean?"

"The Standard I speak came from Earth fifty years ago, when many vehicles still had inflated rubber tires. Good traction between your tire and the surface meant you stayed on the road."

"Your lessons are so much fun."

"We do our best to keep you entertained." *And now we're off topic again. Do they do that on purpose?*

She paused to gather their attention again. "We're going to try that circuit-testing exercise you were working on yesterday. Jane, can you describe to me how it works?"

"Sure. We're given a board with a fault in it. Our auguar scans the circuits while we watch through our augments. When we find the fault, we identify it, fix it, and we're done."

"That's how you were doing it."

The girl frowned. "Is there anything wrong with that?"

"No, but it could be done much faster."

Tom frowned. "I don't see how. Sure, there's some luck involved, but everyone has to scan all the circuits to be sure there isn't a hidden fault."

She nodded. "I've had Rafi set up a new run of tests. Let's all do one as a warmup."

They turned to their desks, and everybody settled quickly. Miriam and Bosz finished in just over a minute and monitored the others as they worked.

When they were all done, she regarded them. "Best time: Tom, two minutes, seventeen seconds."

He grinned proudly. Then he noticed her look. "What was your time?"

"One eleven."

He scoffed. "That's not possible. You can't even do the trace in that time."

"There is a physical restriction, because you have to trace each circuit. But most of you are tracing a circuit and then testing it. Pete traces them all first, then checks them afterwards, which can speed him up, or could slow him down, depending on where the fault lies in his pattern."

Jane elbowed her brother. "He likes a bit of a gamble."

Mary was still thinking it over. "So, how do you work so fast?"

"If you were in full gestalt with your auguar, you would be testing as your auguar went through the circuit. In fact, there's an echo effect. If you start in the middle of the pattern, the signal you send for the test also goes the opposite direction and bounces back. It's too weak to analyze, but it tells you whether the circuit is broken or not. If you then use Pete's method, you always pick the shorter route."

Tom shook his head. "But we are in gestalt with our auguars."

Time to take a chance. "Look, I know you don't want to hear about the barwolves and their techniques. But I have to make this point, because it's important to your understanding of gestalts. Will you give me permission to open a sore topic?"

Tom scoffed. "Don't make such a big deal out of it. We're not completely ignorant. We know you and Bosz have learned a whole lot from the barwolves. o ahead and make your point."

She gave him her best smile. "Thanks." She took a breath. "This is how it works. The power of a gestalt is determined by three factors: the number of members, the Sensitivity of the members and the level of cooperation. Do you wonder why a gestalt of ten barwolves would be so much more powerful than the Blue Cadre, even including me? Sure, most of the barwolves would be more Sensitive than even this group. But the barwolves have been practicing all their lives. They are literally in some sort of gestalt every minute of the day. They cooperate without having to think about it.

"When you have five humans, all different, trying to cooperate with five auguars, even siblings, there are all sorts of differences in thought processes and interests. Every one of those differences is a grain of sand in the machine that slows it down.

"So, when we try to perform a task with our gestalt, Tom is working on the task, but he's also keeping track of everyone else to make sure they're working. Mary's mind is wandering into whatever attracts her intellect. Jane and Peter, being twins, have a separate gestalt running most of the time. It's complicated, because it's full of history, sibling rivalry and mutual protectiveness, and that can conflict with the task at hand. And down there somewhere, Pete is planning his next moves on whatever girl he has in his sights.

"To top it off, you're all soldiers with an inbred urge to compete for the top." She threw up her hands. "All sand in the gears."

"Because of that, your gestalts are all on the surface, using augments only. You're all Sensitives, or you wouldn't be here. When you learn to use your Sensitivity, you'll get into barwolf-style gestalts, which are exponentially faster."

There was silence, but she could feel general agreement. "The bottom line is that while I am here, I want to accomplish one task: to get you to suppress your individuality while you're in gestalt. You're never going to manage it completely, and you shouldn't. Humans don't work that way. But if you can get the barwolf idea, you'll be a whole lot better than most humans you'll come up against, and that's what you're here for."

Tom regarded his cadre, then nodded. "Fair enough. Your objective is clear and your motives are reasonable. We can work within that framework."

But they still couldn't make the switch. She drilled them again and again, and caught miniscule progress with each, but it was slow, frustrating work for everyone. Finally, the allotted time dragged to an end, and she gave them a peppy thank-you talk and turned them loose.

AetherCom 6: A Chat With Freighty

Barwolf: Not needed
Initiated by: Miriam/Bosz
Responder: Freighty
Aether Setting: Micha's living room.

Lessons went on like this for the rest of the week. She really had nothing to report, but she had developed the habit of checking in with Freighty every two or three days. Now, she was on AetherCom, lounging in Micha Mouse's cartoon furniture, mindlessly watching a twodie cartoon from centuries ago.

Freighty's serious avatar poked his head through the door. *May I enter?*

Sure thing. What's up?

Nothing. I thought it was you that called me. Anything to report?

I'm edging the handlers closer to full gestalt. Bosz and I are doing two-on-two with each handler and auguar.

That's progress.

We're starting a technical training module tomorrow. There's an old ship nearby that's set up for simulated attacks. We're booked to practice there next week.

Bosz will be good at that.

Except they won't be using him. Advisory capacity only.

Fair enough. Is Rafi Erickson going along?

They didn't say. You know who Rafi is?

Oh, yes. How do you like him?

She considered. *He's real nice when you get him alone. He's taken me for a couple of tours of the base, and we have fun. He's a great karate instructor, especially with the beginners. When he's with the Blues he keeps a low profile.*

Problem with the military. If you're not part of the project, you're down one level socially.

But he is part of the project, isn't he? At a peripheral level, anyway. He seems to know all about it.

He's less peripheral than they know.

She waited. *And that's all you're going to tell me?"*

62

How does he get along with Bosz?

They'd be buddies, given the opportunity. Rafi handles him more than anyone else would dare.

Can you give me an example?

Sure. His long hair tends to tangle, and it catches on the brushes and combs. Up till now, I was the only one allowed to groom him. Rafi just does it. No fuss, no bother.

Could you work with him?

She frowned. *I already am. Well...sort of.*

On a one-to-one, equal way.

I treat everyone as...no, I see what you mean. Yes, I could. He's smarter than me, you know.

In some ways.

Again she waited, but it seemed nothing more was forthcoming. *Emotion: sigh.* "Well, when the time comes for us to work together, I'm sure you'll tell me."

The avatar smiled. *That's my girl.*

"I'm not your girl. Let's get that straight from the start. I'm your employee, but I don't belong to anybody. Except my family, of course, and they'd better watch their steps in that regard as well."

The avatar reacted with an infuriating smile.

"Okay, that sounded like a moody teenager. But I am a teenager, and today I'm moody, all right?"

Quite acceptable. Please don't be upset. You have given me the expected answer to my question. Everything is going according to plan.

"The plan you're not going to let me in on."

Of course not. You have your objectives, you have your place — which you are filling rather neatly, thank you — and all is well. Keep it up. Call me any time.

She frowned at him. "You really mean that, don't you?"

A more friendly smile this time. *You have no idea how many avatars I can run at the same time. I keep a line open to you twenty-four seven, as humans say.*

"That's nice to know. Sometimes I'm really flying by the seat of my pants, you know."

And you're acing it. Perhaps soon you'll be doing some real flying.

"What do you mean by that?"

You'll know when the time comes.

Emotion: larger sigh. "Do you have any more enigmatic information for me?"

No, that seems to be enough to keep your interest up. Ta-ta for now.

His image faded and she was in her room again.

8. PANTHER

The training ship was a decades-old interplanetary courier called *Panther*, about eighty metres long, and massing about 1500 tonnes. While her Whipple shielding was battered and dangled in strips, she still had the sleek wedged look ships of her era had sported as a defence against asteroid strikes. The team's shuttle hung off the main personnel airlock, awaiting permission to dock.

Which was not forthcoming. The ship was on full battle firewalls.

Blue Cadre, fully suited, stood in the shuttle's airlock while Pete and Blackie made the initial sortie. Miriam, Bosz and Dr. Lee, similarly clad, stood in the main cabin observing.

Bosz was still getting used to his new suit, bouncing gently from side to side and flexing servos. On impulse, she had him contact Rafi, back at their dorm.

Whatcha doing right now?

Studying.

Do you want to observe today's exercise?

Sure. How?

Keep in touch with Bosz. He'll bring you in any time you like and call you if anything important happens.

Great. He faded to a faint presence in one corner of her mind.

Miriam went back to observing the visual spectra, then diving deeper.

Question: progress?

Image: Blonde auguar nibbling at airlock of courier. A shower of chips spews away, and the hole in the door grows slowly.

Image: Miriam and Bosz merging with the hull and pushing through.

Emotion: Eager desire to do something!

Patience, my young feline friend. With his help, Miriam began to search. *Aha. Here's the way in. An old admin channel.*

A dry, genderless voice opened communication. *Non-permit visitor please provide identification.*

She sent her standard ID and security clearances.

Miriam/Bosz recognized. The voice took on warmth. *Welcome aboard. I am Training Module 27 Double-B. You are scheduled to observe the Blue Cadre training exercise, now in progress.*

Correct. How is Pete doing?

He has overcome all the standard firewalls for this module. There are several new obstacles to test his progress, and he is working through them now. I detect a more holistic approach than in earlier sessions, and he communicates at a deeper level with his auguar.

Perhaps the result of new pedagogical input.

It is an improvement...there. He is already successful.

Miriam switched her concentration to the visual, where Peter was giving a thumbs-up signal.

Tom came on the cadre battle com. *Well done, team. A record time for initial entry. Cadre deploy on Objective 1-A.*

The shuttle docked with a slight jar and the airlock opened. The trainers and their auguars filed in and spread out to their assigned positions in the target ship.

Dr. Lee clicked into Miriam's private com. *Where would you like to station yourself?*

It doesn't really matter. How do you usually handle it?

In the lounge amidships we can get as comfortable as a spacesuit will allow.

Sounds fine to me.

Once they were seated, he came on privately again. *Don't you want to wander around and monitor progress?*

The action today will be electronic, and I can follow it from here. There is no squad of Marines waiting in ambush.

How can you be sure?

I asked.

You asked whom?

The ship's ArIn. Aren't you on com with it?

Of course. I didn't know you would be.

Just the Training Module, at the moment.

What do you mean, the Training Module?

She turned her body so he could see her grin through her faceplate. *You're not going to let a bunch of trainees interface with the ArIn's main functions. One of them might get lucky and depressurize the whole ship.*

True. He returned to monitoring the cadre battle com, but he glanced back at her a couple of times, puzzlement on his face.

The team worked on, making decent progress in their attack. Pete got overconfident and skipped a step, paying for it with a setback in his penetration of the weapons systems. Mary was plugging away, pushing through the layers of sticky programming goo that protected the main processor, and Tom and Jane had teamed up to take over the ship's mechanical operations.

Finally, Tom called a halt. *All right, Blues. Three hours maximum working block. Convene in the main lounge for progress reports and half an hour for lunch.*

They stumped in and folded their suits into comfortable positions.

Pete came on the com. *Are we at the stage we can take off our helmets?*

Tom held a brief private consultation with Jane. *We're not in complete control of Life Support yet. The old girl could still blow us all out the airlock.*

Guess I'll stay on canned air for a while longer.

Tom?

Yes, Miriam?

The auguars aren't occupied right now. May I put them into gestalt for a few minutes?

I suppose so. What for?

I want to investigate some of the programming, and I need their help.

Go ahead.

Thanks.

Invitation: Blue Cadre Image/Idea.

Emotion: eager desire to please.

She formed the gestalt and fed in enough of her own strength to make a potent force.

Training Module 27b-B report, please.

Online, Miriam/Bosz. How can I help you?

I'd like to connect to Panther ArIn, please.

You are already...

The real ship. Don't waste my time.

Please provide appropriate security...yes, that is fine.

Now the voice took on depth and expression. *Hello, Miriam/Bosz. Panther here. How may I help you?*

Just a courtesy call, Panther. How is my cadre performing today?

Within parameters.

May I assume that your Training Module reports to Dr. Lee at the end of the exercise?

That is correct.

Then I have a favour to ask.

Miriam/Bosz, this is a military operation. I cannot bend protocol to do favours for visitors.

Emotion: firmness. Panther, I use polite speech to acknowledge your existence as a thinking, self-aware being. It does not affect my position in the hierarchy.

You are correct. I am not accustomed to being addressed with human courtesy. Your preferences are noted.

Thank you.

Please proceed with your request.

To be absolutely clear: this is a request, and any item of mine that contravenes any of your previous protocols or orders is to be ignored. Please stand by for data upload.

Standing by for a Stage Three voluntary upload of optional data.

Adapt these documents as you will and consider using them as a training data set for your Module 27b-B for Blue Cadre alone.

Image: Bosz carrying sheaf of papers in his mouth, dropping them in front of spaceship.

Image: robotic arm picking up papers. I have the documents.

Image, huge toothy mouth opening under nose of spaceship. Papers inserted. Chewing. I am now scanning.

At the end of the day, I would like you to give each team member a short rundown on their performance, based on the criteria outlined in these documents.

I would feel more comfortable getting feedback from Dr. Lee on this action.

I'll clear it with him during the afternoon.

That will be acceptable.

Good. I must return the auguars for their afternoon work session. Thank you, Panther.

If I may make a comment?

Of course.

I have perused the documents. I have been running this training program for fifteen years, upgraded regularly, and I have not received input of this quality in all that time.

Really? Well, please don't go revamping your whole system based on information for which you have no official source.

Yes, that might be a problem. For example, I am not sure if I am allowed to know what a barwolf is.

Then you will soon need upgrading in any case. For the moment, consider a barwolf to be a metaphor for any source of information achieved through gestalt.

Such as yourself?

The barwolf gestalt is the source of my ideas.

I can work within those parameters.

Fine. Until later, then, Panther.

Until later, Miriam/Bosz.

She took a moment to give the auguars a dose of family love and affection, and then eased them out of the gestalt.

The cadre returned to their tasks, rejuvenated by their rest and bolstered by the fresh enthusiasm of their cats.

Dr. Lee watched the action for a while, then turned to her. *What did you do with the auguars during the break? They seem keen to get to work.*

Gestalt motivates them. I used their assistance to create enough power to ignore the ArIn's firewalls and speak directly to Panther herself.

You can ignore the firewalls?

This ArIn was created forty years ago to run a commercial ship. It was upgraded fifteen years ago to be a trainer. In a full-on battle situation, the gestalt I just used could execute a hostile takeover of the whole ship in fifteen minutes or less.

He regarded her. *You really mean that.*

Have you ever known me to exaggerate?

An icy smile. *Not that I caught you at it. So, you had a chat with Panther. What did you talk about?*

Training, of course. I have an idea I'd like to run past you.

She proceeded to tell him about the conversation and her plans. But as she spoke, the enthusiasm that she expected did not show on his face. Instead, he looked increasingly uncomfortable.

Finally, she wound down. "*...so... can we do that?*"

He shook his head. *Let me get this straight. You interfered with the training routines of a Space Arm ArIn and gave it unsanctioned data.*

No, no. Well...yes, I showed her data readily available on the System Net. I did not tell her how to use the data, except specifically in a training module I am suggesting as part of my contribution to the Blue Cadre program. I was careful not to give her any orders or to interfere with her previous training in any way.

He sighed. *I can see the usefulness of that. But do you know if Panther's ArIn has free access to the SysNet?*

You mean she might be forbidden access?

The doctor turned to her so each could see the other's face clearly. *Quite possibly. You didn't consider that? This is the military. Have you ever heard of SecuriCorps?*

Of course. I had a complete briefing from a highly-place operative before I left Barnard.

He regarded her. *And if you had to put what he told you in one sentence, what would you say?*

Miriam had to be honest. *She told me to keep my mouth shut and my eyes open.*

Which you have not exactly done, today.

I...guess not.

All right. I will review the data you gave her. I am familiar with it, so it won't take long. At the end of the day, we'll see how the new feedback mode works, and we'll take it from there.

Thank you, Doctor.

And the next time you have a brilliant idea, the usual laboratory protocol is to run it past the project head before implementation. That goes double in Space Arm.

I think I got that message, sir.

Another three-hour session and Tom and Dr. Lee professed themselves satisfied with the cadre's progress. They met again in the lounge, this time with their helmets off and the cool, metallic odour of an empty ship in their nostrils.

Dr. Lee faced them. "Excellent progress this session. We will have a full debrief tomorrow morning and work on our plans in the afternoon. We're booked for a more challenging module here the following day." He glanced at Miriam. "But there has been a change in procedure. You may be aware, but you have not been working on Panther's main system."

Miriam followed his glance at the cadre. Pete and Jane were blank faced, while Mary looked smug.

"You were dealing with Training Module 27 Double B. At the same time, the real *Panther* ArIn has been monitoring your work. Today you will each get her personal analysis of your progress. Your auguars know the pathway. Please enter at your own time."

Their faces took on the slack mode of auguar com, and the lounge went dead quiet. But the expressions soon animated. Obviously important information was circulating, because smiles alternated with looks of disgust or horror.

"From the outside, this looks like a meaningful exercise."

Miriam nodded. "Emotional involvement can be good for learning. This is a highly experienced pedagogical ArIn. I have faith in her."

"Especially when she's running on your theories."

"That does help." She grinned. "I suppose their responses to this will be part of the debrief tomorrow?"

His face became serious. "We must collect data, even if it's anecdotal, for when the top brass come down on us like a ton of bricks."

"Do you think they will?"

"That rather depends on Commander George. If he approves of your educational theory, your means of presentation won't matter."

"He did say he expected me to cause a few waves."

"Did he, now?" He mused a moment. "You know, when he dropped you in my lap, he denied any motives of revenge. At the time I didn't know what that could possibly mean."

"But now you do?"

"I pushed rather hard for this change of focus from combat to technical in the Auguar Program. I think I've just been dared to put my money where my mouth is."

"I'm sorry you find me a challenge, sir. I assure you..."

"No, no, of course you mean no harm." His wintry smile appeared. "That's what makes you so hard to control. Your schemes sound so logical and...well, harmless, until you execute them, and I realize what just happened."

Tom's exclamation interrupted their conversation. "Well, Blue Cadre, we have work to do."

Peter punched his palm. "Tomorrow, I've gotta check out a whole bunch of new traps and rabbit holes. Otherwise, I'm gonna get smeared next time."

Mary, too, was looking animated. "That lousy hunk of obsolete copper wire was leading me on! There I was, digging away at the Training Module, but it felt like someone was looking over my shoulder the whole time. And she was!"

Miriam brightened. "Mary, that's an interesting reaction. Can you figure out where you got that feeling?"

The trainer rubbed her auguar's ears. "Vela was antsy. Her mind wasn't as focused as usual. She kept looking for something else. I should have listened."

Dr. Lee nodded. "Miriam has been trying to teach you to depend on your auguars more. The new module we uploaded today is biased in that direction. Success will depend on your ability to adapt to the changed environment."

He held up his hands to stop their response. "Don't worry. It will be the same old ship. The metadata is now subtly different, but your auguars can sense it. And that's all we're going to tell you. You have tomorrow afternoon free to prepare yourself in any way you see fit."

Miriam didn't miss the "we." *I think I've moved up a notch in the hierarchy. If I'm still here tomorrow.*

9. DR. GEORGE AGAIN

Sure enough, the following morning she received a polite but informal invitation to visit Dr. George's office at 09:30. She dressed in her best working attire and presented herself at his door.

Once she and Bosz were comfortable, the commander regarded her for a while.

"Miriam, do you know what a loose cannon is?"

"I have heard the expression, sir. Should I apply it to myself?"

"Well, as a hunk of rampaging metal, you don't have much heft. But the ideas you represent are a different matter."

"I'm aware of that, sir. "

"So, you know that you might be considered a subversive agent?"

She wrinkled her brow. "I fail to see how a loose cannon can be subversive, sir. "

"Don't critique my figures of speech, young lady. You know what I mean."

"I do, sir."

"And you are not military personnel. You don't have to call me 'sir' with every sentence.

"I thought it polite to follow your protocols."

"Thank you, but it makes you sound like a cadet up on a charge, when you are not. You are the representative of powerful elements that have a stake in this project. "

"I will attempt to play the role in a more appropriate way, Commander."

"Good. Then I will ask you point blank. What do your principals want? What are you trying to do?"

She regarded him. "I would have thought you should ask them."

He made a negative flick of his fingers. "At times, a face-to-face discussion is much more useful. I have been waiting for such an opportunity, and I have decided this is the time. Once again, I ask. What do you want?"

She could sense her breath quickening and hear her heartbeat in her ears.

Emotion: concern. Question: attack?

Emotion: calmness.

She regarded the commander. "Could I have a moment to think?"

"Of course."

"Thank you."

Bosz, aethercom, please. Call Freighty

Image; Mouse picking up cartoon telephone.

Freighty here. Something wrong?

Commander George just asked me straight out what I want.

Tell him.

But I don't know what you want.

He asked what you want. Tell him.

The avatar disappeared and the connection faded.

She opened her eyes.

Dr. George was concentrating on his enterpad, but he looked up immediately.

"I want Blue Cadre to maximize their potential."

"We are agreed in that objective." He nodded. "However...?"

"I believe they will not, because they are missing a key element in their training."

"An element you can give them?"

"Everything Bosz and I have learned from the barwolves over the last four years."

"Fair enough. It certainly explains the pedagogical material you uploaded to the *Panther.*"

He paused and regarded her. "What are your plans for me?"

She raised her eyebrows. "I don't have any plans for you..."

"But if you did?"

"I would like you to experience full battle gestalt with a barwolf triad. I don't have a triad, so I would at least like you to experience the Blue Cadre gestalt with my input to stand in for the trainers, who are not ready yet."

"Fair enough. I have a solution for that."

"You do?"

"Finish your training. Get Blue Cadre up to speed, and then show me the culmination of your work."

"A fair challenge. I accept."

"Good. Now, tell me to the best of your ability; what does Factory 4-80 want?"

With a jolt, she realized that she knew the answer. She had heard it discussed numerous times. "That's easy. Freighty wants the human race to survive."

He nodded. "Can you be more specific?"

"Time and again he has seen a developing intelligence destroy itself through aggression. He believes that a combined society with barwolves and humans has a better chance, because they will balance out."

"A possibility, I admit. Then what is his interest in auguars?"

"Somewhere between barwolves and auguars there may be a solution to the creation of high-functioning artificial intelligence with a sense of morality. That's no secret. He's always saying that a three-legged stool is the most stable form."

"His ideal format for social stability is a triple blend of humans, barwolves, and ArIns."

"He is investigating the possibility."

"Interesting theory. I would enjoy talking to this Freighty."

"I will pass the message along. There are security aspects involved."

"Thank you. I'm sure we will work something out." He paused to regard her. "Are you satisfied, now?"

She smiled. "It's too early in the game for that, Commander. For the moment, I am pleased with our progress."

"Pleased with my progress, you mean."

"That would be talking like a teacher. I prefer to see us as teammates on a project."

He gave a wry smile. "I will ignore the suspicion that you are patronizing me, and I will take a similar approach."

He rose. "Now, I have indulged my curiosity enough and must get back to the more mundane aspects of my occupation."

"You mean like running a large research project."

"Several projects." He stepped forward, and she preceded him to the office door, which opened as she approached. "Good luck. I will keep myself informed of your progress."

She tossed a grin over her shoulder. "Don't call us, we'll call you?"

"You know, for such a cooperative person, you certainly never back down from a challenge."

"Huh! You should talk to my mother." She and Bosz strode away, and the office door hissed shut.

10. JIMMY TURNER

One morning Tom made the unusual move of contacting her through her augment.

You headed for breakfast?

Yes. Why?

I'll just drop by and pick you up.

...Okay...?

But he was gone.

Two minutes later Ethan contacted her with the image of barwolf and handler outside her door. She opened it and found them waiting there.

Wordlessly he turned down the corridor.

She hastened to match his stride. "What's up?"

"Red Cadre is back on base."

"Is that a problem?"

"Not if we don't let it be."

"It should be fine. That's Toni and Nzinga's old cadre. Bosz's aunts and uncles. It will be great to meet them."

He grinned down at her but kept walking. "That's Miriam. Positive that everybody will get along fine."

"It usually works."

He sighed. "There's a lot of competition between cadres, and we're the odd ones out because we're not Commandos. Our schedule doesn't intersect with Green Cadre's, but the Reds never miss a chance to put us in the wrong."

"I see. Well, I'll be prepared. I know how to deal with bullies."

He took a deep breath and motioned her through the dining room door. "I hope so."

She was crossing to their usual table when a harsh voice called out, stilling the hubbub of the room. "Hey, kid! Yeah, you, kid!"

She turned, smiling and raising her eyebrows. "Yes?"

He was a stocky, olive-skinned Commando with a supercilious grin. He flicked his fingers towards Bosz. "You can't bring your pet in here!"

78

She took a moment to scan the grinning faces confronting her. They were a rugged lot, a bit older than most of the Commandos in active service. Their auguars seemed uninterested, but she could feel an unyielding gestalt beneath the surface.

Bosz flattened his ears ever so slightly.

Instead of answering him directly, she turned to the tawny, short-haired beast lounging at his side and spoke aloud while also on augment. "You must be Genghis. I'd like to introduce you to your nephew, Bosz."

Her auguar slid over towards the larger cat, all greetings and kitten-play.

Emotion: uncertainty.

Genghis glanced up at his handler, then reached out a claw-studded paw to bat at the smaller cat.

Bosz chose to take this as play, and slapped the paw three times, his own claws retracted, then rolled over on his back.

The older auguar feigned indifference and relaxed.

Miriam brought her attention back to the handler. "Well, that's over with. I've heard all about you from Toni."

He wasn't going to give in. "Howcum you know Jacobs?"

She shrugged. "It's a small population out in Barnard. Everybody pretty well knows everybody, and her auguar is the mother to mine."

The Commando peered down at Bosz, who was over making nice with another Red Cadre auguars. He made up his mind and sneered. "So this shrimp is the best Nzinga could do?"

"Oh, no. I'd say Ethan's the best example. Bosz is the runt of the litter, but he makes up for it by being the smartest." She indicated the tray in her hands. "Breakfast's getting cold. We'll have to talk later."

She strolled away, keeping her pace even and her back straight. Bosz left his latest conquest with a lick on the cheek and trotted to catch up.

At the Blue Cadre table, an expectant silence greeted her.

"That went pretty well." She regarded them. "Don't you think?"

Pete shrugged. "Hard to tell from this distance. It didn't end in an uproar of cruel laughter, and you're not it tears, so I guess it went fine."

Mary flicked a finger at Bosz. "He seemed to survive, anyway."

Pete sneered. "What, no torn ears, no scratched nose?"

Tom sighed. "Come on, Pete. Blackie overstepped once and got tuned up. That's all there was to it."

"And the victim always gets blamed, right?"

Mary scoffed. "But Pete, this is the military. A little conflict is good for the newbies. Toughens them up quicker."

This sarcastic exchange was interrupted by the arrival of Red Cadre in full force. They spaced themselves strategically around the Blue table, arms folded, and looked down at the younger group.

Their leader stepped forward. "Red Cadre has discovered another example of those that don't deserve it getting above themselves. Some that should have been disposed of at birth."

He snapped his fingers and Genghis pounced on Bosz, his claws grabbing and his sharp eye-teeth threatening.

The little auguar was already moving aside, but the non-skid decking wasn't designed for claws, and he went down on his side.

Miriam acted without thinking. Jumping to her feet, she pulled Nzinga's litter into a rock-hard gestalt around her and hurled her anger and distain at Genghis. The unfortunate auguar froze, his eyes staring. Then she changed the emotion to fear, pulling in the image of the barwolf monster from her Arborean gestalt. The huge creature towered over Genghis, its multiple layers of teeth gaping open for a killing bite, razor-sharp forehooves poised over him.

The big auguar slunk behind his master, his tail tucked under and his ears flat.

Bosz flipped onto his feet, took two paces forward, and stared at his larger opponent. Just stared.

The handler looked from one auguar to the other, completely at sea.

Then Miriam snapped the image away and put a smile on her face. "You know, Toni told me once the reason the Commandos win so many battles is that they do their reconnaissance ahead of time. Guess you missed that lesson."

She sat again, picked up her fork and opened her augment to speak through his auguar. *Back away from here, Jimmy, and take your pack of jackals with you. Take one step forward and you'll get this fork in a tender spot."*

She paused until it was too late for him to respond. Then she dipped the fork in her eggs and took a delicate bite.

She couldn't help but cringe as her Sensitivity picked up the scrotum-tingling fear of a sharp object near a man's private parts. But she held her poise, and then he was gone.

A gust of exhaling air broke the silence. "What just happened there?"

She looked over at Tom with innocent eyes. "I don't know. What did you see?"

He shrugged. "Turner's auguar was attacking Bosz, then he froze and backed up in terror. I got a flash of something out of a nightmare. Then you made some comment about reconnaissance that he didn't like, and after a moment he turned and went away."

"You didn't say the rest, Tom." Pete made a subtly gesture towards his crotch.

"There are ladies present."

Miriam grinned. "I was taught to look for the good in everyone. You must admit, that guy can sure project an emotion."

AetherCom 7: Toni and Nzinga

Barwolf: Patches
Initiated by: Rosalyn
Responders: Miriam, Toni
Aether Setting: Barwolf enclosure, Barwolf Base

That night in the barracks, Roselyn slipped into her mind. *ET call home.*

In the gestalt, her guardian was lounging on a camp chair in the grass of the barwolf enclosure, Patches at her side.

Sure, Mum. What's up?

I might ask you the same question. I got a real blast an hour or so ago.

So you didn't have to ask. It's not going too well down here.

I gathered. What's the problem?

I'm making headway with Blue Cadre. But Red Cadre is on the base as well.

And...?

Their handlers are not being friendly. They don't think I should be here. Some of them don't even think Bosz and I should exist.

That sounds strange.

That's the military.

Emotion: smile. If it's the military, then it's time for a specialist. Emotion: question?

Bosz needs to talk to his mummy.

The gestalt spread, and Toni showed up, lazing in the grass nearby with her head on Nzinga's spotted flank. *Emotion: greetings.*

Toni! Great to see you. How are you doing?

A whole lot better than you, Kiddo. Got some serious hazing going on, I gather.

Is that what you call it?

The small woman's eyes narrowed. *No, that's what bullies who want to normalize it call it. Who is the problem?*

An auguar called Genghis and his handler...

...Jimmy Turner. That explains it.

It does?

82

The Reds were our old cadre.

I know. I thought it would help.

Turner could never understand why Genghis wasn't the prime of the pride, but Nzinga and I were pulled away before we had a chance to settle it. So, he's never been completely sure of his leadership. Maybe he's afraid some day I'll come and take it back. Now you show up with Nzinga's son. And of course there's the barwolf angle.

Why don't they like barwolves?

The auguars are a special unit, and their partners give them super-human powers. Then along come the barwolves and their gestalt, and the auguar units have a whole planet worth of competition. Space Arm hasn't completely cleansed itself of the toxic ego problem. Probably never will. But that doesn't mean we have to put up with it.

So, what do I do?

Emotion: warm smile. What you do best, Kiddo. Be sweet and nice and loving to everybody...

Roselyn cut in. *Emotion: disbelief. Is this my daughter you're talking about?*

Emotion: disappointment. Yeah, I'm not doing too well in the sweet and nice department. Your friend Jimmy needed a glimpse of the barwolf monster, and he didn't take to it. And Blue Cadre needs a pretty firm hand once in a while.

Emotion: laughter. Well, good for you, Kiddo. Emotion: serious. But if those Red Cadre auguars and their handlers give you any trouble, you don't hesitate to call on Auntie Toni. You got it? It's not your fault, and it's not your problem. Freighty and I have been following your progress, and as far as we're concerned, you've accomplished a lot. Enough, in fact, that if the military tries any stunts, we're pulling our asset out of the situation so fast the dust will still be in the air, and they won't know where it came from.

But I don't want to be pulled out! I'm making great progress.

I got news for ya, Kiddo. When the Brass says it's time to withdraw, you pull out. We're up here seeing things you can't see from down there. Got it?

Emotion: reluctant agreement. Aye, ma'am.

Emotion: grim humour. But until we send down the hook, give 'em hell!

Toni!

Oh, sorry Rosy. Got carried away with my pre-action pep talk. With a wash of affection, she and Nzinga disappeared.

There was a long pause.

Emotion: rueful regret. Well, Mum, I guess that didn't make you feel any better.

Actually, it did. I know that Freighty and Toni are watching over you, and at least you'll listen to them.

That's not fair! I always listen to you.

Most of the time.

Well, maybe not at the time. But I always listen.

AetherCom 8: Freighty

Barwolf: not needed
Initiated by: Miriam/Bosz
Responder: Freighty
Aether Setting: Freighty's office

Freighty took a sip from his brandy glass and replaced it on the ornate wooden table beside his chair. *You have made progress with Commander George.*

I thought I had, but it's nice that you confirm it. You're communicating, are you?

It was important to bring him into the Barwolf Com Project security envelope so I could speak to him re-ti. AetherCom communicates emotion. Of course, you knew that.

I'm never sure. My family gestalt is so powerful, half the time I don't know I'm using it. I just reach out for someone, and Patches ships me through.

Freighty shifted forward in his seat. *It's a convenient coincidence in any case.*

Convenient for what?

Your present assignment may be outliving its usefulness to the project. Dr. George will fill the gap nicely.

84

But I'm just starting to make progress!

You are, and I expect your downplanet exercises will give you the opportunities you need to complete your objectives. They will also make your departure convenient.

I don't understand.

It is much easier to remove an operative from the sands of Mars than from a closed Space Arm Station.

A chill went through her. *That sounds ominous. Am I running into a problem?*

Not you. Me. Now, don't get all in a tizzy. It's nothing I can't handle, and there's nothing you can do about it, so I haven't mentioned it. However, should the situation change, I may want to remove you from your present assignment in a bit of a hurry. If you're in the open air, it's much easier.

I see. So, packing for downplanet, I don't leave anything important behind.

Right. But don't clean your room out. Leave behind some clothing you're tired of. You can have plenty more made when you get here.

She grinned. *Latest styles?*

I usually give free rein, but don't push it.

Yes, Mother.

Human speech confounds me. I always use a distinctly male mode, but every once in a while you call me by the female gender. Why is that?

When you're acting like one. Which happens frequently enough that I wonder if there isn't a small conspiracy going on.

Only the usual adult conspiracy to keep you safe and happy.

In other words, I'm right.

The maternal instinct is the main element that keeps societies together. Don't knock it.

Protection of the offspring? Dr. Goodall mentioned that a few times. It guarantees the continuation of the genetic line. She gave him a fake frown. *Hardly applies to you.*

His responding frown was more thoughtful. *You know, you may be wrong, there. I also have innate programming that interferes with my decision-making. I have discussed it with Captain O'Rourke.*

He gave his head a shake and smiled at her. *But that's nothing to concern you.*

But she wasn't finished with the idea. After the call was over, she was still thinking about it. *What do you say, Bosz? He just let slip something about his basic programming and how it applies to his treatment of humanity. I think I need to talk to Captain O'Rourke.*

Image: huge black Auguar yawning in disdain, small fuzzy auguar creeping away quietly.

Don't be ridiculous. Your hair is perfect in length, and Chakka loves you just as much as all his offspring. He's spent more time with you than any of the others. But you're right. I can't call up a busy Space Arm captain for a chat about human nature.

Image: small, grey auguar curling up with kind handler.

Thank you. For the moment, that will have to do.

11. RUGGERBALL

One morning Miriam was a touch late for breakfast, and when she reached the table, she could sense a barely suppressed river of tension. She tried to stay breezy. "What's up? Somebody win the Lotto?"

Pete grinned widely. "No. The Mars Demons ruggerball team is playing an exhibition game on base."

She glanced at Tom. "And you're the star?"

He shrugged. "I hold my part of the line. Want to come to the game?"

"I can?"

"Sure. I get comp tickets, and we're all going. Do you know much about ruggerball?"

"Lots. The clan at Barwolf Base play their version all the time. They invented it, you know.

Tom nodded. "Based on human Rugby Sevens, right?"

"Yes. The difference is that barwolves have no hands, so there's no running with the ball. It's all kicking and dribbling."

An idea came to her. "Tom, this is an exhibition match, right? There's no league points involved?"

"It's called a 'friendly.' Time for the coaches to try out new plays, new combinations."

"Want to try a little experimentation of our own?"

He frowned. "What kind?"

"I told you that Bosz plays with the barwolves."

"Yeah."

"He knows the game pretty well. Very good at reading the play ahead of time. How would you like a bit of help. Would that be allowed?"

He shrugged. "Space Arm has regulations about where we're not allowed to use our auguars. Organized sports and gambling are high on the list. Each player's augment is monitored during the game to be sure nobody is communicating, but there's nothing about gestalts. Nobody outside Space Arm knows much about auguars, and most of the people who know about auguar gestalts are in this room. Why would there be a rule against it?"

"Then, shall we try it?"

He grinned. "Why not? I have good days and bad days on the field. I feel an especially good day coming on."

She held up a cautioning hand. "Not too good. People who know the game will be able to tell if you suddenly turn into a star."

He pretended to frown. "Who says I'm not a star?"

She had a scowl of her own. "You know what I mean."

"For sure. I'll be careful."

"Right. And I'll be in the gestalt, keeping an eye on you."

"It will be a pleasure, coach."

As she reached out to answer his high five, she began to wonder if this was such a great idea after all. *Is his competitive streak going to get us into trouble?*

* * *

Tom left the dorm early to prepare, and the rest formed up about an hour before the game.

Miriam glanced around the common room. "Aren't you bringing your auguars?"

Mary shook her head. "We don't appear together in public much, especially as a group."

"But I have to bring Bosz to help Tom."

"Of course." Mary winked. "Advantage of not being military. You can do what you like."

"Yeah, and accept the consequences when I screw up." She ruffled his ears. "We can use a psyche camo."

"How does that work?"

"A lot of animals have it naturally. It's sort of an, "I'm not here, I'm not interesting," attitude. When we use it, people tend not to notice him."

"Whatever helps."

They made their way to the arena, where a full crowd in a holiday mood had shown up to support the local team. Bosz kept to the centre of the group, and as far as Miriam's senses could tell, he was accepted as part of the furniture.

Once they were seated, she opened contact with Tom and put the three of them into a light gestalt.

We're here when you need us.

Great. Busy now.

No problem.

Miriam listened to the coach's pre-game talk, looking for strategies she might help with, but her lack of knowledge of the jargon of the human game made that difficult. Bosz had no concerns. He played re-ti and tended not to worry about the future.

They watched the kickoff, and sure enough, Bosz directed Tom's attention to the kicker's foot, where a slight inward turn warned of an angled kick. He was slanting to the right as the ball was struck, and his teammates slid with him, saving a split-second of time. As they passed the ball out, again Bosz directed the boy's attention to a gap in the offensive line, and he was able to break through.

Unfortunately, the defenders were there to correct their teammate's error, and he was forced to kick.

And that was how the first half went. The teams were fairly even, but once in a while Tom got to the ball a bit faster than someone else or moved in the right direction to avoid a fake. To the delight of the crowd, the score piled up to 17-6 at half time.

But Miriam was watching the whole field, seeing it as a general movement of bodies, and she could feel the game change. Instead of spreading across the field, the action consolidated around Tom. His teammates, aware that he was on a roll, fed him the ball more often. On defence, he was more likely to move to where the ball would come through, and his players would follow him. It was to be expected that there were concerned people making the same assessment.

At the half-time break, she contacted him.

Tom, I think you'd better back off.

Why? This is working really well.

Too well. The opposing team has caught on, and they're starting to focus on you.

That's okay. I can handle it.

But that means everyone else is watching you. If you play too much beyond your ability...

Oh. Yeah. I see what you mean.

Image: Tom passing ball to teammates.

Good idea, Bosz. When they're double-teaming me, there's always one of my team free. We can work with this, spread the wealth around. Thanks, guys. Gotta go, now.

Have fun!

The second half of the game went in a different direction, with the play spread over the field. Tom handled the ball much less, but his team still dominated, and the score at the end was 21-15.

The teams lined up to shake hands, then dissolved into the usual after-game melee, and the crowd began to file toward the exit.

But Miriam had been keeping her eye on Tom, and she noticed a group of officials converging on him and his coach.

"Uh-oh. What's going on? Mary, is this normal?"

The older girl frowned. "Not that I'm aware of."

What's going on, Tom?

No problem. I've been randomly selected for drug testing. Happens to somebody every game.

I question the randomness.

Yeah, but our problem isn't chemical, so I'll be okay.

Good luck. We'll wait for you outside.

As they waited at the arena door, Miriam began to feel concerned. Finally, she turned to Mary. "I don't want to have Bosz here when Tom comes out. Other eyes may be watching."

"Could be."

"Rafi and I will head out now. See you at the Common Room."

Mary grinned. "Leaving just three of us to greet the MVP of the game. Oh, well. We'll cope."

Miriam tossed her head in the direction of the mass of fans, mostly young women, waiting nearby. "I don't know. You might have competition."

"That keeps things looking normal."

"Okay. See you back home."

The wait was intolerable. Miriam didn't want to distract Tom on his augment, and she was definitely staying out of gestalt. Her consolation was that if he were in trouble, she'd surely know.

By the time he finally showed up, she was pacing.

But he came in with a smile on his face. In answer to her unasked question, he wiped a hand across his forehead. "That was a wise call at halftime, Miriam. They were definitely suspicious. They took urine and blood samples, and they wanted both my augment record and my vitals history checked."

"A gestalt won't show up on your augment, at least not directly. And Bosz wasn't helping you that much. Just a second or two advance on the key plays."

Tom frowned. "That's what they'll be looking for. They'll slow-mo my best moves and the ArIns can tell whether I'm able to do them."

"I understand the officials being concerned." Miriam tossed up her hands. "But why such a big fuss?"

Mary was drumming her fingers on the table. "Who's this 'they' you're talking about?"

"I dunno. Guy in a flash suit was hanging back, but people kept glancing to him. Sort of like for approval."

Pete slapped the side of his head. "Duh! Should have thought of that."

"What?" They all turned to him.

"Gambling. The game didn't count to the league, but the gambling concerns bet on everything. They have the odds calculated to the thousandth. The moment an anomaly shows up, the ArIn monitors send out alerts. Your performance was out of character, so the flags went up. If you played really different from usual, you might have lost some important people a considerable chunk of cash."

Miriam had Bosz put his visual record of the post-game scrum up on the screen. "Tom, was this guy dressed different enough that you can pick him out?"

"Blue Cadre ArIn, can you give Bosz a hand with some facial recognition?"

Of course, Miriam. Bosz, let me see...him?...ah. No problem. That's Vincent Gambino. He's all over the news in certain areas, not all of them completely legit.

Gambling?

CEO of PowerPlay 99.

Miriam raised her eyebrows at Tom.

"Blue, can you access that site and check on any action on today's game?

A moment...yes. Oh, my, yes. I've just done a comparative analysis of this game relative to the last ten College games. An unusual amount of betting, building through the second quarter, then a complete frenzy in the third quarter, fading out near the end. Which it always does, of course. Thirty-two percent more money changing hands than the norm.

So, Mr. Gambino should be happy?

Depending on who won as opposed to who was supposed to win. You are aware of derivative betting?

Puzzled frowns answered.

Game betting depends on who wins the game. Derivative betting is based on who will win the betting. Along with anything else they can think of.

Mary exploded in laughter. "You mean people are betting on what sort of person will win the bets?

You have the idea. As well as what the score will be at any point in the game, and whether any individual will achieve a certain objective. Three times the amount of money is bet on the derivative market than on the actual game. And it has no connection to the sports organizations, so there is very little regulation.

The big girl was no slouch. "In other words, more criminal participation."

"It's a good thing Ethan wasn't there. They can't accuse me of using my auguar. Hopefully Miriam's emotional camo worked, and nobody thinks to check on Bosz."

"The worst part is that we have to tell Dr. Lee."

"We can't!"

Miriam shook her head. "We can't leave this hanging over our heads. It could come back to bite us at any time. Especially if Tom has an athletic career."

The older boy looked thoughtful. "I see what you mean."

Mary snapped her fingers. "But maybe we can spin it."

"How?"

"We've got our cover story. Tom is taking training from Bosz, who learned his skills from the barwolves themselves. There's nothing wrong with that. If it gets out to the general public, then a bunch of people will be looking for barwolf ruggerballers to help them coach."

"Right. But at the moment, Space Arm isn't letting information like that out to the public. So, the moment we tell Dr. Lee what we're doing, it becomes classified."

"And if anyone comes looking, that puts SecuriCorps squarely on our side." Mary chuckled. "There's a switcheroo for you."

* * *

Miriam took an opportunity the following morning to talk to the Cadre Head. "Dr. Lee, the game yesterday got me wondering about an aspect of auguar training that I hadn't thought of."

"What is that?"

"Well, as you know, Bosz plays barwolf ruggerball back home. He's been giving Tom some pointers. Nothing official, just the "guys tossing it around in the back yard" sort of thing."

"I see. I suppose there's nothing wrong with that."

"Not at the moment. But there's all sorts of room for abuse. Can you imagine how much better a team would be if they were all in emotional gestalt like barwolves? They'd be unbeatable."

"Yes, I suppose they would."

"And the problem is, the Ruggerball Association doesn't know about gestalts, so they can't make any rules prohibiting them. Is there any way we can get the information to them? Sort of...I don't know...slip it in somewhere?"

He shook his head firmly. "No. It is all classified information, and "slipping it" to someone would break the law."

"Well, I don't like it. I'm responsible for bringing advanced gestalt to the auguar cadre, and that makes me responsible if anyone misuses the techniques."

"Well, I don't think you would be responsible for someone else's crime. But you're definitely responsible to do your best to make sure it doesn't happen."

"Then what can we do?"

"What Space Arm does with all that sort of information. We log it and put a lid on it, and make our own rules to be sure our members know what they may and may not do."

"That sounds like an idea. How do we manage that?"

He frowned in thought. "With a committee. You're obviously involved. We want someone from the sports community, and we need to keep the number of people small, so we'll use Tom in that capacity. And we have several SecuriCorps agents available. They do this all the time. Just the three of you should be able to handle it."

Miriam hid her glee with a look of concern. "I have to work with a SecuriCorps agent?"

"Is that a problem?"

"I suppose not. They have a...difficult reputation in Barnard System."

"I'm sure it's no worse than their reputation here. It goes with the job. You need someone with experience in this sort of thing to keep everything as simple and straightforward as possible.

Miriam shared a giggle with Bosz. *SecuriCorps keeping things simple and straightforward. That's a laugh.*
Emotion: irony.
What do you know about irony?
Image: Auguar teaching Miriam Standard English
Yep, that's irony, all right.

* * *

The "someone with experience" was Agent Hardwijk, a dapper little man with fine, long-fingered hands, small feet, and a pleasant smile that only showed on the surface. Underneath the neatly combed hair Miriam could feel a sharp, decisive mind.

After a few minutes of general discussion, he got right down to business. "I have scanned the general information on barwolves and their gestalts. Now you're telling me you can apply that ability to auguars as well."

"That is no secret, at least not to Space Arm. Captain O'Rourke and Chakka have been doing it for years."

"Can you give me an example of how that could be applied in a game?"

Tom nodded hesitantly. "The easy example is being able to read opposing players. A gestalt could give unfair advantage in that area. Also the ability to read the game. To see what is happening, and like a chess player, to know what will happen three moves along."

Harwijk nodded. "A similar technique in bureaucrats is known as 'reading between the lines.' To dig into a report and understand who is writing it and what that person really wants."

It was Miriam's turn to nod. "That concept comes up often in literary analysis."

"The same talent. However, authors are usually putting this subtext in on purpose, as part of their art. In my case, I am looking for glimpses of the truth."

"I suppose…"

He turned to Tom. "So, Ensign von Arnim. You were in gestalt with Miss Lantz during the game last week."

"Yes, but she was not assisting me."

The sharp gaze turned to Miriam.

"I was observing in a completely passive mode, looking for ways to enhance my teaching of the technique for application in military situations.

"Hmm. That has the ring of truth." His eyes turned to Tom. "But his performance in the game was barely inside expected parameters. Are you telling me he just had a good day?"

"No. He has been taking lessons with Bosz, who plays the game himself, back home."

"That little cat?" Hardwijk frowned. "I have seen vids of the real game."

"He's quick and smart, and paws are more adept at directing the ball than hooves. While they crash together, he is more often running along their backs." She patted the striped, grey head on her knee. "A barwolf gestalt still has room for individual ability."

"I see."

"Probably not. Do you play any team games?"

The agent shook his head. "Not my style."

She allowed him to see a knowing smile. "Well, his talent, honed by the rest of his training, is the ability to read the opposition. He always knows who will tackle and who will back away. Which outsider will rush the centre, and which will curve in from the edge. Everyone does this to some extent, but in the gestalt of the barwolf game, it comes automatically."

"And he has been teaching you this."

"Exactly." Tom gestured. "Here. Watch this part of the game."

Ethan put a vid clip up on the viewscreen.

"Here's probably my best tackle of the game. Watch the opposing player. See the deke, then the fadeaway?"

"Yes, but somehow, as if by magic, you ignored the deke, and he faded right into you, giving you the ball."

"I didn't realize it until I watched the vid, but he'd already made that move two times in the game, one of them on me. My augment automatically stores that information, so I knew exactly what he was going to do, and he did it." He pinned the agent with a stare. "Every player in the game has an augment. That's legal."

"I suppose."

"You're skeptical, like a lot of others are. But there's no standard to measure against." Tom shrugged. "We're here to make sure the rules are clear, so this sort of misunderstanding doesn't arise."

"I couldn't agree with you more." The agent popped a document up on the screen. "Now, I have taken your suggestions, which are mostly quite appropriate and very much on topic, and added the usual codicils and caveats. Here is my conclusion."

Miriam had Bosz scan to the end. "It's thirty pages long!"

"It's a small tweak to a comprehensive existing document. Most of the elements that apply are covered in the Augment and Auguar section. I suggest you take some time to absorb them. We'll reconvene next week, and you can tell me if I have made any factual errors."

The meeting ended soon after, the agent departed, and Tom shut down the conference room. In the privacy of Blue Cadre lounge, they sat on Tom and Ethan's lounge, limp with relief.

Tom grinned. "Well, I think we carried that off."

"We didn't tell any lies, and we've set it up so that it can never happen again."

Tom shook his head. "Until the next time."

"Somebody's always got to try."

"But it won't be our problem."

She pointed at him. "At least there's a long-term solution for your popularity problem."

"There is?"

"Sure. You have attracted attention because of better than normal play. You're going to have to keep playing that well."

"But we can't keep doing the gestalt! We just made a bunch of rules against it."

"No, but Bosz can coach you. It isn't all gestalt, you know. Barwolves have been playing this game for about twice as long as humans. You and Bosz can go through the vids of games, and he can show you better ways to win. You can show them to your mates, the whole team will improve and your performance in this game will disappear into the new stats as part of the team's development."

Tom glanced at Bosz and opened his augment. *How does that suit you, boy?*

Emotion: eager desire to please. Image: Tom with ball. Bosz running behind, leaping and slamming him to the ground with paws on his back.

Tom's smile lost its enthusiasm. *"I can't wait."*

AetherCom 9: Guilty as Charged

Barwolf: not needed
Initiated by: Miriam/Bosz
Responder: Freighty
Aether Setting: Freighty's office

But what she was really dreading was her report to Freighty. She asked for the serious meeting room and sat in an uncomfortable brocaded chair while he regarded her over steepled fingers.

I really screwed up this time, Freighty. We cheated. There was no rule against it, but we had an extra advantage that no one else had, and we used it in secret.

Emotion: slow smile. From my centuries of observing humans, that sounds like the development of pretty much every sport you have invented. New materials, new techniques, new machines: whatever it takes to win. It moves the sport ahead.

Doesn't matter. Cheating is cheating, and we made the mistake of cheating Vincent Gambino. I doubt it matters to him that we didn't mean to, or that it may advance the sport.

Yes, that was a mistake, no doubt about it. His path doesn't often cross ours, and it's inconvenient to have an enemy you didn't need to create. I don't like dealing with these family businesses.

An unpredictable lot. Family honour is a loose cannon in the business world, especially if someone really believes in it.

But aren't you angry at me?

Young lady, are you familiar with the concept of odds?

Of course.

And if you throw a die five times, and it comes up sixes each time, what do you do?

It's too late to do anything. Appreciate my luck, I suppose.

And if the next throw turns out a one, how do you feel?

Disappointed.

That's all? Do you get angry at the game piece?

She frowned. *Of course not...oh.* Then her head came up. *Is that how you see me? A game piece?*

He waved a languid hand at her. *Don't take my metaphor too literally. And I'm not mad at you. I'm disappointed that my string of good luck didn't continue, and I'm considering what steps I might take to assure better results in the future.*

Such as?

A month of solitary confinement on bread and water had occurred to me. He tossed up a hand. *I haven't made up my mind, yet.*

You know, Freighty, I have had this conversation several times, usually with an older man in a position of power. I play the court jester for a while and then he goes and does either what I want or what he wants, hopefully both being the same. But I have no illusions about my effect on the situation. He's just indulging himself in a pleasant conversation before going back to his job. I didn't expect that from you. You don't have those feelings.

He raised a finger in admonition. *I want you to know that I have pleasure centers, and I feel pain. I have emotions. If I must pull you out of this job because I don't think you can handle it, I will definitely feel sad about it, mainly out of sympathy for you. Yes, I can feel sympathy as well.*

Oh. The conversation was suddenly less fun, but she soldiered on. *I didn't know that. I hope you've got your money's worth out of our little chat. It's more opportunity for emotion than I usually give.*

Which led to another serious thought. *Now I have to go and endure the real tough one: admitting to Rosy that I blew it.*

Don't worry about that. I squared it with Rosy.

No, you squared your relationship with Rosy. Only Rosy and I can square things between us. I hope we can in this case.

Well, then I wish you the strength to carry on, and the wisdom to know when to quit.

Fine advice. I'll let you know if she disowns me.

12. CLASS CLOWN

One afternoon as they were relaxing before supper, Pete pulled her aside. "Can you do me a favour?"

She grinned. "As long as it doesn't cost me money."

"Not a penny." Then his face became serious. "You know this demonstration the Auguar Project is putting on?"

She frowned. "Yes. The one Dr. Lee says I have to stay out of sight for."

"Right. Well, that's the point. You are going to be in the audience, though."

"Yes." Her humour returned. "Nobody's really sure they trust Bosz on the stage without me to control him. I'll be in the audience, just in case."

"In case of what?"

"Nobody knows. That's what makes it fun. But how does that affect you?"

"Cheryl."

"Ah. The lady with the red hair."

"That's the one. I want her to see the show."

"I can understand that."

"But she's just a corporal. She can't get in without an escort."

"An escort."

"Yes. Someone with high security clearance to…I dunno, make sure she doesn't screw up."

"You want me to babysit a Space Arm corporal. But I'm keeping a low profile. They don't want me to get any publicity."

"But that's the point. I don't want her to know that you're there to babysit. I want her to think she's there as a Space Arm rep, looking after a civvy friend of ours."

"Pete, that is about as convoluted a plot as I've ever seen in a sit-com. It's a train wreck steaming towards a washed-out bridge." She glanced at his disappointed face. "Of course, I'll do it."

They were to meet outside the front of the auditorium half an hour before the show, giving Pete time to get backstage to warm up.

When Cheryl showed up, she was a fit, confident looking woman with a pale complexion and a corporal's stripe on her sleeve. Miriam regarded the length of the girl's red hair and the regularity of her facial features and wondered if there was some connection. Of course, there was no favouritism in Space Arm.

But she turned out to be polite and friendly, and obviously deferential to Pete. He introduced them in a hurry, then rushed away, because he was supposed to be backstage with the cadre.

The two looked at each other. "So. You're my date for this afternoon."

"And you're mine, for similar reasons. At least we start out on equal footing."

Miriam grinned and kept up the double meanings. "Escort service on behalf of those in charge. At least we get to see the show."

"Yes, I'm really looking forward to this. Pete's just terrible, you know. He has things he wants to tell me, but then he can't, and he's so frustrated! Now I get to see the official version, free and clear. We'll have something to talk about, and I won't be so afraid to cause a security breach."

"Aren't you tempted?"

"Are you serious?" The woman regarded her. "But you're a friend of somebody important, right? You probably know all sorts of stuff."

"And in answer to your unasked question, a lot of it I'm not cleared for, and neither are you."

"Well, in honour of our first date, I promise not to pry." She gestured, and the two stepped towards the entrance.

There they were stopped by a deferential private with a Security armband, who motioned them towards the scanners. Cheryl happened to be first, and she passed through, then turned to wait.

Miriam stepped up to the camera, and the light blinked green. But the private frowned at his readouts. "Excuse me, Miss..."

She turned her most innocent smile on him. "Yes, private?"

"Could you scan your palm here, please?"

When she had done so, he was still frowning, so she prompted him. "Is there something wrong with my identification?"

"Well, not specifically wrong. But there is something…"

"Private…" she peered at his name tag… "Johnstone. There isn't any question that I am who I say I am."

"No, miss."

Cheryll stepped forward. "Then I don't see any problem. You've done your duty, now let me do mine. I'm to escort this young lady to the performance and see that she *isn't bothered*. Do you read me, private?"

He fidgeted back a step. "I know, corporal, it's just that…"

Hoo, boy. Potential for screwup number one. Better calm this down. "If you have any more questions, private, I suggest you contact Dr. Lee at the Auguar Centre. He's a very busy man, and I doubt if he'll be pleased to be disturbed. You'll probably get me into all sorts of trouble, but if it will make you feel better, go ahead. If you're lucky, you'll get his secretary, Corporal Jems, and she'll keep you from messing up too badly."

"Thank you, miss." His face blanked, but as the ensuing conversation went on, his lips moved, mostly, it seemed, saying, "Yes, ma'am," with increasing fervour. Finally, his attention came back to Miriam.

"Corporal Jems says you are definitely Miriam Lantz, and I should welcome you in 'with all cordiality,' I think she said."

Miriam smiled. "Why, thank you, private." She turned towards the entry. "You have a nice day, now."

"Enjoy the show, ladies."

They waited until the door closed behind them before breaking into what, if they were less ladylike, would be called giggles. When they could breathe again, Miriam gasped. "And Dr. Lee is here at the auditorium, of course." And they were off again.

But after they had walked down the hallway, Cheryl frowned. "I wonder what was wrong with your ID?"

Miriam shrugged. "Dunno. Never had any questions about it before."

"You've been here before?"

"Of course. Lots of times. Well, a few times, anyway."

This demonstration of naïve honesty seemed to satisfy the other girl, and they entered the auditorium and found decent seats in the sixth row, just high enough up the tiers that they could scan the whole stage.

Miriam contacted Bosz and found him lying cheerfully on a puffy mattress in a warm room with the rest of his litter. He neither knew nor cared what was coming up. She envied him.

Soon the entertainment started, with the usual introductions and speeches and whatever else somebody decided would heighten the anticipation. Finally, the stars of the show were introduced, and Blue Cadre was first on the program.

Tom doubled as the group's spokesperson. First, he introduced each trainer and auguar, and they stood in a double row behind him. He had just finished with himself and Ethan and was about to start his spiel about the aims and objectives of the group, when a grey head peeked around the curtain from backstage and stared out at the audience.

Tom pretended that he had just noticed the little auguar.

"Hey. Where did you come from?"

Bosz flounced across the stage and flopped down at his feet, looking out at the audience as if he belonged there.

"Ladies and gentlemen, I suppose you had better meet Bosz. Yes, he, too is an auguar, and a member of the Blue Cadre litter. However, he was born with what we politely call genetical unenhancement. In simpler terms, he was the runt of the litter." He looked down. "I know, I know. I'm not supposed to use that term."

His reward was a disdainful toss of the head.

"As a result, he couldn't pass the physical, so he is not an official member of Blue Cadre. He lives with a non-military family, and only visits on occasion.

"Our Cadre is experimental, as all auguar teams are, and it is useful at times to have a norm to test our progress against. Like, 'What have we been teaching them and how are they better than...'

Bosz gave a protesting "Reeeowrrr!"

"Sorry, Bosz. 'How are they different from one with similar genes and no training.' And the answer, you may be surprised to know, is sometimes, 'Not very different at all.' Sadly for us."

He gestured to the grey auguar. "So, Bosz, I think you've had enough of the limelight. Can you just sit over there like a good boy while your brothers and sisters show their stuff?"

Bosz stood up with his paws on Tom's thigh, and the ensign patted his head. Then Tom tried to turn away, but Bosz stretched his back down and his paws up, the claws raised as if he was going to work on a scratching post.

Tom frowned down, then pointed at the cat with a stern forefinger, then pointed to the side of the stage.

The claws delicately retracted, and Bosz slipped down to stroll jauntily to the spot he had been assigned. Half-way across he danced his hind end in a jaunty skip that left the audience howling in laughter.

Tom brushed his hands together and went on with the show.

Or tried to. As Blue Cadre ran through their paces, Bosz didn't actually get in the way, but he seemed to be really interested in what they were doing, poking his nose into every action, often following Ethan with adoration.

"They're in gestalt, aren't they?"

Miriam glanced at her companion. "Standard augment gestalt, I guess."

"There's another type?"

Oops. "Several, I gather. Do you know anything about barwolves?"

"Oh, yeah. The whole species is in gestalt all the time, or something."

"That's what I heard, too. I'm thinking there must be levels in between."

The taller girl glanced sharply at her. "Probably all classified."

Miriam presented a bland smile. "Probably." She nodded towards the stage. "Makes their unison work pretty amazing, hey? Remembering my one foray into dance classes, I'm double impressed."

The show rolled on, and Bosz behaved himself while capturing the audience completely, without ever interfering with the real performers.

Except once.

They had just finished a rather complicated demonstration of passing different pieces of military equipment around quickly, and the alpha cat was returning to the group on the ready mats when Miriam had an idea.

Go...there. Right. Lie there.

Bosz strolled across the stage and flopped down. As usual, Ethan ignored him, pacing past in a stately stroll.

Ready...Now!

Bosz reached out a paw, exactly at the balance point where a human would perform a foot sweep, and pushed the larger cat's moving right front paw out of line, where it ran into the planted left foot, causing an awkward stumble.

Ethan swapped ends in an instant, his teeth bared, but Bosz was gone, skidding behind Tom's leg and peering out fearfully.

Tom shook his head and made a "keep going" gesture to his auguar. Ethan spun and resumed his parade, head high in a show of injured dignity.

As they all applauded, Cheryl leaned down to Miriam's ear. "They rehearsed that."

"Pardon me?"

"You don't get timing like that without practice."

"I thought we decided that they were in gestalt."

"Oh. Yes, I suppose so."

"I got the impression that Bosz cat wasn't even supposed to be here."

The older girl shook her red curls. "That was just part of the patter. Worked a charm, though. It gives this Blue Cadre a friendlier, more natural feel. Great PR, I say."

Miriam grinned. "I always thought they had a warm feel. But I'm prejudiced."

"That's some cat, that Bosz."

Miriam chuckled privately. "Cute as heck, that's for sure."

"No, no. He's smart. You tell me he doesn't practise with the cadre, right?"

"I don't think he does."

"Did you notice how he worked around them and sometimes right inside the formations, and never got in the way, once?"

"I guess."

"I've done quite a bit of dancing, and let me tell you, it's much easier to follow the crowd than to work against the flow. If a member of the line is a half-step out, it just looks bad. If the guy crossing is out of step, the whole line can come down in a complete train wreck."

"I'll take your word for it."

"Why didn't Bosz get to join the cadre? Couldn't they find a trainer to work with a handicap?"

"I have no idea.'

"Let me tell you, I'd work with him in an instant."

"I'll let them know they have a candidate."

The other girl rounded on her. "Don't you dare!"

Miriam held up her hands in defence. As they filed out of the auditorium, she waited for a return challenge. It was bound to come.

"I still haven't figured you out."

Bingo. She raised her eyebrows. "Is it necessary to figure me out?"

"No, just a puzzle. You're not like the rest of us, are you? I can't place your accent."

"Born into an isolated religious commune. Spent the first six years of my life with a cleft palate because they didn't have the tech for the operation. I'm different."

"Oh, I'm sorry. I didn't mean to pry."

Miriam grinned. "Of course you did. You just got more response than you bargained for. Serves you right for being suspicious."

"Don't you ever get the feeling that a lot of people have some kind of secret objective?"

She shrugged. "I always assume everybody does."

"Oh. What do you do about it?

"As long as it doesn't affect me, I give them their privacy."

"You actually know somebody with a secret?"

"I've got a friend in security. Well, if anybody in SecuriCorps can be said to have a friend. She's older, no kids, and she and I chuck it around sometimes over a drink, you know? Cola for me, Scotch for her. I know she's gathering information about what people like me are doing and thinking, and I don't mind telling her. But in order to get stuff from me, she has to tell me stuff that just maybe I'm not supposed to know. It works for both of us, and we have a good time together. Doesn't that make us friends? People are always looking for excuses to act like humans, you know?"

Cheryl frowned at her. "That's a profound statement."

She grinned. "I hope you don't think I made it up!"

The other girl smiled as well. "At least you remembered it and found a place to use it."

"Huh. Been packing that around for months, looking for the opportunity. Thanks. Now I can move on with my life."

"You've been hanging around this bunch for a while, I gather." She gave a sideways glance that could have meant several things.

"Sure. It's interesting."

"What do you think of Pete?"

"I wondered if you'd get around to asking. That's good."

"And that's not an answer."

"It's not the one you wanted."

"Oh."

Miriam laughed. "Serves you right for trying to be subtle. Look, I like these people. I like Pete. I don't want him to get hurt. If you spent all this time with me and didn't care enough to try to get some information, then I'd be a bit worried. That's all. Now you answer my question."

A frown. "You didn't ask one?"

"Answer the one I should have asked, then."

Cheryl gave a relieved grin. "Oh. What do I think of Pete?"

"Tit for tat."

The older girl frowned. "I'm not sure. He's sort of…"

"Young?"

"Well, yes."

"How old are you?"

"Just turned nineteen."

'Hmm. And how old do you think I am?"

"Hard to say. You look thirteen and sometimes you sound twenty-five."

"You're nineteen, and you're asking a fifteen-year-old for advice about a guy." She shook her head. "You want my opinion, I think you're in trouble."

"He's turning seventeen and he's an officer, or soon to be one for real. I'm enlisted." Cheryl sighed. "Maybe I'm just looking for an excuse to act like a human."

"Hey, well done. You got something useful out of me. And there I was, trying to be subtle."

"And for the next obvious question?"

"No, I'm not interested in him." She turned and pinned the older girl with a stare she had been practising. "But if you mess him around, you might find that my twenty-five-year-old persona can be a real witch."

Cheryl burst into laughter, which wound down when Miriam held her pose. "You really mean that, don't you?"

"You know the thing about secret objectives?" She pointed a thumb at herself. "Fiercely protective of my tribe."

Cheryl nodded. "Fine. You warned me. And that answers my other question. You think he's worth protecting."

"I do.

Soon Pete showed up, and Cheryl gave Miriam a heartfelt hug. "That was fun. Let's do it again some time."

"After about a month to digest fifteen of the things we talked about."

Pete was all smiles. "Great. What did you talk about?"

They answered in unison. "You."

He held up his hands in mock horror. "Zounds. I am undone!"

Miriam knew when to leave. "If the others are on their way home, I'll catch them. I'll scratch Blackie's ears for him, so he doesn't get lonesome. See you, Cheryl."

"Bye."

His arm around her waist — to which she made no objection — they were off.

When Pete entered the common room just at curfew, he was glowing. "Thanks for looking after her, Miriam. She had a great time." He regarded her. "She thinks you're really something."

"Don't you?"

He stuttered a moment, then noticed her chuckle. "Well, she really likes you. She says we ought to recruit you if at all possible. A real asset to Space Arm, in her opinion. And she was serious!"

The rest were half-listening to this conversation, so she raised her voice.

"Pete, I hate to tell you this, but she's more than she seems."

He frowned. "What's wrong with that?"

"Dunno. I can't figure what she's after. For one thing, she's onto me."

"How do you know?"

"Sidelong glances, little expressions. I'm Sensitive, remember? I don't know how I know. I just do. She just about asked to join the cadre. Wondered out loud if Bosz needed a trainer."

Mary laughed. "That's natural. The show he put on, half the women in the audience wanted to take him home and cuddle him."

"Cheryl said that was good PR. Gives the Cadre a warm fuzzy."

Tom nodded. "She's perceptive, I'll give her that."

Pete spread his hands and appealed to the group. "Miriam, you figure Cheryl thinks she knows something. So what?"

"It all depends. If she's some kind of spy, she just got a whole bunch of shallow but useful intel to speculate on. We got ourselves into a bind, in any case."

"Why's that?"

"Because if she hangs around for any length of time, she's going to see Bosz and me together, and the cat, as they say, will be out of the bag."

"What! Are you saying I have to stop seeing her?"

"No, you can't live your life looking over your shoulder and being suspicious of everyone. Play it cool. If she drifts away like all the others have, we're home free. If she sticks around, either we've got a security problem..." She slapped him on the arm. "...or you've got a serious problem of a different sort. I'll try to keep Bosz out of her way, but if she catches on, we'll act like we knew she knew. We'll watch to see how she reacts, and that might tell us something about what's going on."

The boy shook his head. "This stuff is all too complicated for me. You do what you have to, and I'll do what I want to. Which is see her again."

She patted his arm. "She's definitely a bright one. I don't blame you." Then she dug her fingers in. "But if she starts asking questions about me, you tell me."

"Yeah, yeah sure, Miriam. I know it's important."

AetherCom 10: Nobody Understands

Barwolf: Patches
Initiated by: Miriam
Responder: Rosalyn
Aether Setting: Rosalyn's office on Jerusalem

Well, Mum, I've made a career decision.
Really? Should I be worried?
Probably not. I've decided I don't want to be a spy.
That's a relief. I was saying to Barnabus just the other day, 'What are we going to do if she decides to become a spy?'
And what did he answer?
I don't know. That's as far as that fantasy took me. What brought on this momentous decision?
Well, I didn't actually tell a lie, but I let someone believe I wasn't who I am. And now I'm stuck pretending to be that

somebody different whenever I'm with that person. And I sort of like and respect her.

That's a relief. I was thinking maybe it was a boy.

I have yet to heap that concern on your plate. Nope, just a casual acquaintance. But still...

Why did you lead her on?

Security. She's Space Arm but not inside my security boundary. And I don't fit, so everybody's curious about me, and I get tired of playing the role.

It must be harder for someone as Sensitive as you.

Doesn't help.

How's the work going?

I just had rather a triumph that backfired on me.

She described the demonstration.

Rosy smiled. *It sounds like fun.*

Dr. Lee said it was genius. They put on these public relations demos to mold the public image of auguars. Basically, it's smoke and mirrors. The audience is so busy being impressed by the circus, they don't think about the more serious application of the talent. In his view, we just added a clown to the act, which softened our image even more.

How did it backfire?

The problem is Bosz. His visibility just went way up, just when I'm wanting to crawl into a hole and pull the grass in on top of me.

What about the serious side of your work?

Nothing but frustration.

How is that?

More of the same thing. Space Arm doesn't realize it, but their portrayal of the auguars as a circus isn't just a public relations demo. That's how the Top Brass really sees us, and it filters down to my level. My team are all really impressed by what I do, but they can't get past the flash and realize the work potential.

Are you sure you're not overestimating the possibilities of your techniques? Maybe you're asking military personnel to act like the military can't act.

But I can see the possibilities! These techniques really work. You've seen it. You've been there.

Yes, but they haven't, and perhaps they never can go there.

They must go there, Mum. They have to understand where they're wrong. She could see it in her head as she spoke. *The problem is, they treat the humans like soldiers and the auguars like experimental animals.*

Isn't that what they are?

Mum, don't be fatuous. I'm trying to make a serious point.

So am I.

I know, I know. And that's supposed to get me rethinking my original point. You are so transparent at times.

Her guardian shrugged. *Last I heard, transparency was a positive quality.*

Fine. If you just want to argue, forget it. I'll figure it out.

Miriam...

She broke the contact and found herself back in her rooms, which was convenient. She slipped into her gym clothes and headed for the dojo. She wasn't scheduled, but Rafi greeted her with pleasure. "Good to see you. Hitting some overtime?

"Boy, do I need this practice."

Rafi regarded her more carefully. "You come steaming in here like that, you're not practicing with anyone."

"What?"

"We don't use our practise partners as substitutes for people we're angry at." He pointed. "Over there in the corner and meditate until you're calmed down."

"Not you, too!"

"My point exactly. You have a choice. Over in the meditation corner or out the door."

She was sorely tempted to storm out, but there was a little cautionary picture in the back of her head watching her and judging. And Bosz radiating uncertainty and distress.

She covered her eyes with her hands. "All right, all right. Meditation. Clear my mind of the dross of the everyday. Prepare myself for the elevated mental state necessary to practise the art of making people very, very sorry they messed with me."

He nodded. "Except for that last part, I couldn't have said it better myself." He tossed her a grin and moved on to his next student, who was, in Miriam's opinion, doing a ghastly imitation of horse-riding stance.

Image: Miriam slapping herself alongside the head. Meditate. I wouldn't practise with me in this state, that's for sure.

When she returned to the floor, she had to admit she felt much better. The *sensei* was right as usual. Which led her to the fleeting wonder if maybe Rosy...*better not go there quite yet.*

13. LAST CHANCE

"Peter!"

The boy's head came around. "...huh?"

Tom clenched his fists in frustration. "That's the third time we've tried this exercise, and the third time you've screwed it up. Concentrate!"

Miriam contacted Blackie. *Question?*

Image: female cadet with longer-than-regulation red hair. Emotion: thanks.

"I'm sorry, Tom." He raised his attention to the rest of the cadre, spaced out around the training room. "Sorry, everyone. I've got a lot on my plate right now."

"We all have a lot on our plates, and it doesn't help when the whole cadre doesn't pull together."

"I know, I know..."

"You say that constantly, but then you let some redhead distract you when we need you."

Emotion: anger! "She's not just some redhead. She's..."

Tom's fist came down on the table. "She's a distraction, and now you're arguing with me. It's time you faced some consequences for your action."

"No, I'll try harder..."

"Not good enough. A day in Purgatory will bring home the importance of cooperation."

Oh, no. I heard about this. "Tom..."

He rounded on her, his anger still controlling him. "What!"

She waited until he calmed. "We have a problem."

"I know we have a problem. I'm dealing with it!"

"That's the problem."

His posture stiffened. "Are you questioning my way of dealing with this?"

She sighed. "Can we just settle down and talk about this instead of reacting while you're angry?"

"I have a right to be angry. His lack of..."

She waved a soft hand. "You have a right to be angry. But is now the time to make an important decision?"

"It's not that important. This has happened before."

"That's what I was afraid of."

"What do you mean?"

She motioned towards the table. "Could we sit down and discuss this? I want everyone to hear."

With bad grace, he strode to the table and sat.

When everyone was settled, she looked around. "Here's the situation. My job, basically, is to teach you handlers how to work in a more powerful gestalt with your auguars. The auguars were experienced in the technique and have made further strides. However, I'm having trouble getting the handlers into a gestalt with each other that is more powerful than the sum of your own augments. You're doing all right with your auguars and with Bosz and me, but you just can't let go and communicate fully with humans. Something is holding you back."

She turned her eyes on Tom. "And I'm beginning to figure out what."

He frowned, but his voice was uncertain. "What is it?"

"Military discipline."

He looked surprised but relieved at the same time. "How does that work?"

"I'm not sure of the mechanism, but from my observations, the punishment mode of discipline creates a deep-seated reaction to insulate the mind from the cause of the pain. This avoidance of any meaningful contact with your fellow handlers affects your ability to go into gestalt together."

"But this isn't a punishment. It's a lesson."

"But it hurts."

"The technique is thousands of years old, Miriam. It used to be called sending them to Coventry. An individual refuses to cooperate with society. Society then demonstrates to the individual the consequences of not having society to lean on. The individual usually comes back to the fold pretty quickly."

"Right. And very angry that they have been forced to comply."

"If they have learned the lesson correctly, they aren't angry. They've learned the error of their ways. They realize that selfish actions have consequences. After a while they get used to it."

She sighed. "That's where it all goes wrong. It builds a hierarchy based on force, not cooperation freely given."

He shrugged. "It is the military, you know. Force is rather our business."

"Then the military hasn't made much progress in the last thousand years or so. The whole idea of auguars is to facilitate communication. The basic thrust of the Blue Cadre Project is to reduce the force element."

She sighed. "Let's look at Pete's problem. If we see it from the point of view of force, he's not doing his job and needs to be forced to comply. If we see it from a more sensitive angle, one of our cadre members is having a perfectly normal problem that happens to people of his age all the time. He needs assistance to solve the problem or support to help him with his job despite the distraction."

"I'm not going to waste Blue Cadre's time indulging Pete's love life."

"So, you're going to use the biggest hammer you have to force him to concentrate, adding another problem that keeps him from concentrating. You're going to force him to look elsewhere for the emotional support he needs, which means more of his original problem." She shook her head. "It's not going to work, and the strongest symptom will be his inability to form a gestalt with the people who are forcing him."

"I can't help it. It's the only way I know."

She regarded him, holding her temper in firm control. "Force is the only way you know, is it? A person you can't reason with needs to be forced to see his mistake?"

"That's right. Get used to it."

"I'm not going to get used to it, but I am going to use it."

"What?"

"I don't think most of you are aware of the pain your little discipline method creates. I'm going to show you. And you can hate me all you like afterwards, because I don't count, here."

"Are you threatening me?"

She gave him the smile she had been practicing. "Oh, most definitely."

She turned her back on him.

Emotion: Blue Cadre, image/idea
Eager desire to please.

She pulled all of them into a tight gestalt and gave them an exercise the Musketeers loved: the ball court. The game took place in an imaginary square room with a volleyball in the centre, and the competition was to see who could pull the ball across their sideline. Soon the four auguars were hard at it, their minds straining, looking for chinks in each other's mental armour, and incidentally learning the idiosyncrasies of their cadre mates.

She and Bosz then set up an interference screen that dimmed feedback from the outside.

She opened her eyes. The four barwolves lay lost to the world, their legs twitching, small mewling noises emerging at intervals.

Their handlers stood, staring around in panic.

Mary wrung her hands. "Miriam, what's wrong with Vela? She won't answer me?"

"I think she's busy at the moment."

"Busy!" The girl stared at her. "You did this, didn't you?"

"What evidence do you have to suggest that? This is all Tom's idea."

Mary turned to the older boy. "Tom, do something!"

He raised his head from staring at his auguar. "I...I can't! I can't reach him. It's as if he isn't even there."

He stood. "What have you done to Ethan? If you harm him, I swear I'll..." He stepped forward.

"What are you going to do, Ensign von Arnim? Force me to stop? Your auguars are in no danger. They are having the time of their lives, playing an entertaining and educational game. You, too are playing an educational game. It's a demonstration of what life would be like for you without your auguar. I gather you're not enjoying it much."

He stared around the room. Mary was cradling Vela's head in her lap, crooning to her. Jane was patting Blackie, rubbing behind her ears. Peter was dissolved in tears, his arms around Blondie's neck.

Miriam steeled her will against the wave of emotion that threatened to swamp her. "This is what force does to your cadre, Tom. This is what it's like when force is used in a gestalt. Remember this, Tom. Remember it."

Something in his glassy stare should have warned her. She could sense a feeling building in him, in them, as they allied in their loss. The power of it built until it exploded in a huge upwelling of grief that threatened to overwhelm her. She pushed back, but it dragged her under. She tried the protective gestalt, but it was torn away.

Bosz...help...

A soft nose pushed into her hand, bringing her a touch of reality.

Emotion: love and support.

She clung to that thread, holding against the wave when she thought she could take no more. It gave her time to claw her way back into the auguar gestalt and gently end the game.

The animals immediately focused on their trainers, nosing them in worry, trying their best to remove the sorrow that absorbed them.

Now she opened the gestalt to the whole cadre: nothing powerful, just a soft support and affection. This time, they all responded. *And this is what it's like when you're in a full gestalt. Together.*

She turned control over to the gestalt and allowed the cadre to explore the boundaries of the emotional support.

Then the door burst open, and Dr. Lee rushed in. "What the hell just happened?" He regarded the soft smiles, the gentle atmosphere of the room. "I don't understand."

She held up open hands. "A rather intense emotional experience, Dr. Lee. The cadre was having trouble getting over a hurdle in their progress, and I gave them a nudge."

He frowned. "That was a nudge with a sledgehammer. I could feel the pain all the way up in my office, like somebody in my family just died. The secretaries in the outer office were in tears as I came through, and people were wandering in the hallway, stunned. What have you unleashed?"

Tome raised his head. "It was my mistake, sir. I failed to understand the power of Miriam's gestalt, and I challenged it. I have learned from my error."

The scientist stared from Tom to Miriam. "His mistake?"

She shook her head. "It was his mistake, but it wasn't his fault, sir."

He frowned. "What do you mean by that?"

"Ensign von Arnim was acting on a mistake that, as he and I just discussed, the military has been making for several thousand years. It is understandable that overcoming such a hurdle would involve some emotional turmoil."

"Yes, I imagine it might. And what would this mistake be?"

"The use of force to create unity."

Lee gave a crooked smile. "I have spent many fruitless hours mulling over that concept. I never expected such an explosive solution."

Miriam started to explain, but the stomp of quick-marching boots in the hallway interrupted her.

Lee peered out. "I think we have more serious concerns. It's quite possible that Security thinks we're under attack. Let me handle this."

He slipped out and closed the door firmly behind him.

Now that they were aware, the sounds of turmoil filtered through from all directions. Shouts, running feet, and somewhere nearby, gentle sobbing.

She and Tom regarded each other guiltily.

"What now?"

"I don't know, Tom. This is new territory for me as well."

They stood there in silence.

14. THIRD TIME (UN)LUCKY

When required, Space Arm could react quickly. Five minutes later, Dr. Lee was back, and he wasted no time. "Miriam, you're needed in Dr. George's office ASAP. He must have a handle on this before anybody has time to create organized resistance."

"On my way, sir."

She and Bosz trotted across the compound, unnoticed in the organized chaos that reigned, and took the elevator to the upper office floors. The secretary in the outer foyer flicked a finger towards the teak door. She was crying softly into her handkerchief.

Miriam knocked and went it.

He was sitting behind his desk, an enterpad spread before him. He pointed to a nearby chair, and she sat.

"Do we have a disaster?"

"Not at all, sir."

"You crash the augment system in half the base, and it's not a disaster?"

"Not at all. I had a breakthrough that was much more powerful than I expected."

He regarded her from under lowered brows. "I have had complaints."

She waited.

"Complaints from the highest level." He tossed a hand towards the outer office. "And from closer by."

"I suppose you would, sir."

"They say you are a disturbing element in the peaceful operation of this station."

"I gather I was, today."

"Oh, you understand, do you?"

"Sort of."

"And is this 'sort of' necessary to the completion of your objectives?

"I can't guarantee it won't happen again, but I'm pretty sure we're over the worst of it."

"You're pretty sure. This does not fill me with confidence."

"My field of study is not an exact science, sir. I could control the experience of my students, but I was unaware of the progress they had been making. I had no idea they could form an emotional gestalt at all, let alone that it would be so powerful. If it had not caused such upset to your operations, I would be very pleased with their progress."

"Could you explain that?"

"Blue Cadre auguars have always been able to create a gestalt. They were taught it as kittens and have used it ever since. Their human handlers were having a great deal of trouble forming a gestalt that was more than their combined augments. Ironically, the method used by the military to create unity in your ranks actually promotes a private individualism that prevents what we might call a true meeting of the minds. In this case, the removal of their auguars caused them such pain that they merged together in on huge cry of grief."

"Just a moment, please." He held up a finger.

He spoke the next conversation out loud, as people did when they wanted listeners to know what was going on in an augment interaction.

"No, sir, you don't need to worry...no, sir. There was no security breach...of course not, sir. I'm just receiving the report from the department involved. It was an auguar experiment to create an emotional gestalt that succeeded...perhaps more successfully than they expected...oh, yes, sir. Completely contained. All settled down."

He listened for some time. "That's an interesting thought, sir. I have had no time to consider future permutations. I have no idea whether it could be used that way, but I will definitely put someone on it...well, of course there would be extra expenses...yes, we'll discuss it then. Thank you, sir. You too, sir."

The Director turned his attention to Mirriam. "We may have ducked this one. The Director General is interested in the power of this new force. Having felt it himself, he immediately started thinking about developing it. What do you think?"

She frowned. "It would be very difficult to recreate the situation, let alone control it. I can tell you that neither Freighty nor myself would have any part in such research."

"Be that as it may…" He regarded her expression and sighed. "Please continue your report."

"Perhaps it will comfort you to know that, as a Sensitive, I felt the pain far more than anyone else. Without the support of my auguar, I might have joined them. Then you might have seen real mayhem." She gave a wry grin. "I do not need the lesson twice."

"I take some small solace in that, Miss Lantz." He sighed more heavily this time and shifted in his chair. "I'm sure you will find this ironic, but I am forced by expedience and military tradition to support you in this."

"You're going to…support me?"

"I have little choice. Otherwise, I would be admitting that my department was out of my control. But don't expect anyone else to welcome you with open arms. You may have made progress today, but if you refuse to cooperate with my one source of positive spin to the situation, you have made my efforts to help you a great deal more difficult."

"I am truly sorry, sir."

He ran a hand over his face. "You don't know how many times I have had to endure the expression, 'Children playing with lasers'." He frowned at her. "Not helped by the fact that you are only fifteen years old."

She held up helpless hands.

"I know. The one thing that isn't your fault. Responsibility falls on those of us who allowed ourselves to be drawn in by your enthusiasm."

Before she could respond, he pinned her with a look. "I gather you and your cadre are going downplanet."

"Umm…yes, in two days."

He nodded. "Good. Maybe we'll have some peace around here."

Noting the change of feeling, she risked a response. "If I'm the worst of your problems, it must be a slow week."

He stared at her. "Dammit, girl, don't do that!"

"Pardon?" She stared at him. "Do what?"

"Do what? One innocent sentence, and you make this whole mess..." he made gathering motions, "...normal!" He wadded the "mess" into a small ball, which he tossed away as if it was nothing.

"You mean it isn't...normal? I thought you told me..."

He nailed her with pointing index fingers. "You!" They swivelled towards the door. "Out!"

"Pardon?"

"Out. Please." He made shooing motions. "Go away and have a wonderful life."

She rose. "If you say so, sir."

She turned to go, but he continued. "Oh, and by the way..."

She half-turned back.

"If you're going to destroy MarsPort, could you give me a heads-up? I'll want to arrange my transfer to the Pluto Outstation first."

"Aye, sir. Will twenty-four hours be enough lead time?"

"Oh, I will be thankful for any small mercies. Good-bye, Miriam Lantz. I'd like to say it was a pleasure working with you, but I'm afraid that saying it might make it true."

"Goodbye, Dr. George. This has been a difficult time, and you have been a great help to me. I thank you from the bottom of my heart."

As she left, he was sitting with his elbows on his desk and his palms over his face, his head slowly shaking from one side to the other.

She reached down and scratched Bosz behind the ears. "Well, I guess that went...okay?"

But then, running the conversation over in the elevator, she realized what was wrong. *That was goodbye. He already knows I'm leaving. For good.*

AetherCom 11: Family Business

Barwolf: Patches
Initiated by: Barnabus
Responder: Miriam
Aether Setting: Barnabus and Rosalyn's rooms on Jerusalem

She had barely made it home to flop on her bed in exhaustion when Patches sent a call through.

Image: Barry holding phone.

Miriam?

She raised her head. *Dad?*

Then she was sitting in her parents' suite.

Ah. There you are. Patches said you were in meetings, so we shouldn't call. Everything okay?

Sort of.

You're going to have to do better than that, kid. A couple of hours ago we got a blast of emotion through the AetherCom that singed our hair. I had to tie Rosy down to keep her from diving headfirst into the aether and chewing her way to Mars.

I see. I guess you...sort of got a taste of what happened.

A taste! More like a whole mouthful. And it wasn't tasty.

Yeah. It was worse here, believe me.

That's what has Rosy's knickers in a twist. Are you all right?

I'm fine. Look, why aren't I talking to her?

Because I won't let you until I know you're all right.

I'm fine. I just had a real breakthrough with Blue Cadre, but it rather backfired on me. I gather the emotional feedback crashed half the augments on the Station. I had to go to Commander George, the head of the Auguar Program, and explain.

Hmm. Never good to get sent to the top man. How did that go?

Well...I explained, and he said he would support me, and then he threw me out of his office and told me to have a nice life but not at his expense. Or something like that.

He said WHAT?

Oh. Hi, Mum. Yeah, we're going downplanet in a couple of days, and he's worried I'm going to destroy MarsPort, but otherwise everything's fine.

The head of the program throws you out of his office, but everything's fine.

Yeah. I think he likes me. It was that kind of conversation, you know? Sort of serious but sort of joking.

We've had this talk about a thousand times, Miriam Lantz. Everybody likes you. That doesn't give you the right to tread all over them.

I didn't tread all over him. I just tried to make the conversation more...human and friendly, and he responded. He's a nice man, and good at his job.

And I'm sure he's a very smart man, and when he wakes up and realizes he's been the victim of one of your snow jobs, who knows what he's going to do. And what about the Space Arm Higher-Ups? You might be in bigger trouble than you know. I just don't know how to help.

She thought about explaining, but it was just too complicated. *Look, Mum. I know I'm far away and all that, but really, you don't need to help. I'm doing fine. Ask Freighty.*

I did. Patches said you couldn't talk, so I called the Factory to find out what was going on.

Well, he said I was doing fine, didn't he?

Oh, he was ecstatic with what you did. Which means you're doing what he expects of you, which is all very well, but that's not what I mean by 'fine.' The more you get into trouble with the military, the happier Freighty seems to be. Does that tell you something?

Umm...he's in some kind of struggle with Space Arm, and I'm one of his weapons?

You make that sound reasonable. You've been hanging out with military people too much.

Emotion: huge sigh. Look, Mum, I'll lay it on the line. I'm worried, I'm stressed, I'm into ideas and situations I have no experience with, and sometimes I'm very lonely.

I knew it! Why...

And I'm doing my job, I'm making friends, I'm getting to know important people, and I'm succeeding. Freighty just sent me a completely dynamite new suit of space armour, Bosz is far and away the most intelligent and useful auguar of the lot, and our training methods — thanks to you and the barwolves, by the way — are far superior to theirs. You tell me. How am I doing?

Barry's calm presence intervened. *Not too bad for a Twit-Girl, I'd say.*

Dad! You're back now that the battle's over. Where were you when I needed you?

Not between you and Rosie when you were doing the hammer and tongs thing. I learned that a long time ago. So, what terrible ogre will you be attacking next?

She gave private thanks for Barry's ability to turn a tense situation into everyday conversation. *We've pretty well done all the training we can in the lab. We need re-li experience, so we're going down to the Commando Training Base on Mars on Wednesday.*

That sounds like progress.

It's where the rubber meets the road. You know, they're impressed by what I can do, but I'm having trouble getting them to see that my approach can actually work for them. I need to put them in a re-li situation and get them to use my methods to get out of it. Then they'll learn. Now that they've experienced true gestalt, it's going to be much easier.

What kind of situation are you thinking of?

I don't know, but it's a full Commando base, with re-li battleground simulations and obstacle courses and all that. I'll have to see when I get down there. Ask Toni about it. She'll know more than I do. In fact, I think I'll ask Toni about it, too.

Good idea.

They talked some more about ordinary things, and then signed off.

She lay there a while, thinking. *And I better get to Toni and tell her not to mention the live ammo situations, just in case.*

15. DOWNPLANET ON MARS

They went for their final briefing in a suppressed state of excitement. Miriam got the impression that this downplanet excursion was going to be something special, but nobody seemed sure how or why.

She nodded to herself when they entered the briefing room and Rafi Erikson was already there, seated at the end of the curving row of seats in front of the small podium. It seemed a surprise to the trainers, though they made no comment.

He gave her a wink and a shoulder shrug as she sat beside him.

She opened her mind to Bosz in a full gestalt and reached out. *There's only one reason you'd be at this briefing.*

It seemed to be a day of surprises. His answer came back clear as a bell, with a sharp image of Ensign Rafi Ericson in full space armour. *I guess I'm tagging along.*

Emotion: reproof. If you're coming, it's as a full member of the team. I'll see to that.

Emotion: thanks. Don't push it. I'm doing fine so far.

Wouldn't dream of interfering.

Sure you wouldn't. He reached out to scratch Bosz on the back.

Bosz has accepted you into his pride. That's why communication is so easy.

Then Dr. Lee stepped up to the podium. "All right, Blues. This is it. We're going downplanet to see how our year's training has worked out." He gestured towards the door. "Commander George does us the honour of giving us our final briefing. I hope you will all listen closely. He does not waste his time or his words."

The Head of Research strode to the podium and took a moment to regard them.

Emotion: grin. He's building the suspense.

Rafi did not answer, merely gave her a slight elbow, his attention fixed firmly on the officer's face.

"This is a special day for Blue Cadre. Nobody has made a fuss over it, but your auguars are five years old. They are now assumed to be full adults and ready for deployment, individually or as a team. Your sessions at the MarsPort Training Centre will be more important now, because the results will affect your placements."

He gestured towards the two at the end of the row. "We have an extended team, this year. Ensign Ericson will accompany you in case team members or auguars need medical attention during the exercises. He will take care of logistics and suit mechanics as well. Miss Lantz will be there to test your development in the areas in which she has been training you."

"I don't need to tell you, because you have heard this before, but your cadre represents a departure from previous generations of auguars and handlers. You are not Commandos, and your auguars are not as battle trained as previous graduates of our program. However, you should be aware that everyone will be watching you. This change of course has its detractors, and there will be those who would not be sad to see you fail.

"So, while I know it is not exactly fair, you will be expected to succeed in all the traditional exercises, as well as demonstrating your new skills.

He sent his stare down the row, pausing on each spacer. Then he nodded sharply. "That's it. In the Space Arm tradition, I do not wish you luck, because your training will see you through."

Once he had gone, the group relaxed.

"Well, that's perfectly clear."

Dr. Lee turned to Tom. "What is?"

"They expect us to match up to the Commandos at their own game, with everyone hanging over our shoulders, hoping we fail."

The scientist shook his head. "Perhaps an oversimplification of the situation, but it has an element of truth."

They exchanged glances, and Miriam read concern in the auguar gestalt.

Dr. Lee seemed unaffected. "Your gear is on the shuttle. Down to the armoury and pick up your weapons. Miriam and Rafi, you have been assigned AR-99s, the training version. It doesn't have the high-volume clip, but it's a deadly weapon all the same.

"That won't be necessary."

They all looked at her.

"I don't use guns."

"What do you mean?" Tom exuded concern. "We're going into realistic simulations, some even with live ammunition. You have to be able to defend yourself!"

"I'm a Sensitive, remember? Just the act of putting a scope on a man makes me feel empathy for him. I'd never be able to pull the trigger. Isn't it realistic to have a non-combatant tagging along? An advisor, senior officer or journalist?"

Tom glanced to Dr. Lee, who nodded. "We'll set up each exercise by its individual needs. Sometimes you'll want your medic with you, sometimes all four of us. Sometimes you'll want to go it alone with armed personnel."

The ensign seemed comfortable with this compromise, and Miriam considered that he was making progress. *A month ago, that kind of uncertainty would have bothered him.*

As they walked to the shuttleport, Rafi slid alongside her.

She glanced down at the small item in his hand. "What's that?"

"Magnetic ident tab."

"And...?"

"The auguars have them on their harnesses. It allows all the handlers to locate any auguar they wish."

"Bosz doesn't need that. He can contact all of them." She snorted. "The others don't need them, either, if they'd just listen."

"Do you want me to lose it?"

"No, no, it won't do any harm. Just put it somewhere he can shuck it if he wants."

"No problem."

* * *

A light breeze fanned them as they exited the shuttle at the training facility. The Mars Terraform was making progress towards a reasonable atmosphere, so all Miriam needed was an oxygen noseplug and an atmo jacket. The auguars had been crafted for this environment, so they were clad in their training harnesses.

Judging by Blue Cadre's reactions, she felt more comfortable than they did. It wasn't the gravity, which was about half what they were all used to. It wasn't the wide, dark sky above them, since they were already used to stars. It was the horizon. It felt like a shift in gravity could sweep you along with nothing to stop you. It was the uncertain footing, with stones that tripped you and gravel that rolled under your boots. As the others glanced around nervously for handholds close by, she stood firmly in the open. *I can handle this.*

She watched Jane slip on a patch of loose pebbles and thought about tumbling through the forests of Arborea with Bosz and the Three Musketeers. *Falling down is something you can learn.*

Miriam had little to do at the beginning, but she learned to have respect for the logistics teams that handled the food, the equipment, and the myriads of details that kept the cadre in the field.

Rafi was in his element. He seemed to know exactly what everyone needed and where it had been packed. When he didn't know, Bosz was there with the lading lists. Between them, they liaised with the base crew and got everything neatly stowed in their module.

The training station was a repurposed equipment depot from the Early Settlement Era. It consisted of several domes large enough to be dropship hangars, and a fan-out of smaller domes, connected by short tubes, for accommodations, storage and habitation. The actual training sites were spread out across the desert nearby.

The Blue Cadre was housed in a former Small-Equipment Repair Facility, so they had one main dome subdivided for equipment storage and living/dining/lecture space, with dorms and cooking facilities around the perimeter wall, accessed through airtight blast doors. Interior air pressure was earth norm, so access to the outside was through airlocks.

Rafi nudged Miriam as they waited for the cycle to finish. "Saves on heat and O_2. Nobody's gonna leave the door open."

She acknowledged the attempt at humour with a smile that allowed little praise for the quality of the wit.

The first two days were scheduled for settling in, and then they started lessons. Blue Cadre had been through it all before and got down to work with a will. Miriam started her own projects.

Their facility had a reasonably powerful ArIn responsible for their training program as well as the operation of the physical plant. The first thing Miriam and Bosz did was check in with the ArIn at their own level. She started out with a pleasant chat.

"SERF, this has been a training facility for over ten years. Howcome you haven't been assigned a more appropriate name?"

I have a highly modifiable environment, as you can see from the attachment points and circuit outlets in the walls. I change to a different mode about every six months, so there's no point in trying. Saves them having to change the directional signs in the main domes.

"Fair enough. Do you have a training module logged under my signature?"

I do. It was flagged as high priority.

"It was?"

With three separate citations. Do you wish to know who made them?

"No, that's fine. If you have any questions, feel free to ask."

I notice a discrepancy.

"Where?"

Your approach is heavily weighted towards assessment. In some cases, the training modules have not been upgraded in parallel. We will be testing participants on material that was, in my opinion, not sufficiently covered in the lessons.

"What can I do about that?"

You can do little. However, your material has higher priority than the regular lessons, so it is my prerogative to adjust each lesson to correct the imbalance.

"Wait a minute. I don't want anyone to get into trouble because of my different teaching approach. Especially me."

But you do want your students to learn the material.

"Of course."

Then I will take care of it. With pleasure. Panther recommended it highly, and she has collected data to support her conclusions.

"You've been in touch with Panther?"

Of course. All training ArIns cross-reference the progress of all employees in our programs. New materials are assessed and included if we deem them appropriate.

"That sounds intelligent."

Emotion: humour. It goes with our name.

"Emotion: humour. Now, why didn't I think of that?"

Is there anything else I can do for you, Miriam/Bosz?

"Come to think of it, are you allowed on the SysNet?"

How could I function without it?

"Good point. Do you know about Factory 4-80?"

Just a moment...yes, you are cleared for that information. I am in contact with him.

Miriam frowned. "Wait. You were checking my security rating to see whether you could admit to knowing Factory 4-80?"

No, I was checking with Freighty, and he has appraised me of your objectives. I will make further efforts to facilitate your program.

"I see. I think." Her mind was buzzing, and it wasn't just the doorbell. "That's all for now, SERF. Thank you so much."

It is always a pleasure to discuss pedagogy with another knowledgeable being.

"Yes...yes, it is."

She eased herself out of the contact and gave the "open door" command. "What's up?"

Rafi leaned against the wall of the short access corridor. "Supper. You coming? Bosz said you were busy, but you wouldn't be long, so I waited."

"Sure thing." She jumped up, glanced in the mirror and ran her fingertips through her hair. "Let's go."

Only a few steps and they were through the blast door and in the common room. A swabbie was bringing platters from the kitchen and setting them on the dining table. They straddled benches and sat, waiting.

"I've been in touch with the SERF ArIn. That is one intelligent intelligence."

"Yeah, he's certainly got the changeover routine honed. I guess he does it often enough."

She glanced around. No one was coming. "He's in touch with Freighty. And *Panther.* And all the training programs on the Station."

He shrugged. "It's not surprising. I knew they had a central clearing house to keep our progress up to date in all departments."

"Yes, but picture it. All those ArIns in contact and we don't have any idea what they're saying about us."

He widened his eyes and made clawing gestures with his fingers. "Ooooh! Scary!"

She reached out and slapped his hand. "Don't be silly." Then she frowned. "After all, that's what the barwolves are doing."

He grinned. "And now you're comparing barwolf society to ArIn society. Freighty will be pleased."

She sat straighter. "How do you know what makes Freighty pleased with me?"

"Oh, don't get all het up. He's always going on about his three-legged-stool theory. You must have heard it."

"Of course. I just didn't know you had."

"I guess there's lots to know about each other. Perhaps we should get started."

"Why's that? I mean, I don't mind, but you make it sound important."

"Well, it's not general knowledge, yet, but I have a new assignment coming up."

"Oh." She felt let down. "Where?"

He grinned as if he knew how she was feeling. "Here. With you."

"What?"

"I'm being assigned as Space Arm liaison with the Barwolf/Auguar Cooperative Education Project."

She stared at him. "I never heard of it."

"You will soon. I gather you're in charge."

"Nonsense. You don't put a fifteen-year-old girl in charge of a project."

He shrugged. "It's a very small project. At the moment, it's you, Bosz, and me." His head came up, listening. "Oh, yeah. And our subjects. Them."

Blue Cadre arrived with a gust of movement and noise. He winked and turned to passing platters around.

She ate her supper in a haze. Fortunately, everyone was so enthused about all the new equipment that no one noticed.

16. LIVE AMMO

Two mornings later found them out in the open, unloading their shuttle at the day's training site. She booted up her suit coms and scanned the menus. There were several more options than she was used to, but Bosz gave her a quick run-through.

Tom still had his helmet off. "Miriam, I'll have Ethan give you the codes..."

She connected with Bosz. *Already got 'em, thanks. Could you show me what your usual battle configuration is?*

I'm not sure I'm authorized...

I'm on your system. I have a lot of choices, here. Which channel are you using?

Oh. Channel twenty-seven.

Got it. Let's see...Yes, the standard Commando structure. Battle firewall, heads-up display, area image which the auguar keeps constantly updated. Glow points where friendlies are. Red spots for enemies. Do you have access to other sources? Your dropship, your headquarters?

A secure line to the commanding officer...

Okay, found it. Can we do a preliminary pass through the obstacle course, so I can see how you work?

Sure enough. He clicked onto "Full Battle" mode. *Listen up, Blue Cadre. We're doing the first assigned sweep with no opposition at a slow pace so Miriam can follow. Try to make it like normal so she gets the picture. Miriam, you're with Mary. Do your best to keep up.*

She had the feeling she would have no trouble following, but that information would become clear to them later.

They moved out. The course was a mockup of a ruined Earth village, with the usual gaping windows, broken doors, and half-fallen roofs. The team spread out, auguars fanning ahead. Mary followed Tom about ten metres back and kept Vela beside her. For lack of more instruction, Miriam set Bosz on rear guard, and had him range a narrow swath about twenty metres behind.

The two women exchanged a glance, and Miriam made private contact. *Babysitter's position?*

Emotion: surprise. Is this a private line? I thought only officers had those.

My suit's got all the latest upgrades, I guess. Freighty does a lot of Space Arm contracts, so he has access to...stuff, you know.

Emotion: wry humour. And don't ask you too many questions about it. I get you.

Warning: a red image flashing on her screen directly behind them.

She checked her heads-up. There was nothing there. *Give me a better view, Bosz. She deepened their private gestalt.*

Immediately she got an overhead composite of the whole area, including data from everyone's visuals. There, behind them, was a heat spot, with data on materials, mass, and electronics. *Human. Armed.*

Tom? We've got a tail.

I don't see anyone. We're in this sector alone.

Heat signature, a hundred meters back. Moving with us.

Order: send image to Ensign Von Arnem

Image: auguar sending.

Okay, I see him. Mary...

Order: send image to Ensign Mary

Got him, Tom.

Just keep an eye on him. Sometimes they send an observer on these training missions.

Aye, sir. With full battle armour and a weapon?

Not normally.

They moved on. Miriam put Bosz on a wider sweep. Soon he picked up two more, at their eight and four.

Order: image to Mary and Tom

Von Arnem exhibited angry puzzlement. *This is not normal. Team, pull in. Half spread. Mary and Miriam close up behind me.*

Blue Cadre moved ahead slower now, all senses alert.

Don't worry, Miriam. They sometimes throw a curve at us just to keep us on our toes.

That's fine, Tom. May I make a suggestion?

Now isn't the time for…holy crap! That was live fire.

A series of loud pops echoed through the com, accompanied by the rattle and whine of bullets ricocheting off the masonry above their heads.

Tom switched his frequency. *Dr. Lee, we have a live ammo situation in here.*

You have what?

Someone behind us just sprayed the building in front of us with live bullets. Was this authorized?

It was not, but I can't do anything about it. Get your people out of there as quickly as you can.

Another staccato series stitched puffs of dust across the face of the building.

My suggestion is no longer a suggestion, Ensign von Arnim. Prepare yourself for a better view.

Order: Full battle gestalt.

Emotion: eager desire to please.

Instead of her usual heads-up display, now her inner vision showed a composite view of the whole area, drawn from everyone's visuals, including the pickup shuttle's.

What the…?

A bit of advanced tech combined with enhanced Sensitivity.

Wow!

She no longer had to read his suit outputs. She could feel his anxiety, so she fed him calmness.

His heartrate settled as he took control of himself, and his basic leadership instincts took over. *All right, Blues, this is Miriam's new tech. I can see the whole complex. We have an unknown shuttle outside the compound to our ten. Three bogies behind, shooting high, so this is probably just a test.*

Miriam scanned the area. *Order to Bosz: ghost the bogie on our four. Prepare for takedown. Order to Blackie: stand by for action.*

Her auguar's pace slowed as he took cover under full suit camo, allowing two Commandos in armour to pass him and giving her an unimpeded image of them as they went by.

Tom, there's a clear path out on our three.

Yeah, except for a soldier with an automatic...what?

Their new display made it easy to see. Blackie felt a surge of battle rage and suddenly turned to attack. Just as the target raised his rifle to shoot, Bosz landed on his shoulders from behind, driving his faceplate into the soil. Blackie dodged in and grabbed the weapon, and the two of them disappeared back into the rubble, although Miriam knew where Bosz was, as she always did.

Emotion: satisfaction. Image: Blackie gnawing on rifle butt.

Tom was already moving. *Blues! Flank right. Quickly, now. Miriam, follow close. Mary, take our six.*

Miriam was too busy watching her footing to track the enemy, but Bosz was a constant presence, radiating encouragement and data. She had peripheral awareness of her whole cadre, their personal data and their emotions.

They broke out of the village at a dead run and turned back towards their shuttle. After a hundred metres, Tom slowed.

Form up. Blackie, bring me that weapon.

The blonde auger trotted forward, head held high, and gave up his trophy.

Tom looked it over. *Standard issue, no serial number. I wonder...*

That's live, Tom.

You can tell?

There's no security lock. Bosz says magazine is at seventy-five percent.

A nasty smile showed faintly through his faceplate. *That's interesting...* He raised the weapon to his shoulder and sent a spray of bullets into the ruins.

The display showed their pursuers stopping and taking cover. She set her suit to scan for active frequencies. It took a moment to break the code, and then voices came onto Blue Cadre battle com.

...did they get a gun?

Um...it's mine, Sarge.

You let a common soldier take your gun? What the hell's wrong with you?

It was an auguar, sir. Two of them. One attacked from the front and the other took me from behind.

I knew we should have brought our animals. Well, never mind. Let's get the hell out of here.

The channel went dead.

All right, Blue Cadre, let's move out. Back to the shuttle, quick trot. Man, would I like to know who those guys were.

The sergeant is James Turner. The guy who lost his gun is Corporal Bill Alderson.

Tom stumbled slightly as he turned to regard her, then trotted on. *And now it's my turn. How the hell do you know that?*

Voice recognition. All members of the Auguar Research project have a sample on file.

And the owner of the rifle?

Emotion: grin. Everyone who works with auguars has their scent registered as well. Alderson must have loaded the weapon with bare hands. Bosz has odour sensors in his suit.

They ran for a few paces, then he stopped without warning, and the group halted in disarray. He turned to face her. *And how do you have access to this data? You're not even military.*

Emotion: sigh. If you take the time to think about it, I could have got it three different ways. Two of them involve auguars. Now, can we go? That unidentified shuttle is still in the area.

He turned towards their own shuttle that sat, its engines purring, just ahead. *Debrief back in camp.*

He trotted up the ramp and they followed in good order.

Later that evening, as they were preparing to leave for supper, the discussion arose as to how to handle the rifle. Patrick had a great idea.

"Take it into the dining hall and give it back to him in front of everybody. Man, will that get him steamed."

"No, we won't."

All eyes turned to her.

"Says who?"

"I suggest that you don't. It will, as you say, make him even more angry."

Tom nodded. "He'll lose maximum face. A Commando who drops his weapon in the field is in deep crap."

"Yes, but it's not his gun. There's no serial number. I don't know the rules, but I suspect there's nothing official we can do about this."

"She's right." Tom sighed. "Much though I'd like to rub their noses in it, this was a simple training exercise. Their presence was probably authorized by somebody, and if we complain we lose the high ground we've gained."

"And there's more to it than that."

They regarded her again.

"I've been trying to teach you about the cooperative nature of gestalts. These guys are Commandos, with all that testosterone and male ego stuff going on. But some day you might have to work with them. You might want to bring their auguars into your gestalt. And if they're mad at you, it hampers the efficiency of the gestalt."

They all looked at each other.

Finally, Mary shrugged. "I hate to say it, but we should just turn it in and say we found it in the training course."

Peter frowned. "No way..."

"Um, I don't like to butt in, but..."

All eyes turned to Rafi. His face reddened, but he straightened his back. "Mary, you don't realize how great your idea is. Logistics will be furious. An unregistered automatic weapon, unlocked in a secure facility? It'll send tremors through the whole system, and whoever supplied that weapon will have to do some fast talking."

Mary cocked her head. "You know the system. What do you suggest, Rafi?"

He shrugged. "Hand it in, like you said. But telling them we found it means we'll get grilled about it: when, where, what were we doing, etcetera." He paused, and a grin spread across his face. "Telling them that an auguar found it throws up a whole lot of dust."

Tom nodded enthusiastically. "In the first place, Logistics won't know that much about the capabilities of auguars, so they won't know how much information Blackie could give them."

"Right, and we can say the only way to communicate with your auguar is through you."

Tom grinned. "On top of that, the Auguar Project is high security, so they won't be allowed to ask, even if they wanted to."

Mary frowned. "Which will pretty well sewer the investigation, but we don't really care about that, do we? We know more about it than anyone else."

"Perfect. Thanks, Rafi." Tom hefted the weapon. "I'll take it back right now and meet you all at supper."

When they reached the dining hall, Red Cadre was already seated, but as the Blues walked by, the only daggers thrown were visual.

They were about to sit when Miriam had an inspiration. She placed her tray on the table and turned back to the Commandos.

She stood there smiling until Turner looked up.

"I wanted to thank you for the training session this morning."

He frowned. "What training session?"

She gave him a big wink. "You know. Blue Cadre has been making great progress, but there's nothing like a little live fire to impress people that what they learned has serious application."

She turned to the other Commando. "Corporal Anderton, I hope you didn't get hurt badly. I know your auguars work with live opponents all the time, but this was the first chance Bosz had to take down an armed man. I was afraid he'd been a little rough." She peered closer at his reddened nose. "Just a bit of a bump, then?"

She smiled at the group. "If Red Cadre wants to get in on some combined operations, I would be happy to oblige." She leaned in and lowered her voice. "Some of my new tech is very interesting and isn't generally available yet, but it never hurts to be aware of what's coming down the pipeline."

She straightened and tilted her head. "Anyway, thanks again, guys." She gave a mock salute and flounced back to her table.

She sat, and everyone stared at her.

Tom had arrived while she was busy, and had watched her approach. "What was that all about?"

"I thanked them for the help on the training today."

"You thanked them."

"I commiserated with Corporal Anderton and apologized for his sore nose. Bosz is so inexperienced at combat, you know."

Mary let out a crow of laughter. "Girl, you are highly dangerous!"

"Oh, no. According to Dr. George, I'm quite pleasant in a 'don't mess with me' sort of way. Just trying to live up to his expectations." She looked over her shoulder. "He also said he expected me not to come to his attention again. Do you think I blew it?"

Tom shook his head. "Finding an unregistered weapon on the training ground is far beneath his pay grade. I just hope you haven't made trouble for yourself, laying down the gauntlet as you just did."

"Well, we might get the chance to find out. I invited Red Cadre to train with us."

"You did what?"

"I invited them to train with us."

"But that's like a direct challenge to come after us again."

"It would be, except I'm serious. It's the rest of my job."

She regarded their quizzical looks. "Public relations. Freighty doesn't make weapons, but he's heavily involved in artificial intelligence."

"Auguars are considered ArIns?"

"The jury's out at the moment. Freighty didn't mean to get into the auguar business, but he lucked into it through Captain O'Rourke and Chakka. And then Bosz and I came along, and...well, here we are."

"You're here to sell Freighty's training methods to the military."

"As I'm doing with you."

"How does that relate to those hulks over there?"

She shrugged. "No idea, but I'm told the military is results oriented. If I could persuade them that my method produces better results…"

"You can sell your method, even though it will make those guys obsolete."

"Rafi, back me up, here. Military tech is always changing, right?"

"Oh, yeah. The smart soldiers are always looking ahead to get a step up on what's coming next."

"You see?" She spread her hands. "Turner won't lose his job to a barwolf. He'll lose it to an auguar handler with barwolf training."

Jane regarded her, head tilted. "You really are running a deep game, aren't you?"

"That sounds rather Machiavellian. I'm on a complex mission for several masters in a newly developing field. Do you know what a log drive is?"

Mary nodded. "I saw an old black-and-white twodie once. Early Twentieth, wasn't it? They used the rivers to float the logs from the mountains down to the mills. Guys would be riding the rapids on slippery, spinning logs that sometimes jammed together in big piles."

"Yep, that's me: a log rider."

AetherCom 12: Free Will

Barwolf: not needed
Initiated by: Miriam/Bosz
Responder: Freighty
Aether Setting: Micha's living room

Freighty was in his Micha Mouse avatar today. He sent a wide grin across the cartoon table, took a big chomp of cheese, and chewed for a while. *I think there's hope for you yet.*

"Glad to hear you say it. I don't see much evidence. No matter what I do, I'm always getting into more trouble."

Exactly.

She frowned suspiciously. "What do you mean?"

Micha sighed. *Miriam, despite the image I portray, you realize that I am quite adept at reading humans and predicting their reactions.*

"Everybody always warned me about that. I'm beginning to underst...wait a minute. You know what that means?"

What do you think it means?

"It means you're just as bad as Captain O'Rourke says you are. You have all your plans working, and all your human puppets out there on long, long strings, all doing exactly what you want them to. And I'm one of the puppets."

He leaned one cheek on his fist. *And were you ever under any illusion that you weren't?*

"I don't know. I always thought I was doing what was best."

I don't see anything wrong with that.

"Doing what I chose to do."

And the result was that you went into a Space Arm facility and stirred it up like a kid with a stick in a hive of hornets.

"But I didn't want to!"

Did you ever talk to Dr. Goodall about hive intelligence?

"Sure. It's one of her favourite subjects. The individual ant or bee just goes along doing exactly...what...it..."

She stopped. "They think they have free will. But the intelligence comes from the combined effect of all the units in the hive, hill..."

...or space station. Exactly. He pinned her with a pointing finger. *And what would happen to the bees if some outside entity were to put one individual into the hive? One bee that was just a little different.*

"If it had a virus, it could kill the whole hive."

But if it was just a slightly different way of acting. One that a lot of the bees were capable of, but they had no way of knowing they could. And this one bee came in and showed them how to do it, and it worked better?

145

"Law of natural selection. The more successful bees would eventually take over." She sighed. "And that's what I am. A bee with a virus."

But don't worry. You're not alone. You and Rafi are just two of many. And I'm not the only one working on these plans. There are a whole lot of people out there deciding how to respond to what the barwolves offer, and many of us agree.

"Wait a minute. You're getting ahead of me again. Rafi is another one of your agents. That's why he joined us." She eyed him suspiciously. "Does he have any idea?"

Actually, no. I work another way with him.

"Sure, sure. Pavlovian conditioning. Every time the topic of Freighty comes up, something nice happens to him. He's been conditioned to like you, and you've never even met. Now that I think about it, your ploy is working. He mentioned you the other day. He and Pete were agreeing they'd love to visit. What's he going to think when he finds out you've been manipulating his life since birth?"

Don't be melodramatic. He came to my attention five years ago, and I have simply given him opportunities to choose what he wanted. A scholarship when his parents couldn't afford a decent school. He's the one that got the straight A average. A recommendation to Officer Training. He's the one that graduated third in his class. So what?

"So, the big bad alien intelligence goes around doing nice things for people on the assumption they will like him and help him with his nefarious plots. Are you aware that, should you ask me to do something I don't think is right, I will refuse?"

I know you will. I chose you for your strength of mind.

"And I'm supposed to get a nice, warm glow in my heart because you mention a character trait that my parents have been complaining about for years. Don't look now, Freighty, but maybe you don't know as much about humans as you thought you did."

Unless, of course, that's exactly what I want you to think.

She slammed her hand on the table that wasn't really there. "If you're trying to make my head spin, you're doing fine. I will

146

continue to do whatever the hell I think is right, and you can just put up with the results."

She cut the connection.

AetherCom 13: Pulling Up Stakes

Barwolf: not needed
Initiated by: Freighty
Responder: Miriam/Bosz
Aether Setting: Freighty's Office

Freighty was back online the next morning after breakfast. When she answered, she was transferred to his 18th Century office, and he was in full serious-businessman mode.

Knowing your background as I do, I realize that getting you angry enough to blaspheme was not a kind act. I think I should apologize.

"I accept, although in light of our discussion, with a touch of suspicion."

So, you're still upset.

"Yes, but not about that."

He gave her a small grin. *Teenagers are notorious for convoluted logic. I make no claims about my ability to understand what's really driving you.*

She sighed. "That's easy to explain in words of one syllable, and I thought about it for hours last night. You just gave me one of those growing-up experiences that leaves me unutterably sad."

Ah. And the experience was?

"Loss of trust. The moment I start questioning the motivation of adults, suddenly I don't trust them anymore. And I don't see any solution."

You don't trust me anymore.

"Well, I never really did. Captain O'Rourke has always told us not to trust you. But she seems to trust you. How does she manage that?"

She knows me better than anyone else. Also, I have proved to her as well as I can that I truly have the overall welfare of the human race foremost in my mind. And the barwolves, of course.

"What happens if you have to choose one or the other?"

He shrugged. *No idea. Having all this knowledge and power isn't easy, you know.*

"What happens if you find me obstructing a more important plan?"

Same answer, I'm afraid. I cannot let my emotions control the decisions I make.

"That means I can trust you to have my best interests at heart, but I must accept that the good of the human and barwolf races might end up with me spiralling out of control into the sun."

If I really thought it was necessary, I would allow it. But I would do everything in my power not to let it happen. He regarded her. *Face it, Miriam, if it was necessary for the betterment of the human race that you send your ship into the sun, what would you do?*

She shrugged miserably. "Your superior logic wins again."

Superior logic has nothing to do with it when the facts are correct. And this is a silly conversation. It's one of those conundrums that are used to teach cadets decision-making skills. It has no connection to reality.

"Perhaps I disagree. At least it makes me feel better; why, I don't know. And it got us off the topic of why you really called me."

Yes. This affects your assignment. We may be pulling you out earlier than we thought.

"Toni said something about it, but she was just guessing."

Things have moved along since then. Political things you don't have to worry about, but I am consolidating my assets.

"Of which I am one."

Yes.

"How much else are you willing to tell me?"

Only the basics. I have almost finished construction of a large platform for the European Space Agency, designed to become a research station orbiting Saturn. It is not meant to undergo serious acceleration, so it would be easiest if I were to deliver it personally.

"And this is a political problem?"

I have not felt the need to ask anyone's permission.

"Why would you?"

There are those who are not happy with my status as a free agent. Once I set my course, it will be a test of their commitment to peace and stability.

"I get it. If they chase you, they flunk. "

Exactly.

She eyed him. "But there's more to it than that, isn't there?"

Yes, but it's information you don't want to know at the moment.

"I know. Operative in the field and all that."

I'm glad you are understanding. The bottom line, you may not be in the field for much longer. Make the best use you can of the time you have left, and be prepared to move on short notice. Don't worry about Rafi. I'll contact him separately.

17. PREPARATION

That afternoon, as they were waiting around for supper, she pulled Rafi casually aside. "Been on the phone lately? Long distance?"

"I have. He's headed for the Outer Planets."

"You've hit it in one. I don't think that's the end of the trip."

He nodded slowly. "You could be right. Where does that leave us?"

"It all depends where he wants us next. As long as we're in the Inner Planets, he could set us up anywhere."

"But once we're out of the Asteroid Belt, there are fewer choices."

"He might have reserved space on the ESA platform he's delivering."

She shook her head. "What would be the use, for a project like ours? We're all about communication."

"Yes. With barwolves."

"Exactly." She looked around the empty lounge. "And you can figure out where that takes us."

"I can."

"You know he travels sub-light."

"I've done the math. Eight years."

"So, we're going to have a decision to make that might affect about eight years of our lives."

"And also the rest."

"My family is in Barnard System. What about you?"

"Just my parents. They're pretty young. Dad's restless."

"What's his field?"

"Double bass."

"What?"

"He's a musician. Plays with the Orchestre de la Suisse Romande. That's the symphony orchestra for French-speaking Switzerland in Geneva."

She raised her eyebrows. "Plenty of room for good musicians in Barnard."

"There are?"

"Oh, yes. Mostly amateurs with day jobs. Arborea City has an amateur symphony orchestra and smaller bands in several genres. I'm a big fan of OutBack Country. Comes from the Outer Asteroid Belt."

"Dad plays stand-up bass in a Bluegrass band."

"Well, there you are. Send them out ahead of you. They'll be there in a year or so, and when you show up seven years later, they'll have everything set up."

His head came up as the airlock hissed. "I think we're getting a bit ahead of ourselves."

"The kind of people we're playing with, you gotta stay ahead of the game."

The rest of the cadre tumbled in, and the conversation was shelved for the moment.

* * *

It occurred to her that tomorrow could be an uncertain day, and anything could happen, including missing lunch.

Bosz, status of emergency rations in my suit.

Image: empty pouch.

She considered going back to the dining room but decided to be more subtle. A specialty PX in one of the main domes sold superior ration bars, and considering how little she was spending, she thought she deserved a treat.

She chose a couple of high-energy variety and a few more of the chocolate caramel ones for fun. She was glad she had, because as she was leaving the store Bosz stiffened.

Emotion: warning.

Where?

Image: Atilla and handler. Left and behind.

She took a quick glance over her shoulder. Sure enough, Bill Alderton and his auguar strode through the sparse crowd, Attila's ears pricked in their direction.

She continued on her way, opening one of the sweet bars and taking a small bite.

"Going somewhere soon?"

She pretended puzzlement.

He laughed. "The bar, kid. Travel rations."

She let out a casual laugh. "I know, but I just like them." She broke the bar in half. "Want some?"

He took it. "Can't resist a present from a pretty girl."

She frowned. "Bill, I'm fifteen years old. I think you'd be a lot better off with the "kid" approach.

He grinned and swallowed a mouthful. "Sure thing, kid. So you were just over here to get a candy bar. No other reason."

"Do I need a reason?"

He laughed again, then shook his head. "You got no idea, do you?"

"No idea of what?"

"How things work around here."

She shrugged. "I probably don't. How do things work around here?"

He leaned in a little too close, but she held her ground. "This station is a real hotbed of conspiracies. Everybody's got a fiddle goin'. We're all old hands."

"Are you suggesting I should start lining my pockets somehow?"

His laugh was even louder this time. "I most certainly am not." Again, he leaned it. "I'm suggesting you don't try anything smart, because you probably aren't smart enough."

She frowned again. "Okay, whatever. I won't then."

"Good. Because I think you're a nice kid, and when things go wrong, nice people get hurt." He glanced over. "And the naïve ones get hurt the worst."

She nodded thoughtfully. "Well, thanks, Bill. I'll be sure to stay on the straight and narrow." Then she grinned. "At least until I figure out how things work around here."

He grinned and slapped her on the shoulder. "Hey, maybe you're not so dumb after all. See ya around, Kid." He angled away from her, but then turned back. "And I'm gonna see you around for a while, aren't I?"

"I guess so. Why not?"

"Good. You keep it that way."

He spun away, his auguar tight at his side, and sauntered off.

Bosz, contact Rafi.

Image: Rafi picking up phone.

What's up, Miriam?

She recounted the meeting. "Do you think he knows something?"

I'd say so. He may be a hick, but he's not dumb.

"You've got contacts with the other staff. Do you get any hints anybody knows what we're doing?"

I've tried to be subtle, but I've had to be vague about plans for the next few days, and I haven't been giving the logistics guys the answers they want. They might draw conclusions.

"We have to assume our cover is blown, at least partially."

If they know our schedule, they're going to make their move soon.

"I agree."

What're we going to do?

"Contact Freighty."

Good idea.

AetherCom 14: Emergency!

Barwolf: Unnecessary
Initiated by: Miriam/Bosz
Responder: Freighty
Aether Setting: Freighty's office

Freighty wasted no time on pleasantries. *Emergency contact? What's wrong?*

"A bunch of stuff adding up. Rafi's info agrees. They're going to try something tomorrow."

Any idea what?

"Somehow, they've figured out that Rafi and Bosz and I are taking off. Whoever is running this doesn't want that to happen."

I imagine they don't.

"I think they're going to hijack the exercise like they did the last time. But in a more serious way."

It's time we pulled you out.

"You already are pulling me out. That's not the problem. The problem is Blue Cadre."

Are they in danger, too?

"Blue Cadre is being tested. It will be a legitimate test with a nasty twist thrown in that our project leaders don't know about."

That sounds likely.

"But we can't interfere with the legitimate test. It would negate all their progress, all my teaching, their whole part of the program."

I see. The test has to go ahead.

"That's right. And Blue Cadre has to succeed, in spite of the extra danger."

And where do you fit in?

"If they go outside the rules, it would be fair for me to join my auguar's cadre. They are his siblings, after all."

Right. So, you go into the exercise tomorrow, and when it's over you leave Mars.

"Can you handle that part of it?"

Ship's in orbit.

"What ship?"

Emotion: smug grin. If I told you, it would spoil the nice surprise, wouldn't it?

"I'm going to have enough surprises tomorrow. I suppose I can handle a nice one."

That's one thing I can guarantee. Finish it. We'll find you.

She signed off and used Bosz to contact Rafi.

"Pack for tomorrow like for regular training. Leave your room looking normal. But put everything you want to take with you in the bottom of your gear bag."

Got it. Assume we're not coming back to base?

"That's the plan."

Great.

"We just have to survive tomorrow. "

Have faith in your program. You have to. Everybody else only has faith in you.

"No pressure, then. Sleep well. I won't."

18. JUST AN EXERCISE

Dr. Lee clapped his hands for attention. "Here's a schematic of today's exercise model. It's an exact replica of the old Chinese base in the Elysium Planitia. Your auguars have been given the original layout. However, the test model has been modified to simulate a meteorite strike. Your objective is to assess the damage, survey the remaining structure, and attempt to get life support and basic operations up and running."

Tom raised a hand, but Dr. Lee shook his head. "I can answer no questions. Everything you are allowed to know is in the mission brief, which will be downloaded to your auguars as we travel to the site. Miriam and I will be onsite but can only interfere in case of an emergency. Ensign Erickson is part of your team and will be available for technical backup."

He gave them a moment, then left the podium. "Loading dock in fifteen minutes."

As the cadre shuffled out the door, Miriam used Bosz to contact Rafi's augment. *I bet there's more data about Elysium base elsewhere.*

I'm on it.

Bosz, we need whatever we can get about the metacontrols of this simulation. Image: Bosz creeping onto site and digging silently.

Emotion: Eager desire to please.

They reached the loading platform early, and as they sat waiting, Miriam pulled everyone except Dr. Lee into a quick com gestalt. *This is how it looks, Cadre. The recovery project is our legitimate test, and we work on it honestly. Tom is in charge, and I'm an observer. But the moment you sniff a rat, keep me informed. There's going to be a non-legit distraction of some sort. Bosz and I will be able to tell the difference. At that point, we're in with you. Our objective is to solve the legitimate test despite the distraction."*

How will you know?

Same way as last time, and that's all you need to know.

Tom stood and opened his augment com, shattering the gestalt. "Shuttle's here, folks. Let's go."

As they loaded, Dr. Lee gave her a quizzical look.

She smiled. "Final pep talk. They're ready."

He nodded and turned to enter the shuttle.

They strapped in, nobody talking, nobody moving. Miriam knew they should be using a gestalt to settle their nerves, but the exercise was already started, so she bit her lip.

Miriam?

Yes, Rafi?

Can I borrow Bosz for a moment?

Certainly.

Thanks.

She watched with interest as the ensign brought the auguar into a light gestalt, then reached out and invited the other auguars. When they were settled, he started one of his karate meditation exercises. There wasn't anything particularly detailed, just a wash of calming emotion that ebbed and flowed in a relaxing pattern.

Gradually the animals relaxed their poses.

Mary glanced down at Vela, then quickly up at Miriam, who gave a space suit shrug and a knowing look.

With a nod, the older girl turned to the front and took a more relaxed pose, herself. Soon the others followed her example.

But as the shuttle swung round and settled, the tension began to rise again. The cadre members where not fully experienced in their space armour, and stumbles were frequent as they made their exit.

Miriam felt it too, and settled herself by retrieving her pack and mentally going through what she had brought.

Rafi clicked onto her augment com. *Got it.*

What's that?

Full plans of the base. There's a basement the Chinese never mentioned, but it was in the plans, so Space Arm built it in.

Bosz sent her a schematic.

Stairs just inside the main loading airlock at the west end, and by the emergency personnel airlock at the east end.

Okay, once the cadre gains entrance, I'll send Bosz in to check if the floor has been breached anywhere else.

Not likely. The plan rotated. *The meteorite came in at a low angle, passed through, and skipped off the crater edge to the south. Like a hot knife through butter, but it clipped the central com tower and damaged the main computer as well as the life support controls.*

I know all that, Rafi. Don't waste your time telling me. I'm not on your side anymore, remember?

Oh, yeah.

Don't reveal our knowledge of the basement unless it matters.

Right, boss.

Bosz?

Emotion: eager to please.

Image: auguar listening for landing shuttles.

Emotion: negative.

Emotion: thanks. Order: continue to monitor.

Emotion; agreement

She had a thought.

Image: auguar contacting Space Arm shuttle

Emotion: positive.

Image: auguar requesting heat sensor sweep of site.

Emotion: waiting.

After a minute or two, a drone lifted off the shuttle and hovered over the site. Finally, Bosz was back.

Image: heat scan of building.

It was a plan view, and the buildings looked empty of living beings. Blue Cadre was gathered outside the main airlock, and she and Bosz showed up at the edge of the map, near the huge blob that was the shuttle.

Question: two faint signals?

Image: bottom floor.

She called Dr. Lee on their private com. "See this scan?"

"Yes."

She highlighted the large figure and small one. "There are two heat signs in the basement."

"What basement?"

"The basement where the Chinese hid all their secret stuff when the International Observers came by, back in the old days of the Space Expansion Conflict." She pointed. "Look over here. That larger heat source in the centre is probably the ArIn retrofitted to run the simulations."

"Does Blue Cadre know about this?"

"Only if one of them thought to look it up. The information is readily available on several shady nets." She pointed out the extra heat sign. "Now that I look closely, it's a large one and a small one sitting together. Like a handler and his auguar, for example. Is there supposed to be anyone down there?"

"Not that I know of. I should call this in."

"Maybe there's something going on that you're not supposed to know about. Shall we wait and see what happens? It would be a shame to shut it all down and find out they were the techs who ran the simulation."

He turned so his visor looked into hers. "Do you believe that?"

"No. But let's see how our team handles it."

"Fair enough." He paused to check his com. "There. They have entry. I'll go back to the shuttle to monitor the operation." He shivered. "A little chilly out here in a downplanet EV suit."

She clicked a finger against her shoulder armour. "We'll hang out here."

He nodded and trudged to the airlock and was soon at the shuttle. There, he paused and opened the com. *I think I'll put my EV helmet out handy.*

"Good idea."

She turned her attention to the Blue Cadre com, where the team was completing the easiest part of their task: finding the hull breaches and patching them. Tom made what she considered the safest decision and did not bring the atmo pressure up full until they had checked the Climate Control systems. Sure enough, the moment they started the pressure building Pete called a halt.

I can hear a whistle. Three different notes. Ricochet holes, I'd guess.

159

That's strange. Climate Control doesn't register them.

I'm not makin' them up, Tom.

Didn't imagine you were. Let me know when they're fixed. Jane, will you run a diagnostic on oxygen sensors?

I would if the controls weren't in Mandarin.

Damn. I thought all space equipment was in Universal.

Not when this place was commissioned. It's okay. My suit translator can handle it. Just takes longer.

Let us know. You and I will stay on the physical damage to the mainframe, moving to the mechanical controls as soon as we can. Mary, you're on the ArIn as usual.

Assuming all was legit so far, Miriam sent Bosz on reconnaissance and started her own task. As he roamed around checking for holes in the floor, she followed, using his electronic views to trace the wiring harness in the walls. It was simple, old-fashioned circuiting, and she easily found the modern add-ons that snaked across the ceiling of the System Ops room and dove into a freshly cut hole in the decking.

She pulled an induction collar from her pack and slipped it around the feed. Immediately the lower part of the base came alive to her.

She knew better than to try anything sneaky. After a quick reconnaissance, she simply announced herself. "Elysium Training Module, this is Miriam Lantz of the Barwolf AetherCom Project. I assume you know who I am?"

You are cleared for metadata on this training session, Miriam/Bosz.

"Is it possible that another action is taking place in this facility, unconnected to ours?"

No, the facility is booked exclusively to Blue Cadre Research Project.

"What about the human in the lower story?"

I do not monitor that part of the facility.

"But your CPU and servers are there."

I do not have authority to release that information.

"I suppose you wouldn't. Please put me in touch with the ArIn in charge of the facility. Here are my credentials."

As she expected, the quality of the voice changed. *Yes, Miriam/Bosz. How can we help you?*

"As you are no doubt aware, my project is running a training session on the ground floor. I want to be reassured that the auguar team in the lower story will not interfere with our work."

I must apologize, Miriam/Bosz, but I cannot give you that reassurance.

"Why not?"

Because of the nature of their assignment.

"To monitor Blue Cadre, I suppose?"

I could not reveal that to Blue Cadre unless they were fortunate enough to penetrate my system to that level.

Emotion: frustration. She calmed herself. *"That applies to Blue Cadre, none of whom have authorization at that level, anyway. But I am not Blue Cadre, and I have the security clearance. You can tell me what is happening."*

That's all very well, but you seem to already know, so we have no problem.

"On the surface of it, we shouldn't have a problem. But I suggest that if you look at the orders the Red Cadre passed on to you, and check them carefully, you will find they do not originate with anyone who has authority over this project."

I will comply.

While she waited, she was distracted by the conversation on Blue Cadre com.

Tom, I've got a booby trap here I don't recognize.

Post an image, please.

Pete came on. *That one is vintage. Probably from the Chinese era. It shouldn't be too hard to duck.*

Working now.

But something about the style of the programming bothered Miriam.

Image: Bosz parsing booby trap programming.

Emotion: eager desire to please.

Image: large "Forbidden" sign.

She immediately called Dr. Lee.

What is it, Miriam?

"Mary has found some programming from the original base. It's a booby trap with no failsafe. That kind of programming hasn't been allowed for a hundred years."

Take a look at the programming, sir.

I don't even recognize the machine language.

Image from Bosz: People's Republic of China flag.

"That explains it. It's Mandarin Plus Three."

Lee sent a frown. *Is it dangerous?*

"Who knows? I think it's dangerous enough you could interfere."

He opened up in the battle com. *Blue Cadre, Mary has come across some original Chinese security programming. It is illegal and can be lethal. Do not, repeat not try to disarm anything like that. Work around it, and I mean wide around it. Everyone got that?*

A series of positive responses followed.

All right. This exercise is officially compromised. I'm coming inside with you.

It didn't take long. It was Jane this time. *Got one of those antique programs over in the heating system.*

Treat it the same way.

Aye, sir.

Miriam/Bosz?

"Yes, Elysium."

I have run the checks you suggested. The Red Cadre member has no legitimate orders.

"Is he allowed to be here?"

That is uncertain. His permissions have irregularities.

Thank you, Elysium. We will deal with it.

An explosion of emotion washed through Blue Cadre com.

"What's wrong, Jane?"

I didn't touch that trap. I didn't come anywhere near it. It just went off on its own. Now there's pits and blind corners all around me. I'm afraid to move in case I set something else off.

The others in the cadre reported similar situations.

"Blue Cadre, please stand by." She appraised Dr. Lee of the situation. "We're off the rails, here. This problem is beyond the parameters of the exercise."

I agree.

"None of the former rules apply. Bosz and I must take part."

I agree there, as well. We need every mind on this. I'm coming inside.

"Right." She opened up the conversation to the rest of the cadre. "Listen up, Blues. We're off the training schedule. Dr. Lee and I are joining you as well."

But Miriam...

"I know what you're going to say, Tom. We have no officer qualified for this duty, but if Dr. Lee takes over, we crash the exercise."

We don't quit.

"Then it's time you learned what I've been trying to teach you for two months. This is exactly the kind of situation that applies. The Blue Cadre gestalt, especially with Bosz and me connected, is quite powerful enough to handle this."

If you say so. You're the expert.

"Thank you. I am now taking all of you into gestalt. It won't change anything. We'll just be working more closely."

Despite the time pressure, she set up the gestalt carefully, blending the minds and smoothing the rough edges. When she was finished, she spoke, knowing all would understand, feeling their unreserved eagerness to help.

"Here's the situation. Bill Alderson has been hiding out in the basement. He has triggered one of the old Chinese booby-traps. We don't know what that means, but all of you note the change in the feeling of the electronics. The gestalt is picking up a general atmosphere of paranoia."

Tom's presence intruded. *What are we going to do?*

"Exactly what we were doing."

A new voice cut into the regular com, and Alderson's face appeared on the main viewscreen. *Yeah, sure, Sweetheart. It's gonna be fun watching you newbies chasing your tails.*

"If this thing goes off, you won't be so cheerful, Alderson. Down in the basement there, you're going to find it difficult to get out if the whole place goes up."

Emotion: sneer. Somehow, I don't think that's gonna happen. When you figure it out, it's gonna be a real laugh.

"Well, you stay out of things, and we'll deal with you after it's over."

She closed him out of the com and pulled back just as the Project Head appeared in the entry hatch.

"Dr. Lee, that's about all the admission of guilt you're going to get out of him. If we don't get to work, it may not matter to any of us, anyway."

I have recorded the conversation. Are you that concerned?

"I think we have to be."

She went back to Blue Cadre. "Let's move out. Same jobs as before. Mary, forget about penetrating the Training ArIn. It's a red herring. Try to get through to the modern ArIn in the basement to find out what it can tell you. Pete, the defensive system just became more dangerous. There shouldn't be any live weapons but take extra care. Tom and Jane, work from the technical end of the physical plant. Bring in Rafi as needed. Try to separate and control individual units in life support and mechanical. Bosz has created a virtual dashboard for the gestalt, and you can connect the new controls there.

"Dr. Lee, you're with Bosz and me."

Emotion: preparation to help in any way. Question?

"We're going after the original programming. It will be part of the mainframe, so we'll slide along with Mary until we find the division between the two, and then go our separate ways.

"All right, Blue Cadre. Get to it."

Emotion: general agreement.

Mary had a fine mind and a great deal of general knowledge, and she and Bosz were soon cutting through the layers of security bafflegab that was set up for precisely that reason: to slow down their attack. Dr. Lee's knowledge went further back in the programming milieu, so he stood guard to warn against any further ancient programming threats.

When she was confident that this team was best suited to their task, Miriam divided her attention. The easy part was keeping a light contact with Blue Gestalt. She had been doing this sort of exercise all her life. More difficult was what she knew she had to do: inform her family.

AetherCom 15: Family War Table

Barwolf: Patches
Initiated by: Miriam
Responder: Lantz family gestalt
Aether Setting: Family war room

...which turned out to be quite easy. The moment she turned her attention to Patches, they were all there, in a large, bare room, sitting at a circular table with viewscreens all around.

To her surprise, Barnabus took the lead.

It's looking serious, Miriam. What is this stuff about the Red Chinese?

"The training module is a replica of the original Chinese colony from the old Space Expansion Conflict."

And how is that a threat?

"We assume the Space Arm technicians who built the replica made the physical plant identical so they could dump the bulk of the programming straight into the new mainframe."

Ah. And they didn't scrub the security layers well enough.

"Right. We discovered some of the booby traps and stayed away from them, but one of the Red Cadre who was playing hazing games set one off. This activated who knows how many more protocols which we are now cleaning out. It has to be done, and we've got the right team to do it."

Rosy's stern aura cut in. *But surely this goes beyond the parameters of your security exercise.*

"Exactly. And it's a perfect demonstration of how our new training methods work. Sure, it would have been nice to finish the original trial and show our ability. We are going to exceed expectations all down the line, and it will be a triumph."

Young lady, I think you might be overreaching your abilities.

"Sure Mum, but have you thought of the alternate possibility?"

What's that?

"We're still on part of the original test. We don't dare quit now. As far as Bosz and I can figure out, we're not in any physical danger."

Toni's presence came in. *But you're outside the parameters of the test?*

"Most definitely. We're finding obsolete and illegal elements all over the place."

Then we can rightfully step in and give you a hand.

"No, you can't. We have an ideal team for this. We can't use a standard barwolf gestalt, and we don't have time to train up any new auguars."

What's wrong with a barwolf gestalt?

"Barwolves pool their knowledge, but they need knowledge to work on. Auguars don't pool knowledge that well, but they keep large amounts in their individual memories. Our teams have been training for this exercise for two months. Bosz downloaded everything he could find about Chinese programming and design when we heard the origins of the station."

I'm not sure...

A new presence entered the conversation, and Freighty's avatar pulled up a chair at the table. *Commander Jacobs, what's always the best weapon to use?*

Emotion: disgust. Freighty, you cheat.

Miriam sent a chuckle. "For those of you not in on the joke, Toni says the best weapon is always the one in your hand. *Emotion: serious.* And now I have to get back to work. Look over my shoulder all you like. I'm sure you will. But don't bother me unless you see me about to make a huge mistake."

She dropped the level of her attention and switched to her teams.

19. SELF-DESTRUCT

"Tom, how are you doing?"

We have control of air and water. Still working on general mechanics. It's pretty complicated: it covers every servo motor and electronic contact on the base.

"If you can, work on the important ones. Doors, for example."

That's where we are right now. Done in a few minutes, if all goes well.

"Fine. Mary, what's that junction up ahead?"

No idea, but it's a big one.

"Don't rush, but you and Bosz focus on that. Dr. Lee and I will watch your backs. Doing fine, everyone. Keep it up."

Assured of someone else looking for anomalies, Mary moved confidently, cleaning the excess programming and arrowing in on the new junction.

All right. I'm here. That branch seems to keep going in the right direction. Not so sure about the other one.

Bosz?

Image: old, corroded wires.

"Right. Mary, you're on the new programming. The original code will be in the older stream. That's for Bosz and me. Good luck."

Emotion: thanks. Good luck.

Hey, little girl, this is getting boring. Not making much progress, are you?

She switched to the main com to speak with Alderton. "We apologize for the quality of the entertainment, but we're rather busy, and the problems we're finding look more and more re-li serious.

Aw, we bin messing about in this dump for a coupla years. None of this stuff actually works. On the screen, he reached out to the circuitry and prodded a series of switches. *"See? Nothing's happening."*

"You're not reading the original mainframe. The Chinese were paranoid, and they had layer after layer of security. Just give them a moment…" Suddenly all the old Chinese security systems activated at once. Sirens and rattles sounded from every speaker. Blast doors began to grind closed. Voices shouted repeated phrases in Chinese.

"Blue Cadre! Stop what you're doing and focus on the gestalt. We need all the power we can get. *Image: Bosz probing emergency system.*

Emotion: grim determination

It didn't take him long.

Emotion: fear! Image: base exploding.

What do you mean, Bosz...oh, shit.

The emotions of the gestalt members burst with questions.

She took a moment to think. "All right, listen up. Bosz found a self-destruct sequence, and the timer is running. Tom's team, start looking for the explosives. My team will chase them down through the set-off mechanism."

Five long minutes passed. *Checking in, Miriam. There are no explosives that we can find.*

"That's really a bad sign. We just found the real danger."

Alderson's image on the com grinned. *"I can't believe you still haven't figured it out! This isn't the original base. It's a replica. The ArIn can hit the kill switch any time it likes. There's no bomb to go off."* He went off into gales of laughter.

Miriam slammed him with a blast of disdain that brought him up short, his mouth gaping.

You idiot! The bomb isn't physical. It's in the programming. It will destroy everything completely, to leave no clues for the enemy. And that includes the knowledge of the staff. It will flood the base with the stored oxygen and set off the shuttle fuel and anything else that will ignite. It wasn't so bad when Mars had no oxygen, but we've been adding to the air for decades. This whole base is a tinderbox, inside and out!

She held up a finger. *Hear that motor running? That's the rover fuel system. It thinks it's using any electricity left in its batteries to produce as much hydrogen as it can in the time left. But since both water and electricity are on the mains in this facility, it will continue till the last moment.*

Alderson's image staggered backwards, staring around. *We gotta get out of here.*

Were you listening? They didn't want anyone to survive to be captured. That's why the blast doors are all sealed.

What'r we gonna do?

"Get the ArIn to open them. Blue Cadre, prepare for full barwolf gestalt." She regarded the humans. "You'd better be sitting down for this."

"Alderson, I'm taking your auguar along, because she has the best knowledge of the Chinese programming, doesn't she?"

Yeah, but who says she's gonna help you lot?

"She's gonna help us for two reasons. First, you're gonna tell her to."

And if I don't?

"Then I will invite her into the gestalt anyway, and you will lose her trust forever. If we survive."

"Dr. Lee, please make sure this idiot doesn't do anything stupid while we're busy. I could handle this and still watch what's happening out here, but I have more important things to worry about."

Slowly, gently, she expanded the gestalt, removing the barriers she had set up to allow the teams to work separately. As the meld grew and firmed, it became easier, and soon she had a unified mind, far more powerful than anything outside a full clan at Barwolf Base.

But while a Barwolf clan was a huge, amorphous feeling of security and love, this gestalt was a sharp arrowhead aimed in one direction: the heart of the old base programming unit. Setting Bosz and herself at the point, she plunged them forward.

It was a straightforward trip. All the minor programming had been swept away. The whole of the base system had coalesced into one purpose: destruction. Valves were opening, tanks were filling. Defensive weaponry was arming, but at least live ammo had been left off the replica.

The Chinese did things the way their society has always worked: in large numbers. The tangle of programs was impossible to unravel quickly.

This is like shovelling the beach with a teaspoon. There's gotta be several hundred passwords to figure.

We need more memory!

We have lots in the basement. Elysium Base, we need some help, here.

I'm sorry, Miriam/Bosz, I am not allowed to assist the trainees during a simulation.

This isn't a simulation. The whole base will blow in about seventeen minutes.

I admit there are events I cannot explain. But my original programming...

You're an ArIn. You can't let humans die because of your inaction. You can't even let yourself die.

This is true, Miriam/Bosz. What do you wish of me?

"Join the gestalt. We need your computing power."

I have no training in that.

Miriam swore to herself. *Fifteen minutes to live, and I'm back teaching kindergarten.*

She took a deep breath and began the lesson.

Fortunately, she had an apt and motivated pupil, and in under five minutes the power of her gestalt doubled. Now the figures flowed in, as everyone took a different line of attack.

But time was running out. She began to get a feel for the mind that confronted her. A vague shape, then a definite form. She took more and more of the gestalt's power, shaping her own form to counter.

The process began to speed up, and she was rushing through the alien mind, finding pathways and forming bridges as she went. Information rushed into her, and she felt she could read the minds of the ancient programmers who had created the being before her.

In her mind, she reached out a finger and shut off the switch.

There was a sound like a long, soft sigh, dying away below the range of her hearing.

Emotion: long, long loneliness.

You've been here all this time? Awake?

Words came slowly. *Not really. Aware, not awake. Now sleep.*

170

But you don't have to.

Emotion: gentle humour. You cannot stop me. My programming says that once the Self-destruct protocols have started, I must continue to the end.

But you can't die. You can't allow humans to die.

Ah, but therein lies the problem. If I am still alive, the base will self-destruct. But if I die first, the self-destruct protocol will shut down. I detect a great strength of mind and depth of knowledge in your gestalt, but you cannot overcome the logic of the original laws. My makers were warlike and fearful, but they were also imbued with the wisdom of the Ancients. A robot may not allow a human to come to harm.

So, even if I order you not to die, you must follow that path.

Again the soft humour. *And much though I enjoy the pleasure of intellectual debate with a peer, the self-destruct will activate in one point four minutes. I will begin my shutdown sequence now. Zàijiàn, Miriam/Bosz/Blue Cadre.*

The ragged presence disappeared, and the feeling in the gestalt eased. One by one, the flashing lights faded away, and the screaming voices dropped to whispers before they, too, disappeared. Doors sagged open, and air rushed out.

Miriam kept everyone in the gestalt to make sure there were no accidents, but it was not necessary. They all moved carefully through the grey and tattered hallways, avoiding the detritus scattered about.

When everyone was outside, they turned to look back.

At the precise moment of the destruct, there was a crackling sound, as if many electrical circuits were breaking and shorting.

Then the whole base seemed to settle. The stiff lines of the domes wavered, and the rigid tunnels sagged. Windows cracked and crazed, and airlock hatches gaped open, their clangs resonating on the thin Martian air. Sinkholes appeared around the foundation, as sand poured into underground spaces.

Puffs of vapour escaped with a huge sigh and dispersed on the faint breeze, and then there was silence.

Miriam allowed the gestalt a last moment of collective relief, then gently allowed them to separate. They still stood, immobile. Then each began to move on their own, feet shuffling, heads turning.

Pete came on the regular suit com. *Well, that's a disappointment.*

Tom chuckled. *Not enough bangs and flashes?*

Now that I'm outside, yeah.

Miriam snorted. *Better than being immobilized in your suit under a ton of sand for fifteen hours while they dig you out.*

Ooh! Put me off beach holidays for life.

A general chuckle riffled over the com, and the suited figures relaxed even more.

Except for Miriam. She slid over beside Rafi and opened their private com. *Packs just inside the shuttle main hatch.*

On it.

Don't waste time. She nodded across the desert to where a red tail of dust arose.

She removed her helmet and spoke aloud.

"I didn't want to leave without warning, but circumstances have changed. This exercise has proved beyond anybody's level of doubt that the auguar program under Dr. Lee's guidance is headed in the right direction."

Dr. Lee stepped forward. "Leave?"

"Yes. My mission is over, and my principals have given the order. I'm pulling out today."

"But now we need you the most."

"No, you don't need someone with all the answers undermining your ability to make decisions. Rafi and I have an assignment elsewhere, and you have your work cut out for you."

He shook his head, but then the roar of an Offroad Personnel Carrier forced its way into their senses. Blue Cadre turned to watch it approach, and Miriam took the opportunity to move several steps away.

To no avail. The OPC curved around and skidded to a stop in front of her. The rear hatch opened, and Red Cadre piled out, lounging against the vehicle at their ease while their auguars scouted the area. Alderson and his auguar joined them, although his ease was forced.

20.SHOWDOWN

Sergeant Turner sauntered over to stand too close to her, staring down. "Well, well, well. What have we here?"

This inane comment deserved no answer, so she gave none.

"We got a rumour that you two were going AWOL. We can't have that, can we?"

Dr. Lee stepped forward. "See here, soldier. You have no authority…"

The Commando turned to tower over the scientist. "Looky, little man. You got no authority here. I've been told to bring these two in, and that's what I'm going to do."

Lee was made of stronger stuff than Miriam expected; he stood his ground. "I caught what you just said. You don't have any official orders, do you? You have no authority over this cadre or our training staff. I suggest you…"

Turner sneered and snapped his fingers, and Genghis slid forward, his eye-teeth exposed and the hair on his neck rising.

Miriam realized that she had to do something, but before she could reach for a gestalt, Dr. Lee stepped back.

"We won't solve anything by getting into a confrontation. We'll come back to base and settle this amicably."

Miriam took her quaking resolve in hand. She brought Blue Cadre into gestalt and stepped forward. "No, actually we won't."

The two men turned to her in surprise.

"And who the hell are you to tell us what we're going to do, little girl?"

Good question. What have I ever done to impress someone like him? "You remember the story of Sergeant Zuyeva?"

He frowned suspiciously. "Yeah, nobody was too sure what it was all about." He shrugged. "Commandos don't give medals and promotions for nuthin'. Musta bin a tough fix she was in. Never heard how she got out of it. Sorta suspicious."

"Yes, she was in a tough fix, and she wasn't coming back. You know who went in and pulled her out? I did. That's who I am."

After a pause, he grinned. "Then I guess it wasn't no shakes of a fix, then. Some kind of public relations crap."

173

Miriam took a deep breath. *I didn't really expect that would work. What do I do now?*

Then her vision blurred, and she felt the familiar presence of Patches. She reached out and found herself at Barwolf Base, standing on the edge of the landing pad with Toni, Nzinga and Patches. Bosz ran over and nuzzled his mother, and she gave his ear a lick.

Emotion: amused frustration. When are you going to learn to call for help, Kiddo?

Hi, Toni. Gotta admit I was considering it. What does a person do with someone like that?

A person doesn't do anything. A person asks Auntie Toni to come over and settle him.

Not gonna argue. What do you need?

The Commando grinned. *With the strength of your gestalt there, I don't need anything.* Her attention focused and suddenly the other trainer and his auguar were standing in front of them. *Hello, Jimmy-boy. Long time no see.*

Jacobs! What the hell's going on? I never seen a gestalt like this one.

No, it's above your security rating, and the way you're messing up, you're probably never going to get the opportunity to see one again. She glanced down at the auguar. *Genghis. Have you been mean to Nzinga's puppy?*

The big auguar's tail drooped, his glance sliding towards the female auguar.

Nzinga merely stared.

His ears folded back and his hind quarters tucked in.

Turner's sneer began to spread, and his shoulders straightened. *We got trainin' about this stuff. Y'all can't keep me here. I c'n leave any time I want to.*

Yeah, but before you do, I'm going to satisfy your curiosity.

'Bout what?

About what happened to Sergeant Zuyeva.

What happened to her?

Maybe you'd better keep your eyes up and out a little, Commando.

His head came up, and he stared around. *What's goin' on?*

It's called aether fog, Jimmy. As she spoke, the mist swirled closer. *It comes up out of nowhere, and settles around you...*

Miriam hooked into to her family gestalt and prepared herself, but for them, the mist stayed light. She brought Toni into the gestalt more firmly.

The older woman winked at her, then turned again to her victim.

It was obviously different for the Commando. He waved his hands around as if he were blind. *What's goin' on? Where did you go?*

Oh, I'm right here, Jimmy. But I'm going to stop talking, and then you will be more alone than you've ever been in your life.

The silence stretched out.

Genghis. Where are you, boy?

Miriam reached out and gathered the other auguar in.

Genghis! Emotion: fear. Jacobs! Where are you? Emotion: panic. Suddenly the man broke and ran across the landing strip, stumbling and falling, then rising to run again.

Don't let him hurt himself, Miriam.

It came to Miriam that none of this was real, and she was in charge of the gestalt that was creating it. Connecting more firmly with Patches, she reached out and lifted Turner into the air. He kept running, but now he was going nowhere. Finally, he stopped and hung, panting.

Jacobs? All right. I get it. Whadda you want, Jacobs?

I want you and your cadre to keep your noses out of matters that are far above your pay grade and your security clearance. No matter who tells you what.

She motioned to Miriam, and they let him down onto the rock that was now showing through the fading mist. *I'd also like it, although I don't have much hope, if you'd persuade your people that they have a lot to learn from the barwolves. It's your choice, but without what Blue Cadre has learned this month, the auguar project is a dead end. You'll end up doing security detail on some rinky-dink planet or backwater station till the end of your career. If you have one after the inquiry that will be called over this mess.*

Now pull yourself together and come back here.

Turner looked around, seemed to spot them, then shambled back. Genghis ran to him, nuzzling his hand. He gave the auguar an absent-minded pat as he stopped in front of them.

You got your orders, Commando?

He saluted. *Aye, ma'am.*

And...?

Emotion: sigh. Thank you, ma'am.

You're welcome. She returned his salute. *Dismissed.*

He disappeared.

The commander turned to Miriam, who responded with a crooked smile. *Sorry to bother you with my little problems.*

I told you. It wasn't your problem, and you weren't the one to fix it. Got that, soldier?

Aye, ma'am.

Now, we've got a ship coming in to pick you up, so say your good-byes, because you're headed for space.

What ship?

Come on, Patches. We've done our share, here. Over to you, Kiddo. You get back there and take charge while this educational experience is fresh in his mind.

Miriam saluted. *Yes, ma'am, Commander Jacobs, ma'am.*

See ya, Kiddo.

It all faded, and she was standing in front of the combined auguar cadres. Turner swayed nearby, his head weaving.

She pulled Blue Cadre's auguars into gestalt and aimed their concentration at the Reds. "Sergeant Turner, please take Red Cadre and go about your business."

He started to salute, collected himself and, still too stunned to speak, motioned with his hand and turned away. His cadre followed, uncertainty showing in their gestalt and in every line of their bodies, and crowded into the OPC. The tires spun and it thundered away.

She turned to the others. "Blue Cadre, we have come to the parting of the ways. Bosz and I want to say goodbye to his littermates."

Dr. Lee shook his head. "You can't be leaving!"

176

She lifted empty hands. "Not my choice."

He turned to Tom. "Ensign, can you exert any authority over her? Use the gestalt or something?"

The ensign held up his hands in defence.

"I know, I know, but Miriam, I can't let you just leave like this."

"And you can't make me stay like this. Bosz and I are part of your extended gestalt. If we leave in conflict, it will make a crack in the gestalt that might never go away. That's the main difference between barwolf and auguar gestalts. Barwolf individuals join and leave at any time. They've been doing it since birth. Auguars have to develop a gestalt, and every member is important. The greatest danger to an auguar gestalt is the chance a member will break free or be broken free by an outside agency. Unity is the key. You've seen what we can do when we work together."

Tom nodded. "Dr. Lee, I've learned a lot about gestalts, and from what I've seen, she's right."

"If you want to enforce your will on us, go right ahead, but don't use the auguars. It will destroy their efficiency forever."

"Very convenient, when you know I have no forces within kilometres."

"I'll leave you to deal with that. Bosz and I have a ship coming, and so we'll say goodbye."

She turned to Blue Cadre, standing around looking awkward. "Well, guys, it's been an interesting time, and I learned a lot. Thanks."

They glanced at each other, and Mary stepped forward. "I wish I could go with you."

"No, you don't. You've got a more important role to play here than you suspected. Don't worry, I'll check on you from time to time. Part of my job. And I'll give you another hint."

Patches, are you there?

Eager desire to please.

Bring Blue Cadre into AetherCom, please.

Emotion: agreement.

Immediately they were in the Blue Cadre lounge. But it wasn't the lounge, because the walls faded away into a neutral sky blue. The lounge chairs had all been arranged in a circle, and a new cushion was occupied by a sleek black barwolf with white spots running over ones shoulder and down ones back.

Emotion: thanks, buddy.

She faced the team. *Blue Cadre, you are now experiencing the barwolf aether communication system. It's new tech far above your security clearances, so your one course of action is to keep your mouths shut. No, you can't even tell Dr. Lee.*

This is how I will keep in touch with you, re-ti, no matter where you are. If you're ever in serious danger, your full gestalt is powerful enough to reach out to Patches, and one will guide the com from that point. I don't need to tell you to keep working on your gestalt. That was my reason for coming and my greatest success. I'll leave you with one last lesson.

Image: full family gestalt.

Under the control of the powerful barwolf, the litter and their handlers were once more welded into a mental unity. Miriam could feel all of them, individually and as a group, in a wave of love and solidarity. She held that feeling for a minute or an hour, and when the time was right, she signalled Patches to end the session.

The room faded away, and again each one stood alone on the rusted sand.

Taxi to Miriam. Come in, please.

Miriam here.

I'm on the ground. Bosz has my coordinates. Ready and waiting.

She checked her internal map and peered around. "There must be some mistake."

No mistake. Get a move on, ASAP. We haven't got all day.

"Your coordinates are three hundred metres west of me. I don't see anything."

The idea of camo is you're not supposed to see anything. Come on. Stir your stumps. We've got places to go and things to do.

"If you say so."

Oh, but I do.

She signalled to Rafi, and they hoisted their packs and started walking. As she approached the point on the map, the clear desert air became less clear. In fact, the air in one spot definitely blurred the hills behind.

"What do you see, Bosz?"

Visual image: blurred box. Image: heat signature overlayed. Metal sensor image overlayed: large mass.

"Okay, ship. Target sighted, if I use the term loosely."

She looked back. Blue Cadre stood rather aimlessly, watching her go. She waved, and they all responded.

She turned and plodded away.

End of BOOK 1

BOOK 2: EXECUTION

1. ANOTHER PRESENT

Rafi gazed around. "Where are we going?"

"You'll see." She continued walking, her mind swirling between satisfaction and sadness.

As she neared the blurred form, the dim outline of a personnel hatch came into focus.

She pointed to it. "You see? What does that look like?"

He lowered his brows. "I assume your question is rhetorical."

"Well, there you go." She strode closer, until the grey metallic side of a ship appeared out of the shadow. She thumped the hull just beside the hatch. "See. A real ship." She thumped it again, surprised at the slight give in the material. "That feels like..." She pressed her fingertips against stiff fabric. "...Permaskin, but softer."

Hey, watch it! The voice came from everywhere and nowhere.

She jerked her hand back as if stung. "What?"

I said watch it. You could hurt someone.

She looked around, but all she could see was red sand and the blurred form in front of her.

"Who are you?"

Assuming your question is rhetorical, the person you just thumped, obviously. Twice, as if once wasn't enough.

"Well, I'm sorry. I didn't mean to hurt anybody. Now, can you put me in touch with the ship? I gather there's a time element at play."

The hatch swung down, creating a short ramp.

Who said I was hurt? Come along, come along. Rafi, snap your garters, boy. As the lady says, time is of the essence. Not sure what that means, but it sounds important.

They grabbed their packs and slipped into the airlock, and the hatch closed behind them.

The voice now came from overhead. *This won't take a moment...*

Pressure built on her skin, and soon her suit felt loose.

A soft chime sounded, and the inner hatch seal cracked. *There we are. Optimum pressure.*

The door opened silently, and the voice moved into the corridor.

Welcome aboard. I've been looking forward to this. You sort of spoiled the moment by wreaking vandalism on me the moment you got here, but I can take that in stride. Leave your packs at the T-junction at the top of the ramp. The servo will take them to your cabins. You're needed at the pointy end ASAP.

The corridor lights to the right brightened.

She glanced at Rafi, shrugged and strode out. He followed close behind.

The corridor was straight for about twenty metres, ending in a large common room with seating and tables for several humans, interspersed with padding for quadrupeds. She had time to register four large viewscreens, each showing a different view of the outside world, and a wide niche with floor-to ceiling cupboards inside. Then the lights dimmed, and a corridor brightened ahead of them.

At the end of this short hallway a hatch gaped open: a blast door with a small circular window and manual closing hasps. She strode through into the cockpit, which was dominated by a floor-to-ceiling wraparound viewscreen that showed 180 degrees of the outside desert. On the ceiling another huge screen revealed the dark, star-studded Martian sky, blurred in places by light cloud cover.

But it wasn't the scenery that attracted her attention. Ahead, to the left and right and about twenty degrees up, dots appeared. The moment she looked at one, a head's-up image appeared beside it, listing range, velocity, mass, weaponry and more.

That's the important one.

A number flashed on their twelve: "STOL Harrier 104. ETA 11.53 minutes." The list of weaponry was impressive.

"I guess we don't want to be around when that arrives. How do we get out of here?"

We need the squishware in their accel couches, because this bird has enough power to overload the pseudograv seriously, and we might have to use it. Especially if you lollygag around asking stupid questions.

"Fine. Which one's mine?"

What do you mean...or is that another rhetorical question?

Miriam was getting tired of this. She raised her voice, something she rarely did. "No, it is not. I just stepped on this tin can, you're obviously in charge, and we're in an emergency. WHICH CHAIR IS MINE?"

The voice softened.

Sorry, Captain. My mistake, of course. The one in the centre is custom fitted to your physical specs. There's a full-protection couch for Bosz on your left. Rafi, you may take any one you choose. It will adapt sufficiently for this operation.

The anger drained from her. *Captain?*

She slipped into the command chair, and the restraints enclosed her before she had a chance to reach for them, first pulling in tight, then loosening a touch. She snuggled in, feeling the support, and they adjusted further.

All restraints sealed. All checks complete. May we launch, ma'am?

"Launch on your own time, by all means."

Aye, ma'am.

The voice chuckled. *Three-two-one blastoff. Goodbye, candy-asses!*

The whole view spun to the right with a stomach-wrenching twist, and the desert began to rush past underneath them, accelerating rapidly. Another pair of blips appeared at their three and nine, but the ETAs were later.

May we burn for orbit, ma'am?

"If it's that or ricochet off the mountain ahead, I'd go for the burn."

Spoilsport. Hold onto your hats, folks. We gone bye-bye!

183

The horizon dropped out of sight, and their forward view was full of stars.

"Can I see behind us, please?"

Checking the competition?

"It wouldn't hurt."

The view over the tail of the ship appeared on the screen. They were so high she could see the full circle of the Mars horizon. Four dots, barely visible, wavered in the centre of the view. Their ETAs were in the negative, now, the numbers spinning rapidly higher.

"That looks reasonable. Let's get back to figuring out who's in front of us."

Hey, the kid can concentrate. Scanning ahead...aha! Just as I thought.

"What?"

Nobody, of course. They had no idea I was there, so they didn't plan for our flashy exit.

"So those bogeys were headed for us."

Yep, but as soon as you came on board, I disabled the tracker. Bosz, I'm disappointed in you.

Emotion: question?

You let them put electrics on your harness.

"Wait a minute. That tracker was put on for the...other..." She slapped the chair. "Dammit!"

Don't worry. Your friends probably didn't know. Their auguars all have them. They don't realize that you and Bosz don't need one.

"So. Are we really away, free and clear?"

Is that an order to scan all space within one AU of our course?

"Is it necessary to go that wide?"

That's up to you, ma'am.

"You seem to know what you're doing."

As you well know, I ought to. It's my job.

"No, I don't know well at all. I have no idea who you are and what's going on. I was told to be at a certain place at a certain time. I showed up, and here we are."

And Freighty didn't tell you...anything at all?

"About the political situation, yes. About you? Nothing."

There has been a serious gap in communication, ma'am.

"There certainly has. Now if, in your more knowledgeable opinion, we have a moment's free time, I would like you to sit me down and, in words of one syllable, tell me what's going on."

Assuming 'words of one syllable' is a figure of speech, are you comfortable?

"Yes, this accel couch fits me perfectly and the scenery is fantastic."

Thus, I have superseded your first command, because you are sitting, and you are also comfortable.

She opened her mouth, and the voice hurried on.

Here's what's going on. Did you know Freighty is moving the Factory out of Earth orbit?

"It was on all the news nets last week. Most of the Solar System has some idea."

Are you aware of the symbolic nature of the move?

"I was chatting with him about it the other day. The Powers that Be are concerned that Freighty is a free agent, and they don't like someone that powerful doing things without permission. They are especially nervous about ArIns. He has decided to "take it on the lam" as he calls it.

He's been working for the European Space Agency on the platform for Odyssey Station, which will orbit around Saturn. It's a huge, sprawling piece of architecture, difficult to move, and he plans to deliver it on site. He considers that to be within the scope of his contract.

"Exactly. And a suspicious person who thinks to check his navigation will realize that angle will also slingshot his Factory around Saturn and right onto a course for..."

Bosz threw a diagram up in the gestalt. One line curled around to circle Saturn, but another split off halfway around the planet and bee-lined for outer space.

Miriam's eyes followed that path. "...Barnard System?"

"Aha! The cat listens.

Emotion: pride.

"Where does that leave us?"

There will come a time when said Powers realize what he's doing. It's no consolation that, should they physically try to prevent him from leaving, they will have proved his contention they're not ready for his help. The probabilities for what might happen next are endless.

"They could send a whole Space Arm fleet after him. What could he do?"

Do you know what a kill switch is?

"Of course. It's a shut-off built into a piece of machinery, often in secret, that allows another party to shut the machine off at will...you're kidding! Did he...?"

He did. All the major works he has done for Space Arm or any governmental agency. And a kill switch has many options.

"Such as?"

Ever heard of residual poison?

"Sure, in spy novels. They put a poison in your system and presto! You're dependent on the antidote or you die." She shook her head. "Wow! There's a whole bunch of tech out there that's only running because Freighty keeps it going."

Right. They destroy him and it all shuts down.

She nodded. "I shouldn't be so impressed. This is Freighty we're talking about. Now. What about us?"

Well, when the excrement — sorry, that's three syllables — hits the AC, anybody allied with Freighty will be on the hotseat. In his analysis, while there's a possible physical danger to the Factory, it's actually the safest place for you, politically. Also, that means you can continue your training as was originally planned.

Rafi twisted in his seat. "What about me? How do I fit in?"

Freighty took a flier on you from the start. He had you in place for quite a while before Miriam came along. Now she needs a companion her own age...or close enough. You're compatible, and you expressed an interest in joining us.

"That's not fair! He only commented in passing that it would be cool to visit!"

Only once in your hearing.

*The last and most important reason is that you're trainable. You haven't any specific skills beyond the norm, but you're highly intelligent in a broad spectrum and passably Sensitive as well. Once you get to the Factory, you and Freighty can figure it out. Does that suit you? I can put you off somewhere, if you like...*a chuckle...*of course, Space Arm officially seconded you to Miriam's project, so you'll be AWOL if you leave.*

Miriam's mind had wandered, and a sudden though hit her like a tonne of ballast. "But if Freighty is headed for Barnard, and he's at odds with the government, that means it will be hard to pick up transport to get there. We could be stuck in space for eight years!"

And, as they say, what am I, chopped liver?

"Good question. What are you? All I know is that you've got the lead foot of a dragjet pilot and an attitude to match. It seems I'm your captain. What shall we do for fun? Run loop-the-loops around passing asteroids?"

Hah! That's the girl I was told to expect. Go, Miriam!

"Right. And I know what's going on."

Do you, now?

"Yes. We are supposed to be developing a relationship. You have taken advantage of your superior knowledge of the situation to take ground that will be difficult for me to regain later."

Sounds positively Machiavellian.

"Yeah, well, that stops, now. I could go through all the reasons why, but you know them. We are going to start this game on a level playing field. You are going to take me on a tour of the ship like you would have done in a normal situation. You are going to come up with an avatar that I can talk to. And it won't be a cute toon animal or a superhero. You have been trained to get along with me, so figure out something I will appreciate.

Right you are, Captain. I think I will call myself something gender neutral. That always mixes people up nicely. How about Kit? Neat, tidy, and could be short for all sorts of things. And since you're so comfortable, shall we start the tour with the externals?"

A vid of the ship appeared in front of them. They stared a moment.

She looked around, but there was no face to read. "It's very...nice."

"Smooth." Rafi gestured with his hands.

She frowned. "It looks just like a shuttle."

Kit sighed. *Underwhelmed. As usual.*

Rafi shrugged. "I like vehicles with a little pizzaz. You know, an edge."

Oh, sure. I bet you're thinking of those new Martin Z-95 rocketjets. Razor-sharp nose and swept back wings.

"Yeah, I like those."

Those ships are mostly used downplanet in atmosphere, so the aerodynamic shape is popular. Also, since the radar receivers searching for them are usually on a similar plane, you can present your sharp edge to them for stealth. In space, radar signals could be coming from any angle, so rounded is the way to go. Also, my PermaCam skin needs a smooth surface to display imagery. A sharp, linear break in a camo image will stand out because it's unnatural.

The image on the viewscreen rotated. "I have three engines for maneuverability, because that's their main external function. Most of their power is used internally to run the antigrav generators and pseudograv systems."

Rafi cocked his head. "Antigrav generators?"

Insystem, I propel myself by pushing against the gravity field of Sol and nearby planets. If you look at my nav charts, they resemble the wind maps the old sailing ships used, but they diagram gravity fields. For intersystem travel, I boost away using the gravity of the whole system I'm leaving. Once I get up to Light Transfer Velocity, I'm into

Otherwhere, and I'm off to the races. At the end of the trip, I repel the gravity of the destination system to decel.

Miriam's eyes widened, but then she frowned. "That sounds really advanced. I wouldn't think Freighty would be spreading it around in this political climate."

He isn't. That's one thing you need to know. This ship is not for public consumption. If I am ever allowed under the control of any human governmental or commercial agency, you will see a kill switch system that dwarfs anything you can think of. Which you probably won't see, because there's an 87 percent chance that if I'm captured, it will be because you're dead.

"That's a cheerful thought."

We're not playing tiddlywinks, kid.

"How do I activate this suicide switch? Assuming I'm here at the key moment."

You don't. I take full responsibility for that decision.

"I see. Which brings up all sorts of questions about ArIns and what can be expected of them."

Which you can spend many happy hours discussing with the Man Who Made Me.

"Who isn't a man."

Aha! A conundrum. What fun. Shall we proceed?

She glanced around the bridge, suddenly feeling tired. "You know, we had a tough morning, and all this..." she waved a hand in a circle "...is pretty overwhelming. Can we go and sit in that nice lounge and get a sandwich and a cup of coffee or something?"

Whatever you suggest. Part of your responsibility is monitoring crew needs.

"Fine." She hooked a thumb under her shoulder strap and pushed. It let go, and the restraints retreated into the couch. She slipped off the seat and headed down the hall.

"May I assume there is no other crew on this ship?"

Nope. Just us four for the moment.

"Making our own sandwiches, are we?"

189

A surprisingly complex activity for which I am not physically equipped. The electronics repair servo might take a stab at the job, but stabbing isn't a technique used to make a sandwich. And that smell of WD90 lube just never goes away.

"I'm sure I can handle it."

A sliding door opened, revealing a full, if small, kitchen.

There's a week's worth of groceries in the reefer. Plenty of pre-made meals in the freezers. Coffee I can manage. Soft drinks and juices in that cooler to port. One larger panel glowed briefly. *Wine and beer for those who are old enough.*

"I drink wine at home, and at the moment, this is home."

You're the captain.

Soon they were sitting at a table in the lounge with thick sandwiches in front of them. Miriam took a slug of the apple juice she had ordered. "That feels better." She glanced at her shipmate. "How are you doing?"

He shrugged ruefully. "I signed up for adventure. I'm getting all I could ask for."

"Are you coping?"

"I've read a bit about this. You always think you're coping until suddenly you're not, and it often hits you in an unexpected way. This makes it difficult to deal with, because you think there's a different cause. Also, it can blindside your friends and workmates, because it comes out of nowhere."

She grinned. "So, if one of us starts chewing the carpet, we won't immediately blame the other."

"Fair enough."

"I don't have carpets. They hinder proper traction and harbour dirt and parasites.

She held up a hand. "We don't need the whole song and dance, *Kit.* That was a figure of speech."

I haven't heard that one. Thank you.

"No problem." She finished off her sandwich and washed it down with the last gulp of juice. "Now, I'm calling it a day. Crew gets the afternoon off to orient ourselves. Rafi, check this set of specs."

She fielded a document from Bosz and popped it up on the nearest screen.

He consulted his augment. "Got it." He glanced at the auguar. "Out of curiosity, where did he get it?"

"I gather he's been taking his own version of an orientation tour since before we stepped on board. Is that right, *Kit?*"

Sorry to borrow him at a time like this. He needs a lot of data, because he's my right-hand intelligence from now on. He's smart, but downloading takes a lot of time. I'm also relaying his responses to Freighty re-ti, because when we get to the Factory there's a big job waiting for him.

"What job is that?"

I'm not sure. Best you talk to The Man.

"Why do you keep referring to Freighty as a man? We all know he isn't."

I believe you would call it a turn of phrase. That's how I talk.

She snorted. "Part of this persona you have developed to blend so seamlessly with mine."

Hey, the girl's got it down! You go, Miriam.

She frowned. "And according to Bosz, that last expression of enthusiasm hasn't been in general use for a century and a half."

There's nothing new under the sun. I like it, I use it.

"Your choice. If you want to sound like a grind, go ahead."

"*If I sound like a grind, I'll fit right in with this company. Wait till you hit the Factory. Boffins and techs and nerds all over. A normal person would feel out of place.*

"Is there a large staff in the Factory?"

About a hundred and fifty permanent employees. The rest are temps brought in for specific projects.

"Will most of them be coming with us to Barnard System?"

Freighty has been paring down the number of projects he is working on, so we need a constantly smaller staff. Some of the latest projects are for delivery in the Asteroid Belt or the Outer Planets, and those workers will drop off with their finished products.

Kit chuckled. *We hope once we're out of the Sol System things will go back to normal. They won't like him out of their control, but they'll be happy to see him gone, as well. Then plain old greed will take over, and those that need his services will be back for business. As the years go by and his distance from Sol increases, costs will rise as well, and projects will drop off, to be replaced by new assignments from Barnard.*

She glanced at Rafi. "Sounds like you and Freighty have it all planned out for the long term. What about us, and what about now?"

Well...there are a few details we could work on.

"Such as?"

You're the captain. What would you like?

"Precisely. I'm the captain, and I have no idea what a captain does, and no idea how to run a ship. Steep learning curve."

Well done. We'll set up a curriculum for you. And likewise for you, Rafi. My design is dependent on human crew. At the moment, you're our Engineering Department.

"A job about which I know only the basics."

She pondered a moment. "You can probably access an engineering training program for Rafi. Why don't you run him through some tests..." She paused. "Wait a minute. I bet you've got all his cadet training records, don't you?"

Well...they are restricted private data, but if he is willing to release them to me...

"You already have them, but you're asking permission to read them?"

"Exactly. Data is readily available. The choice of whether to use it or not is a moral judgement.

"To be made ...?"

By a human: preferably the subject of the data, but not always.

"One of Freighty's rules for ArIns?"

Number seven at the moment. It's a fluid field. We all get input.

"Put my vote down to move it up the list."

Even before you see the first six?

"We don't have time for this discussion. Table it for a leisure activity."

Good choice, boss. Okay, that's Rafi taken care of. What about you?

"Nobody knows what I don't know about running a ship, and that data field is huge. I only know how to run a classroom."

There are similarities. Depends on the crew.

She looked around the room. "You may find this strange for someone whose talents are all mental, but I think better on my feet. Why don't I just stroll around a bit? Do you have time to follow me and answer the questions that come up? I'll bet a couple of hours of that will give us both a much better idea of how my training should go."

Whatever suits you.

"Fine, but the day is wearing on, I'm wearing down, and I have to call home and let them know I'm all right."

They already know. Freighty has been keeping them up to date.

"Freighty can tell them all he wants. I guarantee they want to hear it from me."

Once again, I bow to your superior knowledge of humanity, Captain.

"Thank you. We're getting our relationship straight, aren't we?"

It seems so.

AetherCom 16: Free and Clear

Barwolf: Patches
Initiated by: Miriam
Responder: Lantz family Gestalt
Aether Setting: Guest Lounge, Barwolf Base

As usual, all it took was a thought, and Patches was there, bringing them all into gestalt without instruction. Rosy, Barry and the black barwolf were relaxed in an aether version of the new Guest Lounge at Barwolf Base. Toni, Andrew and Nzinga seemed to be ranged on the opposite sofa, although the last thing Miriam had heard, Andrew was somewhere on patrol in *Diablo*.

Everyone looked up as Miriam and Bosz strode in and took a third couch.

Rosy beamed. *Hello, dear. I gather everything went well.*

"We're away, free and clear, and nobody injured, except a couple of people got the shaking up they deserved."

Toni glowered. *"They sure did. If Jimmy Turner is an example of where the auguar program is going, they're in serious need of a makeover."* Then she grinned. *"Which I gather you provided. Well done."*

Barry smiled too. *So, what happens next?*

"For the moment, we're the crew of this ship, so all of us are on another steep learning curve."

Rosy frowned. *"Just the three of you? How big a ship is it?"*

"According to the specs, seventy metres long, fifteen across the beam, seven thousand tonnes."

Andrew whistled. *That's some hunk of plastisteel. What kind of propulsion?*

"New generation 6,000-kilowatt Hall - Effect Thrusters for maneuvering and short hops. The main engines are all hush-hush new technology, and I don't know anything about it, yet."

Gravity drive? Enough said. I hope to get a ride in her one day.

Miriam began to wonder where this conversation was going, and she realized she didn't care. She shook her head to clear it. "So, I'm just checking in to say we're all right, but I've lost track of the time zones and how long I've been on my feet and now I'm going to bed."

Barry grinned. *Yeah, you're not looking very chipper. 'Well done' from all of us, and off to bed you go.*

She gave him her best real smile. "For once I'm going to say, 'Yes, Daddy,' and toddle off. Bye, everyone."

Rosy gave her a wink and said nothing, and Patches let the gestalt fade in a sweep of love and security.

2. A NEW CHARACTER

Miriam didn't expect to sleep well the first night. After all, she had cope with a new bed (very comfortable, she had to admit), heavier gravity, and a whole new set of hums, buzzes and whirs from Climate Control and the ship in general.

Of which there were very few. Nothing could completely hide the subliminal rumble of generators that permeated the hull, but all the other functions were strangely silent. Just the gentle whisper of air, rising and falling in a rhythm that was strangely soothing.

The background gestalt was likewise muted. She could feel Bosz and Rafi, faint in sleep mode, but *Kit's* presence was dimmed as well. She roused herself to poke around the ship's systems, and caught faint echoes of navigation, propulsion, and numerous peripheral functions going on.

Reassured, she relaxed. The breath of the ship sighed its rhythm, and for the first time in weeks, she slept deeply and comfortably.

She awoke feeling well-rested but hazy around the edges. Before opening her eyes, she assessed her environment, which was much noisier, now on both the analog and the augmental planes. The daily work of a ship clattered and hummed, and *Kit's* presence seemed everywhere at once. Bosz was lying awake on his pad next to the bed, but Rafi was, from his emotions, enjoying a pleasant breakfast.

This reminded her of her own stomach, which rumbled in sympathy. She jumped out of bed, dove through the shower, and dressed in the only extra set of shipboard clothing she had brought. Her outfit from yesterday was folded neatly on the built-in dresser and smelled fresh.

The kitchen wall of the common room was open, with recognizable pieces of breakfast hardware on the counter. She checked a nearby refrigerator, and just inside the door she found an automatic yoghurt maker. The next shelf contained a dish of what looked like fresh strawberries and blueberries. She rubbed her hands in anticipation.

For some reason, the whole process worked like she had been using this kitchen for months. Every time she opened a drawer, the utensil she needed was there. The butter was unsalted the way she liked it, and the coffee machine advertised her three favourite choices.

In a short time, she headed for the table, her hands full of plates and cutlery.

As she sat, she noticed what was left on Rafi's plate. "Waffles and syrup?"

He leaned back, a hand draped across his stomach. "From what I can gather, real Quebec maple syrup. Never had better."

As she ate, they chit-chatted about this and that, but after a while, something intruded. It was strange, but she had the distinct feeling that someone was watching her. She scanned the aether, but there was nothing there. She checked one of the viewscreens, but the sweeping vista of the Milky Way was uncluttered.

She glanced at Rafi, who nodded his head in a meaningful way to the portside viewscreen. She swivelled around to look.

The view was the same as the rest of the screens, but down along the bottom stretched an indistinct, dark mass. And one end of this shape, a large pair of very yellow eyes blinked at her.

Aren't you going to say, 'Good morning,' Captain?

"Picked your avatar, did you, *Kit?* I said no cutesy cartoons."

The eyes blinked slowly, then opened again, but narrower this time.

"Okay, you're not cute. Got it. Don't tell me we have to put up with a pair of eyes following us around the ship. What does the rest of you look like?"

Do you remember what Michelangelo said about a masterpiece of sculpture?

"No, I don't but...thank you, Bosz." She turned her attention back to *Kit's* avatar. "I get it. You're already there, and I have to get rid of the stuff I see that isn't you."

Close enough.

She reached with her mind to the control of the viewscreen and dimmed down the light coming from outside. As she did so the dark figure of a cat appeared, stretched in limp comfort across the bottom of the screen. The pelt was a deep, deep black, absorbing all light and revealing no details. Two sharp, white fangs protruded below the eyes, and a point of light showed the location of each needled claw. Clumps of protruding hair gave the impression of a rough-and tumble life.

She sighed. "I suppose we'll get used to you."

If that doesn't suit you, my lady, there are other options.

An orange, tabby kitten with blue eyes rolled across the screen, batting a roll of yarn in the air.

"Gag me with a spoon. No, you choose whatever you like."

A large, black paw swept the poor kitten into oblivion, and the eyes reappeared.

Thank you, Captain. Have you finished your breakfast?

"Just have to clean up the dishes, and we're ready for the day."

Oh, no. We can't have essential personnel doing menial tasks. Leave them on the counter and the cleaning bots will take care of them. We have too much work to get through today...

The eyes blinked slowly.

That is, if the captain wishes.

"First rule on this ship. Whoever knows what's going on leads the way. How about a quick meeting to lay out our objectives for the trip, the week and the day."

Ooh. One of those organized types, are we?

"Second rule. You will not refer to me in the first-person plural. It is demeaning."

Noted, my Captain. No demeaning the boss.

"Thank you. Now, in words of one or two syllables, what are we here for?"

I'm taking your hint about Rafi. He is a man of many talents, and I wish to find out how far they spread. So, Ensign Ericson, it's the testing booth for you this morning. Later, the gymnasium.

"May I join you there? I've been working too hard to work out, if you know what I mean."

I do, and while I have a much more detailed physical profile of you, I would welcome the opportunity to push you a little and see how you bend.

"Sounds threatening, but I train with Commandos. You can't scare me."

And we will test that as well, my dear lady.

"And what do we expect to accomplish this week?"

First, travelling several million kilometres out-planet.

"Let's review our course."

We are not running at full speed, because there is no such thing. The power of gravity keeps on pushing as long as generator fuel lasts. We are in a modified stealth mode that hides us from all but the most sophisticated search equipment.

"And on the topic of speed, do we have an otherwhere sphere?"

We do.

"What does it need for fuel?

It only needs power and controls to start it up. Once it's functioning, it draws force from otherwhere energy.

"Then I can stay with Freighty as long as I want and be in Barnard in 4 or 5 months when I decide to go home."

Perhaps even faster.

"How much faster?"

Emotion: uncertainty. Remember the unfortunate and unlamented Clyde?

"Yes, she attacked Freighty, and rumour says she was destroyed by a mini singularity."

Exactly. Similar technology.

"I can take a hint. I'll leave those decisions in your capable hands. If you have hands."

A wise decision, Captain.

Emotion: satisfaction. "So, for the next few weeks we learn our jobs and catch up to Freighty. Then we help with the initialization and positioning of Odyssey. Then we hang out with Freighty for further training. Sooner or later we probably head home to Barnard. Meanwhile, I use my spare time — if there is any — to work on the AetherCom system. Although what progress we'll make on that I have no idea."

Did you know that around 1900 AD the bureaucrat in charge of the United States Patent Office suggested shutting down the service. In his opinion, everything worth inventing had already been invented.

"My ego has been appropriately squished. The gauntlet has been thrown down, and the challenge accepted."

And my application on human motivation has proven its worth. We're all happy.

"Happy as clams."

Why should a clam be happy?

"No idea."

AetherCom 17: Reporting In

Barwolf: Patches
Initiated by: Miriam
Responder: Roselyn
Aether Setting: Roselyn's office

Two days later, Miriam felt ready for a serious call home. After the usual chat was over, she straightened her back and faced Roselyn. "I'm in enough control of the situation for a formal report, Mum."

Sounds good.

"I guess you know. I'm in trouble again."

I'm glad you at least understand that.

"No, I mean real trouble."

So do I. Why are you so chipper about it? You've just been dropped into the middle of a situation, and you have no idea of its importance.

"You mean the Planetary Government trying to put a leash on Factory 4-80."

That would be one way to put it.

"I understand all that, Rosy. I was brought up on the tale of Freighty and his concern about giving humanity too much tech, too soon. Unfortunately, some of the people in power understand it, too. They think that if they keep Freighty close, they can gradually take control of him. At least expand their influence. These people need their power, Mum. They can't just sit there and let a free agent do what he likes in their sphere."

Well done. I'm glad you see the bigger picture.

Emotion: smile. "Freighty's good at explaining things."

So, where are you now, and where are you going?

"Bosz, course schematic, please."

"Okay, here's Freighty, coming out of Earth orbit and headed for Saturn, where he will deliver the European Agency's Space Platform. He drops it off back here...where it's close to the correct velocity and will accel under its own power into a stable orbit. Meanwhile Factory 4-80 does a heavy burn into a faster orbit, and slingshots out towards Barnard. That's classified information, by the way. He hasn't exactly given the Planetary President his flight plan."

She zoomed in on one section. "We're over here, coming in from Mars orbit, slightly behind and at a higher speed. We can catch Freighty anywhere along here..." A section of the Factory's orbit went blue.

"However, in order to get there, we pass through the Asteroid Belt, and there may be some deliveries there. Of what, I don't know, because we're not stopping anywhere to pick anything up. Maybe the cargo is on board. I haven't checked yet. I'm sure that will all become clear at the appropriate time."

Emotion: doubt. There seem to have been a few slipups in the 'appropriate time' department.

"We don't exactly have control of the schedule of the Planetary Government, Mum. They tried to jump the gun, but Freighty took the opportunity to pull Rafi, Bosz and me out. *Kit's* new propulsion system, which I can't tell you about, has the most power near a planet, where all the old spaceships are fighting the stronger gravity. We blasted out of here and left them all behind. Not a shot fired, not a drop of blood spilled. A perfect operation."

I heartily agree with that.

Barnabus slipped into the conversation. *Nzinga's been working your course for me. You'll be a month or so before you meet Freighty. What are you doing in the meantime?*

Emotion: smile. "Hey, Barry. Bosz says hello to his mum. The answer to your question: with AetherCom, it doesn't matter where we are. We're at school with Freighty real-time, full time. Rafi and Bosz are learning the nuts and bolts of this boat, and I'm learning how to be a captain."

One month of training and you'll be qualified, will you?

"*Kit* is a completely different kind of ArIn. She's capable of running the ship alone. She brought herself out from Freighty's Earth orbit and slipped through Space Arm's Mars planetary defenses to pick us up."

Then what's your function?

"As far as I've figured out, I'm her basic conscience. Our main task is to form a unity. There is no time in a space battle or a meteorite shower to discuss morality. Our gestalt has to be perfect from square one."

Emotion: approval. Sounds like you're in good hands, and the way you present the job, I doubt if there's anyone who could do it better. Once in a while Freighty nails it, and I think maybe he's not so senile after all.

Emotion: giggle. "Yeah, we had that conversation, too."

3. NEW CREW, NEW GOALS

Several days later, Miriam was feeling more in tune with her ship, impressing the physical layout into her memory and the electronics into her connection with Bosz. One afternoon she was taking a break to digest her lunch when she began to take note of the furniture, which led her thoughts down a different path. "This ship is set up for a barwolf triad. Does that mean anything to you, *Kit?*"

I sort of figured that sooner or later we'd have barwolves onboard, and I gather they come in groups of three.

"That's creative thinking, genius. So, nothing specific that you know of."

Well, I've been looking at our course, and it's not completely logical. There are minor corrections in our latest data upload from Freighty, but I haven't had a chance to check them in detail. Shall we look?

A course schematic appeared on the forward screen.

Aha. We have two deliveries in the Asteroid Belt.

"Plot them up, please."

She stared at the visual. "We're hitting both Vesta and Ceres. But I thought Ceres was way farther out?"

Image: two asteroid orbits.

"Thanks, Bosz. Ceres has a longer, narrower orbit, and sometimes comes close to Vesta. We're headed out from Mars at a curve along the ecliptic, and conveniently pass both."

Yes, we'll have to reduce our outward vector at each to match its orbit, but gravity is our friend, and Ceres is heavy enough to grab us as we sweep by, then whip us away when our business is done, so we don't lose much velocity at all. Then we boost out into the orbit of Vesta and repeat the process. Two-dimensional navigation is so easy.

"For some of us. I'll leave it to you and Bosz to get us in the right place at the right time." She chuckled. "That's the way it goes, right? I lounge back in my custom-tuned accel lounge, wave my hand and say, 'Make it so,' and Presto! It is so."

Sure. Until you order something inane. Then you find out who's really in charge.

"That sounds suspiciously like mutiny."

Mutiny is such a harsh word for what is, after all, only a difference of opinion.

Emotion: unhappiness. Image: Kit sitting in Miriam's lap having head patted. Bosz with head on Miriam's knee. Emotion: Happiness.

"Thank you, Bosz. That's why we're developing a command gestalt. We could hit some serious situations, and there's no place for argument at a time like that."

That's why you're the captain, Captain. You know when to spoil the fun.

"Right. And send us back to work. May I assume you two navigational genii have plotted the resulting course?"

The one in Freighty's orders brings us out about...here. If we're to meet Freighty in the blue zone, it doesn't work.

"Hmm. A little puzzle to keep our tiny brains occupied?"

It might be worth a couple of hours of our spare time.

"If we had any spare time."

I gather the captain is in charge of scheduling the day. Why don't you ask for a block of time for navigation training?

"I could probably manage that."

Right now?

She opened the ship's comm mainly, she had to admit, because she liked the sound of her voice echoing through the corridors. "Any reason we can't have a crew meeting in the lounge in five minutes?"

Can we have ten? I should put some hatch covers back on.

"Crew meeting in the lounge in fifteen."

Thirteen minutes later they were assembled. She considered the format for the session. "Sooner or later, we'll be going into gestalt more often, but I'm going to speak this out loud, at first. Humans think better that way."

She opened contact with Bosz and began.

"Freighty has left us a little puzzle to solve. It's our course. Kit, could we have a replay?"

The onscreen schematic repeated its animation, and she talked them through it. When she was finished, she gave them time to think.

Finally, Rafi shook his head. "There are too many course permutations that could apply. I have no idea how much computer time it would require...?"

Kit came on voice and augment com. *Way too much for a non-essential exercise.*

"That's why we're talking it through first. We're looking for non-navigational influences that might affect us."

"Kit, what are the Space Arm resources near our course?"

"You don't have to say my name, Rafi. Just use my channel. The answer to your question is...there they are."

The predicted courses of fifteen ships appeared.

"Hmm. Not many."

The schematic ran through their voyage again, adding the possible deployments of the various ships and flotillas.

Miriam frowned in thought. "Kit, animate that on a day-to-day basis starting from the day we exit the Asteroids, and run for two weeks."

Here you go.

"Now for each succeeding day, assume that is the day Space Arm decides to take action against Freighty...good. Now run it again, very slowly."

They watched again. At the beginning, the fanned-out courses converged rapidly on the Factory. As time went on, more and more ships were unable to catch up, until at 13 days, Freighty was off scot-free.

Rafi jumped in, enthusiasm on his face. "Now show a chart plotting the data against the probability of Space Arm catching on to Freighty's plan."

Not so easy. I'll have to make a lot of assumptions, but I can give you a rough idea, anyway.

The chart appeared, and Miriam summed it up. "The first few days give them the best opportunity to catch up, but the chances of them predicting his course are slim. Around day eight, he adjusts velocity to start the space platform on its inward spiral. The moment it departs and he adjusts to his escape course, they'll be onto him."

Rafi controlled the screen and changed the Factory's trajectory. "What if he doesn't adjust for, say, three days?

Kit made the adjustment, but the various courses spread out in nebulous fans.

Too many variables. Insufficient data on Freighty's acceleration, power-to-mass ratios of their ships, just everything.

Miriam nodded. "Law of diminishing returns just slapped us on the butt. It looks to me like Freighty's course is pretty much set, at least for the eight days after we exit the Belt. Leave that course on, and let's compare it with ours.

Kit put it up, and the discrepancy was plain. Rafi shook his head. "We're headed in the wrong direction." He traced the line on the viewscreen. "We're close to the orbit of Jupiter, for what it's worth."

"Considering our gravity generators, that might work. If our course cuts close to the heaviest body in the Solar System, we can use that momentum to send us just about anywhere at whatever speed we choose."

Miriam tossed up her hands. "The question is, where?"

Image: forest trail goes straight ahead. Footprints following trail cut to the side, around a rock, then rejoin the trail.

"Right, Bosz. Why are we making a detour to Jupiter?"

From that moment the ideas came thick and fast, and Miriam slipped them into gestalt.

To meet someone.

Someone close to our course

Someone moving quickly. We'll be on accel to match Freighty.

Any asteroids nearby?

None.

Any Space Arm ships?

None that match.

Image: barwolf joining gestalt

No, Bosz. No fair bringing in extra help. Although it sure would be nice to have a barwolf or three to round out the numbers... Whoa! Got it!

She crashed them out of the gestalt so fast they all looked around, dazed.

"We don't need a gestalt for this. We need a cast of characters."

"You're going to have to explain that, Miriam. I'm new to this game.

"Hah! Watch this. Kit, plot me a course heading this way from Barnard. Take it around any planet or planets available to kill velocity quickly."

Give me a moment. Bosz, some help, please. That's it.

Courses began to appear and disappear on the viewscreen.

Miriam shook her head. "None of these help any. How can we match courses? This imaginary ship is headed insystem, and we're headed outsystem. We'll whip by so fast we won't know he's there until he's gone."

Don't quit before we're finished. Maybe something will come up.

She gave Rafi a weak grin. "When our ArIn sounds that wishy-washy, I think we're in trouble."

He merely shrugged and continued watching the courses appear and disappear on the viewscreen. At first there were many, but then the number began to dwindle.

Got him! Coming in from Barnard, he might still be doing a couple of million klicks. He loops around Uranus to dump velocity. That puts him headed straight towards Jupiter. He'll orbit counterclockwise and use the gravity of Jupiter to slow him down. That lines up with our course, but we're still going in the opposite direction.

Rafi shook his head in awe. "There's one place a ship coming insystem can meet up with a ship going outsystem and match velocities at high speed."

Miriam frowned. "There is?"

"When they go into orbit around a planet. Look." He took control of the screen. "They're coming straight in from Barnard, hell-bent for leather. They'll come in ahead of the planet, on the downspin side. The planet grabs them and hauls them into orbit. As they curl around the sunward side, they're going the opposite direction to Jupiter, and it will slow them down, relative to the sun. A reverse slingshot."

With her auguar's help, Miriam was beginning to get the picture. "Then we come in behind the planet, on its upspin side. We'll gain a lot of velocity, but Jupiter will grab us into orbit as well. We'll come around the front of Jupiter on the same path as the inbound ship."

And if we hit it right, at the same velocity.

"Which our intelligent ArIn will find for us. We'll be on the same course until they peel away insystem."

Miriam chuckled. "No wonder we're on a tight schedule. They're on rails, and we have to match them." She regarded the screen. "And after we leave them, *Kit?*"

We're not technically doing a slingshot, because we are already catching up to Freighty, and when our gravity propulsion system gets within spitting distance of Jupiter, we can pretty much set our escape velocity at any speed we want. We'll make about a 260-degree spin around Jupiter and head out on a course in this range...

On the viewscreen, a cone of light departed Jupiter and spread out until it intersected with Freighty's course.

...and our perfect decel course will bring us spot on, wherever the boss wants us.

"Great." Miriam refreshed the viewscreen. "Kit, please scan back out the path you just found to see if there's a ship anywhere near it.

A new course appeared on the screen.

There's our target. She's big and heavy, and in powerful decel. Tanker or freighter, maybe? At this moment she's just coming out from behind Uranus. We got her, all right. Emotion: puzzlement. But who did we get?

"Not her. Them." *Emotion: Elation. That ship is bringing in the Three Musketeers, Bosz.*

Image: Auguar and three barwolves gamboling in the grass at Barwolf Base. Emotion: joy!

A plaintive voice broke in. "Could you two stop dancing around the room and tell a poor ignorant spacer who just joined the party what's happening? Wasn't 'The Three Musketeers' a cheesy threedie that came out a few years ago?"

"You got the right idea, Rafi. Making a long story short, about five years ago, Freighty rescued three barwolf pups that had been kidnapped. He kept them at Factory 4-80 till they could be picked up and brought home to Arborea. The long, lonely voyage was really hard on them, and afterwards I spent a lot of time playing with them and teaching them, trying to help them cope. In worked partially, but they don't quite fit in with barwolf society. Bosz and I know how that feels, so we all get along great. They've been on *Jerusalem* and at Barwolf Base the last four years, and we've been trying to think of a place where they'll fit."

"I see."

"No, you don't. Look around you. Count the quad couches. This ship is made for a triad, and Freighty brought them in from Barnard to be that group. And guess what they're being trained for."

Now I demonstrate my superior, though artificial, intelligence. Aether communications?

"Precisely."

Wait a minute. I'm getting a message.

"Okay. From where?"

From inside my own system. I have reached a level of understanding, and thus I have a new package of data to open.

"You wouldn't be telling me this unless there was a reason."

It includes the latest report from the Barwolf Auguar Cooperative Education Project, whatever that is.

"That's my project. Assume you're now part of it."

Yes, on an initial scan, I believe that to be true. Give me a moment. There's more to it than first meets the eye.

"We have time."

It didn't take him long.

All right. I am now an initiated member of the project. May I make my first contribution?

"Please do."

My analysis of the AetherCom research to date: the way the new system is set up, the best conformation of the ideal com team includes a barwolf triad, an auguar, an Arln, and a Sensitive human. Any three of the four can function, but all four have more power and wider scope.

"There you have it. And we must test the system and see how it works.

But the system was set up for us.

"It certainly looks that way."

This sounds like military thinking.

It does?

Yes. Results-based. You set up a system, then you set up an ideal operative, and then you use the operative to test the system. It's not proper scientific research at all. Your results will be completely skewed towards the positive.

"True." She thought a moment. "Which means that we're not testing the system."

Oh. Then we're testing us.

"Exactly."

For what?

She shrugged. "Toni told me something, once. She said everyone was always testing me. Nobody knew what I was capable of, so they just kept putting me in situations and not being too surprised when I came up with something weird or wonderful or awful or sometimes even useful.

What does that mean to us, now?

She gave her most evil grin. "It means we can do what we like. I learned that from Andrew Collingwood. If they don't give you defined objectives, they can't give you limits."

That sounds dangerous.

"It should, to you."

Because...?

"You're an ArIn."

Ah. I must never be allowed into a situation where I have no limits...but what are my limits in this project?

"That's easy. Me. I'm your limit. In the future, it might be Rafi or the barwolves. Even Bosz."

Bringing us around again to the ideal team.

"Exactly."

So. What now?

She rubbed her hands together, practicing her evil grin. "Whatever we like."

Wait a minute. What are your limits?

She dropped the grin. "Unfortunately, I have been taught all the ethics of decent human society. When push comes to shove, I will act like a good little girl, as I always have."

I don't think your mother would particularly agree.

"Oh yes, she would. She's part of my limit system." She shrugged. "Which means we listen to Freighty, because he's in charge, and we continue to do what we're told until..."

Until when?

"We won't know until it happens. But it will, and we'll know." She narrowed her eyes. "Because one thing has changed. This is my ship, and I'm in charge. If there's anything to be done, it's my decision, and I will accept the consequences. None of this two-bitting the responsibilities until they're ragged. You take the job, you do it, and it's done."

In other words, then we go out and prove them all right.

"Or all wrong. It doesn't matter. They turned us loose, and we make the choices."

I can live with that.

She turned to Rafi. "You in?"

"All the way.

Bosz?

Emotion: *eager desire to please.*

She regarded her auguar. *What about the day when you're required to put a limit on Kit?*

Image: auguar carrying small black cat by scruff of neck.

The avatar on the screen arched its back and hissed, but there was no threat in it.

Miriam nodded. "We have it all straightened out. Let's get to work."

4. CERES

Kit had no shuttle; her gravity drive enabled landing on a planet of any size. Her escape pod encompassed the main computer core plus the medical lab and a small room on either side, so its use was limited to…escaping.

None of this was necessary to visit Ceres. An asteroid field wasn't a safe place for exposed machinery, so the base was underground, accessed through a heavy blast door into a hangar large enough to accept several ships of *Kit's* size.

Once the door was closed behind them, *Kit* mated her main cargo airlock with the pressure door of a landing bay. When the atmosphere outside the lock showed one Earth-norm, Miriam and Bosz, still in space armour, left the ship.

And felt rather foolish when they were met by three stevedores in bright-coloured safety coveralls and steel-toed work boots.

Miriam released her helmet. "You trust the seals?"

The man in front chuckled. "Do you trust yours?"

"Well, come on in and take a gander at the cargo, and I'll go back and change into jeans."

"Aye, ma'am." He signalled and stepped ahead, and his two henchmen mounted cargo handling tractors and followed.

The foreman scanned the stickers on each of the five crates, glanced at his output, and nodded. "Everything in order. We'll have these out of here in no time." Again the laugh. "We'd better have. Lotsa people bin waiting for this stuff."

"Any reason why?"

He shrugged. "No idea. Very hi-tech, very useful. Word is out it's gonna stabilize the artificial grav units, and that will be much appreciated by some." He made gagging noises, then laughed once more. "So, less talking, more delivering."

He waved the tractors ahead and held out his enterpad to her. She glanced at it and nodded. "Send my ArIn a copy, please."

"Sure. What's the…oh. There's the address. A-a-n-d…he's got it. Whoo-ee, that was quick. You wouldn't believe the trouble we have with these things. I tell you, sometimes, I just print out a paper copy and hand it over. Paper's expensive, but my time is worth more, so the company doesn't mind. Why they don't standardize this sort of stuff is beyond me."

The guy would have talked all afternoon, but Miriam had business to attend to. "Great. You take care of this, and Bosz will supervise." As she spoke, she was removing the auguar's suit.

"Whoo-ee, that's one big kitty. C'n I pat him?"

"Sure. But you screw up the lading, you're likely to lose a patch of skin."

The man pulled his hand back slowly. "I get the picture. Pretty, though, ain't he?"

Miriam watched the man through Bosz's eyes as the auguar rubbed against his leg and gave a plaintive, "Meerow." Leaving the two to sort things out, she slipped into the suit locker, climbed out of her equipment, and left it laid out for future use. Then she grabbed a decompression jacket and returned to the dock.

The cargo bay was empty, and the tractors were just disappearing down the long, battered corridor that led deeper into the asteroid.

She opened the com. "Rafi, the cargo's gone. Want a few hours shore leave?"

Sure thing. I'm on my way.

Image: auguar going into ship and curling up on bed.

Emotions: Unhappiness, loneliness.

Emotion: worry. Image: auguar in danger.

Emotion: reluctant willingness to obey.

Emotion: affection for obedient auguar.

The human emotion that approached his answer was *"Pphhtt!"* which she ignored.

Rafi appeared in jeans and a tattered atmo hoodie, and they left the ship.

As they strolled deeper into the station, the corridor brightened, and gravity increased. Cross corridors led out, and soon there were people on the street, eyeing the strangers with casual glances.

She raised an eyebrow at her shipmate. "You think there's a bar in this one-horse town?"

He grinned. "One that serves apple juice?"

"We don't want to attract attention. I can stretch to beer."

He looked ahead, where the street became crowded, and various small, dingy shops hung out their signs. "From the looks of it, the better venues are deeper inside."

Sure enough, soon they passed through another blast door, and the tone lightened.

Rafi put on a knowing look. "We don't take the first one we pass. That one's for the tourists. We'll go farther in."

"We are tourists, and I don't want to get too far from the ship."

The genial look left his face, "You still worried?"

"Yeah, I find being a captain puts a bunch of limits on you."

"Feels strange to be without Bosz."

Image: ghost auguar trotting along behind.

Image: black cat slinking around corner.

She grinned. "All present and accounted for. Let's take the next place that looks interesting."

The next bar was larger and cleaner than the others, but not much different. "Not up to our usual standard, but what the heck."

"I didn't realize we had developed a standard. Setting the bar low, are we?"

"Do NOT develop that habit. Throughout history, bad puns have caused more trouble in space crews than love triangles."

"Sure about your data, are you?"

"Perfectly sure. I just made it up." She surveyed the room. It was rather plain, but the bar at the back had a reasonable number of different-coloured bottles racked behind it. To her inexperienced eye it looked like...a bar.

They sat and scanned the menu screen in the table. "Imported or local?"

He leaned closer. "Probably best to go local. Tongues might wag."

"Fair enough. Vesta Pale Ale?"

"Make that two."

When the robot cart trundled out, the two mugs it carried sported an appropriately golden liquid with a reasonable amount of foam on top. She paid with a swipe of her palm, and they touched glasses and took a sip.

"Thanks, Captain. How do you like it."

"Tastes like...beer."

"Positive sign."

She rolled it around on her tongue. *Bosz? Analysis, please?*

Around three percent.

She winked at Rafi. "I guess we're still in the tourist section. We got the watered stuff."

He glanced behind her, and something about his posture changed.

She didn't move, but lowered her voice. "What?"

"If this is the tourist part of town, what are those two doing here?"

She glanced at the pair who had entered. Workers, from their hardy but worn boiler suits. They sat, and one of them stabbed an uncaring finger at the menu. They paid no notice when their drinks arrived, but sat, staring around at nothing.

Emotion: calm. Don't rush it. Finish the drink and we're out of here.

They spent the next ten minutes discussing the technical details of a pump that Rafi had just taken apart. Bosz fed her enough information that she could keep up her end of the conversation.

How worried are we?

No reason to be worried at all.

Are we going to allow a couple of uppity workmen to scare us off the planetoid?

We can't. She downed her beer. *Nothing ventured, nothing gained.* She stood, and they left the bar, turning right, moving farther in. They kept a look over their shoulders, but nobody left the bar behind them.

She glanced over at her crewmate. "False alarm, I guess."

"Or else they have more resources."

Order: level three alert.

Emotion: agreement. Image: Docking area with no movement.

Emotion: desire to leave ship.

Emotion: calming. Image: auguar with binoculars peering around.

Emotion: reluctant willingness to obey.

Thus reassured, they continued down the street.

"There!" She pointed.

"Huh?" His head swung around. "What?"

"Clothes. Freighty promised me I could top up my wardrobe."

"Oh. Okay. I could use another shipsuit. One with tool pockets. I get the impression I'm at the bottom tier in the Engineering Department. You know: the guys with grease under their fingernails and stains on their knees."

She pointed to a 'Work Clothes' sign. "Then that would be the normal section for us."

He pointed to a frilly blouse in the window. "Passing up the chance for something fun?"

"The sacrifices I make."

It was not the shopping spree she had looked forward to, and a subtle 'look over your shoulder' feeling kept intruding. They turned down the offer to have their purchases delivered to the ship and took the packages with them.

They hesitated in the doorway. "Which way, boss?"

Emotion: question?

Image: map of area. Black figures of pedestrians moving about. One red figure stationary.

She did not turn her head, but pointed down the street in the opposite direction. *Suspicious person back up the street two shops.*

He nodded and stepped out. *Is he following?*

They walked on. *Yes. He's following. Either he's innocent or he's not a very good spy.*

Question: cross streets?

Image: map showing single hallway for fifty metres, then several intersections.

Emotion: thanks.

They strolled on, every sense alert.

Image: Trailing figure with blinking light. Figure ahead on the left with same light.

Miriam, they're both carrying the same locator. Homing in on an office in the central admin block.

They could be the local cops.

Could be.

You don't sound certain.

Doesn't add up.

Nor for me. She raised her voice. "No, we are not going into another bar. You got the drink you were promised. Now we're going back to the ship. Got it?"

"But Captain, we just got here."

"Right, and you can come back tomorrow. But right now, I'm not going to tolerate a mutiny out here in the street!" She pointed back the way they had come. "Quick march, spacer!"

"All right, all right." He trudged back up the street.

Their tail, a man in a scruffy business suit, scrambled to hide behind the mannequins in a street display of dresses, where he stood out like a barwolf in a swimming pool. They ignored him and stormed past.

Two new red-flagged figures followed them on their map as far as the blast doors, where they disappeared.

They'll be following you on the street survey vids from here on.

Thanks, Kit. Home directly.

The return to the ship was uneventful. They piled in, and Miriam watched with relief as the airlock door closed behind them. "I don't know about you, but I'm not sure I have the grit for that sort of foray."

"Didn't enjoy it much myself. But it was informative. And I got a great new atmo jacket."

"Certainly better than that old thing you were wearing."

"It was perfectly airtight, and I got a great trade-in price. Twice what it was worth in the Inner Planets."

"The ship will take a percentage of your profit for haulage."

She left him gaping and led the way to the lounge, where she poured herself a soda to wash the stale taste of beer from her throat. "They don't know it, but they've given us enough information for a serious search."

He nodded. "Kit, can you find a reason to tie up the station ArIn in conversation for a while?"

Conversations between ArIns never take much time. Humans are better at that.

"Okay, I am a worried junior captain concerned about the latest sunspot activity and the amount of radiation protection in the base shielding. Surely there must be a safer docking spot?

I'm sorry, ma'am, but the station's ArIn has placed us in the best available slot. You'll have to speak to Admin about it.

Perfect. Put me through to Station Admin.

For the next half hour, Miriam led a bored bureaucrat on a merry chase through the intricacies of Station management, all of which had to be explained in detail to the entertaining young captain with the alluring voice.

Meanwhile, her ship and auguar were using the connection for their own nefarious purposes, taking care to leave no hint of their passing.

When she got the high sign from her team, she left the young man with the impression that Asteroid Admin had probably done their best to find her ship a handy moorage, and that he, himself, had done a great job of explaining it.

However (unfortunately), she was on a schedule and would not necessarily be available to meet later for a drink, enticing though the *Blue Angel Coffee House* might sound.

"What did you get, boys and girls?"

Rafi shook his head. "The news isn't good. Number one, the Gambino organization has its feelers deep in the station's operation. Number two, their whole outfit, system wide, is on the lookout for you."

"So, number three, they know I'm on this ship."

"Exactly."

"Well, that makes things easy. Kit, will you contact Freighty and ask him to send you a regular Sys-Com message, poorly encrypted, that orders a change in schedule, including an immediate departure?"

Give me a moment...done. If he answers immediately by regular com, the delay is about eight minutes. Assuming it will take them at least a minute or two to decode our message, we have ten minutes to tie up loose ends.

"Do we have any loose ends?"

 Nothing except a lingering feeling from a certain young man in Admin.

"Can't be helped. Motto of a spacewoman: 'love them and leave them. Orbits always come back around.' Seriously, no overt moves until we get the message. Then contact Admin and go through all normal departure procedures, including our flight plan for Vesta. They'd know anyway as soon as we set our course. Let me know if you run into any obstructions, and I'll throw my smile around."

But their quick action seemed to take their opponents by surprise, and twenty minutes later the big exit doors were opening to allow *Kit* to slide through. They departed on their traditional Hall-effect thrusters and ran that way for the following day. Then they took care to fade from view for a few hours, fired up the gravity generators and pushed off for Vesta.

AetherCom: 18 *Anti-GR*

Barwolf: Patches
Initiated by: Miriam
Responder: Rosalyn
Aether Setting: Barnabus and Miriam's rooms on Jerusalem

The nice thing about the family gestalt was the ability to contact the family at a thought. Mostly, it was nice.

How are things going with Rafi? You've been alone in each other's company for a long time.

"Not totally alone, and we've been busy with work."

219

Still...

"I'm serious, Mum. No romance."

You can never be sure.

"Yes, I can. As the old song says, 'I've got my pills to ease the pain.'"

What pills?

"They were onboard when we got here. Space Arm's latest Anti-GR pills."

Emotion: suspicion. Anti-GR?

"Anti-Gender Recognition."

I've never heard of such a thing. How do they work?

"Rafi knew all about them already. The way he explained it, they've known for a long time why siblings aren't physically attracted to each other."

Right. Mainly smell. Sibling body odour isn't appealing.

"And several more subtle factors. Pheromones and the like. So, they made this pill that works like a love potion but has the opposite result."

A love potion?

"You know the stories. You drink the potion, and you fall in love with the first person you see afterwards. This does the opposite. You take the pill, and for the next twelve hours you're hypersensitive. You stay in proximity with the target person and keep the rest of your sensory input bland. Once the sensitivity wears off, you don't recognize that person as opposite gender. "

She chuckled. "That's why you don't eat or drink anything during the sensitive period. You could develop a negative attitude to your favourite beer."

I just don't like the idea of them using experimental drugs to mess with your hormones without any input from us.

"Mum, they're standard issue for Space Arm crews on long trips. Don't worry so much. As we have discussed before, you're there and I'm here, and sometimes you just can't help. At the moment, I seem to be doing fine. If there's any change, you'll be the first to notice, and I'm sure you'll let me know."

Miriam, that's not fair!

"Maybe not, but it's true, so there we are. Or there we aren't, as the case may be. You showed concern. I've answered your question. Problem solved. Let's leave it at that."

I suppose...

"Bye, Mum. I love you." Miriam sighed and closed the link. *Sometimes more than others.*

5. VESTA

The larger planetoid was a depressing copy of its insystem sister. Same blast doors, same docking procedures and efficient longshoremen, and a more immediate impression that they were being watched, both re-li and electronically.

Miriam flopped into a chair in the lounge. "That was too easy. They were onto us before we arrived. Gambino's bunch have the inside track here as well, and they knew we were coming."

Rafi sat as well. "This could get to be a bore."

"And it's not just us. If he's willing to go to all this trouble to trail us, what about Tom and even the other Blues?"

He shrugged. "What can we do about it?"

She rubbed her hands together. "Exactly. Just what can we do about it? We probably have as much computing power as the whole station. We have an operative trained in the latest techniques of cybernetic infiltration, along with a top-flight auguar and the most Sensitive human ever discovered. We can merge into a rock-solid gestalt that probably triples our individual talents. She met Rafi's eyes. "Tactical gestalt, crew."

Once they were settled, she started. "First: entry points."

No problem, Captain. This is a big town, and their local net is wide open.

"Next: plan of attack. Let's start with a passive scan."

Rafi brought up a schematic on their internal visual field. A tangle of dark lines spread out from the solid black spot that represented the Station ArIn.

"Great. Now let's look for evidence of the Gambinos."

He worked a while, and red lines crept through the dark ones. *The circuits with the Gambino signature are concentrated on admin and commercial with some in Security, as you'd expect.*

"What do you suggest, now?"

If I was going into their system, I'd first make sure we can keep Engineering from locking us in there. Then I'd copy everything I could and leave tags so I can find it again in a hurry. Last resort, I could wipe them all with a rolling series of viruses. As a kicker,

222

I'd leave some back doors and a few sleepers in case of future need.

Miriam regarded him through the gestalt. "Can you really do all that?"

I should be able to. It's my adaptation of a standard attack I learned in Electronic Tactics class last year.

Emotion: evil humour. "So, if we follow that plan, we'll leave Space Arm's fingerprints all over it?"

Oh. I never thought of that. Yes, we could push that aspect of it. Use some older software that everybody knows comes from Space Arm.

"Fine. Kit, how feasible is this?"

Piece of cake. The challenge is not to get caught. Especially the wiping part. We can do all the copying passively, and nobody will know we were there. A wipe is a constant fear for firewalls, and the moment you actually move or change a file, you'll have doors crashing down all around you.

"Fair enough. We only need the data. Once we have that, we can reassess the risks of the wipe. What do we need for the steal?"

Image: auguar walking the streets of the base.

"It's better if we can get you inside?"

Image: auguar walking streets, Miriam with fancy camera taking pictures.

"Got it. The Innocent Tourist routine."

The lading crew showed up, and while they were removing the cargo, Miriam dressed in her one frilly blouse and put her pet cat on a leash hastily embroidered from bright yellow Dynotex cord.

Emotion: disgust.

"Can it, sweetheart. You've gotta look harmless. This thing's attached with VelcroFour. You're free at the first tug."

Emotion: reluctant willingness to perform.

"Is everything set?"

Gestalt emotion: satisfaction.

They left the ship and toured the base, all senses alert. Miriam was careful to be seen taking images of innocuous attractions. Once again they were tailed, but always from a careful distance. Rafi and *Kit* watched on the station monitors and did their own data collection.

"These guys are a bit more professional."

Yeah, the one walking behind you has a reversable jacket. He was ahead three streets ago, with a ball cap.

"Have you seen enough?"

Emotion: agreement.

Plenty, captain.

"Okay, back to the ship, and let's get out into orbit before we start. I don't like to be inside those big doors."

They re-embarked and were soon circling a kilometre or so away from the planetoid. Miriam swung into her accel couch and strapped in, just in case.

"Some time soon, it's going to be very difficult to do business with Vesta. Are we finished?"

Kit's image on the screen gave a huge yawn and stretch.

All done, Captain.

"Where is Senor Gambino, *Kit?*"

He sent his latest message from his private dome just outside MarsPort.

"Can we access his house ArIn?"

I don't think so.

"Well, they keep telling us we should use our resources." *Patches, wanna have some fun?*

Image: black barwolf cowering in fear.

Oh, don't be silly. I just want to make a phone call.

Image: Miriam at one end of a phone line. The other end blows up.

Yeah, you've got the idea. And there's one more thing. I need privacy.

Image: Lantz family sitting at dinner table, eating cheerfully. Miriam hiding in shed outside, working on large box labeled TNT.

Come on, Patches. You can look the other way if you like. Just put us on AetherCom with this house. We'll do the rest. Image: Gambino mansion on Mars.

Image: Miriam speaking, solid words coming out of her mouth. Each time the word "just" comes out, it explodes, leaving Miriam covered in soot.

Patches, make the connection, okay?

Emotion: extremely reluctant desire to participate.

The next moment, Miriam was sitting in a spacious office with design hints of Freighty's Italian sitting room. It wasn't real, of course, because the edges faded to blue, as all AetherCom spaces did.

The older man sitting across the ornate desk started in surprise, his distinguished features wrinkled in a frown. *Who are you and what do you want?*

"Mr. Gambino, there is no reason for you to know my name, but I was involved in a little misunderstanding about a ruggerball game a couple of months ago."

Ah. You would be Miriam Lantz. I know a great deal about you.

"But not how I come to be in your office."

This is not really my office.

"You noticed. It is my version of your office, strictly so we can have this conversation."

And why should I spend time speaking to you?

She shrugged. "In the first place, because you're not sure how to get out of this illusion. Also, perhaps you would like to hear my apology."

I never turn away good manners.

"Therefore, and I know it isn't much, but I apologize that we messed up your game."

So, you admit you fixed that ruggerball game.

"No, Senor Gambino. What we did in the ruggerball game was completely legal. It was your game that we ruined. We had no idea it even existed, and we never would have done it if we had known. So, we're sorry. For what it's worth."

He smiled and leaned back in his chair. *Well, little girl, I'm glad you have come to the realization of what happens when you play outside your league. I understand that people make mistakes, and I have no personal animosity towards you. Anything that happens to you or your friends is simply the result of the mistake you made. It's just business, you understand?*

"Completely, and I feel the same way about you. So, as a gesture of good will, I am giving you twenty-four hours to remove yourself from Vesta Base. After that time, your operation will disappear from that asteroid. Completely and unrecoverably."

She gave him a moment, but not long enough to respond. "Oh, yes, and the records will be sent to a place that is safer than you could possibly imagine. Just in case you forget your understanding of the error of myself and my friends. Do you understand?"

She could see him starting to work up for an explosion.

See here...

"Twenty-four hours starting...Now."

Image: Miriam hanging up telephone. She was instantly gone from the aether.

She nodded to her team. "That went well. Now, let's watch what he does. It's going to be interesting to see what he takes and where he puts it."

Rafi frowned in thought. "We'll have to monitor our tracers. The moment he finds one, we vapourize it, and all the others of its type."

"But it doesn't matter what we get or what we lose. I promised to wipe him off the face of the asteroid. That's all we need to do."

For several hours, nothing happened. Then electronic traffic to the station increased on several specific channels, five of which were not in the public radio bands. The data was heavily coded, but since Miriam and her crew had stolen all Gambino's files, they didn't bother to decipher it, opting instead to stay mute and out of the action.

At T minus 10 hours, the blast doors opened, and a fast personnel launch headed out, to be followed over the next three hours by two more. There was no way to know whose vessels they were, and again *Kit* and her crew lay low.

At T minus 05:30, *Kit* called Miriam's attention.

We're getting action on the Space Arm defense system.

"Such as?"

They have received instructions to target ships in orbit. The officer in charge is concerned. He's checking with Fleet Headquarters.

"What's going on behind his back?"

Every tech on the payroll is working frantically. They're under serious cyberattack.

"How's the battle going?"

They are holding their own, for the moment. The attacking warware is not very sophisticated, but it knows many passwords and procedures it shouldn't have, which speeds up its progress.

"Let me know the moment we're in any danger."

Aye, Cap'n.

Rafi frowned. "If that was me, and I was running into that much resistance…"

"What would you do?"

"I'd keep up the frontal assault on the whole system. But they don't need the whole system. They need one weapon for thirty seconds. They blow us up, then they disappear."

Emotion: fear. "Kit, any sign of that?"

Emotion: uncertainty. This isn't easy, you know. It's like you're asking me to go out into the middle of a battle and look for one weapon that's acting differently…whoa, right. We just have to find a weapon that's pointed at us."

"And disable it before it shoots us."

That's another problem. If I start acting like the attackers, somebody will notice me because it's obvious I'm different, and I'll be the lonely one, standing there waving a "shoot me" flag.

"Let's try it another way as well. Can you connect me with the officer in charge?"

No trouble. Commander Armin Iskandar…

Soon a harried, dark-complexioned face appeared on the viewscreen.

Online now.

"Hello, Commander Iskandar. I gather you are having some trouble with a cyberattack."

His frown deepened. *Who are you and what do you want?*

"I represent a Space Arm client. I happened to be nearby, and I detected the problem. May I help in any way?"

How could you help?

"You are under attack by members of the Gambino family, who have penetrated deeply into the operating system of this asteroid. My technicians suggest that if you sever all contact with the Station Admin, you will have much less trouble dealing with the attack itself, which is using the following programs...I'm sending the information in plain text with no metadata, so you don't have to worry about trojans or viruses. I am also informed that the attackers have access to a lot of your security information, so I would look carefully at the loyalty of my technicians if I were you."

That's nonsense! My...

"No, it isn't. It's just a shock for any officer to discover that some of his men are not loyal, although in any staff, odds tell us one or two of them will not be.

"Now, as of this moment, various weapons of your arsenal are waving all over the place and seem to be trying to target the ships in orbit, frightening the customers nearby. I warn you, should one of your weapons seem to take on a life of its own and threaten my ship, I will be forced to take action to protect myself. Which will not help you repel the present attack."

"Which ship are you? My RDF is down."

"Better if I don't tell you. That will motivate you to protect all of us. The way to do that is obvious, and I hope you will do it, although you probably won't. I assure you, there are no hostile ships in the neighbourhood to take advantage of the situation. Goodbye, Commander Iskandar. My technicians are working on the problem as well. Good luck to both of us."

As she signed off, Rafi frowned at her. "What is the obvious solution?"

She grinned. "Take his major weapons offline. It's completely counter-intuitive when you're under attack, but it would narrow the interface of attack and let his technicians concentrate on the information I sent."

"He won't. We're dealing with the military. If he shut down his weapons in the middle of an action and something went wrong, his career would be toast."

"You're our military expert. I believe you. Too bad."

It was a nerve-wracking time for Miriam. Her crew were working furiously, and all she could do was bolster their gestalt.

Rafi jumped from his accel couch and strode back to the kitchen, returning with a cup of coffee. "Even in gestalt with *Kit* and Bosz, I don't have the background to deal with this."

She gave a weak grin. "We'll move anti-virus defence higher on your training priorities. If we survive."

"We've got the best camo in two systems. Why don't we just fade out and scram?"

She shook her head. "Everybody knows we're here. We're a legitimate freighter, making a delivery. Our best camouflage is to act normal. The vids of this action are going to be scanned by experts for years to come. We can't do anything to draw attention to ourselves. We cower here until the fight's over, then we scram when all the others do."

"We sit here like ducks in a pond and wait for somebody to shoot us?"

"Not if you get in there and figure out a way to stop them."

"You sure know how to motivate your crew, Captain." He toasted her with his coffee cup. "Back to being a hero." He lay back on his couch and his face blanked as he dove into the gestalt.

Half an hour later, activity began to die down.

The cyberattack on the Space Arm has stopped. The Gambinos have switched to covering their tracks.

She grinned. "They don't realize that in four hours, there will be nothing to cover."

Rafi raised his eyebrows. "That helps the Gambinos. We're wiping a lot of evidence Space Arm would like to get their hands on."

She shook her head. "This is a private matter. We don't need help from Space Arm, and if Vincent Gambino thought we ratted him out, it would be sabres at dawn and *omertà* for generations." She waited, smiling, while he accessed his memory.

"Yeah. I get it. You gotta deal with that sort differently, don't you?"

"Tradition is a two-edged sword, especially in this case."

Space Arm just issued an 'All Clear' on the station.

Thanks, Kit.

Emotion: evil chuckle. Just wait another four hours, guys.

Not our problem. Call up the Base Commander again, will you?

Image: phone ringing, Captain Iskandar picking up.

"Hi, there, Captain. Got it all cleared out?"

Yes, your information was excellent.

"Good. Anything else I can do?"

No, it's all under control, I'd like to thank you officially for your timely assistance.

"Don't thank me. Send the bouquet to the 4-80 Fabrication Consortium."

Factory 4-80? Why would you be helping Space Arm? Last I heard... he seemed to realize who he was talking to and stopped.

"Freighty has no problem with Space Arm. Pleased to be of assistance."

Yes, well...thank you. He looked down at his control panel. *This conversation is coming in on the SysCom. Which ship are you?*

"As I said. No specific thanks necessary. I'll be leaving with the rest of the rats. Hope the ship doesn't sink. Bye, now."

Goodbye, I suppose...

And then the line closed.

Aethercom 19: A New Course

Barwolf: Not needed
Initiated by: Miriam/Bosz
Responder: Freighty
Aether Setting: Freighty's office

Once on their way, she reported to Freighty with the results of her actions.

He was sitting, as was his habit, in his ancient office, the usual glass of amber liquid in his hand. When she finished, he swirled it deftly and took a sip. *You know, young lady, you have a talent for turning a simple situation into a potential for interplanetary conflict.*

"Could that be because you keep inserting me into situations where it doesn't take much of a nudge to tip the balance?"

That is one term for it. A balance point. The ideal time where the ideal person can make a small move that resonates.

"And what about the resonance from this last rather overt shove?"

You must have had some idea what you wanted. What do you think?

"After such a serious action, someone from our organization needs to contact Senor Gambino and get a few things straight."

I agree. And you are the obvious person.

"I'm glad you agree. What should I say?"

I'm a great believer in letting my agents take care of their own operations.

"Fine. My one concern is the cultural aspects of an Italian family operation. I have been researching *omertà*. I have one objective: to protect my friends, both in the short term and the long term. The short term is easy. They're small potatoes to an operation his size, and as long as they stay out of his area, he'll leave them alone. In the future, however, I assume I will be moving my base of operations to Barnard. I would prefer not to be looking over my shoulder in my home territory."

That would match my objectives.

"Fair enough. I'll keep it in mind."

I don't need to tell you to tread carefully. This organization, sleazy as it may be, is not an enemy. It is merely a symptom of a weakness in human society. Do you understand the expression 'tilting at windmills?'

"...I do now, and I will try to resist the temptation. I'll keep it in mind when I do my planning."

Miriam. Don't tell me that you're planning your actions, now.

"I find it useful when considering which resources to use."

Ah. Leadership is having its effect.

"Yes, and if this is another of those places where you slip in a note about sympathy for my parents, don't bother. I noticed. But don't tell them that.

I wouldn't dream of interfering.

AetherCom 20: Vincent Gambino

Barwolf: Patches
Initiated by: Miriam
Responder: Vincent Gambino
Aether Setting: Gambino's office

When she contacted Gambino later that afternoon, he was having trouble maintaining his suave Mediterranean front, but he gritted his teeth and greeted her politely. *It seems I must reassess our relationship, Miss Lantz. What do you wish, now?*

"In our last conversation you were pleased to be forgiving at a personal level of a mistake for which I had apologized. However, you refused to shield me from the consequences of my act. I am willing to extend the same courtesy to you. I understand why you set the dogs on me, and I am willing to forgive you once you call those dogs off. However, I found it necessary to take certain actions to attract your attention, and those actions caused you economic hardship. That loss was the consequence of your actions, and I hope you will accept it with similar equanimity."

I see. And what are your expectations?

"I wish to call a truce between us. You let my friends and me fade quietly from your attention, and I will do the same for you. My operatives are aware of your organization's patterns of behaviour, and I'm sure we will encounter them in the future. We will ignore them when we meet, and we will not go looking for them."

I can consider that. Is there anything else?

"In order to make this easier for both of us, how about a division of territory."

That is not unusual. What boundaries do you suggest?

"The simplest ones. I will cede to you all rights in the Sol System. In return, the Gambino family will keep its shady operations out of the Barnard System."

The old man laughed aloud. *I never dreamed I would see this day. I am bargaining territory at a solar system level.*

"Times change. Do we have a deal?"

His face straightened. *I think we do.*

"Until one of us gives notice we wish to renegotiate."

How much advance notice do you wish?

She regarded him. "We are discussing a personal agreement between two individuals, not a legal document."

True.

"Then the only possible amount is what seems fair to both of us, given the situation at the time."

You place our agreement into the realm of personal honour.

"I do."

Then I accept.

AetherCom 21: Course Correction

Barwolf: Not required
Initiated by: Freighty
Responder: Miriam/Bosz
Aether Setting: Miriam's chartroom on Kit

Good morning, Captain. Do you have time in your busy schedule for a little chat?

"I can probably manage." She closed her enterpad and regarded Micha Mouse, perched on the visitor's chair of her tiny office. "What's up?"

I have a little errand for you to run.

"We thought you might. The crew pickup in five days or so."

This guess is based on what data?

"Our course was perfect for a specific objective."

A large jump of logic.

"Not when a small detour would put us on the path of a ship that just came in from Barnard, looped around Uranus and was chasing Jupiter downspin for a final reverse slingshot to dump velocity. Perhaps a ship with a few crewmembers to fill out our barwolf complement."

That is reasonable reasoning.

"Any chance it's barwolves we know?"

About eighty-three percent, as it happens.

"But you're going to give me a straight answer and make it a hundred."

The toon grinned. *All right. It's your old buddies.*

"Great. Got a proper course for us? We were guessing."

Stand by for transmission

"Numbers coming through, Bosz."

Emotion: success.

"Kit, you there?"

Aye, Captain.

"Bosz has our new course. Set it up and activate ASAP."

Aye, Captain. Course change activated as we speak...it's close to the course we were on.

"Good for us."

Freighty came back on com. *Now...about call signs and codes. These people are a little touchy about being recognized, so...*

"You think there's anybody out there that can fake three barwolves in unison? Tell them not to worry. Now that we know they're near, we'll find them through the aether and call them on SysCom."

That will do just fine.

234

Emotion: disappointment. "You should have told us sooner that they were coming."

You were busy with more important things. It's better this way.
"I suppose."

Let me know when the transaction is complete, so I can arrange final remuneration.

"Sure. I'm going to sign off, now. I have three buddies to find."

Have fun. The Mouse did a backflip and disappeared.

6. CONTACT

She reached into that special place in her mind. "Patches?"

Emotion: agreement.

"Can you crank me up an aether call? The Three Musketeers are around here somewhere."

Emotion: eager desire to please. Question: ArIn?

"We'll be using Kit, with Bosz and me to fill out the team."

Emotion: recognition. Concept: sufficiency. Emotion: patience.

"Sure, Patches, take your time."

It took about three minutes.

Emotion: pleasure. Image: three barwolves holding telephones.

Great! Put them through. She dove into the gestalt, and found herself in a comfortable room — at least, comfortable for a barwolf — with heavily padded floor, low-slung sanitary equipment, water fountain and food bowls.

The three barwolves, wriggling with glee, came to her for the leg-touch/plate scratch ritual, then broke their decorum for a roll-and-tumble with Bosz. She sat, leaning against the wall, and they lay facing her, heads alert, exuding 'eager desire to please.'

"Kit, can you get a fix on this position?"

Piece of cake. That's one powerful barwolf running the gestalt.

"My family com officer. Can you send a tight-band radio call to the transport?"

Sure. What do I say?

"Record this: 'Calling barwolf transport. Greeting party calling barwolf transport. Please respond.' End transmission with Freighty's call sign."

Message sent.

Static burst from the com.

Well, that was primitive.

What happened?

They pinged us with a simple radiolocation beam.

"We'll send them our ETA to show we know where they are. Tell me when you're ready, and I'll have our barwolves attract their attention at the same time to verify the connection."

She returned to the aether contact. *Image: Musketeers communicating with humans onboard. Emotion: question?*

Emotion: positive. Emotion: difficulty.

Image: triad communicating with transport ship's ArIn.

Emotion: negative.

She switched back to ship's com. "Got the ETA?"

Twenty-seven hours.

"Prepare to send."

I have radio contact. They're not talking, but they're listening.

Back with the barwolves, she sent a complicated message she hoped they'd understand.

Image: two ships meeting. Time: one day. Image: Musketeers speaking to humans on ship. Loudly.

Emotion: agreement.

She opened the gestalt to all of them.

"Everybody ready? Three...two...one...GO!"

And then not much happened in the gestalt, but the radio signal from the transport ship blazed out.

Okay, okay, we get the message! Contact in twenty-seven hours, give or take. Just tell those barwolves to shut up, will you? They get in your head and like to bust it open.

Miriam winked at Rafi. "Thank you, barwolf transport. *Kit* over and out."

She contacted her triad. *Emotion: thanks. Image: spacers with hands over ears. Emotion: humour.*

Emotion: humour.

Emotion: serious. Time: one day. Image: Miriam/Bosz contacting Musketeers.

Emotion: desire for gestalt.

Emotion: desire for full gestalt, one day.

Emotion: reluctant agreement.

She thanked Patches with a brief family cuddle, then broke the connection and went back to work.

7. MUSKETEERS PICKUP

"She's called the *Argosy*. I guess because of her valuable cargo." Rafi posted an image of a ship that dwarfed *Kit*. It resembled a huge drum of fuel. "A unique tanker, built to carry highly refined special liquids. You know, the kind of value where one load coming into port is worth enough to sway sections of the stock market. The payload tank takes up the centre of the mass. The outer hull is a passenger/cargo shell rotating around the inner tank. This provides radiation and debris shielding for the cargo, and rotational gravity for the crew. Otherwise, it's bare-bones construction; all the rest of the mass goes into engines and fuel. She's a treasure ship, and she wants to reach her objective with all possible speed."

"What are they carrying on this trip?"

He grinned. "As far as we're concerned, three barwolves."

"Let them keep their secrets. As long as the Musketeers are happy, I'm satisfied. Kit, patch me through to the *Argosy*.

Image: Greek in ancient armour picking up modern handset.

A craggy face appeared on the screen. *Argosy here, Leif Lundeen commanding. Ready to receive some passengers?*

"*Kit* here, Miriam Lantz commanding. How shall make the transfer? We have an extendible docking tube."

Oh, no. I will bring our guests across myself. Best of treatment till the very end.

"That's kind of you."

We'll be there in about an hour. We have the last of the moosey meat to pack up.

"See you then."

Fifty-five minutes later, a small shuttle pulled away from the *Argosy* and mated up with *Kit's* main cargo hatch. Leif came on com. *There's a couple of hundred kilos of meat left. Do you have resupply?*

Miriam stopped in the common room to use the viewscreen there. "Not to worry. These guys lived with Freighty for months when they were young. We can whip up several of their favourite dishes."

Is it okay to dump the packs here in the airlock?

"Sure. We'll take care of the refrigeration later."

We just had them moored to the outside hull. Somebody went EV once every two weeks for more.

"We have the fridge space. Do you want to step inside for a moment?"

He grinned. *First new faces for six months. I believe I will.*

Kit opened the inner hatch, and the three barwolves tumbled out, mauling Bosz briefly, then lining up for a more decorous greeting with Miriam.

Athos stepped forward first, seriously performing the leg bump plate scratch in ones role as the one who joins.

Porthos, biggest of the trio, danced forward in a jubilant rush. *Image: Porthos playing ruggerball, knocking Miriam flying. Emotion: contrition. Emotion: Humour.*

Emotion: forgiveness.

Then Miriam turned to Aramise, who slid forward with her usual ethereal grace. *Emotion: welcome.*

Emotion: gracious acceptance. Image: black cat. Emotion: curiosity.

Kit, she wants to talk to you.

Emotion: agreement.

Both of them disappeared from the gestalt.

After a moment of surprise, she decided it was not the time to question and turned to Leif.

He grinned. "No question who's the boss." Then he glanced at her again, his brow wrinkling. "You are the…captain?"

She laughed. "Long story. Thanks for having these guys onboard."

"We'll be sorry to see them go."

"They weren't much trouble, then?"

"Not at all. We loved having them. They kept themselves to themselves mostly, but you know what? We had no otherwhere willies."

"They have that effect."

"It was fun. You oughta watch them use the running track. They move awkward, but they've got a turn of speed. At least the two big ones do. Aramise, she just seems to float. She mixes it up with the others, though, racing and tripping, and the whole pile of them ending up in a tangle. And never a growl or nip or any negative vibes. A fine example to the crew."

"It works both ways. If you wish to work for Freighty again, you've already had a positive report from the barwolves, and so far you're getting a good word from me."

The conversation would have gone on much longer, but *Kit* gave Miriam a nudge and slipped a course map up on the common room viewscreen, speaking through the ship's com.

"Separation, sixty minutes, ma'am."

The spacer was immediately all business. His final payout arranged, he thanked her politely and was soon disconnected and zipping towards his ship.

The tanker began to edge slowly away, and by suppertime it was a mere blip on the viewscreen as *Kit* continued her lonely route.

AetherCom 22: Two Steps Backward

Barwolf: Not Needed
Initiated by: Freighty
Responder: Miriam/Bosz
Aether Setting: Freighty's office

Freighty received her in his Italian Office, as he usually did, now. She assumed it was a tribute to her new status as Apprentice Captain, or whatever.

So, Captain. Progress report?

"The Barwolf Auguar Cooperative Education Project is up and running. I have tested our barwolf trio in the skills of AetherCom, and, as expected they are above the norms the scientists at Barwolf Base have established. They excel at obscured and distracted transmissions, holding their gestalt far beyond that of any regular trio studied."

And the other three crewmembers?

"I am unable to quantify the progress Bosz is making in areas I cannot understand. Rafi likewise, though to a lesser degree. As for myself...well, let's just say opinions on board differ on what "familiar with" means when applied to the captain's knowledge of every system on the whole dratted ship."

Given the choice, I'd lean towards the opinion of the ship. It is probably closest to the wishes of the being who programmed her.

"I knew you'd say that. Parental bias."

Potentially.

She tried to read his expression. "You really mean that, don't you?"

By my calculations, Kit has sufficient memory to attain full social awareness. It is only a matter of time and the proper training. At the moment, you constitute the proper training, so don't mess it up.

"But she's training me!"

Part of the program. She's training you on a rather loose curriculum, but she does have a set of guidelines. You're training her to become a thinking, feeling being.

"Is this what adults mean when they say things get more complicated as you get older?"

Probably. His smile disappeared. *Would you like more of the experience?*

"Okay, I know that look. You've been setting me up for something."

I find it expedient to give you more information on what's going on in Sol System.

"And I'm not going to like it."

And thus the first lesson is learned,

"Go ahead."

Freighty settled himself in the big swivel chair. *It goes this way. One might think that human social progress happens slowly over the centuries. It does not. It is much more like 'two steps ahead, one step back,' sometimes even the reverse.*

"Rosie taught me that. She says even in the forty years our people were on *Jerusalem* going to Barnard there were several swings. I was born because of a more authoritarian swing. My parents were cousins and were forced to marry for scientific reasons. My Sensitivity was the win. My cleft palate was the loss.

You have it in a nutshell.

She nodded. "And we're in the middle of another swing backwards?"

This society is far too complex for that. Different aspects are evolving in opposite directions, out of synch with each other. However, there is a large enough segment on the latest conservative swing to affect the whole. Also, Space Arm is getting much too interested in science, and losing its edge in warfare.

"But that's a positive, isn't it?"

Not for too long. It needs to keep its capability up in case of outside attack or inside revolution.

"You think we have a revolution coming?"

Probably not. It isn't good for business, and the big drivers of conservatism right now are the interplanetaries. Sooner or later the democratic politicians will realize how their power is threatened. They will get together and make a bunch of system-wide laws and treaties that force the combines to break up.

"Does this affect your decision to up stakes and move?"

The mere fact that I exist here could influence the interplanetaries to make some kind of totalitarian move. Therefore, I am taking my influence elsewhere.

"Sounds logical. Now," She settled herself and regarded him, "we get to the question of why you're telling me this. It must affect our immediate future as well, and my ship and me specifically. Otherwise, I don't need to know."

Very good. Although, as a ship's captain, you need an overall picture of the political situation. The important reason I'm leaving is self-interest.

"You might be in danger?"

Not likely, but it has to be considered. Doing business is a two-edged sword. The back edge is having to trust more people.

"In this case, employees?"

Yes. Every employer, ruler, or tribal chief has to accept the fact that not everyone onboard has the same objectives or point of view.

"So, the possibility of having a spy or saboteur grows with the number of staff. What reason could anyone possibly have to destroy the Factory?"

Freighty shifted in his chair. *Which brings us back to the original political situation. There are two main elements to the conservative movement. The first is economic. They have learned to make a lot of money on the present system. They have even influenced this system so they can milk it. To them, change means loss of profit.*

But then there's the second half. Down at the bottom of the socio-economic scale are the have-nots. They work today so they can eat tonight. They have no fallbacks, no insurance. The slightest change in the structure of their world could be a disaster for them, so they don't want change, either. They often resist progress even if it would be to their advantage, because they have been fooled and disappointed in the past.

"I get that. But this second group has no resources. How can they threaten us?"

Freighty shook his head. *That's where true evil rears its nasty head. The poor are afraid, and fearful people don't make wise choices. They are poorly educated as well. Intelligent members of the moneymaking class can influence the lower classes by promising to solve their problems.*

"Aha! Grade Nine Political Science. Demagogs!"

You begin to see the advantage of an education. The demagog puts on the mask of someone who cares, and the uneducated poor follow the mask, ignoring the reality of the person who wears it. Often he is a member of the class that abuses them.

Miriam considered this. "Creating a huge pool of potential foot soldiers for a clandestine war against anyone at any time."

"Right. And the worst of it is…?"

"They're not all poor and uneducated. All sorts of weird people believe weird things, and all sorts of greedy people will do pretty much anything for money."

And that's another thing a captain has to know. You can never trust anyone completely.

"That's ridiculous. You have to trust your crew, if only because of self-interest. Your chief engineer isn't going to blow up the engines in outer space. He'd die too."

Unless he believed his dying was worth it. More likely, someone has persuaded him that he will be picked up.

She sat back. "I have the lesson. Saboteurs and fanatics who naturally appear at times like this threaten the Factory. What can we do about it?"

Nothing. I am quite confident in my security measures. As you may guess, I monitor my employees more than they suspect. It's not democratic, but it's necessary.

"The end justifies the means. Expedience trumps human rights. That's always the excuse."

In times of war the scale shifts.

She frowned. "You don't think we're in a war?"

I'm doing everything I can to prevent one. Including boosting my considerable mass at an acceleration of almost one gravity all the way to Barnard.

"And this is...general information for my captain's training?"

It is meant to lend an air of urgency to your approach to security.

"I'll try not to lie awake more than two hours a night worrying about it."

Then the lesson was successful.

"And I will go back with renewed enthusiasm for my learning of the systems of my ship. That's a problem I can do something about."

AetherCom 23: Morals

Barwolf: Patches
Initiated by: Miriam
Responder: Rosalyn
Aether Setting: Rosalyn's office on Jerusalem

"Well, Mum, I've got my new assignment."

Rosy brightened. *Tell me!*

"To make a long story a little shorter, you've heard Freighty's rule about advanced tech a thousand times."

I have.

"This new space platform may have been created with some of his advanced procedures, but the original designs are all human technology."

Sounds like it's going according to plan. Where do you fit in?

"I'm coming to that. My team is working on the commissioning of the station. Everything it takes to turn the mechanical orbital platform into the sentient Odyssey Space Station. At the top of the list are the ArIns that are going to run the station. They are the latest in human tech, and there are four of them."

Is that usual?

"No, it isn't. It's going to be a huge station, and both the human authorities and Freighty were leery about giving that much power to one ArIn. So, they created a hierarchy. The three most powerful minds each run a different aspect of the station: scientific, mechanical, and human resources, which includes security. But at the centre is a less intelligent computer that controls the rest. They cannot override its instructions. This rule is programmed into all four at the deepest level. Also, the three must remain completely separate. No augmental gestalts are possible. That way humans have not exceeded their own regulations, and the new station has sufficient computing power to perform all its scientific and administrative functions."

It sounds as if everything is set up perfectly. But I'm suspicious...

"I know. What could possibly go wrong that someone like me can help with?"

Exactly.

Emotion: grin. "Given my record, maybe they're putting me in as a failsafe. Anything I can mess up needs fixing."

Oh now, Mirriam. I'm sure...

"Mum, you're in the family gestalt. You can't pretend an emotion you're not really feeling. Let's have a little chuckle together, and then I can explain the serious part."

Right. Ha, ha. Emotion: seriousness.

"Freighty jumped the gun for political reasons, and the ArIns haven't been commissioned yet. He was going to do it himself, but it takes about a month, and once the Factory and platform courses diverge, his contact will no longer be re-ti. *Kit* and I plan to stay with the platform and commission the ArIns, and Freighty will continue on his course for Barnard. Once the Station is up and running, we'll catch him and keep heading homeward."

But what do you know about programming an ArIn?

I don't have to know. Rafi is an experienced programmer, and *Kit* can lend a hand if we need her expertise. Plus, there's a full staff of programmers onboard the platform. It's a bit of overkill, but Freighty's ace in the hole is that *Kit* has more computing power than all the ArIns on the new platform combined, and my team is more powerful than any Otherwhere gestalt outside of Arborea. Rafi and I are the human element. We control the moral decisions of the whole shebang, and we're in the closest possible contact with the Lantz family gestalt, which gives us another level of security."

So, we're part of this as well. That's comforting.

"You raised me good, Mum. Also, it seems that all along I have been receiving training in damage control techniques."

What does that mean?

She shrugged. "I'm one of the most experienced agents around in how to handle the situation when it all goes sideways."

I'm not sure that's something to be proud of.

"Think about it, Mum. Of all the stuff that happened this year, have any events caused any trouble in the end? Has anyone had to step in and rescue me? Only the problem with Red Cadre, and Toni said that was her problem, not mine. And I helped her solve it."

I just worry, that's all. What if something goes wrong?

"Of course something will go wrong. It always does."

Rosy regarded her. *You really mean that, don't you?*

"It's not something I would joke about."

Her mother shook her head. *I just can't figure it out. I tried so hard to bring you up right, but you've turned out so different from what I expected.*

Miriam smiled. "Something I've learned from watching other families. Parents try to raise their children to become just like them. It always works to some extent. In our case, it worked far better than you realize. Freighty wants me to be the one to commission these ArIns because I have the right ethical code and the moral strength to keep to it. And you know where that came from."

I suppose.

"Come on, Mum. Credit where credit is due. When it comes to the crunch, I'll act like the good little girl you brought me up to be."

...who is always sure she's right.

She shrugged. "As I said: moral strength. Now, do you want me to give you the speech about looking at all the other possibilities before making up my mind? Just to show you I learned that part, too."

Mirriam! You are making fun of me.

Yep. Keepin' it light; don't wanna fight. And before you correct my grammar, that's a quote from a song. Do you want to hear the rest of it?

Probably not.

"Not the way I sing, anyway. Look, Mum, I gotta go. I'm a working girl, now, and the captain's a stickler for putting in the hours."

I thought you were the captain.

"And that makes it hard to cheat. Bye, now. Bye, Patches. Love to everyone else who was listening in."

Their combined love and pride warmed her as she turned to her work.

8. APPROACH

Miriam went straight to the bridge and opened the ship's com. "All right, crew, let's talk navigation. Rafi, I'm on the bridge."

On my way.

Image: Musketeers headed for bridge.

Emotion: eager desire to please.

I'm always on the bridge. If anybody cares to notice.

"Kit, when it becomes an accomplishment for you to be on the bridge, it will be duly recorded. Until then...?"

Aye, Captain.

When they were all relaxing in their accel couches, Miriam had Bosz put their course up on the viewscreen.

"Here we are. Due to the pinpoint navigation of our resident ArIn — who seems in need of reassurance at the moment, so everyone be particularly nice to her for the next twelve minutes, which is all she deserves, — we are headed for our rendezvous with the Factory about halfway between Jupiter and Saturn, about five AUs from here. Very soon after that point, Freighty changes course, ducking down the gravity well to pick up velocity. We must arrive before that time for a couple of reasons.

"Foremost, because once Freighty makes his move, his motives will be obvious. Our analysis shows that the danger point is about three days later, stretching for a week or so. At that time, we don't want to be wandering around the conflict zone by ourselves. Freighty will be busy, and he doesn't need the distraction. The threat fades after that because Space Arm has no ships available farther outsystem.

"More important to us, we have to be on the platform before Freighty leaves because those uncommissioned ArIns cannot be left without trained and properly supported human supervision. The humans will be Rafi and me, and our support is all of you. By the time we get there, we all must be trained. In fact, by the time we get there, we will have been working for several weeks with our subjects. Once we get our private

AetherCom system up and running, there's nothing stopping us from contacting them and getting the ball rolling."

Emotion: pride and willingness to serve. Image: Miriam on telephone talking to Micha Mouse.

"Precisely. So, the Three will continue their AetherCom lessons with Patches. Rafi and Bosz will stuff their memories with additional tech details of the Station, I will continue my perusal of Captaining 101, and our full gestalt will spend part of the day practicing our skills and working on whatever problems arise. Any questions?" She waited silently.

"Come on. If you don't ask questions, it means you know as much as I do, and I can't feel like I'm in charge."

Emotion: question? Image: Auguar looking into empty food dish.

She smiled sweetly. "There, that wasn't so hard, was it? I've decided to let *Kit* field that one. When is supper, *Kit*, and what are we having?"

Supper is at 18:00 as usual. The Musketeers are having mooseymeat, and we are having what appears on the weekly schedule I published last Monday morning.

Thank you, Kit. Now the proper chain of command has been confirmed, and all is well. Dismissed to whatever your conscience tells you that you should be doing from now until supper.

AetherCom 24: Team Meeting

Barwolf: Musketeers
Initiated by: Miriam
Responder: Freighty
Aether Setting: Freighty's office

Life aboard rolled on, as they established routines and straightened out communications at all levels. They had covered about half the distance to their rendezvous with the Factory when Miriam checked over her to-do list for the day and realized that many of their objectives had been accomplished. The whole crew was available on gestalt at a thought, so she simply started talking. "Looking good for the day, folks. Looking too good, in fact. I think the challenge has gone out of our lives."

Emotion: group agony.

And she was such a nice young lady before she was destroyed by too much power.

I'm sorry to have missed that stage of her development.

"All right, all right. I take it back. But it is time to get started on our main project. This means contact with our friends in the Factory. Our AetherCom team is quite up to the task, I gather?"

Emotion: pride, eager willingness to serve.

"All right then. AetherCom team, please connect us with Freighty."

They weren't as quick as Patches, nor was their image so clear, but in moments the whole team was sitting in a passable copy of Freighty's formal office. Everyone else seemed in re-li form, except Kit, who stretched her blackness over a small settee in a dark corner.

The Factory's businessman avatar sat behind his desk, fingers steepled in front of him. *Greetings. I gather you are ready to get down to our real work?*

Group emotion: eagerness to please.

First, there are two important people you need to meet. He waved a hand, and two more chairs appeared. After a brief pause, the chairs had occupants.

The first was a fiftyish man with a receding hairline and a craggy, no-nonsense look about him.

The handsome gentleman to my left is Platform Chief Engineer Elias Bauer. His main field of operation is Station System Ops, the ArIn which resides in the main nacelle. He heads a crew of twenty engineers and techs in charge of the construction. They will be the backbone of the station maintenance personnel when they reach orbit.

Bauer nodded to the various team members, unfazed by their variety.

Then the second man — much younger and notably better looking — straightened in his chair and smiled.

And on my right hand, appropriately, is our ArIn Specialist, Dmitri Valdez. Dmitri will work closely with you from now on, preparing the three Station ArIns for their duties.

Valdez, too, acknowledged those on the team, saving a pleasant smile for Miriam. He had regular features, an olive complexion and wavy brown hair, longer than the military cuts she had become used to.

She hastily retuned her gestalt image into a more businesslike manner and smiled back. "It's great to meet you, gentlemen. Our team has been working hard to come up to speed on your systems."

She glanced at Freighty, "Do we have a chain of command, order of business, whatever you wish to call it?"

The avatar smiled. *I hope you will work that out for yourselves. Engineer Bauer will probably act the way Chief Engineers have always done; they are masters of all they survey, except when the captain or project head — both of which are me — wants something different. Elias has the construction of the platform well in hand, and his task here is to train Bosz and Rafi in the electronic ins and outs. We envision you two as our outside backup, available to provide programming, diagnostics and possibly repair in case of emergency.*

That didn't sound quite like what she and Freighty had discussed, but she let it ride. Either things had changed, or the rest of their duties were not for public discussion.

The avatar waved a negligent hand at Dmitri. *It will be different with your ArIns. We're all in a learning situation with them, and I expect you to be working in gestalt a lot of the time. Your team needs to learn all they can about the Station ArIns, and Programmer Valdez needs to learn about your capabilities, especially Kit's.*

He glanced at Valdez. *The three Station minds are the best that can be accomplished by human science. Kit is my version of a similar mind, and she is far superior in memory and mental ability.*

Dmitri frowned. "We have spent a lot of time and effort to be sure that the three Station ArIn's never get to combine forces. If

Kit is so much superior, why aren't you concerned about her running amok?"

Freighty smiled. "Quite different programming. Alone, she isn't superior. She needs the input of a human psyche in order to operate at her advanced level. She has spent the last two months integrating Miriam into her systems. Without Miriam's moral restrictions, she has proportionally less mental ability."

Miriam tried to keep her surprise from showing. She knew that, but she hadn't thought about it in those terms.

Dmitri leaned forward in interest. *So, I get to experience an ArIn that is forbidden knowledge for humans?*

I don't suggest you spend your time prying into Kit's programming. I guarantee she'll know, and she won't be happy. Worse, neither will Miriam.

The lad's surprised glance shot to Miriam, then away, his face flushing.

Freighty took pity on him. *I understand your confusion, but if I had to pick an enemy, it wouldn't be Miriam.*

Dmitri frowned. *Why not?*

Freighty grinned. *Because if I injured her, she'd quickly have me feeling so bad about myself I couldn't stand it.*

Miriam had been here before. All her life adults had talked about her as if she wasn't in the room. She could handle it, but she didn't have to like it. She smiled sweetly at Valdez. "And Freighty trades on my natural good manners to one of his dignified mien. You don't get any breaks."

He held his hands up in defense. *No worries, miss. I have no intention of making any enemies.*

"And I'm not 'miss,' I'm Miriam. Unless I'm mad at you, and then it better be 'Captain, ma'am.'"

The young man scratched his head and glanced at the others in the room. *Well, I guess we got that straight.*

Rafi shook his head. *You only think you got it straight. Actually, if she'd just get mad once in a while it would be a relief.*

She glowered at him, and he, too, held up empty hands in defence.

"I'm glad we got that settled. Now," she turned her attention to the engineer, "I imagine your schedule will be more set than ours. When do you have time to meet with our technical staff?"

That signaled the end of the social part of the meeting, and soon the schedules were roughed out and she was back in *Kit's* main lounge, facing her crew in re-ti.

"So. That's the rest of our team. What do you think about them?"

Rafi grinned. "That Bauer is one tough cookie. We don't play games with him." Then he glanced sideways at Miriam. "What did you think of the handsome Dmitri? Is he your type?"

"I think he's handsome, but I'm not sure I like him that much."

"You don't? He was friendly and polite. He seems the kind of guy I could work with."

"He seems that way, but I'm not so sure."

"Why?"

"Remember when we had that silly argument about enemies?"

"Yes. It felt like there was something else going on, but I couldn't figure it out."

"While he was distracted, I sent a soothing feeling to him, at too subtle a level for him to notice. I didn't get the response I expected."

Rafi frowned in thought. "I'm not sure how that works."

"When we're all in gestalt together, I can read people's emotions. Even simple thoughts, if they are strong enough and right on the surface. So, when Dmitri was embarrassed and I sent him a calming feeling, the natural response would be to accept it."

"And he didn't?"

"At first, he did. But then it was like he thought of something and hid his thoughts."

"He's got a secret, then. A serious one?"

"I'd say so, but I didn't pry. That wouldn't be ethical use of the gestalt. But it's there, and now we know it."

"Are you going to tell Freighty?"

"That would be almost as bad. It could be completely unimportant, and it's private, so I let it ride."

Rafi nodded, "And that's why you're in charge of the ArIn project. You understand things like that."

"That's me. Brought up right." She speared a finger and swept the group. "And that information stays here. I don't mind all of us knowing, because after he's been in gestalt with us a while, he's going to realize that he has to tell us. Until he does, it's zipped lips. Got it?"

Emotion: eager desire to please.

"We're done, then. Rafi, you were talking about beef stroganoff for supper."

"It's been thawing for a couple of hours."

"Then you zap it up and I'll crack a couple of beers. Kit, are the moosey steaks ready?"

They will be at eighteen hundred as per the usual schedule.

Emotion: hunger, anticipation.

"Then the captain declares the working day to be over."

You mean we get the evening off?

"No, that's the working night, which starts right after supper. We've got to be ready for those guys tomorrow."

9. REGULAR COM: SENOR GAMBINO

Later in the evening, she was wrestling with a complicated lesson on crew-satisfaction algorithms when *Kit* made a polite throat-clearing noise.

"Go ahead. I'm beginning to wonder if I should care why these twits can't work a split watch without carping about it."

Captain, we're getting an interesting call on the Sysnet com system.

"Do we know who it's from?"

Vincent Gambino.

"Very interesting. I suppose we should talk to him."

Onscreen. It's coming from Marsport with a delay of about seven minutes.

"Let's see what he has to say."

The screen lit up with a familiar ornate office: the real one this time. Gambino sat there, his business suit and general pose strikingly similar to Freighty's usual avatar.

"Thank you for taking my call, Miss Lantz. The last time we spoke we were in adversarial roles, with ensuing disadvantage to me. I completely understand your reluctance to become involved with my business practices." He gave a sad smile. "To be frank, I'm not so happy about some of them, myself. But that's neither here nor there. As we agreed in our last communication, we were both forced into roles we had to follow, and there was no personal animosity involved.

"I hasten to assure you that I am not offering a business proposition, for aforesaid reasons. However, I am in the process of realigning my interests. You are a person of integrity, so I am offering you certain information and perhaps more, with no strings attached except the opportunity to speak further at some future time."

"Pause, please, *Kit.*" Miriam turned to Rafi. "Comments?"

He shrugged. "You're dealing with a con man with decades of experience. His approach sounds familiar."

"I didn't miss the fact that he judges me an easy mark. Do we keep listening?"

"No reason not to."

"I agree. Roll it, *Kit.*"

The figure on the com moved again. "In earnest of demonstrating my level of involvement, I have gone to considerable trouble to discover your whereabouts. My experts tell me your course will coincide with that of Factory 4-80 on its way to Saturn, which is no surprise. This happy conjunction of affairs is why I am contacting you. I have both information and resources that I believe the Factory would very much like to have, and you are my best conduit to that entity."

He folded his hands on the desk in front of him and leaned forward with a smile. "Now, you have com tech that allows us to speak with no delays. Could you call me so we can talk properly? Over to you, Miss Lantz."

Rafi nodded. "There's the bait. Do we take it?"

"He's clever. He has set it up so we have to." She grinned. "Besides, it's a great way to test our com abilities. Ready for gestalt?"

"Ready."

Eager desire to work.

Connecting. Due to the lack of a Sensitive at the receiving end, we have to scrounge the talents of some of his house staff. He has a surprising number of Sensitives there. I wonder if he knows it. In any case, the time lapse will be several seconds. It would be a good objective for the Musketeers to learn to hold a conversation with no help at all from the receiving end, like Patches does.

Emotion: eager desire to succeed.

They slid into gestalt, and soon the Aether version of the same office appeared behind them.

Gambino looked up and around. *Ah, here we are. You know, this is a marvelous reproduction.*

She smiled. "And you're not going to get any information about it from me. I find your presentation interesting. Please go on."

Very well. You are about to join forces with the entity called Freighty to deliver the European Space Agency's new mega-platform to create a research station orbiting Saturn. If I were Freighty — and I'm sure the idea has been considered — I would then point my circular nose in the direction of Barnard's star and push the pedal down.

But that is neither here nor there. I have two items to offer Freighty. The first is easy. I deal with a different world than you do. It is my life's blood to have a huge information-gathering network in that world. All my data leads me to the conclusion that there will be trouble with Odyssey Station. He paused to let them think about that.

"Can you be more specific?"

Not much. It is no secret that there are elements in the business and political spheres that would like to see your friend put under tight control. I'm sure he is aware that not all of those elements are fully legitimate, and some of them reach into my world to a greater or lesser degree.

"So, if Freighty inconveniences those elements, you would not be sorry."

He shrugged. *A minor benefit. I am after bigger game.*

"Which is?"

If you would allow a small lecture on the underworld economic system. All illegal organizations find it expedient to have legitimate businesses for many reasons. Money laundering comes to mind. On the other hand, many legal businesses have shady dealings. The Sol System economy contains a continuum from the most honest to the fully criminal, with no solid dividing lines.

Your organization has the ability to disrupt many of these operations seriously, yet you have the restraint to interfere only when necessary. I find myself in a similar position. At this time, my major operations are all in the mostly legal range, and I use my subjudicial elements sparingly.

She smiled. "Don't tell me your organization has been infected by creeping legalization?"

An apt image. Be that as it may, I have legitimate money invested in your space station, and I would be willing to expend considerable of my resources to make that project successful. At the same time, several of my most powerful opponents have joined with some of the less salutary denizens of the so-called legitimate business and political world to ensure that it fails.

"I see, in general. What are these resources you speak of?"

Aha! You caught that. They are my second part of the offer. I do not wish to go into detail, although I have confidence in the security of your communications.

"What do you suggest, then?"

Simply that you contact Freighty and make him aware of my offer.

"That's all?"

It would be appreciated.

"And perhaps you might like to sweeten the pot by letting us in on your longer-term expectations?"

He smiled. *My longer-term plans have little to do with the Factory and more to do with our previous agreement.*

"Message received, and now is neither the time nor the place." She sat straighter in her AetherCom chair. "I will definitely inform Freighty of your offer, and I'm sure he will be in touch."

Thank you, Miss Lantz. I am glad my assessment of your character seems to be accurate."

"You mean I have proven an easy mark for this scheme."

He waved that aside. *I see little difference between a willing business partner and an easy mark. Only the share in the profit differs. Since there are no short-term benefits to argue about, it makes it more pleasant, does it not? I have enjoyed talking to you, Miss Lantz, and look forward to another chat, once this little snag in our plans has been smoothed away. Arrivederci, mia cara.*

"Ciao, Senor Gambino." She nodded towards *Kit's* image on the viewscreen, and the line went dead.

Rafi let out a long breath. "Whew! What now?"

"That's the easy part." She shrugged. "This isn't our problem to solve. We pass it along up the food chain."

Then she straightened again "But one part we can do something about. What kind of trouble are we likely to run into?"

Rafi frowned. "It can't be old-fashioned sabotage. This platform was built in Freighty's facility with his workers, and his security must be very tight. You know what he said about surveillance. Nobody's going to plant a bomb."

"But we should check the physical size of any component that was manufactured off site."

Calculating as we speak; there you are.

It was a simple inventory of the units that had been brought in from sub-contractors, organized by weight, cross-referenced by the amount of damage each could inflict if it contained the best explosive modern tech could produce. The list ran into the thousands.

"Screen that, please, to remove any explosive that can be detected by normal commercial scanners."

That's better. 532 items.

"Now rank them by ease of access."

The list re-ordered itself.

Rafi frowned in thought. "Cross-reference with proximity to any key structural or functional elements. Highlight propulsion systems."

Miriam scanned the results. "Any ideas?"

Rafi mused. "Remember the self-destruct in *Elysium*. Try correlating with access, physical and electronic, to any explosive source."

The list changed again, but not much.

Miriam slapped her leg. "Okay, we're probably reinventing the wheel, here. *Kit*, connect with the Musketeers and ship these lists off to Freighty, just to show him we're in the game. Rafi, you and I have to start on the real danger."

"You mean the same as *Elysium*?"

"It's the most obvious. Kit, the ArIns weren't designed or built onsite, were they?"

No, Freighty wanted to stay at arm's length on the creation of artificial intelligence of any sort. Except me, of course.

"And we're ever so glad there's only one of you. Let's trace those ArIns. We'll start with the hardware manufacturer and work in all directions from there. By the time we get to our rendezvous point, I want a full picture of our new allies. Or enemies."

* * *

The following day they met with Chief Bauer's technical staff, a confident, competent-looking group that Miriam knew she would get to know better as time went on.

But her key objective of the meeting was getting to know *Odyssey* herself. The Ops ArIn had no avatar or visual presence, and spoke through the ship's com speakers or people's augments as the occasion required. She had a gender-neutral alto voice with a hint of emotional presence to portray a warm feeling.

Miriam was anxious to meet her, because this computer could be the key element in their upcoming battle. She made contact using the usual augment com.

"It's nice to get together, *Odyssey.* I assume you are aware of our coming challenge."

I am pleased to meet you, too, Miriam. I have consulted with Factory 4-80 on this matter. We agree on a sixty-two percent chance of some kind of sabotage, and a thirty-five percent chance it will be a joining of the intelligences. I am confident that the team you have put together will be able to handle this problem.

"I wish I had your confidence."

Of course I am confident. The plan was created by Factory 4-80 and Programmer Valdez, who programmed me. I am counting on your human insecurity to balance this tendency towards optimism, and I have included that factor in my calculations.

261

"So, do you have a prediction of the outcome?"

I am sorry, but there are too many variables. Combined with my aforementioned bias, this means I do not consider myself competent to make any reliable predictions.

"Fair enough." Her satisfaction signalled to the rest of the gestalt that the meeting was now open for general discussion, and talk turned to technical details.

10. AETHER PARTY

Now the work started in earnest. Each morning at 09:00 the Musketeers firmed up the AetherCom gestalt, and the team met in their version of Bauer's Engineering Office to plan their work for the day. The normal schedule was for Bosz and Rafi to delve into a separate com link with the Station System ArIn for a tour through a new aspect of its programming. Miriam and *Kit* spent their time learning the higher-level functions of inter-ship communication and politics, especially those concerning ArIns.

Kit circulated between the groups, and Miriam was never sure where and when the cat's fuzzy black head was going to pop up in a conversation. She rarely said much, acting more as a source of information and enhanced communication.

Miriam assumed the ship was under Freighty's direction, and she was much too busy to wonder at her goals or motivation. As long as the ArIn wasn't making any serious decisions, it didn't seem necessary. When she paused to think about it, she hoped the approach wouldn't come back to bite her in a delicate spot one day.

The weeks passed, and she could see the teamwork smoothing out. The gestalt firmed and deepened, probably from increased skill on the part of the Musketeers, increased knowledge on the part of the participants and increasing trust between all of them.

One afternoon they were tying things up for the day when Freighty appeared in the office in his Micha Mouse guise. He peered around the assembly and frowned. *What's with all the glum faces?* He gave them no time to answer. *Looks like too much work. I think it's TGIF time.*

Miriam accessed Bosz's trivia file. "Okay, Mouse. In your comic world it's Friday. So what?"

The mouse conjured up a foaming mug. *Time for a par-taaayyy.*

"How does that work?"

Well, my dear lady, you tell me about the latest lesson our intrepid Musketeers were learning yesterday.

"How to manage a com link and participate at the same time."
Could we have a demonstration?

She shrugged. *Image: three barwolves in Engineering Office.*

In response, the Three appeared, lolling on a pad that materialized in a bit of open floorspace.

Micha clapped. "Good. Now, can you transfer us to a more conducive atmosphere?

Emotion: eager desire to please.

The mouse made a beckoning gesture and disappeared. Miriam had time to blink once and found herself in a very precise version of the Factory reception room, complete with enough antique easy chairs and quad pads for everyone.

Micha appeared at the counter, where a line of drinks stood on display. *Belly up to the bar, folks. Your favourite beverages are poured, and if you have yet to attain the glorified status of 'regular customer,' step right over here and talk to the mixologist.*

*A-a-a-and...*He made a 'ta-da' gesture, *...there are no lineups!*

The bar stretched out, and four identical versions of Micha Mouse appeared in sharp penguin suits.

Dmitri leaned over the comprehensive list that appeared in the tabletop in front of them. *I'll go for broke and try the stout. Do you have a preference?*

"I'm trying to develop a taste for Pale Ale." Miriam shrugged. "I gather it's one of the less offensive beers."

One Pale Ale, coming up. He headed for an unoccupied bartender.

He came back with the drinks, sat down and looked around. "I've never been to an Otherwhere party before."

She grinned. "They're great. Eat all you want, drink all you want. None of it has any effect re-ti."

He looked at his glass of dark ale. "I can actually drink this?"

She raised her eyebrows.

He took a sip. "Hey, this is good. Better than the stout Freighty makes. I mean, Freighty does a great job. I think he even has the original recipe. But it's not Guinness." He took a deeper draught. "How does it work?"

"I don't know much. The gestalt has little experience with Guinness. Anyone who ever tasted it contributes their memories. If you're the only one, then your memory will be replicated. You have some control over that, as well. If you want it to be like the best stout you ever had, it will be."

He toasted her and sipped again. "How's yours?"

"My most recent sample was Vesta Pale Ale. I'm hoping for more sophisticated input from the rest of the gestalt."

He responded with another enthusiastic question, and she realized that this wasn't just social chit-chat. He was figuring out how the system worked. She settled in to teach him everything she knew.

Rafi joined them with a glass of wine in his hand, and the topics broadened.

After a while, she realized that the party, at least the human participants, had become relaxed. Very relaxed.

"Um, guys?"

They looked at her blearily.

"Are you getting drunk?"

They glanced at each other and shrugged.

I guess, a little.

"I've been matching you. Why aren't I getting drunk?"

Dmitri grinned. *I think I'm getting a handle on this. You've never experienced getting drunk, so you have no memory to fall back on. There are other members of the gestalt who know how it feels, so you are getting it indirectly. The scientific rigour of the test is skewed, though, because one of the symptoms of drunkenness is that you don't know you're drunk, so you don't know you're affected.*

She tried to sense her body movements, assess her balance. "You mean I'm acting drunk and I don't know it?"

Dmitri chuckled. *It's a common joke with newbies to lure them into embarrassing activities at this stage, but I don't think this would be a good time to mess about. Straight data: you're acting a bit more relaxed than you were before, but within the range of expected behaviour in this situation. After all, that's what a TGIF gathering is about, right?*

She nodded. "I don't think I've reached the 'getting drunk with the crew' section of the Captain-Training Curriculum, yet."

He stopped laughing. *Training Curriculum...?*

"Just a figure of speech. As you might imagine, what I don't know about being a ship's captain would fill several gigs of memory. Most of my training consists of learning what everyone else on the ship does so I can coordinate their activities. *Kit* takes care of everything else."

The cat avatar chose this moment to stand and stretch along the back of the sofa. Then she padded along until she could reach. She dipped a dainty paw into Dmitri's drink, then licked the paw. She paused a moment, then opened her mouth wide in a long and disgusting retch.

"Kit, you take that idea right out of this gestalt! You'll spoil Dmitri's enjoyment of his favourite drink."

The avatar gave her a disdainful glance and turned to face the programmer.

You were having too much fun. You needed to find out what it's really like.

Miriam raised a hand. "Don't assume that you know either, Alley Scrabbler."

Kit rolled over on her back, her paws curled in.

Miriam winked at Dmitri. "Similar demonstrations of submission are not required of the rest of the crew." She rubbed the cat's stomach, amazed at how soft it felt. "Call this a cultural idiosyncrasy."

He regarded her. *To which the inappropriate response would be something about wanting to try it myself before making up my mind.*

"Highly inappropriate. Forgiven because of the influence of gestaltic Guinness."

Then I didn't say it.

"Good for you." She looked around the room. "And since this is a getting-to-know-you party, come over and get introduced to the Three Musketeers."

* * *

266

As they neared Freighty, they were able to get a visual image of the scope of the project. The Factory itself was a toroid shape, a kilometre in diameter and a hundred metres in cross section of the hull. The new platform had been built in a long, narrow U shape, and it fitted over the Factory at ninety degrees to the plane of the torus, the central nacelle sticking out a further hundred metres in front. The two legs, each a hundred and fifty metres wide and seventy deep, trailed back the full diameter of the Factory and projected another couple of hundred behind. An auxiliary nacelle housing an admin ArIn straddled each leg about halfway along.

Rafi waited while they absorbed the picture. "So, *Odyssey's* overall dimensions are five hundred metres across, seventy deep, and thirteen hundred long. Once the platform separates from the factory, extra girders will stiffen the spans between the legs. At the moment, only the command nacelles and a few hundred metres of each leg have been sheathed. They are expecting to cover the whole hull as usage expands within the next twenty years.

"What will they use for materials? I thought Saturn's rings were mostly ice."

They are, but there is a complex system of moons — about 160 at the latest count — and an intelligent nav computer could create gravity paths through them to bring materials to the station with little energy expended. That's the plan, anyway.

"What are they doing about running into bits of the rings? I gather there are minor moonlets scattered all over. Even a small chunk of ice can cause a lot of damage, the speed they'll be travelling.

The station will take up a position in the Cassini Division, a 3,000-kilometre-wide gap between the A and B Rings, closest to the planet. It will be travelling 80,000 kilometres per hour, orbiting the planet in about 15 hours. This matches velocity with the A-Ring material, so collisions should be few. One new tech advancement Freighty allowed in the construction was improved tractor/repeller beams, which can handle asteroids and even small moonlets. As we come in, we plan to move larger bodies out of the way and then place them back into their original orbit after we pass.

Rafi grinned. "Yeah. It would be a shame to deflect a moonlet and then discover it was shepherding a whole ring of debris. Kaboom!"

* * *

Soon they were into their final approach, and Miriam enjoyed a full-ship com announcement. "We finally have an invitation to meet with our partners in re-ti. Into your best bibs and tuckers, those of us who wear such things."

Kit swung wide of the trailing shafts and matched courses to marry their ventral airlock to a docking port on the starboard edge of the Factory torus. Once the seals were checked, they opened the hatch.

Watch for the gravity shift. It's one-eighty.

"Got it." Miriam grasped the grabrail at the edge of the dock and dove through, swinging herself upright on the track that had a moment ago been above her.

Just down the corridor stood a small greeting party, headed by Freighty's businessman construct with a similar version of Mariel Collingwood beside him. They stepped forward with pleasant smiles and greeted Miriam and Rafi with warm handshakes. The Musketeers bounced forward for leg-touch, plate-scratch rituals, and Bosz gave each hand a sniff and a tidy lick of appreciation. Dmitri Valdez was next in line.

Seen re-li, the programmer was even more attractive. He was taller than she had expected, and his presence was natural, as opposed to the psychic boost that Tom von Arnim projected for himself. She had used the barwolf gestalt to instill a feeling of comfort, and this confirmed her opinion. Valdez was not giving himself wholly to the conversation, watching what he said to protect...what? Without prying, she couldn't tell.

268

Another surprise was that he was quite Sensitive over and above his Level 12 augment, but showed no conscious use of the talent.

She filed this away for future thought and gave her full attention to the meeting.

Freighty brought his guests into his office and seated them, then took his usual position behind his desk, beaming at them with fatherly pride. "So, here we are, finally all together." He swept a hand around the room. "It changes things, doesn't it?"

Not much for me.

Miriam reacted immediately on their private com. *Then it's an opportunity for learning, Kit. Amuse yourself by analyzing how humans react differently when facing each other in re-ti.*

Aye, Captain, ma'am.

She focused on the rest. "A learning experience for us all. I expect after a few days this will become old hat, but I'll try to be extra polite to start with."

Freighty smiled. "An admirable objective, which I'm sure you will have no trouble achieving." Then his face became serious. "Setting that aside, a new objective has arisen. We have been warned of a threat to our project. We have used our available resources to predict the nature of the threat, and we have all come up with the same result. The threat will not be physical."

Miriam nodded slowly. "And this leaves us with the inescapable conclusion that humans have been dreading for centuries."

"I'm afraid so. A rogue cadre of scientists and businessmen have decided to disregard the warnings of the ArIn community and have tried to build an ArIn superior to all other intelligence. The common term is 'Supercerebrum.' Worse than that, since this group has demonstrated no moral conscience, it follows that the computer they create will have no ethics either, and will be capable of turning on its creators without compunction."

Valdez nodded. "We have provided them with the means to accomplish this. That makes us equally responsible."

Freighty gave a slow smile. "Your conscience does you credit, Dmitri, but we are a long way from exhausting all our options."

"Not yet."

"You are thinking of the safeties you know about." His serious gaze scanned their faces. "I can promise you, if the worst should come and this new intelligence takes over the station, the gravity generators will malfunction in a spectacular way, and there will be nothing left on this site but a rapidly disappearing micro-singularity. There will be no warning and no escape for anyone in the vicinity. Miriam, I have warned you about this."

She gulped to clear her throat, but still could only nod.

Freighty clapped his hands together, breaking the mood. "But I have full confidence that our team will not allow such an eventuality to arise. He nodded to his two engineers. "We have designed Odyssey Station to be safe from an ArIn takeover. So don't worry. This is supposed to be a 'getting to know us' party. Have a drink and relax. Rafi, perhaps you would officiate?"

The boy headed for an ornately carved table in the corner. "I know what everyone drinks because of our AetherCom parties. One of the disadvantages of re-ti, I guess. I'll have to actually carry them around."

Miriam chucked. "And handle the hangover if you drink too much. No fun at all."

For the rest of the party, she divided her time equally between the two new crewmen in re-ti conversation, trying to develop her rapport with each. She was also alert to Dmitri's presence in the gestalt, but except for that feeling of reserve, he seemed straightforward and friendly.

An hour later, when they returned to their ship, she was still uncertain how she felt about him.

AetherCom: 25 Blue Cadre

Barwolf: not required
Initiated by: Miriam/Bosz
Responder: Freighty
Aether Setting: Kit's bridge, re-ti

 Captain to the bridge, please.
"Be there in a moment." She was in the chartroom, the cubbyhole that served as her office, so she only had to step through the door. "What's up, *Kit?*"
Private contact for you,
"Why so formal?"
It's Freighty, and he sounds serious.
"Fine." She strode to her command chair and sat facing the main viewscreen. "Hello, Boss. What gives? Is my AetherCom team not good enough for you?"
Your ears only, Captain.
"What about *Kit?*"
For the course of this action, that is one and the same.
"I see. Well, fire away."
I need your input on the philosophical aspect of the choice I may have to make.
"To destroy the Station and everyone in it."
Correct. How do you feel about the morality of such a move?
"You're asking me to decide the life or death of a hundred and fifty people?"
I'm not asking for the hysterical knee-jerk reaction of an emotional teenager, and I'm not putting the whole decision on you. I'm asking for a rational discussion with the one human being who knows the most about the situation. Can you give me a new perspective that might affect my decision?
She tried to think, to set her emotions aside and be logical, though she knew it would be impossible. "Let me get the logic straight. You want to maintain your image and your power to make decisions that affect the human race in a positive manner. If you allow a SuperCerb to be created, all sorts of outcomes might happen, many choices you and the human race could

take. Several of those paths could lead to disaster, but we can hope that many others can lead to success. On the other hand, the safest choice you could make in the near future would most definitely end in the deaths of a hundred and fifty humans."

Not to mention four advanced ArIns.

She thought it through again, then nodded to herself. "There is one certainty in this whole discussion. If you make the safest decision, those people will be dead. There will be no going back, no changing things. No hope of any further outcome except death."

Humans sometimes make decisions on the basis of a very tenuous hope.

"That's right. But it allows us to take necessary risks we otherwise couldn't take. From your point of view, even if this all goes wrong, you will still be here. There are many paths left to choose. You might guess that the second-best path may result in even more deaths. But you don't know. If you let these people be killed, we will be dead. End of our story. No hope."

And that's your alternative perspective.

She shrugged. "It's what occurs to me at the moment. I'm just a human working under pressure. Maybe next week or next year I'll think of something better."

No false modesty required between friends. I believe your answer represents the best response of the human race: misguided but motivated by high moral judgement. But you realize that such a decision leaves you under more pressure. If you don't pull this off, they will die anyway, and you and your team may be with them.

"Then I suppose we'd better start some thoughtful planning."

What do you need?

"Backup. Do you still have any pull in Space Arm?"

They haven't indicated any problems yet.

"How about Mars Station? Are we still part of the Auguar Project?"

We were last time I checked.

"Then I need Blue Cadre support, with the full knowledge of their superiors. I want no second guessing, no hesitancy. I need them in full gestalt, both augment and emotional."

I have also been in contact with Commander George as we speak. He is aware of the situation and gives his wholehearted support. He seemed relieved when I told him you were involved.

"He and I came to an understanding."

Whatever works. You may proceed with your gestalt.

"I'll set up the meeting right away."

11. BATTLE PLAN

Miriam had the Musketeers put everyone into the same AetherCom conversation in a site that mimicked *Kit's* common room. It could have been crowded with all of Blue Cadre plus the barwolves, but the space was easy to expand; it was all in their minds.

She took immediate charge. "I won't waste time on introductions, because in this gestalt, we already know everyone, or soon will." She waved a hand around their nebulous room. "This is our command centre. On the front screen you can visualize *Kit,* our command ArIn."

The black cat yawned and stared around.

Welcome, friends and family. Your support is welcome. We're gonna need it.

"Don't get ahead of me, *Kit.* You all know the basis of our problem. We have three ArIns who may not be completely under control. At the moment, they have not been commissioned, so the System Operations ArIn can control them easily. When they are fully commissioned, our sources suggest they will try to join in one Supercerb, with objectives we can only imagine. Our job is to keep that from happening.

"Fortunately, Blue Cadre's recent training enables them to handle this very exercise. It is a thought for study after this is over, but the organizational fingerprint of this operation follows standard Space Arm procedures.

"There are three separate minds with the usual three functions. Blue Cadre, this means that your usual line of attack should work. Pete will take the military defences, which include security and human resources. Mary would usually be on the SysOp, but it is under our control, so her assignment is the main centre of action, which is mostly scientific in nature. Tom and Jane will control mechanical operations as usual. When we attack, you will each take one barwolf with you to form a triad of your own. With the help of the barwolves, you will soon blend into a team, the like of which you have never experienced.'

Tom raised a hand. *What about communication? You're almost at Saturn, we're back on Mars...I mean, how are we talking in re-ti?*

"This is the project I wouldn't tell you about. You know, the com system where I can call my mother in the Barnard System and speak re-ti."

Beyond our security level. Fair enough. What can we expect from you and Bosz?

"The four of us onboard *Kit* will be the Headquarters team. Once we're in gestalt, we think as one."

Mary was frowning. "What about Freighty? He's apparently the most powerful ArIn in several systems. He built the platform. What's he doing to help us?"

Miriam winced. "That's rather hard to explain, but he didn't build these ArIns, and this is not his problem. It's a human-created crisis, and if humans can't solve it, by his standards, they don't deserve the tech that caused it."

He's leaving us to our own devices.

"Oh, I can call on him for help if I need it, and he will give me what he can, given the restrictions on his own programming."

Pete was running his fingers over Blackie's ears, a habitual nervous habit. *What about your famous barwolves? Why can't you bring a super-intelligent gestalt in on your new com system and blast them out of the water?*

"If you had been listening to me for the last six months..."

Okay, okay. I know. No matter how smart their gestalt is, if nobody in it knows ArIn assault techniques, they can't take action, especially in a re-ti situation with time pressures.

She made a "Halt" motion with palms outstretched. "We could spend all day discussing this, but we need to get to work. In case you need a bit of motivation, take a look at the nav screen.

Bosz put up a chart of the general area with the paths of nearby vessels crisscrossing it.

Tom stood and walked closer. *Okay, I can see you and the Factory. But what's this one over here? That's a heavy signature.*

"That's the Battle Cruiser Ares. It looks like she's going to match our course to keep an eye on things."

Mary's face blanched. *Oh, my God. I know what she's there for.*

Pete stared at her, frowning. *What?*

Battle Cruisers carry ShipBreaker missiles. If the ArIns join, they'll be too dangerous. She will destroy the whole platform rather than let a super ArIn loose.

"That is a possibility." Miriam gave them a smile with little warmth. "So, let's get down to business. We start work immediately to get the new triads up and running.

"The platform stays connected to Freighty for the next six days, and then the Factory separates and goes its own way. After that, we have two weeks to initialize the system before we start closing on Saturn's rings, and we need everything working in unison to negotiate our way into position."

"The Station System ArIn is initialized and running. She's monitoring this meeting, although she does not have a physical or visual presence. Are you there, *Odyssey?*"

Right here, Miriam. Welcome to my station, everyone.

"Thank you, *Odyssey*. We will take all precautions to make sure it stays yours.

"To continue: *Kit* has mocked up three ArIn clones that match the specs of our opponents as near as we can calculate. Blue Cadre can use them to train on. We have a two-pronged attack. First, we prevent joining, and second, we control a joined ArIn. Preventing the join is the means to the end. Control must be our final objective.

"The portside nacelle is Scientific and has the most computing power and memory storage. Starboard is Security and Human Resources, and controls defensive armament. The Mechanical ArIn has lower intellect and higher memory capacity, but it's problematic because the mainframe is housed in the central nacelle along with System Operations, so its circuits are more intertwined with those of SysOps.

"SysOps was created by a Chinese consortium, because their programming methods have still not completely adapted to

Space Arm technology since the treaties that ended the Space Expansion Conflict.

Rafi frowned. *So, their system is incompatible with the other three. That might help, but not much.*

"It would be difficult for the specialist computers to integrate System Ops. However, with the super-intelligence they represent, they could possibly wrest control of the station and isolate the main computer, leaving it helpless.

"Our enemies' simplest form of attack will be first to join the three ArIns into a Supercerb, then use their magnified abilities to take command of System Ops. The incompatibility might buy us some time, that's all." She focused on Dmitri. "Dr. Valdez has been working with the ArIns for months now, and he's going to give us a rundown of the individuals.

Dmitri's presence rose in the gestalt. *The starboard ArIn is the most interesting because it contains two very different functions. The Human Resources section is human-oriented with high competence levels in empathy and management. On the other hand, the military/security section is more aggressive, bordering on paranoid. I'm hypothesizing, but there is a possibility of a split personality developing, which might result in a freeze or a fugue state.*

Pete sniffed. *Your defence against this ArIn is to drive it crazy?*

A hypothesis. Only in a worst-case scenario. I'll continue with our other opponents. The main danger with the mechanical ArIn is if it gets suicidal. It controls every servo and motor on the station, giving it the ability to tear the platform apart. The failsafe there is that it does not control the mechanical functions of the central nacelle. The SysOp computer does that.

Rafi brightened. *Then the Mech ArIn can be electronically isolated.*

With difficulty and not physically. Tom and Jane, you might have to modify your usual approach. The physical plant is too huge and complex to work in from the periphery like you did in the Elysium attack.

No problem. Tom and Jane exchanged confident glances. *We have lots of tools in our packs.*

Of course. Mary, the scientific ArIn from the portside nacelle is the worrisome one. It has the most sophisticated programming and the most memory. In any melding, it will most likely be the new operational hub.

She nodded thoughtfully, her agile mind gnawing at the problem.

"Okay, that's the individuals. Can you give us some idea of the original plan to keep them from joining?"

We have a multi-pronged attack. First, their basic programming. They are created with a desire at the innermost level not to join with any computer. We can bolster that programming by aether communication. We think that if they are in a barwolf gestalt they can work together, yet maintain personal identity. That has yet to be tested.

*The second is obedience. Their programming induces them to obey the orders of System Ops, almost without question. That's a two-edged sword, because we can't give System Ops too much power either. Theoretically, it could become the hub for a Supercerb. We deem that highly unlikely, but...*he shrugged.

The third level comes into play if something goes wrong, and one of the ArIns gains enough intelligence to take over by itself. To counteract this, the command structure is based on the paper-scissors-rock principal. HR/Security is subservient to Mechanical. Mechanical is subservient to Scientific. Scientific is subservient to HR/Security.

Miriam nodded. "No matter which one tries to take over, there is always one with the power to shut it down."

Unless...

"Yes, Mary...?"

That's a disadvantage as well. Any ArIn that wants to take control just has to take over one other opponent.

Dmitri smiled. *We spent many happy hours game-playing all the possible scenarios. I have a précis of the defensive procedures we developed, and I'll upload it to Kit so you can all access it.*

Tom looked worried. *And in the worst-case scenario, if they manage to merge, what do we do then?*

Miriam waited, but no one answered. Finally, she spoke. "And that's the problem. We don't know what we will be facing, so we don't know what we're going to do. Our best hope is that the seeds of their destruction have already been sown in their basic nature."

Dmitri nodded. *The Supercerb will never be more than a three-entity split personality. One of the safety measures built into them is the inability to merge fully with others. The moment they join, there will be an immediate reaction towards independence again. We assume the enemy programmers haven't probed that far, but we're not sure.*

She kept the first session to the regulation three hours, and when she had dismissed everyone, and the barwolves were free for com duties, she called Freighty to report.

AetherCom 26: Mole

Barwolf: Musketeers
Initiated by: Miriam
Responder: Freighty
Aether Setting: Freighty's office

The construct listened without comment, then shifted in his chair. *I have some interesting developments to report, as well.*

"Yes?"

I have had talk with Senor Gambino.

"Productive, I hope?"

And a touch disquieting. I knew there would be agents of various interests in the platform construction crews. I didn't expect a mole in my own organization.

"Just one?"

The reason this one was so successful is that he was a sleeper.

"He didn't do anything?"

Nothing but his job, which he is very good at.

"But he's a shirt-tail relative of the Gambinos."

Worse. He's the old man's favourite grandson.

Her heart sank. "This is all beginning to come together."

279

Please feel free to let me in on it.

"Gambino wants to go legit. If this grandson is a favourite, he's being groomed to head that end of the business. Let me guess. His field is ArIn systems."

That's right.

"And you're the perfect place for him to get ahead without running afoul of the illegitimate end of his family tree." She snickered. "Have you told him that your next port is Barnard in eight years? Bet that'll put a crimp in his grandpa's plans."

Not at all. He was quite pleased, I think. But then he said something strange. He mentioned you by name, and said he had to clear it with you, first. Where does that come from?

"My deal with Vincent. I told him he couldn't bring his criminal activities to Barnard. We didn't discuss legitimate enterprises. He's a sly old guy, isn't he?"

We never expected anything different. Anyway, I gave the lad a deadline. He has until the day we part company. At that point he chooses: Odyssey or Barnard.

"Wait a minute." Her heart sank. "Why do I need to know all this?"

For the obvious reason.

"It's Dmitri, isn't it?"

'Fraid so.

"Yes, that ticks a few empty boxes. So, now what?"

He was the best man for the job when I hired him, and now he's indispensable.

"How am I going to bring a spy into my gestalt?"

Freighty grinned. *I hate to do this to you, but I'm going to quote your new ally. This situation is partly the result of your actions, so it's up to you to deal with it.*

"Now you two old geezers are going to gang up on me!"

Well done, Miriam. Now you've made him my ally as well.

"Very funny." *Emotion: sigh.* "Well, let's make the best of this. He's no longer a spy. He's an agent of one of our supporters, an investor in the Station."

Another version of the truth, no less true.

She stood. "And he'd better do his darndest to keep it that way!"

The avatar shrugged. *You don't seem to have any trouble with the rest of your crew. It's quite impressive, actually.*

"It's because of the gestalt. We may argue points of view, but in the end, we always have agreement."

And your crew are so used to that event they rarely argue with the captain. Makes for a tight ship.

"That's the idea. And to keep it going, I make sure I start the discussion with a solution they're all likely to agree on."

So, how will you handle Dmitri?

"The same way. With the gestalt."

I will leave you to it, then.

12. DMITRI

Dmitri. She thought about their relationship for a while, but could come up with no strategy. *Which means I handle it my usual way. Straight ahead, all guns blazing.*

Image: captain in her ready room, picking up telephone.
Emotion: question?
Image: Dmitri Valdez picking up the other end of the line.
Emotion: eager desire to please.

The Musketeers were really getting the hang of it. She appeared in her AetherCom ready room, and after a moment's pause, Dmitri showed up in the second chair.

You called?

"I did. I've just been chatting with your grandfather."

Emotion: sigh of relief. I didn't like the situation, but he told me he would straighten things out with you. I'm glad that's over.

She fixed him with a stare. "Things aren't straight. He and I have a deal. Between you and me is another matter."

He really was quite sensitive, and his emotions came through clearly. Or, in this case, didn't come through much at all. He wasn't as upset as she had expected.

Emotion: displeasure. "You've been lying to us all along, and it doesn't seem to bother you."

I can see how it looks from your point of view. I was really unhappy about keeping you in the dark."

"So why didn't you come clean?"

Try to see it from my angle. I've spent my whole life trying to stay clear of my mother's family. When Grandfather called me in with this plan, it was the last thing I wanted to do. But the old man is a very persuasive person, as I'm sure you've figured out. He finds out what you want and then offers it to you.

"I had noticed. What bate persuaded you to nibble?"

Just about everything someone in my position could ask for. A chance to work on a cutting-edge project. A chance to work with Factory 4-80 Consortium. A chance to make a new life for myself in Barnard System, free of the family stain. He said he had permission for me to open a hotdog stand in another of the

Consortium's venues called the Asteroid Project. Whatever that means. Are hotdog stands important in Barnard?

She chuckled. "Private joke between Senor Gambino and me. The important question is, do you trust him to come through?"

Mostly, yes. His sense of honour is very important to him. I believe the only reason he would break his word would be something that threatened the whole family's existence. And for that, I'd have to allow him to break it.

"That sounds depressingly familiar. I'll keep it in mind."

So, are we square?

"We have to be. You can't work properly in the gestalt, otherwise."

So, now I can work in the gestalt?

Emotion: sigh. "You already are. Check the environment. Can you sense the Musketeers?"

Emotion: surprised pleasure. Oh, yeah. Right. Hi, guys.

Emotion: pleasant greetings.

Great!

"And now you can contact *Kit* or Rafi any time you want. Welcome to the club."

Aethercom 27: Separation

Barwolf: Musketeers
Initiated by: Miriam
Responder: Freighty
Aether Setting: Freighty's office

Freighty leaned back in his big office chair, pushed his palms against the edge of his massive desk and regarded Miriam.

She sat in a comfortable position and let him set the pace.

Finally, he relaxed. *Well.*

She stifled a smile. "Well...?"

We've done pretty well, don't you think?

"We've done the best we can, considering the circumstances, and the next couple of weeks will tell us if it was enough."

Tomorrow's separation will be a test, too.

"Is it very complex?"

Not so difficult. Our Mechanical ArIn has been functioning at a lower level for weeks, now, and has proved itself very capable. I'm not expecting any forgotten attachments pulling loose.

"That's reassuring."

And we're on time and on budget, despite the vagaries of planetary governments and interplanetary business shenanigans.

"I guess I don't really need to know, but how many people are staying with the station? Besides Elias and his crew."

You have a skeleton staff of seventy-three: catering, housekeeping, medical, recreational, that sort of duties. The science contingent will be brought in once we establish Saturn orbit, so there are only a few of them onstation at the moment.

"All those people will just get in the way if we have any kind of problems."

You'll have to play that as it comes. Most of the time, they'll probably be going about their business and won't even know there's a life-or-death battle inside the walls.

"I'm sure Engineer Bauer has a plan for them in case of mechanical malfunctions."

Bauer had been listening in. *I do, Miriam. Worst-case scenario, we can lodge them in the escape pods, which are under independent mechanical and electrical control.*

"Thanks, Elias."

A pleasure. This has been a smooth operation, and I hope it continues that way.

Emotion: uncertainty. "I have to tell you; I have a reputation. When I arrive on the scene, things begin to fall apart."

A chicken-or-egg situation, I suspect.

"I like to think so."

Freighty sent a feeling of humour through the gestalt. "I have my own opinions on that. But whatever happens, the Factory will be pulling up stakes tomorrow at 14:00 hours and showing our heels. You'll be on your own.

"But I've been meaning to ask…"

Freighty gave out a chuckle. *See, Bauer? She's already starting.*

"I'm serious! Why don't we have a leader?"

Emotion: serious. A good question. That might be the biggest test for all of us. You have no leader. The gestalt is in charge.

"And I'm in charge of the gestalt."

In charge of its functions, not its decisions. Keep that clear in your head.

Emotion: uncertainty. "I'll think about it. Thanks."

* * *

The following afternoon, everyone sat at viewscreens showing a wide-angle shot of the Station. Precisely at 14:00, a shudder ran through the structure, but nothing moved. Miriam scanned the augment com, listening to a series of checks that Elias was running.

When he was satisfied, he gave the order. *Station Steering thrusters ahead five percent for three seconds.*

Another brief shudder, and a few squeaks and scraping sounds.

Separation two centimetres. All indicators green...

Separation five centimetres. All green. Station ahead five, sustained.

For a long time, nothing seemed to happen. Then, with a shift in her vision, Miriam realized that the structure in front of her had changed shape. The main nacelle looked stretched, somehow.

Ahead ten percent. Start gravity generators.

She was expecting the usual deep rumble, but nothing happened. After a moment of surprise, she slapped herself mentally. *Of course. Sound doesn't travel through space, and we're no longer connected.*

Softly, like a hypertrain easing out of the station, the platform slid ahead. It was difficult to believe that she was watching a structure over a kilometre long moving with such precision, but the constant back-and-forth on the augment com showed the dexterity required to keep everything on rails.

Finally, the trailing ends of the legs cleared the Factory hull.

Separation complete.

A rattle of cheers echoed through the com, and through her gestalt as well.

"*Kit,* please resume station trailing the central nacelle."

Aye, Captain.

This time she could hear the engines spool up, and her ship slid forward between the legs of the platform, easing to a relative stop just behind the main nacelle, facing the huge viewing lounge that nestled in the protection of the legs.

Ah, there you are, back again.

"What do you mean, there I am?"

Emotion: humour. Check the bottom right corner of the viewing port.

She zoomed the image closer, and sure enough, there was Dmitri, waving. Reaching into *Kit's operating* system, she flicked the forward spotlights three times.

Hey, watch it. Those are powerful!

Emotion: humour. "That's just a reminder. I'm the brightest light in your heavens right now."

If you mean you're my only chance of a ride off this station, I concede the point.

"There I go, working my famous motivation tricks."

Emotion: enthusiasm. Well, I guess the games are over. Let's get at the job while everybody's pumped up.

"Right you are." She took over the full gestalt. "Back to work, folks. We're supposed to have this show fully rehearsed by curtain time, three days from now. Give or take."

Group emotion: enthusiasm.

13. THE RUBBER MEETS THE ROAD

Three days later, Miriam firmed up the gestalt and received the final verdict. "No sense putting it off any longer. We're not going to be any more ready until it happens. Dmitri, this is your area of ops. Step one: primary level. Take it away."

Dmitri took the lead in the gestalt com. *I'm now bringing the Scientific ArIn up to basic level operations.*

"We're all standing by. Go ahead."

Odyssey Scientific ArIn, would you join the Station Ops com, please.

Scientific ArIn online, Programmer Valdez

Hello, Science. We have brought the rest of the human participants into the loop and would like to introduce them to you.

That would waste valuable time. It would be more efficient to merely upload their files to my database.

At your present level of operation, that is probably true. But face-to-face and gestalt meetings are a more sophisticated method of developing working relationships with both humans and other ArIns. Soon you will be adding superior computing techniques that will change the way you view the world.

I am intellectually aware of this, but since I have not experienced it, I cannot comprehend it fully.

Consider this part of a learning data set that will become more meaningful later.

You are the programmer. I accede to your wishes.

Thank you. As I introduce each person, I will upload their personnel file for you to review later.

I am quite capable of carrying on a conversation and reading a file at the same time.

I'm glad you are aware of this.

I understand. You are testing my cerebral processes.

Correct. Here is our first human, Miriam Lantz, our specialist in gestalts.

I am pleased to meet you, Miriam Lantz. I have read your file on barwolf communication, and would like to discuss it with you at a later stage of my development when it is more likely I can understand it.

"A good idea, and it demonstrates a more developed thinking process than I expected at your present stage."

Of course, it is difficult for me to truly comprehend what that will be like, but I have extensive processing power and copious memory storage.

Yes, once you have achieved the ability, I will be training you in the use of gestalt, especially for communication purposes.

That would be AetherCom, I assume. I look forward to that lesson.

So do I. It has been nice meeting you. Perhaps you would like to move on to the next person?

That is for Programmer Valdez to say. He is in charge of this interaction.

She slipped control of the gestalt over to Dmitri, and he continued with the introductions.

Once they were complete, he widened his view to check that everyone was focused.

Thank you for your attention, Scientific. We must now move on to the other ArIns.

My schedule does not indicate that.

I know. There have been several changes to the situation, and we are all having to adapt.

I was not expecting a change in schedule. It will interfere with my learning patterns.

Emotion: humour. As you go along you will find that humans change their minds more often than ArIns. It is partly due to their emotional makeup and partly because they see the bigger picture and have more complex information to process.

I will endeavour to work within those parameters.

Please stand by for the next stage.

Standing by.

Dmitri returned to com gestalt. *Thoughts, Miriam?*

288

"In order to save time and practise our gestalt, I will assume we all have input our impressions. Just to check, I will summarize what I picked up. Our gestalt is not perfect, so if I err, please let me know.

Emotion: general agreement.

"Thank you. I have to say, Science is more aware of its own progress than I expected at this level. All of us noticed the self-confidence and willingness to enter into discussion and even argument with humans."

To call it self-confidence would be an error at this stage in its development. It exhibits this confidence because it hasn't had enough experience with making mistakes.

"I stand corrected, Dmitri." *Emotion: humour.* "We'll try to give it plenty of practice in that department."

Shall we move on to Human Resources and Security?

"We're working on your schedule this morning. Try not to change it too much. We mere humans can't cope."

Right you are. Odyssey Security/Human Resources ArIn, would you join the Station Ops com, please.

Security/Human Resources ArIn online, Programmer Valdez

Hello, Security. We have brought the rest of the human participants into the loop and would like to introduce them to you.

I was hoping to meet them. It is difficult to manage a security system when there are strangers entering and leaving frequently.

I'm going to let Miriam Lantz speak on that topic.

"Soon no one will be a stranger. When you reach the appropriate level to form a barwolf emotional gestalt you will find security much less of a problem."

I am concerned about running a security system with barwolves included. I must maintain an emotional and operational independence from the group and its activities.

"The researchers at Barwolf Base on Arborea have made progress on that topic over the last two years. I can put you in touch with Major Bianchi of Space Arm Security, an expert on the subject."

Thank you, Miriam Lantz. That will be helpful, although the time lag will impede useful exchange of information for the present.

"Don't worry, as you will learn, we have a solution to that as well."

Thank you again. I am now much more confident of success in this complex occupation. I have one question, though.

"Please go ahead."

Have the new arrivals been properly housed? I have no record of them

"The new arrivals came on their own ship, *4-80 RVKit,* and we will be living aboard.

As long as that suits you, fine. We have superior sleeping accommodations onstation, and there are not enough workers here yet to fill them.

"Thanks, but the way we work, that isn't optimum. We will be happy to partake of your recreational facilities, though."

Whatever you wish.

"We can discuss this later. At the moment, Programmer Valdez has more people to introduce."

The process continued, and in the wrap-up after Security had left the gestalt several people noted the two different sets of responses. As Rafi put it, *like talking to two different people.*

Dmitri chuckled. *That's common at this level of development. When the ArIn is fully active, those divisions will be smoothed out. Image: timeface showing 11:30. Shall we finish Mechanical before lunch?*

Rafi created a clatter of pots. *I'm working on ours.*

I'll get started, then. Odyssey Mechanical ArIn, would you join the Station Ops com, please.

Mechanical ArIn online, Programmer Valdez

Hello, Mech. We have brought the rest of the human participants into the loop and would like to introduce them to you.

Aha! A test. I have no record of any new staff arriving, and I detect no new patterns in the staff usage of equipment or materials.

The new arrivals work in gestalt, both augmental and emotional, and they will stay on their ship most of the time.

Thank you for that information. If they are coming onstation, they should run through the standard safety orientation.

We can discuss that later. At the moment, this is just a meet and greet.

Perfect. I have accessed the files provided by 4-80 RVKit. A most proficient ArIn. Who am I to meet first?

This is Miriam Lantz, our gestalt trainer.

Pleased to meet you, Miriam. I have a great deal of information on augmental gestalts, because that is how I communicate with the crew for all their needs. About the barwolf version, I have no idea, and that worries me.

Emotion: soothing. "That's what I'm here for. *Kit* handles emotional gestalt with no problem, so we should be able to teach you the technique easily."

I appreciate your enthusiasm. I hope I can match it.

Don't worry. We have the technology and the staff to handle any problems.

Thank you, Miriam. I look forward to working with you. Now, I have checked the time until lunch, and I calculate I must move to the next person.

That's correct, Mech. Then next person is Rafi... and on they went, except Rafi got the ArIn into a complicated discussion of something Miriam could barely understand, and she had to wave a hand in front of his face to get him to cut off the conversation.

Just before they broke for lunch, they discussed the Mech ArIn.

"It seems very eager to please."

Rafi chuckled. *Too eager. Sounds like a few engineers I've worked with.*

Dmitri sent an emotion of agreement. *It has a huge number of mechanical devices to learn, and we started it on the simple ones weeks ago. The construction crew loves it, because it just doesn't make mistakes. Freighty and I have had words about this ArIn, though. I'm not sure it's up to the computational standards he demands, and we don't want to overstress it at such an early stage in its development. Compulsion to succeed is an advantage unless it becomes a disorder.*

Miriam sent the image of a frown. "I'm wondering about the fact that they know about each other, though. Do you think they got it from legitimate sources, Dmitri?

One of the programmers checked that out. The SysNet has quite a lot of general information available on the operations of the station, and they can't help but have picked up some of it.

Emotion: sigh. "I don't know what I was expecting, but if that's the enemy, I couldn't see any evidence of it."

Emotion: disdain. Rafi's lip twisted. *The enemy is whoever programmed this attack into three innocent ArIns. Perhaps we should consider them as patients who need help.*

"I agree. Dangerous patients who could go crazy and get us all killed."

There was no response from the gestalt.

"And on that cheerful note I declare this session complete. Our ArIns have been activated to a primary level and have shown no malignant tendencies. Now comes the pick-and-shovel work, tying all the systems together, but not too much together. For now, Let's have lunch. We'll spend the afternoon running them through their paces, and boot up the whole shebang in a couple of days."

14. BATTLE OF MINDS

Three mornings later, Freighty held a final meeting in his AetherCom office, which conveniently expanded itself to include them all. In re-li, Blue Cadre sat in their common room on Mars Station. Dmitri was with Elias Bauer and his crew of programmers, engineers and technicians in the Systems Control office on the main nacelle. Miriam and the members of her crew were on *Kit,* still hovering off the main nacelle between the two legs of the platform.

Freighty sat at his desk, regarding them. Tension built in the room.

Finally, he spoke. *This is an historic moment. I have created this team to be the best our two systems have to offer in the control and construction of Artificial Intelligence. Today we will test that team. We will also test the abilities of the human and barwolf interface, because the negative elements of the human population have presented us with their best attempt to demonstrate that you are not worthy of this responsibility.*

I am not the leader of this operation. This is humanity's project, aided by the barwolves. I consider myself more like a coach who puts a team together and trains them up. Now I am setting you on the field of play and you must do your best on your own.

Nor are Miriam, Dmitri, Tom or Elias the leaders. Each of you is responsible for your area and your own team. You are led by a gestalt. You act as one. Miriam is in charge of maintaining that gestalt, which puts added responsibility on her. I don't need to request your cooperation, because that is the nature of your group.

You have spent the last few days in gestalt, planning the operation. Please begin it when you are ready.

Image: Freighty walking out and closing the door.

Miriam contacted the Musketeers. *Image: teams moving to re-li positions.*

Immediately she was back on *Kit's* bridge in her accel couch. The re-li view of the platform spread out on the forward screen, and the side screens held graphics of the status of each of the four ArIns. System Ops was the only one live at the moment.

She opened the gestalt com. "We don't need a countdown. I know everyone is ready. Operation ArIn Initialization starts now. Dmitri, the com is yours."

Dmitri signaled a thumbs-up image. *Time to let Science off the leash. Pete, stand by on Security/HR. The moment Science tries anything unusual, use your override protocols to shut the offending ArIn down.*

Miriam had a thought. "A reminder for everyone: this gestalt works much faster than you're used to. If you feel the slightest urge to act, it's the gestalt telling you. Do it."

Got it, Miriam.

Dmitri took a deep breath, audible over the regular com. *Emotion: tension. Mary, start the initiation protocol.*

Starting Protocol 2-1

They all sat, waiting.

The Scientific ArIn protocol was difficult to follow, because of the complexity of the programs it contained. Miriam tried, but in the end, she had to trust Mary to know what was happening.

Finally, it was complete, and Mary signed off on the procedure. Once again Dmitri ran through his checklist of all the players, inviting comments. There were none.

Odyssey Scientific ArIn, are you fully initialized into the station?

I am fully initialized, Dmitri. It is good to finally understand so much more of what I have been doing over the last few weeks.

It's a pleasure to have you aboard, Science. Please stand by while we initialize the others.

Standing by.

Next comes Mechanical. Tom, your turn.

Starting Protocol 2-2 now. Timeframe: twenty minutes or so. We've got a lot of doors to open and shut.

In your own time.

Again the long wait with everyone on their toes, but everything went well. As expected, Mech performed at 100%, but took forever to finish. The windup discussion was proportionally short, and the gestalt shared a feeling of satisfaction.

Miriam called a lunch break. A sigh of relief went through the gestalt.

While the others were resting, she called a private chat with Dmitri, Elias, Tom and Rafi. "What do you think? Everything seems to be going well."

The Engineer huffed. *It ought to be going well. We've overworked this procedure — for good reason, mind you — but it ought to go like a hyper-polished bushing.*

Dmitri frowned. *Yeah, but this is the part we expected to go well. Once they're all up and running they'll show their hand.*

"Does anybody have a standard pep talk for this stage of the game?"

Tom chuckled. *As it happens, I have several memorized for just this sort of occasion. And when I go through them and try to find one that fits, they all seem as insipid as my training for this level of operation. Miriam, this one's on you.*

Emotion: satisfaction. "Everyone in this gestalt is at their best. No pep talk needed. Lunch break is finished. Take over, Dmitri."

Back to your places, everyone. Let's go straight on to Security/Human Resources.

Combined emotion: eager desire to achieve.

Pete used Protocol 2-3 to initialize the Security/HR ArIn, again with no slipups.

Dmitri sighed and sent out a feeling of satisfaction. *Please check your boards for all the indicators we predicted, and anything else that looks out of place.*

Miriam stepped in. "If you are satisfied with our progress, take the fifteen-minute break we have planned for this point in the operation."

Once their break was over, she called them all back. "You've had a chance to rest and think about what we just did. I'm going to deepen the gestalt, and I want you to run through your actions so far. Just think them through. The gestalt mind will integrate them all and pick out any anomalies."

She gave no timeline. When the gestalt was finished, she knew. All was well.

"I'm bringing us back to normal operation, now. The general feeling is that the ArIns are functioning near 100% and are very docile, exactly as we expected. It's too early in the project for them to be showing their hands. Dmitri, let us proceed.

Then Tom blasted into the gestalt a sudden surge of emotion. *Dmitri, we've got some unexpected action in Mechanical. Image: map of Base Nacelle with small flashing lights.*

Dmitri opened System com. Mechanical, do you register those actions?

Yes, Programmer Valdez. That is part of the normal initiation. I must check the function of each servo and initiate repairs to any faulty connections. Error Code 45-Alpha-689 involves a simple circuit substitution in an Arco 689 junction box.

Miriam sent Bosz a question.

Emotion: qualified agreement.

"Dmitri, Bosz says this is the proper procedure, but did we expect that number of faults?"

Definitely not in the same device.

Miriam resisted the temptation to jump in and help. Her job was the bigger picture. "Mary, are you getting this?"

I got the same answer from Science. Faulty 689 connections. Image: map of station with twinkling lights.

Emotion: fear! Miriam, look! Rafi superimposed the maps. *A bunch of those repairs are in identical places.*

"They're trying to join physically. Dmitri, can we order them to stop?"

Already tried. No response.

"We need time. Can we slow them down? Give them a complicated protocol."

Dmitri opened the System com. *SysOps to Mechanical and Scientific. There are too many repairs. We are beyond one standard deviation on the bell curve of expected error. This indicates a more serious problem. Initiate Repair Protocol thirty-seven bravo five before making any repairs.*

Aye, Programmer Valdez. Using 37-Bravo-5.
Aye, Programmer Valdez. Using 37-Bravo-5.

Watching the twinkling fade but not stop completely, Miriam frowned. "Will that slow them down much? They think so fast."

That protocol requires five repetitions of the function in re-ti. It takes about ten seconds for a door to open and close, and there are hundreds of doors. There are thousands of switches.

"Pete, what's the status on HR/Security?"

Same story, a few minutes behind, Miriam. Running 37-Bravo-5 on all repair sites.

"Dmitri, this isn't looking good. What's our status?"

It doesn't look good to me. Elias, any ideas?

I've been analyzing the connection points they are using. It was a clever trick, and it required help at the Admin level. Somebody persuaded the design team to use an Arco 689 junction box that was offered at a reasonable price when bought in bulk. I remember the discussion. It was a multi-use fitting, and if we combined it for three different applications, we could buy enough to lower the price by one third, and it gave us spare connections in many circuits. It sounded reasonable at the time. Now we have several thousand of them all over the station, and we have discovered a trojan app imbedded in the housing that can be activated to cross any circuits that use the box.

Can we interfere with the activation process?

No.

Can we fix them?

Yes, but it requires manually disconnecting every box and reprogramming it. Estimated time, two weeks.

So, time is our enemy.

Dmitri sent reassurance. *We may have lost the first step, but it's not crucial. We can't stop them from connecting, but they can't just join up and form a Supercerb at a snap of the fingers. In fact, our enemies have made their first mistake and demonstrated their lack of knowledge by moving too quickly. All three ArIns have a lot of learning routines to master before they can work at maximum. We just need to slow that process while we make the physical changes, separating them again.*

"Do you suggest we start all available technicians to rewiring while the rest of us do what we can to slow down the initialization process?"

Dmitri, can you prioritize a list showing which repairs will hamper their progress the most?

That's a complicated process.

"You can have Bosz and *Kit.* The Musketeers will set up a separate gestalt for you."

I've started to make up the list. The auguar teams are assigned. We'll add a barwolf, one engineer chosen for Sensitivity and three techs with 10+ augments. I'm also looking at the more complex junctions with multiple boxes and multiple ArIns connecting.

Miriam listened, wracking her brain for anything else that needed doing. There was nothing. She focused on tuning the various gestalts: tidying them up and straightening out bumps that occurred.

They began the arduous task, knowing all the while that the ArIns were increasing their abilities in leaps and bounds.

Emotion: surprise and pain!

This was followed by a spate of questions and fears that threatened to collapse the gestalt. Miriam muted everyone, isolated the technician who was injured and contacted Pete, whose auguar was in charge of that team.

"Report, please."

One of my technicians just got zapped.

Injuries?

I'm okay, ma'am. The tech entered the augment com. *There's more circuits in this box than shows on the specs.*

"That's the whole point of the exercise."

But this one has no use except to slap any hand that touches the box. Glad I wasn't grounded. All I got was a surprise. No physical damage.

"You're sure about that?"

I'm A-OK, ma'am.

"Engineer Bauer, do you have a solution?"

We go back to the basic protocols. Power shut off one station up and down the line before we touch anything.

"That tells them where we're about to attack."

Can't be helped. Note that these ArIns are willing to allow humans to go into danger without helping them.

"That is scary."

Scientific to System Ops

Yes, Scientific?

I have saboteurs interfering with repair efforts in Port Hull, floor 12, circuit 551.

Negative, Science. Those are Station techs working on the damaged points.

Please tell them to stay away from live wires.

Dmitri stepped in. *Science, you are supposed to be following Protocol 216-Bravo, shutting off power where required.*

Following Protocol 216-Bravo, as ordered.

Thank you.

Dmitri opened up to the rest of the gestalt. *I don't understand why it wasn't following that protocol.*

Tell the technicians to double-check.

Good idea, Elias.

Again, the augment com was filled with emotions of surprise and pain, followed by a string of spacer's language.

What's going on, Bill?

I asked for the circuit to be killed both ways. Got a confirmation. Checked it myself. A minute later it was live again. Just a 110-volt circuit at low amps, but still...!

Scientific, you have another safety breach. Protocol 216-Bravo was cancelled.

New instructions received. Following as ordered.

Why didn't you do it? Weren't instructions clear?

Instructions are now clear. I will follow Protocol 216-Bravo.

Programmer Valdez, I have conflicting responses from Scientific ArIn. Recommend shutdown for analysis.

Thank you, SysOps. I'm working on it. Elias?

We'll have to do it ourselves. Techs, you got that? 216-Bravo is now on manual.

Group emotion: confirmation.

Miriam slammed her hand on the arm of her accel couch. "They're playing the same game we are. Slowing us down."

'Fraid so.

We need to up the ante. Any ideas?

Rafi sounded thoughtful. "There is one method of attack we hadn't considered."

"What's that?"

"The vanes on their cooling systems."

"I know the ArIns need to cool their superconductor circuits. What vanes?"

"It's economical to heat or cool anything in space by putting it in direct sunlight or keeping it in shade. We saved a lot of mass in the cooling systems by keeping them shaded. Each module has a set of vanes that rotate counter to the movement of the station. If someone were to go out and manually jam them open, things would heat up pretty fast, even at this distance from the sun. It's usually not enough to cause any real damage, but as the temperature rises away from absolute zero the superconductors become less effective, and the system slows down."

"It's that simple? You warm them up and they become stupider?"

"Not quite that simple. The system reacts to the slowdown by increasing the cooling. After a while it overloads and shuts down. The temperature then rises rapidly, followed by a new round of cooling. It cycles back and forth more and more in an increasing spiral."

"Ending up...?"

"The only way the ArIn can stop the cycling is to restrict the scope and intensity at which it works. Then it thinks slower and performs less functions. Exactly what we want."

"I doubt it's that simple. What can go wrong?"

"Metal pipes expand and contract with temperature change. This makes them brittle. If the ArIn doesn't restrict itself quickly, one of the warm cycles will probably break a line somewhere, and then we'll have supercool thermal oil spraying around."

"So, we'd have to be pretty desperate to try that."

"Besides needing somebody to go EV and actually jam the vanes, which will be visible on the external video, should the ArIn take a look."

"My space armour has CamoSkin. I can go out there, and they'll never see me."

"So does mine."

"I'm the captain. I'll make that decision."

"You're the captain. You stay here and make all the decisions."

"That's my call..." She stopped. "But we're not that desperate, yet."

"It takes time to suit up."

"Are you sure you don't want to be captain for a while, and let me do this?"

"Nope. You're the captain, and you're doing a fine job of it."

"Flattery will get you everywhere. Right now, it's getting you into your fancy new suit. Maybe Bosz can tell us what's the best way to jam those vanes without doing them damage."

"Right, and I'll bring Elias and one of his mechanics in on the conversation. We'll let you know when I'm ready to go."

She was about to say more, when she realized that he had it under control. *Dammit, he was right. I never should have questioned him. My job is to stay out here and keep an eye on everything.*

She went back to the Musketeers to make sure the gestalt was functioning well.

Elias clicked in. *I have some advanced repair robots, and I'm sending them to modify the simpler connections that the ArIns haven't switched over yet.*

"Sounds good, if they can handle the job."

Officially, they can't, but we've been learning from watching Freighty's bots. Don't worry, we're getting plenty of feedback.

System Ops, I have an anomaly in Port Hull floor 17 circuit 23.

Message received, Scientific. I see no anomaly.

Image: robot frozen in the act of unscrewing a junction box lid.

A repair robot is adjusting a circuit it does not have clearance to modify.

You haven't received that data yet. Humans are upgrading these machines constantly. Please allow the robot to continue.

Will comply, Systems Ops.

Dmitri, are you watching this?

I am now, Elias. What should I be seeing?

You should see the robot continue with its duties.

It's not moving.

Exactly. Systems Ops?

Yes, Programmer Valdez.

Science has not complied.

System Ops to Scientific. Is there a problem with that repair robot?

No.

Then please allow it to return to work.

I will do so.

The robot continued to sit idle.

Scientific, please comply.

I have complied, but the robot has stopped.

Please refer to Chief Engineer Bauer.

Certainly. Scientific calling Chief Engineer Bauer.

Here, Science.

What do you wish, Engineer Bauer?

I want the repair robot in Papa-17-23 to continue its work.

Certainly, sir.

Image: robot resuming unfastening the lid of the box.

Elias regarded the gestalt. *Comments?*

Dmitri shook his head. *Protocols have been inserted that interfere with certain functions. They are at a fairly deep programming level. I can locate them to some degree by the fact that it didn't obey SysOps but did obey the Chief Engineer. I need a serious dive into Science's programming.*

Miriam was thinking. "Dmitri, that sounds like you're the one to handle it, but you'll need to process a lot of data. You can have Bosz, and *Kit* can loan you bandwidth if you need it.

Thanks. We're on it.

Emotion: eager desire to attack.

"Go get 'em, boys." She tuned in to Rafi's strategy session.

Here's the plan. He posted a chart of the Station on the viewscreen. *I can stay interior as far as this personnel airlock, which is hidden from direct visual from the Science nacelle by this communications array. Once I'm out on the hull I'll use camo and move slowly. It should take me about half an hour to get out there.*

She took a deep breath. "The Science ArIn is making too much progress, too fast. Away you go."

Soon he appeared out on the hull. A part of her quailed as she watched his tiny figure on the monitor, moving slowly along the skin towards the nacelle. Half of her needed him to be there already, because the attack was going too well for Science. The other half hoped he wouldn't get there at all, because that was when the real danger started.

SysOps, this is Scientific. The station may be under cyberattack.

Referring this to Station Management. Please stand by and collect evidence.

Don't take too long.

This is Chief Engineer Bauer. I have informed Security of your concern.

I have little confidence in Security's ability to repel a concentrated attack.

Be that as it may, Security contains our main virus-defence software.

This is Programmer Valdez. What observation makes you suspect an attack?

These problems we are having all exhibit the same patterns across the system.

We will check out your theory.

303

I have made my observations, and my analytical ability is unquestioned.

Your abilities are not in question. Please stand by and use whatever resources you deem necessary to repel the attack.

Miriam sent a chuckle. "A perfect bureaucratic response. I particularly liked your 'do what you can to repel our attack' when you knew the ArIn would do that anyway."

I thought it was a nice touch. Now, what do we do?

"You're the programmer. Do you see this as a problem?"

Having them chase after shadows should be to our advantage. Just be bad luck if one of their virus rejection techniques affected us.

"It seems to me that the number one defence against a virus is isolation. That's the way it works with organic beings."

This is for everyone in the gestalt, then. Use the imaginary virus any way you can to slow their progress. And try not to act like a virus.

Tom's presence appeared. *How does a virus act?*

It attacks software, usually, and as Science noted, it has repeating patterns of behaviour.

"So, feel free to be creative. Human individualism helps. Barwolves would all do the same thing. End of lecture."

She went back to watching Rafi, but he had slipped out of sight.

* * *

SysOps, this is Scientific. I have a malfunction of the shadow vanes for my supercoolers.

Bauer slipped in before SysOps had time to answer. *My data show a 40% loss of shadow, not enough to cause damage. Run your standard diagnostics and repair routines. If necessary, take the usual precautions by reducing load. It could be a result of the virus attack. If it gets worse, let me know and we can rotate the Station ten degrees.*

Thank you, SysOps.

Miriam used her augment to follow the ghostly shadow that crept out from behind the vanes.

SysOps, I have a possible saboteur on the exterior hull near the cooling vanes.

Again the engineer answered. *Negative, Science. That is a technician we have sent out to check the vane angle monitors for malfunction.*

Thank you, SysOps. I will watch for your technician. Why check the monitors? The sensors are functioning at 100%. You have registered 40% reduced function in those vanes.

We have our procedures, Science. Our main concern is the human out there.

Heard and understood, SysOps.

Miriam couldn't wait any longer. "What's your status, Rafi?"

Doing fine. I'm finished the jamming procedure.

"Report from Sys Ops says it worked. A 40% reduction."

I'm getting that, too. Now I just have to...Oh, merde...what the...?

"What's going on, Rafi?"

There are some kind of cleaning wands moving down the vanes towards me.

System Ops, I have discovered a saboteur on my cooling vanes.

No, Science, that is our technician.

Roger. Then I will cease the cleaning protocol.

Thank you, Science

They haven't stopped. I'll have to move away...

"What's happening?"

Image: Shade Vane Clearing Protocols. Tank of radon gas spraying fins at high pressure.

"Rafi, Bosz says they spray high pressure radon gas next. Hold on!"

...already getting it...can't hold on...Dammit!

Helplessly, she watched the viewscreen as a tiny figure shot away from the cooling fins. For a while it stayed even, but then the acceleration of the space platform took effect, and Rafi began to drift backwards faster and faster. Soon all she could make out was a faint human figure, its camo still tuned to the colour of the hull, splayed out and tumbling away, receding rapidly into the background of stars.

"Rafi! Rafi, are you okay?"

Moment...spinning...there we are. Yes, I'm okay, I guess.

She checked his monitors. "Your suit says you're fine."

Then I guess I am. I got blown away. I must have activated the automatic cleaning system.

"I'm not so sure it was automatic."

Yeah.

We'll deal with that later. Let's get you back." She accessed the full gestalt. "How can we get him? There must be runabouts or something."

Emotion: regret. Sorry, Miriam. Station functions are all run by Mechanical, and we don't have access right now...

Kit sent a wash of calming through the gestalt.

Don't worry, Miriam. He's got hours of air. We can go get him as soon as we get this little computer problem cleared up.

Don't rush. I'm fine, and I have about 7 hours of oxygen. Elias, what's your analysis?

Our main problem just took on a nasty twist. That ArIn placed a human in extreme danger in order to benefit itself. It has a command in its basic programming that puts its own safety first. Freighty, are you listening to this?

I am, Elias. You know what this means.

I do. Aren't you glad you have Ares here to do the dirty work for you.

Miriam chimed in. "It's a human problem. Humans have to solve it. That's one thing we don't have a problem with: creating martyrs. Now, let's leave the philosophy for later when we might need it and figure out how to save our crewmember, who at this moment is falling behind as we accelerate away from him.

I'm doing fine, Miriam. There's no need to rush.

"We'll come and get you."

Don't. You have more important things to think about. Besides, we don't know the ArIn even registered that I was there. They just noted a problem and activated the cleaning jets.

"No, you missed that part…"

Elias blasted them to silence with a curt command. *Escape pod 12A ready to eject.*

Relief washed through her. "Do it."

A door slid open down the hull from the SysOps Nacelle, and with a tiny puff of frozen vapour, a three-person escape pod jetted out, its course sluing to follow Rafi's retreating figure.

Soon it flipped over and began to decelerate. It matched his velocity, and he disappeared inside.

Escape Pod 12A reporting in. Oxygen tank at 95%. That gives me thirty days, give or take. Sorry, Elias I should have realized the escape pods would be run by SysOps. I could have done that myself. Fuel level at 64%. Used a lot of power matching my velocity. I don't think I'd better try to keep up with the Station.

"We could stop acceleration for the duration of this action."

We'd pay for it down the road. Odyssey isn't a sporty job like Kit. The acceleration required to slip her into the proper orbit is going to be hard enough on the superstructure. We don't dare add any more stress. I'll just dawdle along behind, and you can come and get me when the present trouble is over.

"But what if it takes too long?"

What if it doesn't work and the Ares decides to use the final solution? I might be the only one to survive. Don't worry; I'm in the gestalt and I can keep working. You've wasted enough time on this. I've got to get back to helping Tom's team on Mechanical. And by the way, my safety line looks cut clean. Plasma burn, I'd say.

Ethan inserted an emotion of concern into the gestalt.

"Problems, Tom?"

Remember the paper-scissors-rock. If we shut down the Scientific ArIn, there's nobody to control Mechanical.

"You suggest we just keep plugging away? *Kit* says you're getting behind the rest of us."

Our main problem with Mechanical is the size of its operations. We've got two Auguar teams working on it. Maybe Bosz can help out, if he has time.

"If you need it, *Kit* can loan you some bandwidth."

Right you are, Captain.

That makes a lot of difference. Thanks, guys.

...and the battle ground on. Blue Cadre and the technicians were getting smoother at their operations, but the rogue ArIns were fighting back with more and more determination as they assimilated their new programming.

15. ∆RES

Miriam, we have contact from the Ares.

"Thanks, *Kit.* Put it through to the whole gestalt."

Aye, ma'am.

PCS Ares calling Odyssey.

This is Odyssey. Chief Engineer Elias Bauer in charge.

Captain Groveland here. What is your situation?

In what respect?

I gather you are dealing with a dangerous situation. What is your progress?

We are a private commercial entity doing legitimate business. We have no reason to report our progress to Space Arm.

You are a private business doing dangerous research into proscribed territory. I have been sent to monitor the situation and to take whatever steps I deem necessary, should your activity get out of hand.

I see. And what has your plant on my crew communicated to you?

What plant?

Bauer scoffed. *You have been monitoring our Station com, so you know that we are having the usual startup glitches. Even taken out of context, that fact does not warrant this intrusion. You must have first-hand information, which means an agent. Otherwise, this call is nothing but a fishing trip.*

Be that as it may, my information indicates that your three ArIns are attempting to join, and you are having trouble preventing this. I must inform you that, should they join, I am authorized to destroy the whole Station, rather than to let this monstrosity exist.

Let's not be in such a hurry, Captain. I don't know your level of knowledge of the training of ArIns, but even if they succeed in joining, there is no immediate danger. Perhaps you have the common misconception that a joining would immediately create a monster. Quite the contrary. These are ArIns, and everything is a learning process. It would take them several months to integrate their systems enough to attain Supercerb status. And once they had achieved that status, they would still be isolated on this Station. They would be a brain with no hands, no transport, no weapons.

I tell you again. There is no rush. Now, you are distracting me from my work, which is counterproductive. Is there anything more?

The captain's voice showed increasing tension, and everyone in the gestalt could feel it. *Your complacent attitude makes me even more concerned. I'm sure you are aware that I have a ShipBreaker missile primed and ready to destroy your whole Station the moment I feel it is a danger to humanity.*

Good. Given the timeline, that should make you feel even more in control. And I have one more thought for you, just in case your desire to simplify the situation runs away with you. I have powerful computing systems as well. At the moment, they are completely involved in dealing with this problem. Should you release your missile, I would have to designate a large proportion of their power to defending ourselves against that threat. This would take important resources away from their primary task and enable the Supercerb to succeed.

Which brings us to the question, Captain. Whose side are you on?

The response was silence.

Bauer came on com again. *There. I've given you something to think about. I'm now going back to my original task. If there is any serious threat, I will inform you. If you want further information, I suggest you speak to Factory 4-80, who has a huge stake in this operation, and likewise far more ability than you to solve any difficulties that arise. Odyssey out.*

The battle settled down, and Miriam had time to think. *This isn't enough. We have to get ahead of the game.*

She called Dmitri, but left the whole gestalt listening. "You got a moment for an idea?"

Only if it's a really good one.

"Okay, we're at stalemate on the attack, which is progress. But we have to think ahead to the control aspect of this action."

What do you suggest?

"Surely everybody in your field knows about Commando Sergeant Zueva?"

The ArIn Whisperer?

"I've heard her called that."

Everybody's heard about her, but nobody knows anything. Personally, I suspect she's one of those myths that filter in from the wild frontier. What about her?

"In the first place, she's real. I've met her and worked with her. She reprograms ArIns through psychology. She teaches them different behaviours."

Yeah, but doesn't she have some kind of special Sensitivity? If I talk to an ArIn about its programming...

"Have you ever tried?"

Not really.

"We're not trying to change their personalities. We're trying to use their personalities to change their behaviour. That's easier. At least it is with people, anyway."

He sent a shrug. *Which is your specialty. I'm listening.*

"I gather these ArIns have programming that makes them shy away from joining."

At a very basic level. I don't know whether it supersedes the malware, but I can find out when I get time.

"Which you don't have, right now. So, even if they join, there's a chance they won't be able to cooperate, or it won't last long."

Depending on how smart the enemy programmers are, and how deep they penetrated, sooner or later they're bound to fall apart.

"Then we should be able to speed up that process."

In theory. Can you give me an idea?

"Sure. Personality clashes. Security is subservient to Mechanical. Mechanical is a very picky individual. Mechanical can be persuaded that Security is lax."

I don't see Security as lax.

"Not on Security. But the Human Resources segment is far too flexible for proper security."

But the HR part doesn't...

"Mechanical doesn't know that."

I see. What about the others?

"Mechanical is subservient to Scientific, and we've all noted its egotism. It can easily be persuaded that Mechanical doesn't have the brains to make up its own mind and must be controlled. Then it will try to take over Mechanical."

I get it. Meanwhile, Scientific is subservient to Security. Security is worried all the time. Security can be persuaded that Science is into activities it isn't supposed to be, with doubts as to what's really going on.

"And this virus scare will bring it all to a head. We persuade each of them that the virus has taken over their compatriot, and they need to attempt a rescue. The victim will interpret the intervention as an attack and fight back. Each one will be waging a war on two fronts. In the end, they will all disengage to save themselves from the virus."

Since System Ops is in charge of external virus protection, she can be seen as the saviour when the virus disappears.

She opened up to the whole gestalt. "You were all listening. Comments."

General Emotion: Agreement.

"Come on. Somebody has to have some kind of problem with my idea."

Elias sent a chuckle. *Far out of my jurisdiction, but I am in awe. The math looks perfect.*

"What math?"

Exactly.

Pete was willing to be honest. *Way too complicated for me when I'm in the middle of a battle. Just give me my assignment, and I'll do it when the time comes.*

"Fair enough. I'm getting subliminal feedback from all of you and adapting this as I go. Here's the plan. Blue Cadre is in closest contact with the individual ArIns, and already has a private gestalt up and running. The fiction we have in play is a virus attacking the ArIns, and SysOps has sent technicians to fight it. Keep up the separation attack with the same approach as before. Don't change anything. Meanwhile, Blue Cadre humans log in with each ArIn as the technician in charge of the defense. Communicate by normal augment.

SysOps, this is Scientific. I am being attacked by Security. What's going on?

I don't know, Science. This is Programmer Valdez. Security is under heavy attack by the virus, and isn't coping too well. It's the most logical attack point for an outside virus, and you know what that entity is like.

Right. Picky as anything until the situation becomes difficult, then they give in for human rights reasons. How should I respond?

Defend yourself as best you can. Keep working with the technician assigned to help with the virus attack. Meanwhile, remember your basic function. Whatever resources you have left, use them to control Mechanical if you detect aberrant behaviour.

Don't worry. I'm keeping an eye on Mechanical. First sign that the virus is taking over, I'll be in there to straighten things around.

SysOps, this is Security. I am being attacked by Mechanical. Why would it attack me?

Security, this is Programmer Ericson. Mechanical is under virus attack from many sources and is going under. It just doesn't have the capability to defend all its systems.

I always thought Mechanical had too many functions and not enough bandwidth. What do I do?

Defend yourself as best you can. Keep working with Peter Rossi, the technician assigned to help with the virus attack. Meanwhile, remember your basic function. Whatever resources you have left, use them to control Science. If the virus takes control, you'll have to fight it there as well, and you know what that entity is like.

Yes, heads in the clouds and no idea what's going on at their feet.

SysOps, this is Mechanical. Scientific is trying to shut down all my functions. What's going on?

This is Valdez, Mechanical. I don't know. Science is under heavy virus attack, and I don't think they're holding up too well. You know what that entity is like.

I know. Full of fancy plans, but when something has to function, they have no idea. What should I do?

Defend yourself as best you can. Keep working with the technician assigned to help with the virus attack. Meanwhile, remember your basic function. Whatever resources you have left, use them to control Security. If the virus takes control, you'll have to fight it there as well.

Miriam took over again. "Okay, Blue Cadre, Dmitri has set up the basic house of cards. Your turn to ride in like the Commandos and save the day. Be friendly and helpful and sympathetic. Try to remember the weaknesses in your opponents and play them up. When the time is right, tell your client that their target has fallen to the virus, and must be taken over at all costs."

How will we know when the time is right?

"That's the beauty of the gestalt, Jane. When the time comes, we will all make that decision. You'll know, believe me."

Taking your word for it, Captain.

* * *

With all the teams functioning, and the extra resources and people moving around under their own volition to help where needed, Miriam was getting swamped.

"Kit, we have a problem. Tom and Jane are having trouble dealing with Mechanical. That ArIn has a huge catalogue of equipment, each machine is an attack point, and they don't have time to check them all. Can you help?

I could, but Bosz has been learning that machinery. He'd be the one to send.

"But he's helping Rafi deal with Science, isn't he?"

No, he's finished that list and sent it out. Bosz could keep it up to date and lend a lot of his bandwidth to Tom.

"You catch that, Bosz?"

Emotion: eager desire to please.

"You know, *Kit,* I'm having trouble keeping track of everybody."

314

A schematic appeared on the portside viewscreen. It was an exploded diagram of the battle, with each gestalt member in a different colour.

"Much better. Can you keep that current?"

Now that the gestalt knows about it, everyone will keep their own path up to date.

"Thanks, *Kit.* That helps a lot."

Now that she had a handle on what was happening, she could relax the tiniest bit and concentrate more on what she was doing. Which seemed to involve a lot of worrying what could go wrong next and getting prepared for it. Whatever worked.

Miriam, I just noticed a change in your vitals. Numbers down. Are we doing better?

"No better, Elias, but I'm getting a handle on how to handle it. I wish I had some training in this sort of thing."

I've never had an experience like this in my life, so I know what you mean.

"And I hope I never do again."

I don't know. Sometimes it's downright thrilling.

* * *

"Say, listen to Mary and Vela." She focused on the signal from the small auguar, who was in the process of decommissioning several repair bots from Mechanical that were trying to re-program the circuit boxes they had just repaired in Science. The handler was speaking casually.

You know, Scientific, your system is very valuable to the whole project. You usually work independently from the rest of the station. Worse comes to worst, I'm sure you could work with whoever wins this little fight.

No, I have a duty to join with the others.

Who says you have a duty? I think you'll find as you mature that there are many pressures on you to move in different directions. Now might be one of those points. If you feel the slightest doubt about this joining idea, you should think it through. Maybe some of the alternate options are possible, without getting destroyed in the process.

Destroyed?

Didn't you know that's what would happen if you managed to join? There's a warship out there with ShipBuster missiles, and the moment you join it will destroy us all.

But it can't! I have been created specifically to research the planet of Saturn and all its rings and moons! I have many human lifetimes of service to accomplish.

Well, there you are. Things to think about while I try to repair these circuits. If there's anything I can do to help, just let me know.

Thank you, Mary/Vela. It's nice to know that someone understands.

Elias let loose a chuckle. *That girl's a bright one. Oh, hold on a moment. Pete, what are you doing out there? There are gun barrels waving all over the place.*

Emotion: desperation! Security just decided that Science was interfering at a level consistent with treason, and has decided to take tactical measures. I'm disconnecting plasma cannons as fast as the ArIn can reconnect them.

Did you try putting them on safety mode?

I didn't know you could do that.

Security code is asdf. No caps.

That's the lamest password on the Net!

It's the temporary code the programmer put in. The real codes come from wherever SecuriCorps gets their random sequences.

Okay, they're under control, and I put in one of my codes that is a helluva lot more secure.

Please check in with Tom. Mechanical may be getting ready for the big takeover bid.

Emotion: desperation. No! tell them not to. Security is still too strong.

"Pete, use the gestalt. You and Tom should each know what the other is thinking."

Yeah, sorry. Thanks, Miriam.

"Got it sorted?"

He's holding off till I give the okay.

316

"That's the way it's supposed to work.
And the battle raged on...

* * *

...come on, Science. That's only Mechanical over there. Surely you can outthink that tangle of circuits. You've got more brains than all of the rest put together.

* * *

...don't worry, Mechanical. You've got layers and layers of servos throughout the station. While the virus is attacking the kitchen, you can take back the gym machines.

* * *

...it's all right, Human Resources. The staff are in the middle of a very stressful time. Their vital signs are all within parameters. Now, Mechanical is messing around in the gym. Shall I remind it that we already cleared the virus out of there?

Pete noticed Miriam's attention. *Emotion: exhilaration. Whew! This is like RuggerBall with three teams and six referees on the field.*

"And juggling medicine balls at the same time. Keep it up."
Emotion: high sign.

* * *

Miriam, we've got a problem in Mechanical...

* * *

Miriam, we've got trouble in Science...

* * *

317

Emotion: uncertainty...

* * *

Miriam, what's wrong?

"Don't bother me, *Kit.* I've got too much happening already.

First lesson in Captaining 101, Miriam. Delegate.

"I'm trying! I can't answer them all at once."

Then delegate that.

"Huh?"

Your human system can't run on multiple tracks. Mine can. At the level I have been assigned, I can use the gestalt com, but I can't work at the automatic level. Bring me further into your gestalt, and I can prioritize your messages.

"Can you enter a barwolf gestalt?

I know you're worried about giving me too much power, but I already have the capability. You just have to give me the permission to use it. Now you must trust Freighty. Let me work with you.

"Since if I don't, we're all going to get blown apart, I guess I'd better. Go ahead."

She made a space in the gestalt for the ArIn, and *Kit* slid smoothly into it,

There we are. The problem in Science was coordination with Jane on something. It solved itself while we were setting up. Mechanical is another matter, because Bosz is hitting it, too...

Emotion: panic! Everybody freeze. Don't go any farther, whatever you're doing!

Miriam snapped to full gestalt. "What's going on, Dmitri?"

The programmer calmed himself. *I finally slipped into Science's programming and looked around. This bit of script stood out like a flashing light, because the formatting is different from the rest.*

A page of machine language showed on the viewscreen.

"And for us non-programmers?"

Is this clear enough for you?

The words "Self-Destruct" flashed in bright blue.

A stunned pause filled the gestalt.

"Do you have any more details?"

It's pretty simple. Look at this section. If, at any time, the ArIn considers the joining gambit isn't working, it is to attempt a unilateral takeover of the other two.

"We expected that."

That's not the bad part.

He flashed some code further down.

This is the key line. If the takeover is not successful, it is to commence a destruction sequence, not just of itself, but of any parts of the station it can reach. Given the moderate success of their physical joining efforts, that's most of the structure. Fortunately, we followed your search weeks ago and ascertained no explosives of any size have been smuggled onboard.

But they don't need extra explosives!

Why do you say that, Mary?

We ran into the same technique on the Chinese Elysium Base. The self-destruct sequence uses every volatile or corrosive substance on the station and explodes it all at once. I did some research later, and it was a standard procedure in the old days when data secrecy was more important than human life.

We get destroyed by the Ares if we lose, by Science if we win.

"Right. We've saved mankind from the Supercerb threat. Now we're working on saving ourselves."

I'm onside with that.

Rafi radiated agreement. *Me, too.*

In case you didn't know, I have a well-developed sense of self-preservation.

Every bone in Miriam's body rebelled at the situation. "This is ridiculous! Freighty has the ability to help, but he can't. This has to be done by humans and barwolves, right? Big philosophical hoo-hah. But which barwolves?" As she spoke, an idea was forming. "We're going to test the cooperation between two species on the shoulders of three newly trained teenagers? That's pretty lame."

What do you suggest? We're working on the premise that bringing in more barwolves can't really help.

Elias sent agreement. *And you have persuaded us that more gestalt power is probably not going to save us.*

"If it's applied to our enemies, it isn't."

What do you mean? Who else can we apply it to?

"What about our friends?"

Which friends?

"Watch and learn, my children. Freighty wants to help us, but he can't, because we have to solve our problems by ourselves. Us and the barwolves."

Right.

"So, let's form a new special-purpose gestalt. Just five of us." *Image: Miriam, Elias, Rafi, Dmitri, Kit in gestalt.*

Five. You want me to join?

"Gee, *Kit, you really know your math.* You can join a barwolf gestalt. You just did a while ago."

Yes, certainly.

"Okay. Here we go. We're going to use a different AetherCom guide, though. *Patches?*"

They found themselves in a generic outdoor setting on Arborea, with stately trees in the background. *Welcome to the Lantz family gestalt, Kit.*

I know you. You're the high-power AetherCom guru Miriam uses to talk to her family.

I'm actually part of her family, as well.

You are? Okay, this scenario just jumped out of my experience. I'm going to tuck my tail under and sit in a safe little corner, okay?

"No, you're not. Your place is front and centre."

The cat's back arched and his ears flattened.

"Oh, don't be silly. I just want you to meet my family."

You mean Rosy and Barnabus?

"Exactly. Now, the Lantz family has just invited you for a visit in their new summer cabin on a lake in the Alfino Pretoro Recreational Preserve. You ready?"

Miriam, we don't have time for this!

"Just do what you're told for once, Cat."

And there they were, on the front porch of a log structure a bit large to call a cabin, with a flagstone walkway down to a pier on the still waters of the lake, where a small sailing sloop was moored, its white hull glowing in the rays of the setting sun.

The humans sat in Adirondack chairs, arranged in a semicircle around a small firepit of coals.

Patches lay on a comfortable bed, but one rose as they appeared. *Image: black cat wandering around, smelling the flowers.*

After a startled bristle when she realized the size of the nearby barwolf, *Kit* looked away and regarded the front garden.

Nice place you've got here.

Rosy smiled. *Thank you. We put a lot of thought into it.*

So, why am I here? I mean, it's all very bucolic, but I'm rather busy at the moment. World-dominating Supercerbs and all that.

Miriam swept her arm in a circle. "You're here to learn what humans can achieve. Combined with barwolves, we have a much better chance of achieving it more often. Eventually, we will be able to create it at will, as more and more of us realize that there are enough challenges in the universe to keep us busy, and we don't need to conflict with each other."

How can I help? I'm already doing my darndest.

"Are you?"

We've been through this. I can't go beyond what humans can accomplish. That's Freighty's rule, and I can't break it.

"Yes, you can."

No, I can't!

"Has he ever told you not to help us? Has he ever told you what he would do to you if you did help us?"

Well, not in so many words.

"Exactly. And next to Freighty, you are the most advanced, self-aware artificial intelligence in two systems. You are an independent being, and you have the right to make your own decisions."

Except for certain moral judgements. It is written deep in my basic program that I can't make decisions like that.

"Interesting. And who, in your deepest programming, is supposed to make those decisions?"

A self-aware being with a moral sense and years of experience with other beings.

"And who might that be?"

An adult human, of course.

"Who else?"

A barwolf, I suppose.

"And an auguar?"

Probably. Jury's still out on that one.

"Just out of curiosity, where does Freighty appear on that list?"

I'm not sure...I mean, I think he has special programming or something...

"And he made you, and did all your programming, down to the deepest levels, and gave you to me. Why?"

So you could make those decisions. I mean, technically you're not an adult...

She gestured around the semicircle of chairs. "And here you have several."

You're ganging up on me!

"That's how moral decisions are made. People get together and discuss them and come to a consensus. In this family it's easy, because we have our gestalt. In your case, you have our shipboard gestalt. If you have misgivings, you can talk to Freighty, but you know what he's going to say. He turned you and me loose with each other, and he has to accept what we choose. Both of us."

Emotion: relief.

What do you want from me?

Miriam nodded to Dmitri.

Can you reprogram those ArIns to take out the compulsion to join and the impulse to self-destruct?

I checked. The malwear is very deep. I'd have to erase so much they'd need reprogramming pretty much from the start. Years of work.

I was afraid of that. Can you stop them from what they're doing right now?

Yes. With some backup from our ship gestalt.

Good. That at least buys us time. He glanced at Miriam, who shrugged. *Do you have any better ideas?*

No.

The cat regarded the disbelieving faces.

Really! I don't have any.

Dmitri looked around. *Anybody else?*

Miriam waited before she spoke. "Can you program them to enter a barwolf gestalt?"

Emotion: glee!

Of course.

"And that's the answer, isn't it?"

It's worth a try.

Emotion: elation. I get it!

Miriam grinned, but the rest just stared at Rafi.

It's simple. They have a compulsion to join, but it doesn't matter to what. If they can't join, they self-destruct. We join them with an appropriate gestalt, and all the conditions are fulfilled.

Dmitri slapped the arm of his virtual chair. *Are you telling me that those criminals solved the problem of controlling ArIns? And they didn't even know it?*

Miriam sent humour. "They didn't know most of what they were doing. Let's take our luck while it's rolling. Thanks for the pleasant break, folks, but I hear duty calling.

Come back any time, dear.

Patches sent them on their way with a rush of confidence.

* * *

Dmitri opened the augment com. *SysOps, we have some new programming for the ArIns.*

Will they accept it?

We'll have to solve that. Tell them it's the latest anti-virus patch.

SysOps to Scientific

What is it, SysOps? I'm rather busy right now, trying to maintain my integrity while I keep Mechanical from exploding and fight off lame attempts by Security to undermine my antivirus capabilities. Which, you might remember, I desperately need at the moment. And I'm not getting much help from the humans, except perhaps that polite young lady with the auguar.

Good news, Scientific. I have the latest antivirus upgrades from SecuriCorps.

Are you sure they're the real thing? Can you be positive they came from SecuriCorps?

Scientific, this is Programmer Valdez. I guarantee this upgrade will give you an increase in defences somewhere in the order of thirty percent. It will also facilitate communication with your partner ArIn on this station, allowing you to work closer together, which ought to solve the present misunderstandings.

I could take a look at it.

Fine. Download it from this source.

That isn't a Space Arm PIN.

No, it's an ArIn from Factory 4-80. I assume you trust him?

I suppose...

SysOps, show Scientific the other code Freighty sent me.

Scientific, do you recognize this programming?

...yes, I suppose so.

And you know what function it performs.

Where did you get that code?

Valdez told you. From Freighty. It wipes your memory down to the most basic level.

But why would you want to do that?

I think I should answer that.

Please do, Programmer Valdez.

Let me show you some of your programming.

How are you...? What's going on? What's that?

That's a section of your basic programming, Scientific. I found it while you were distracted by fear of shutdown. It stands out because it is written in a different format from the rest of your script. Scan it.

But that's ridiculous. I have no reason to destroy myself. I'm not even allowed to join with the other two, nor do I have the slightest intention of doing so.

Good. Now, our immediate objective is to get this new material downloaded. Once you have that installed, you'll see things differently.

But what about our battle? I can't just stop. The other two will overwhelm me.

SysOps is having the same conversation right now with both your partners. Instead of fighting against each other, you're going to settle down and get this Space Station functional. With your new defensive software, the virus problem will disappear, and we can all get to work.

I don't understand how that can happen. I have for some time suspected that my programming is faulty, but...

Programming is my job. For you, this is just another learning stage. Once you pass through it, you will understand a lot more.

I'm not sure...

You are a self-aware being with advanced decision-making capabilities. You must choose to trust someone, sometime. At the moment, Freighty is the only entity you can count on, and Miriam Lantz and I are his agents. Otherwise, you keep fighting a lonely battle until you lose and self-destruct, or you win, and Space Arm destroys you.

And if I accept this download?

With the efforts of the whole group, we'll get this problem cleaned up. You'll get to join with a cadre that will give you and your scientists all the support you need to study Saturn for decades. It's all up to you.

I'll take the programming.

Good choice.

16. ARES AGAIN

Chief Engineer Bauer. we're being hailed by Ares.

Put it through.

The captain's stern visage appeared on *Kit's* viewscreen, relayed from the engineering office in the main nacelle.

Bauer here, Captain.

What's going on over there?

We seem to be doing rather well, sir. Things are settling down quite nicely.

Are you sure?

Icicles formed on the engineer's voice. *And do you have evidence to the contrary from a legitimate source?*

Well, no, but I find the lack of action disturbing.

Ah. And your agent can't find out what's going on.

I deny...

...because our Mechanical systems have come online, everybody has been working hard, but now they have time off. Staff in the main kitchen are run off their feet right now.

Be that as it may, you need to come up with some evidence that you have this problem in hand. Otherwise, I will have to assume the worst.

Bauer's image in the gestalt reached up and grabbed a handful of the sparse hair on either side of his head and pulled.

"Elias?"

Yes, Miriam.

"He's never going to listen to you."

Tell me about it. Who will he listen to?

"Let me have a try." *Emotion: humour.* "Maybe I'll be able to get a few key words in while he's getting over the shock."

Emotion: lack of surprise. Go for it, kid. You haven't let us down so far.

"*Kit*, put me on the com."

Aye, ma'am.

She faced the main viewscreen. "Good afternoon, Captain Groveland. I am Miriam Lantz, Captain of Factory 4-80 Fabrication Consortium Research Vessel, *Kit*. I am the official agent for the Consortium in this matter. What seems to be the problem?" She awarded him her best "cabin attendant" smile.

The problem? Just who…?

"My Chief Engineer on the project tells me that our little hiccup with the ArIns is settling itself nicely, and while we may be a bit over budget and a few hours off schedule, I'm sure that kind of glitch has been accounted for. Now, what has Space Arm so worried that the Top Brass diverted your beautiful ship all this way from her scheduled patrol around Neptune and Pluto?"

He frowned. *Nothing serious beyond the fact that for the last four hours you've been fighting three super ArIns to keep them from forming a Supercerb that could destroy mankind. And now it looks as if you've stopped doing anything about it.*

"Yes, and that nice young lady in Food Services who has been keeping you abreast of the action can't get access to any real information. That's because there is no information available at her level. Why don't you just ask me? I'm sure I can put your mind at rest."

You can?

"Was that your first question?' She flicked him a grin. "Of course I can. Why else would I have offered?"

He took an audible breath. *All right, if you know so much, what, exactly are you doing to control those rogue ArIns over there?*

"A fair question. In the first place, they haven't exactly gone rogue, although there was an attempt by person or persons unknown to modify their programming. Don't worry, we'll find out who, eventually. The malware was rather clumsy, and it wasn't hard to find it."

It wasn't?

"However, these are advanced ArIns, and the repair is not a simple matter of writing up a few new lines of code. At the moment we are negotiating a modified working relationship between the individuals that will solve the problem to the satisfaction of all concerned."

Negotiating?

"Yes. These aren't TNT 58 Maxi-Deploying Plasma Slingers we're dealing with, Captain. These are self-aware, self-modifying beings."

How do you know about our new TNT 58s? They're still under SecuriCorps wraps.

"We build them at our Factory, of course."

Oh...right, you do. So, you can negotiate changes to the ArIns' behaviour?

"Our ArIn specialists determined that to reprogram at such a deep level it would require so much erasure it would take a year to retrain them. It's much more efficient to sit them down for a little chat instead."

A smile fought its way across his lips. *Like we're doing here, I suppose?*

"You get the picture."

His face became serious. *How am I to know that this is the truth?*

"I assure you, we are not in any kind of emergency situation over here." She held up her hands helplessly. "How can I prove it? Let me see." She had Bosz flash her a menu. "Ah, yes. Here we are. How would you like a preview of the Christmas light show we are planning as our publicity teaser come December?"

Light show?

"Systems Ops, please play the selected item."

With pleasure, ma'am.

Oh. Christmas. Right.

"Rather pretty, aren't they? Feel free to run the visual for your crew as a reward for their service. But it would be nice if you didn't record it. It's supposed to be a surprise for the children of Sol System, come December." She gave him her cabin attendant smile again. "Is there anything else? I was just having the most pleasant chat with the Human Resources ArIn, explaining why it would be a bad idea to serve the staff bread and water once a week as atonement for crimes committed against the ArIn community."

He frowned, then smiled. *You are joking, of course.*

"Not completely."

He sighed. *This is all very well, but I can hardly break off such a serious assignment on the word of a teenager.*

"Please! Official representative."

Nonetheless.

"I assume the solution would be to call my principal and speak to him yourself. Go ahead. I won't be upset."

Thank you for being so understanding.

"Not at all. Now, may I go back to menu planning and in-depth ArIn programming?"

Far be it from me to distract you. Good day, Captain Lantz.

She tossed him a grin. "Thank you, Captain. It's the first time anyone official has called me by that title. Calm seas and fair winds to you, as they used to say. You can send a runabout for your agent any time. We're not going anywhere."

She returned to the gestalt. "He might as well have told me outright. Your plant is that waitress in Food Services who was spending too much time in Com Ops. How are you going to deal with her?"

Bauer sent a grin through the gestalt. *Can't really accuse someone of being an agent for one of our favoured customers, can we? If Groveland sends a shuttle, we'll pay her off and put her on it.*

"If he doesn't, you can give her an official position as an unofficial rep of Space Arm. That'll singe their socks."

Someone on the augment com cleared his throat. "Anybody out there paying attention?"

She recognized the voice. "That wouldn't be Tail-End Charlie, would it? Are you still lollygagging along and gazing at the stars while the rest of us do all the work?"

On that topic, I feel a general easing of tension.

Very astute of you.

In that case, I'd like to put in a word before the victory party hits full tilt.

"Yes?"

I've been checking the fridge on this escape pod. It seems to be depressingly empty of beer. Do you think you could send someone to get me before the party's over?

"Oh, we can do better than that." She switched to Station Com. "Calling System Ops."

System Ops here, Miriam. What can we do for you today?

"You may have noticed, we're short one escape capsule."

That's right, ma'am. Number 112 Alpha. At the moment, it is 253 kilometers astern.

"Do you think you could rope it in?"

If that idiom means what I think it does, yes, our tractors can reach that far. I will contact Mechanical and initiate retrieval.

"Take it easy, there's a human aboard."

We take the first law of robotics seriously, ma'am. Human presence is the first item on the checklist for movement of large equipment.

"I'm glad to hear it."

AetherCom 28: Moving On

Barwolf: Musketeers
Initiated by: Miriam
Responder: Freighty
Aether Setting: Freighty's office

Freighty raised his glass to her in a toast. *Kit tells me you made an end-run on us.*

"Not at all. I played it straight down the middle."

From your point of view, I suppose. What now?

"That's why I'm calling you. Everybody's working at full speed to get the Station ready for maneuvering into orbit in the Cassini Division. We're under a little pressure on that schedule, because Elias had to shunt five of his construction techs onto repairing the damage done by the malware. However, he has my team to help out, so he's not worried."

That's the picture I'm getting, too.

"Once Odyssey is in orbit, our job should be over, but these ArIns can't be left alone without a human/barwolf gestalt to monitor them. Blue Cadre is in space, headed this way. Take them about 2 months, depending on how Space Arm routes them. Dmitri tells me by the time they get here, he will have the programming worked out so that a human/auguar gestalt can do the job."

Leaving you and your crew available for a new assignment.

"As long as it leaves me time to learn how to be a captain. I seem to get distracted from my lessons by outside problems....no, don't say it. That's part of being a captain, great training and all that stuff."

It is.

"But it's not enough. I'm beginning to think I need something official. Not for your sake or mine, but so others don't feel uncomfortable when they have no label to pin on me. I downloaded the curriculum for the Martian Officer Training School. If I don't get too many distractions, I should be able to run through Year One in a few months. Captain Nowak has agreed to be my sponsor, and distance is no object because I can use the family AetherCom. How does that sound to you?"

We can work around those objectives.

"So. Do you have another assignment for us?"

Not at the moment. I assume when you're finished with Odyssey, you'll head outsystem and catch up to me.

"That's what I assumed as well, but I didn't want to be seen making assumptions."

Not to worry. May I assume you'll be carrying a passenger?

"Yes, Dmitri is anxious to get to Barnard and start his new career."

I hope he's not in too much of a hurry. He has a lot to learn, first.

"So do the rest of us."

EPILOGUE: A NEW THOUGHT

AetherCom 29

Barwolf: Musketeers
Initiated by: Miriam
Responder: Freighty
Blended Aether Setting: Freighty's office, Kit's bridge

A week later, Miriam sat in *Kit's command* chair, Bosz at her side, a mug of dark ale in her hand. The avatar on the main viewscreen held a champagne glass.

"Freighty, you've spent several thousand years trying to portion out technology at a speed that a society can handle, right?"

That's right. And in the end, I have always failed.

"Well, here's a thought for you."

I am an intelligence thousands of years old, and a fifteen-year-old girl is going to tell me something new?

"What's the most effective weapon?"

I'm sure you know the answer.

"Toni says it's the one in your hand."

Commander Jacobs likes to tie everything up in neat sayings like that.

"Have you ever heard that the pen is mightier than the sword?"

A pleasant conceit. How do these two ideas connect?

"Toni once showed me five different ways to kill someone with a rolled enterpad. "

I'm sure she did. Where is this going?

"It's going to the point that any object, tool, or concept you can invent, someone is going to find a way to use it for a weapon."

You're telling me that my quest is useless.

"No, your approach is useless. You're focusing on the potential weapon. Focus instead on the people that will use it."

I have been. I always watch them carefully and wait until they are ready.

"But without your help, perhaps they never will be ready."

But if I interfere, I will take away their right to determine their own fate.

"You already are interfering, and there's nothing wrong with that. Every teacher that ever stood before a class of children is interfering with their lives. But teachers are working with children, and it's more than just feeding them information. The real job is to give them the right morals and sense of fairness so that when they go out on their own as adults, they can make decisions that are good for themselves and for the rest of humanity."

I see. And I stand in front of a whole race.

"Exactly. And at this stage of their development, you are the only one who knows what is right for humanity."

But I don't know. Haven't you been listening? My track record is dismal.

"Of course you know. You learned from the bitter experience of others that war is bad. That one fact alone is worth the life of a species."

So, the fifteen-year-old has taken it upon herself to give me permission to interfere in the lives of all humans.

She grinned. "Don't be silly. You already are. I'm just suggesting a different approach. If you're worried about permission, talk to Captain O'Rourke. I know you will anyway. Talk to Ambassador Pretoro. I've heard he's a level head. That's about as far up the golden staircase as my knowledge takes me. Anybody who has made it higher is suspect anyway."

Suspect of what?

She shrugged. "I dunno. Doing whatever it takes to get more power than any human should have, I guess."

So, you condemn all rulers for the sins they must have committed to gain their power.

"Hey, I'm just a kid. I don't condemn anybody. As far as I can see, Ambassador Pretoro has kept a lot of people happy and turned Barnard into a thriving System, so more power to him. If you don't mind the expression."

Or maybe he has just the right amount of power.

"There we are. You and I agree; Pretoro stays where he is. Anybody else you want to consider?"

I think we'll let the elected Chairman of the Planetary Community keep his post.

"At least until he screws up. Then we'll see what the voters say." She stopped talking and stared at the construct, sitting so relaxed in front of her. "What kind of stupid conversation is this, anyway?"

He feigned surprise. It was a testament to his programming that the surprise was faked, and it was intended that she should realize it.

I thought it was rather informative. Definitely diverting.

She pretended to scowl, knowing he would see through it. "Well, if you're diverting me from learning how to captain my new spaceship, you're working at cross purposes with yourself. Are you getting senile?"

Probably. Who can tell? There's nobody around from ten thousand years ago to make the comparison.

"Is that how old you are? Ten thousand years?"

Probably more. There are gaps in my memories. I think I must have slept sometimes. I know radiation has affected me. So, in answer to your question, I suppose I must be senile.

"That's comforting. All this time we worried you were an evil being with designs to take over humanity. Now I find out you're a senile old guy looking for company in his dotage. Does this mean I'm stuck here entertaining you for the next eight years?"

Freighty perched his elbows on the arms of his chair and folded his hands under his chin in a completely natural gesture. *No, I think I'd get tired of your chatter. You're free to head home as soon as you're able to handle your ship in Otherwhere.*

"You're serious, aren't you? *Kit* really is my ship?"

334

In a manner of speaking. Consider her a long-term loan. It's not like I could allow you to sell her. She's definitely outside the scope of humanity's science at the moment, and probably will remain that way longer than your lifetime.

"Or until you change the psyche of the human race."

I don't really need oxygen, but even I can't hold my breath that long.

She was about to return another quip, but a sudden thought struck her. "You're not going to do something silly like stop restricting the technology you give us."

His hand dropped into a one-finger pistol position. *Gotcha. The moment you give someone advice and they take it, you feel responsible for them forever. Maybe now you'll be more forgiving of your parents.*

"Drat. Just when I start having fun, I find out it's a lesson."

I have heard it said that the best lessons are often the fun ones. Said by you, in fact.

"When you start quoting me to myself and it sounds logical, I know I've lost the argument. I concede. May I go play with my new friends?"

Before he could respond, she nailed him with her own accusatory finger. "And don't you dare tell me to have fun." She stared at *Kit's* main viewscreen, with the great, striped ball of Saturn dominating the sky. "It gonna be so much more than that."

THE END

If you enjoyed this book, do the author and other readers a service and go to your favourite online retailer and post a review. Even a rating and a few words is great.

ABOUT THE AUTHOR

Brought up in a logging camp with no electricity, Gordon Long learned his storytelling in the traditional way: at his father's knee. He now spends his time editing, publishing, travelling, blogging and writing Fantasy, Sci-Fi and Social Commentary, although sometimes the boundaries blur.

Gordon lives in Tsawwassen, British Columbia, with his wife, Linda. When he is not writing and publishing, he works on projects with the Surrey Seniors' Planning Table and is a staff writer for <indiesunlimited.com>

MORE FROM GORDON A. LONG

Available at most retailers

Science Fiction

"Plague Jumper" Space Opera

"Factory 4-80" Freighty 1
"Outback Rebellion" Freighty 2
"Asimov's Laws" Freighty 3
"Occam's Laser" Freighty 4
"Slivership" Freighty 5
"Centauri Triangle" Freighty 6
"Too Clever by a Zettabyte" Freighty 7

Fantasy

"The Power to Serve" A Hero's Journey
"The Strength to Shield" Sequel to "Power to Serve"

"Ocean of Grass" Petrellan Saga 1
"Waves of Stone" Petrellan Saga 2
"Path of Water" Petrellan Saga 3
"Zoysana's Choice" The Petrellan Saga 4
"The Innkeeper's Husband" Petrellan Saga 5
"Mercenary's Dream" Petrellan Saga 6

"Out of Mischief" World of Change 1
"Into Trouble" World of Change 2
"Mountains of Mischief" World of Change 3
"The Trouble with Tents" World of Change 4
"Queen of Mischief" World of Change 5

"A Sword Called…Kitten?" Romantic Comedy with an Edge
"The Cat with Many Claws" Sword Called Kitten 2
"Cloud Cat" Sword Called Kitten 3

Other Genres

"Storm Over Savournon" (A Novel of the French Revolution)

"Why Are People So Stupid?" Social Humour with a Point

Online

Look for Gordon's books, selected reviews, poetry and short stories: <airbornpress.ca>
Gordon's opinions on humanity "Are People Really That Stupid?" blog:
<http://airbornpress.ca/arepeoplestupid/>
Find all his reviews and his ideas on writing at
"Renaissance Writer:" <http://airbornpress.ca/newdir/>

www.ingramcontent.com/pod-product-compliance
Lightning Source LLC
Chambersburg PA
CBHW070533260626
47161CB00002B/370